Praise for *The Bright Lands*

"There's a darkness lurking in *The Bright Lands*, and it's apt to give you a case of the shivers... An enticing read any way you s

"A fascinating and suspenseful read."

"Fram's ambitious debut takes a critical, terrifying look at a small town in Texas... This offers as many weekend frights as celebratory lights."

—*Publishers Weekly*

"A confident and thought-provoking tale that explores complex family dynamics, sexuality, religion, and coming-of-age anxieties within a solid horror frame. A great choice for fans of Victor LaValle or Ania Ahlborn."

—*Library Journal*

"[*The Bright Lands*] is bold, brash, and disturbing, boasting an assured, righteous young voice calling out the contradictions, hypocrisies, and repression that allow the horrors of abuse to root and grow generational damage as history repeats itself."

—*Lone Star Literary*

"John Fram carves quite a niche with his debut... *The Bright Lands* admirably lives up to Fram's 'Stephen Queen' moniker."

—*Shelf Awareness*

"[A] rich and complex debut."

—*Lambda Literary*

"This is an excellent tale soaked in atmosphere that takes readers into some disturbing places as it examines small-town life and queer experiences in rural America."

—*Mystery Scene Magazine*

"For the lovers of mere murder mystery novels with a horror twist, this is a perfect match; for readers who like their stories to have a bit more depth, this is a highly recommendable read as well."

—*Rainbow Reviews*

"John Fram's novel marks the debut of an already accomplished novelist. *The Bright Lands* is a dark tale luminously, and compellingly, told."

—John Banville, Booker Prize winner

"Absolutely enthralling. Written with the rhythm of the game Fram writes of. A mystery to get the skin crawling even as you unbury the secrets of those trying to solve it. Despite its nature, there is a warmth to this thriller, and you'll feel like you've come home...a home that still haunts you."

—Josh Malerman, *New York Times* bestselling author of *Bird Box*

"*The Bright Lands* is Gothic and Faulknerian: smooth, original, haunting. And very sexy."

—Edmund White, author of *A Boy's Own Story*

"John Fram's *The Bright Lands* is darker than you think. Fram begins with a *Friday Night Lights* supernatural mystery, then lures the reader into an insidious labyrinth of human cruelty, voracious supernatural evil, and startling malice. Unsettling, and compelling as hell."

—Christopher Golden, *New York Times* bestselling author of *The Pandora Room*

"I am stunned—I haven't been able to step away from this book since I started it. An earnest, thoughtful exploration of the monstrosity inherent in our American myths surrounding masculinity and sexuality, *The Bright Lands* is a kind of horror I've never seen before. Fram's done something exquisite here."

—Sarah Gailey, author of *Magic for Liars*

"Fram has delivered a powerhouse of a debut that is certain to be one of the year's most bracing thrillers. Unapologetic in its queerness, cruelty and heart, *The Bright Lands* will sink its teeth into you."

—P. J. Vernon, author of *Bath Haus*

"*The Bright Lands* is a chilling and fast-paced supernatural thriller that also manages to be a heartbreaking meditation on shame, repression, denial and regret. This strange and beautiful novel is a stunning debut and I'm already hungry for whatever Fram does next."

—Shaun Hamill, author of *A Cosmology of Monsters*

THE
BRIGHT
LANDS

THE BRIGHT LANDS

A NOVEL

JOHN FRAM

HANOVER
SQUARE
PRESS

HANOVER
SQUARE
PRESS™

Recycling programs
for this product may
not exist in your area.

ISBN-13: 978-1-335-45773-8

The Bright Lands

First published in 2020. This edition published in 2021.

This edition published by arrangement with Harlequin Books S.A.

Hanover Square Press
22 Adelaide St. West, 40th Floor
Toronto, Ontario M5H 4E3, Canada
HanoverSqPress.com
BookClubbish.com

Printed in U.S.A.

For Matt and Nance.

Sorry I couldn't finish in time.

THE
BRIGHT
LANDS

People everywhere, young and old, were already dreaming of heroes.

—H. G. Bissinger, *Friday Night Lights*

This country makes it hard to fuck.

—Fever Ray

SUNDAY

DREAMS AND OTHER HAZARDS

JOEL

His brother's message came late.

The little party which had started in Tulum on Monday had somehow only just ended at Joel's apartment a few minutes before the text arrived. An international bender. It sounded fun on paper. Joel had goaded the last of his bleary guests out the door and made sure his wallet and cologne were still concealed behind the suits in his closet. He used an app to pay off his drug dealer, used another app to order a housekeeper for the morning, poured himself a tall glass of seltzer and settled into bed next to the empty space where he had hoped, earlier in the weekend, he might now find some company resting. He swallowed two Tylenol. He wondered why nobody ever warned you it was possible to feel this alone before you were thirty.

His phone lit the ceiling a cold blue. Joel was so exhausted he mistook it, initially, for some new breed of ghost.

This place is bullshit, wrote Dylan, his brother.

Joel studied the message for a very long time before responding: Everything ok?

Dylan was eleven years younger than Joel. He was a senior in high school this fall, if Joel's addled brain was doing the math right, and still lived in Bentley, Texas, a rotten rind of a town which Joel had escaped the moment he could and hoped to never see again. When Joel missed his family, he flew them to Manhattan. Which was most Christmases. Some. Twice.

As he waited for his brother to respond, Joel scrolled up to see the last time they'd spoken: three months before, when Joel, likely drunk, had sent Dylan a picture of a football player tackling a massive rooster mascot. Dylan had responded, wordlessly, with a GIF of two handsome underwear models colliding with one another on a catwalk.

The brothers' relationship was a muted one.

Joel's screen slid back down with the arrival of a new message.

lol sorry wrong person.

Joel typed a message, deleted it and tried again. It's cool. He added after a pause: What's up?

Joel watched his screen. The status of his message changed from Delivered to Read. Joel waited, waited, but no reply came.

Joel was almost asleep again when his phone lit up for the second time.

actually it's not ok.

Joel tried to call. It went to voice mail after two rings.

can't talk rn, his brother wrote. sorry.

Lil D, Joel wrote—an old pet name that felt rusty from disuse—What's wrong?

dumb dreams. bad dreams. i'm stupid.

This was followed by a GIF of a linebacker shaking his head on the sidelines of a game.

i fucking hate football

Oh.

what's stupid about hating football?

how else i'm gonna get out of this place?

Joel climbed out of bed. In the kitchen he poured himself another seltzer, debated for a moment and splashed it with vodka.

The way their mother described it, Dylan was the best thing to happen to Bentley's football program in a decade. He'd made varsity when he was just a freshman and had been the starting quarterback the year after that. The team had flourished under Dylan: they made it all the way to state quarterfinals his first year as quarterback, had made it to semifinals last year and now, according to the breathless calls Joel had received from his mother over the summer, the Bentley Bison had a shot at the state championships for the first time in a generation.

In all of his Instagram photos, Joel's little brother had never once appeared to be anything but affable and handsome and casually, ruthlessly charming in the way of Southern boys who knew their towns were made for them. Now, sitting on the chilly bar stool in his kitchen, Joel debated how best to approach the idea that Dylan had anything resembling a problem in his life.

He took a long drink.

Tennis worked for me, Joel typed.

can't, Dylan wrote. they killed it.

The fuck?

to make more money for football.

Fuck.

ya.

Basketball? Baseball?

coach says my numbers are shit.

You mean your grades?

their ok. They're* lol

Joel smiled at his phone. maybe just scholarships for college then.

not that ok

Oh.

cause football. i can't ever study.

Why don't you quit then? You've got a year to turn shit around.

hahahahaha that's funny

What is?

quit football. Joel waited out a long pause. sorry, Dylan finally wrote. i shouldn't be bothering you.

You're not bothering me, Joel typed. Dylan talk to me please.

i thought about it a lot really i want to but i can't quit i can't

Why not?

Another long pause. u don't remember what it's like down here.

Joel left his phone unlocked on the counter. He gathered empty glasses into his sink, tossed out a stuffed ashtray, picked up small baggies that a few hours before had held cocaine and molly and every other palliative he could get his hands on and rolled them into a wet towel to bury in his garbage. He gagged at a sharp whiff of gin uncoiling from somewhere beneath his counter. He *did* remember what it was like in Bentley, Texas. Or, rather, there was plenty he had made himself forget.

Joel had made a name for himself upon arriving in New York with an economics degree from a nowhere school and a plaque from his tennis scholarship and a smile on his face. He had established himself as an analyst with an *itch*, an *instinct*, the ability to look at a pile of data and spot flaws, opportunities, dangerously optimistic projections. That itch had served him very, very well. Just look at this custom kitchen, at the Italian sofa in the living room from a designer whose name brought a pause to even the most jaded of the Hamptons set.

And what was Joel's itch telling him now?

This is serious.

There's something wrong with that town.

This is your brother.

i can't quit football. i just fucking can't but i can't keep playing neither if i don't play i don't got no college cause who's gonna pay for it? mom? and if i don't got no college i'm fucking stuck here and if i stay here i'll go crazy bro—i can't sleep i can't eat i can't go to the bright lands it's not the same no more i can't with this fucking place

Can't go to the what?

i hate it here. it's like i hear this town talking when i sleep.

Joel looked at his absurd apartment, at the well-appointed wreckage of his late twenties, and told himself he wasn't afraid. He googled How much does college cost today and priced plane tickets and pretended he wasn't scared out of his mind at the thought of what he was about to do.

u there? yo joel u there?

I'm here.

Joel took a hard sip of vodka straight from the bottle. He sent Dylan a screenshot of a ticket confirmation.

He told himself it was time to start being an older brother for once in his life.

Maybe I can help.

FRIDAY

HOPE AND HALOGEN

JOEL

Five days later his plane pierced the cloud bank and great squares of Texas prairie rose up to swallow him. Watching the flatland take shape out his window, he felt a familiar anxiety wind its fingers around his throat.

His brother was not the first troubled football player to confide in Joel. All week in Manhattan he had thought of nothing but a sticky summer afternoon a decade ago, of a truck cab spiked with the smell of spearmint, of a man with shocking green eyes and a bad neck shaking his head with effort and saying, *"Don't play that game if you can help it, Whitley."* Joel would cut off an arm to ensure Dylan never suffered the same fate as that ruined man.

If Joel could jab a finger in his blighted hometown's eye, so much the better.

He chewed an Adderall and texted his brother.

* * *

An ugly thunderhead was rolling in from the Gulf. When the Enterprise attendant led Joel to the parking lot to collect his rental—a low-slung convertible with a gleaming black hood—the twilit air felt ready to burst. One sniff and Joel knew he was back. There was nothing quite like the smell of Texas in the hours before some fresh calamity.

The open convertible tore away from the encroaching storm with a moan. Joel passed through towns with names like Thrall and Spree and Thorndale and wove around trucks and horse trailers, their drivers and passengers all regarding him (and the pop music blaring from his speakers) with a courteous suspicion.

There were fewer cows than he remembered. Great miles of scrubby flatland unrolled to either side of the highway, punctuated only by a lonely water tower, a totemic bale of hay, a sunken barn with half the country visible through a hole in its side.

BENTLEY: 18 MILES. Joel didn't smoke and yet he craved a cigarette. He caught a casual crackle of gunfire somewhere in the distance—*there* was a sound he'd forgotten—and slowed to allow a rusted Chevy to merge ahead of him. Something caught his eye in the truck's bed. A hulking stuffed bison wobbled on stiff legs, a letterman jacket fastened around its furry shoulders, its black glass eyes catching the last of the sunlight through the grill of a green Bentley football helmet.

It was a challenge not to stare into those eyes. With a queasy flutter in his stomach, a creep of gooseflesh up his arms, Joel suddenly felt he'd seen those eyes before, though he was also certain he'd never seen this stuffed bison in his life. He had the strangest conviction—almost like déjà vu—that those black eyes had watched him on a very bad night a very long time ago. They had watched him then just like they were watching him now: with a hungry, inhuman intelligence, like a lizard waiting for a fly to buzz just a few inches closer.

Jesus, Joel thought. He wasn't even home and already he was jumping at taxidermy.

Joel caught sight of the first sign of fresh paint since Austin. A billboard that read MY HERD MY GLORY appeared, listing the names and numbers of every player on the team. He strained to spot his brother, though he needn't have bothered. Just past BENTLEY: 2 MILES his brother's face rose up from the fields. DYLAN WHITLEY, SENIOR, the sign read. "THE BOY WITH THE MILLION DOLLAR ARM."

The convertible's speakers sputtered, the music playing from Joel's phone cut out. Bentley took shape on the flat horizon. As the truck ahead of him rumbled toward town, a dark light rose in the bison's dead eyes. Joel jumped. He would have sworn he'd just seen the thing blink.

As if in reply, a cold voice seemed to whisper through the static of the convertible's speakers:

imissedyou.

CLARK

On what she would later consider the last easy night of her life, Sheriff's Deputy Starsha Clark pulled her cruiser into the football field's parking lot and spotted two other police cars near the end zone.

Deputy Browder smiled as Clark pulled up. God help him, when Browder smiled he looked too young to drive. Hulking Deputy Jones, his uniform black with sweat, was propped against the end zone's fence, bellowing something down the field.

Clark's heart stuttered when she saw the score: 14–13, favoring the Rattichville Cougars, the Bison's competition that evening, and with only a minute-three remaining in the half.

"We been lucky as the devil tonight," Browder said.

Jones spat a sunflower seed into the grass. "With them Cougars o-line against us, we need him."

Dylan Whitley stood at the sidelines: even from downfield

the boy was unmistakable. He stood just north of six foot, making him one of the shortest quarterbacks anyone in Bentley could remember, but he was broad-chested and long-legged and possessed the sort of sturdy shoulders a town needed to drape its hopes on. He paced near the water coolers, poker-faced, only the mouth guard that bobbed fitfully between his teeth betraying any hint of anxiety.

Jamal Reynolds, the team's backup quarterback, stood a few steps behind Dylan in a pristine jersey, murmuring something that made Dylan nod his head and chew his mouth guard harder. Clark struggled to remember the last time she'd seen Jamal play.

Crouched beside Dylan, adjusting a stubborn knot in his laces, was KT Staler, the wiry tight end whose performance on the field fluctuated so wildly he had earned the nickname Mister Powerball—with Staler you either got the jackpot or nothing at all. If Clark wasn't mistaken, the skinny boy looked like he'd somehow lost even more weight lately.

Luke Evers, the Bison's running back, stood beside the team's offensive coordinator, raising an arm with a bicep the size of a honeydew to point at something on the coach's clipboard. Evers was the sort of strapping boy that Texas athletics bred on a yearly basis. He only seemed to be getting bigger.

Interesting, Clark thought. Luke Evers had grown and KT Staler had shrunk. Clark's mind, conditioned by three years on the force, began to speculate on reasons for this before she quelled it with a cigarette. She turned her attention back to the field. For an hour, just an hour, she would prefer not to be a cop.

The Bison readied their line to block the second play, the tight Lycra of their pants gleaming as they bent low. T-Bay Baskin, the Bison's defensive captain, shouted and spat into the grass. The Cougar quarterback caught the snap. For a moment Clark lost sight of the ball as the Rattichville offense pulled a sweep to the left, spotting it again in the hands of the Cougar halfback. The boy was trying to hustle the ball wide, running toward the Bison's exposed flank and looking for all the world like he was about to make it around.

Garrett Mason, the Bison's safety and one of the biggest players on the team by a wide margin, took the halfback down at the waist. The slap of the two players colliding set Clark's teeth on edge. The play had been a very long, very illegal flying tackle, and as the Rattichville halfback struggled to his feet, his body shaking as he held in a retch, Clark was certain the Bison had just earned themselves a penalty.

From somewhere behind her, she heard an odd scraping noise. Heard it again: a rustle, a hush. There, in the dark, she saw a man shuffle between two trucks, his crooked left foot trailing through the gravel behind him like a dead dog on a short leash.

"Do my eyes deceive me," Clark said softly. "Or is Mr. Ovelle back in town?"

The deputies turned. Jason Ovelle, the man in the shadows, had been a miscreant since before he'd crossed the graduation stage of Bentley High, a few steps ahead of Clark herself. Unaware he was being watched, the man tugged on a truck's door handle.

"And he brought some burglary with him." Browder smiled.

Clark stubbed her half-smoked cigarette on the fence rail and tucked it behind her ear. She would have to be a cop tonight after all.

Ovelle, apparently still oblivious to their attention, limped into the shadows as the officers made their way across the parking lot—a galling cheer rose from the stands the moment they turned away, of course—but as Clark drew near she spotted the man digging beneath the seat of KT Staler's rusted Tacoma. She started to run.

Ovelle froze at the sound, turned his head slowly to face her. He made no effort to escape.

"Evening, Officer." He smiled. "Those boys is something, ain't they?"

"They are indeed. Why ain't you watching the game with us, Jason?"

The last decade had not been kind to Ovelle. A milky scar ran from his brow to the crown of his buzzed scalp. He was skinny, almost frail, and he stood with a permanent stoop. According to one story, an angry con had taken a folding chair to Jason's ankle when he was serving a dime up in Huntsville on drug charges, but there was no telling if this was the truth. Jason had the sort of reputation that attracted stories the way a wound attracts flies.

He made a show of patting his pockets and turned back to KT Staler's open Tacoma. "I would enjoy it, Clark, ma'am," Jason said. "But I'm a little short. These bag boys owe me, see, and I—"

This was quite strange. Jason was a fuckup, a small-time hood, but Clark had never seen him do something so brazen as rooting through the door well of a star Bison player in plain view of an officer. She wondered what sort of wolf was pawing at his door tonight.

And then she saw the weapon on his hip: a nasty-looking hunting knife, a good eight inches long.

Clark's hand hovered over her gun. Another cheer rose up from the field, the marching band boomed to life: the half had ended. If she and the other officers didn't hurry they were about to have an audience, and God help them then. The men that ran Bentley could not abide a single joule of the spotlight being stolen from their Bison on a Friday night.

"Let's talk about this at the station, eh, Jason?" Clark said.

"The station?" Ovelle stared at her, horror in his eyes. "But they'd kill me if I went to the station. I ain't even supposed to *be* here."

"No, you surely ain't." She nodded at the Tacoma. "We would normally consider this breaking and entering."

Panic fell over Jason's face. He finally made to dash past Clark, his bad foot throwing up a little cloud of dust in his wake, but the moment he was within reach she tossed him against the rusted hood of the Tacoma. The air flew from his gut with a soft *pfft*. Clark pinned his wrists against his shoulder blades, slid the knife from his belt, tossed it in the grass. "That's enough now." She shushed him like she would a child.

"You've killed me, Clark." Jason gasped. "You've killed me."

"Wrists, Jason. Please."

Officer Jones appeared from the other side of the Tacoma and picked up the knife, glanced at the rust on its serrated edge, shook his head. "You alright?"

Browder appeared from behind a Jeep. "Audience incoming."

Sure enough, there was a rumble of voices in the parking lot. Clark clicked home the second cuff.

"You're as bad as your brother," Jason whispered.

Clark went cold. She felt a sudden urge to slam the man into the truck again. "What did you just say?"

Deputy Jones patted her shoulder. "Want me to book him?" he asked her.

Her mind shifted gears. With the sheriff's department's small staff the general rule with booking paperwork was *you caught it, you clean it.*

"You'll miss the second half," Clark said.

Jones shrugged and slid the knife's sheath off Jason's belt. He squeezed Jason's scrawny arm until the little man yelped in pain. Jones's flat face didn't register the sound. "I seen enough of these games."

Clark hesitated, but only for a moment. Whatever Jason had to say about her brother she could pry out of him at the station. She thanked Jones. She let go of Jason's arm.

When she and the two other deputies stepped into the glare of the parking lot's sodium lamps they were greeted with polite applause. A small crowd—housewives in baggy Bison T-shirts, men under ball caps and Stetsons—watched as Jason was loaded, shouting and cursing, into the back of Jones's cruiser. Clark wore her most stoic face.

You're as bad as your brother.

Pulling the dented cigarette from behind her ear, Clark finally regarded her audience. She saw that their faces were turned not toward Jones's departing police cruiser but to something over her shoulder. A little charge of anticipation still hung in the air, as if everyone were expecting some kind of encore.

She spotted the black convertible first, a sleek little Mustang she had never seen around town. A man stood next to it, watching her. He was implacably urban: tall, well built, sharply dressed in dark clothes of the sort no one in Bentley ever wore.

Clark recognized the man's bashful smile. Only one man in her life had ever smiled at her that way.

Her lighter froze on its way to the cigarette. "Son of a bitch."

JAMAL

Jamal Reynolds, the Bison's second-string quarterback, followed the rest of the team into the locker room and kept his head down. Deputy Clark might not have remembered the last time Jamal had played in a game but he certainly did. He knew, down to the minute, the total length of time he'd ever had the good fortune to strap on his helmet and step onto the field: forty-six minutes. Forty-six minutes after almost four years on the team. And that number didn't look likely to go up tonight.

Talented as he knew he was, Jamal never complained about this. He'd learned long ago that in Texas there were some things you just had to accept.

"Do you feel the wind out there yet?" Dylan said, sidling up beside Jamal to open his locker and check his phone. The game's first half had ended moments before, just as the Bison defense had (miraculously) prevented another Cougar goal.

"You made the right call at the toss," Jamal said, thumping Dylan on the shoulder, because that was another thing Jamal had learned: the true role of the backbench player was to be a cheerleader in the places the girls couldn't reach.

KT Staler, the Bison's skinny tight end, opened his locker. "You hear the way that kid was choking?"

Dylan raised his phone, pushed his hair out of his eyes, pulled KT and Jamal into frame. "Cheese to my brother." He smiled deftly. The screen flashed white.

"My eyes look funny." KT peered at the photo.

"He's here?" said Jamal.

Dylan typed something. He didn't look up. "Landed an hour ago."

"About fucking time," KT said.

Coach Parter's voice came booming from the doorway. "Aches? Pains? Whitley, how you faring?"

Dylan hardly glanced at him. "Fine, Coach."

When Parter was out of earshot, Dylan murmured to Jamal, "I'll try and get you some field time in the fourth. The Fat Man's barely looked at you all season."

An unwelcome voice came from behind them. "If this wind turns around it'll be right in our faces."

Luke Evers, the team's muscled running back, approached them with his gloves still on.

"It won't turn," Dylan said.

"Brazos is already flagging. Malacek too. We should have hit them harder at the kick, Whitley. We could have had this in the bag by now."

Dylan grinned. "You don't trust this arm?"

"I don't trust your head."

"It ain't your call, bro," Jamal said to Luke.

"I'm the offensive captain, Reynolds."

"They'll remember that when they make the movie," said KT.

"Fuck off, Staler."

"Boys. Whiteboard. Now." Coach Wesford, the offensive coordinator, snapped his fingers. "I said *now*."

With Dylan gone, KT's attention turned to his phone. He typed a message, stared at his screen, typed something else. He concealed the screen deep inside his locker.

The sight unsettled Jamal. Since when was KT able to keep a secret?

Jamal went to fill his water bottle. The players were raucous as usual tonight—athletic cups lobbed and dodged, nipples twisted, shoulders knuckled—but as Jamal made his way around a puddle of what he could only hope was water he felt something taut and anxious in the air, a muted electric charge, as if the storm brewing outside had trailed into the field house on the tops of their helmets.

"Is it j-j-just me—" Benny Garcia, one of the other back-benchers, stood beside the rusted water fountain and scratched his nuts. "Or d-d-does it l-l-look l-l-like they're p-p-plotting something?"

Jamal looked over his shoulder. B-B-Benny was right. It wasn't just KT. At every other locker stood a player staring intently at a phone. Jamal caught Mitchell Malacek, the team's starting halfback, murmuring something to the Turner twins. The twins shared one of their eerie mirrored smiles.

"I can't believe it." Garrett Mason, the massive defensive safety, shuddered at something on KT's phone as Jamal returned to his own locker. KT flipped the screen over when he saw Jamal watching.

Garrett had a scowl that could knock a bird from the sky. He licked blood from his lip. "You ain't got enough business of your own, Reynolds?"

Jamal forced a grin, said nothing.

A few minutes later, Dylan returned. "Hey," Dylan said, scooting up to Jamal's locker. "You've got my back, right?"

"Of course, bro," Jamal said, though he found it odd Dylan would even ask.

When he looked up, he saw that Dylan had spoken not to him, but to KT.

At the sound of Jamal's voice, Dylan gave an embarrassed little laugh. He draped his Million-Dollar Arm over Jamal's shoulder. "I never have to worry about you, do I?"

When Dylan's attention was turned away, Jamal saw a little frown cross KT's face, a pinch of something pained and frightened. Ashamed.

And then it was gone.

"I got you, man," KT said.

"Always?" Dylan said, smiling to the two of them.

"Always."

Jamal wrapped his arm around him. Skin to skin, muscle to bone. They were, briefly, unbreakable.

JOEL

His analyst's mind ran the odds. Of all the residents of Bentley, how could the first person Joel met upon his arrival be the one woman he was truly afraid to see? The woman who had been just as unpopular in high school as he but ten times harder, the woman permanently outshone by her famous older brother, the woman who would always be Joel's first and final girlfriend: Starsha Marilynn Clark, though God help the man dumb enough to call her by all three names.

Three thousand to one, he thought. He supposed his luck could only improve from here.

Joel went for a handshake, saw her hesitate. Nodding toward the dim line of trucks, where he'd just enjoyed the pleasure of watching an old bully's arrest, Joel said, "You're a professional."

"And we have an audience." She shook his hand quickly, lit her cigarette.

"Jason turned out about how I expected."

"We've all gotten a little worse for wear around here."

She held the cigarette with her teeth, adjusted a bun of muddy brown hair. She'd always been short and oddly proportioned: legs too long, arms too brief—"the velociraptor," they'd called her in school—but there was a nervy strength to her limbs now. Her nose had been broken at some point. She still had her brother's startling jade eyes, and Joel saw that she was running odds behind those eyes, just like him. She wasn't happy.

In a way, Joel was grateful for Clark's chilliness. After everything he had put her through ten years ago—and wasn't *that* a polite way of putting it—he was relieved she hadn't decided to knock a few bright teeth from his mouth.

The young deputy beside her, a cute guy covered in tattoos, smiled with a cordial scorn Joel remembered well from his time here. The man nodded at the convertible. "You think that little beauty can handle these roads here?"

"I'm sure Mr. Whitley will put on a good show if it can't," Clark said.

Whatever Joel might have said in response was lost to a little whoop of greeting from the crowd. "My goodness, Officers, y'all never catch a breath of peace." At the sound of her voice, Joel felt a knot loosen in his chest. He wasn't sure he'd ever been so grateful to know his mother was nearby.

She strode toward them with a hot dog in either hand, a massive leather bag dangling from the crook of her arm and a goggle-eyed Bison cap perched on her head.

"My Lord," she said, looking Joel up and down and turning to Clark. "Don't he look expensive?"

"Good to see you, Mrs. Whitley," Clark said.

Browder tapped the brim of an invisible cap. "Your son's a hell of a boy, ma'am," he said, and turned very seriously toward the field as if to leave no doubt which son he meant.

"You two are pure charity," said Joel's mother. "Let me

get this instigator out of y'all's hair, no? Tell your father I said hello, Clark."

Before Clark could turn away, Joel produced a business card from his wallet. A soft breeze toyed with the card's corner. Clark looked at Joel, at his mother. With a puff of smoke, she plucked the card from his fingers.

"My Lord Jesus, will the ladies ever have words about *this*," Joel's mother murmured when they had cleared the crowd of onlookers. The man at the little ticket booth waved them through with a surprised "Oh" of recognition. "And folks only just stopped talking about all that business between you and Starsha back in the day. Not to *mention* all that sadness with her brother—oh, shit fire—did I not send you a jersey this year?"

Joel shook his head.

"Dylan said I should bring you an old one. He thinks of everything." She handed Joel a hot dog. "There. Now it looks like you're trying."

Joel nibbled at the hot dog and took in his mother as she shouted her hellos and thank-yous to the folks who greeted her on their way by. Paulette Whitley, his indomitable mother. Her hair looked incredible and her makeup heavy: highlights and lowlights and two thick tracks of eyeliner. She was slimmer than Joel had ever seen her before—somehow her forearms were tighter than his own—yet he couldn't help but notice that when she turned her head the skin of her neck was finally beginning to crack. With a sudden lurch of guilt, Joel saw that in his absence his mother had begun to grow old, an indignity he thought had been reserved entirely for him.

"We're celebrities now, you know," Paulette said, turning to Joel with a laugh. "Your brother calls me the Real Housewife of Pettis County."

Joel smiled vaguely at this, at the familiar faces milling behind the stands. Curiously, there was no sign of that strange stuffed bison he'd encountered on his way in. Already Joel had written off the whisper he thought he'd heard in his speakers as road noise, written off the way the animal had seemed to study him from the bed of that truck but, still—Joel was glad he didn't have to write it all off again.

"It sounds like Dylan is the real deal," Joel said.

Paulette snorted. "You should hear the phone calls that boy gets."

"Phone calls for football?"

"All the big schools is circling like sharks." She counted her bright green nails. "Baylor, Notre Dame, Provincetown—"

"Princeton?"

"Penn State—they're getting ready to spend some money on their college football, they say. Rumor has it there's a baker's dozen recruiters here tonight, but my bet is they're waiting for the Perlin game next week. *That's* the match you should have come home to see. These Cougars ain't got much fight in them this year." Paulette stopped as Joel took another bite of his hot dog. A shrewd look came into her eye. "Dylan still ain't said why you decided to come down so sudden."

Joel chewed slowly, considered all the ways this conversation could work against him. "Where's Darren?"

"Houston. Killed him to miss this. He says hello."

"I should call him."

"He can text now." She fumbled in her bag for something. "When Darren moved into the house, Dylan taught him how to use the little yellow faces. Tulum looked lovely."

"More like salty."

Paulette made a little *hmm* he remembered well. Some of Joel's friends had mothers who gossiped with them about men and their attendant escapades as gleefully as they would with a daughter. Not Joel. He knew that, like subway travel and foreign food and apartment living, his queerness was the sort of thing Paulette could understand conceptually, could even see the appeal of in certain lights, but would rather not imagine in practice.

Why, he wondered, had she even brought it up tonight?

"Oh my word, look who it is!"

Joel turned to see a slim lady with a perfect shell of blond hair staring at him like he'd been fished from the lake.

"I had to come see for myself," the lady said to Paulette. When she shook her head not a single strand of that hair moved. "Has he been here long?"

"You remember Mrs. Malacek, Joel."

He didn't. "Of course."

"Mayor Malacek's wife," Paulette said. She always knew when he was lying. "Three terms later."

"Soon to be four. My son loves your brother." Mrs. Malacek let out a cackle like a wineglass striking a pool deck. With the most bizarre combination of pleasure and reproof Joel had ever heard, the woman added, "It takes a real talent to outshine the mayor's firstborn, you know."

"Oh my goodness, it *is* him!" called another thin woman, hustling to prevent any hope of escape. A small terrier trembled at its station in the woman's purse.

"I told my husband, I told him it was you. Sweet mercy Lord, don't you look growed? We needed a chest like that when you was in school."

"Mrs. Mason," Joel said, giving her a curt nod. Her nephew had gone well out of his way to make Joel's high school years unbearable. "A pleasure."

"He just arrived," Mrs. Malacek said knowingly. "All the way from San Francisco."

"New York, actually."

"Have you met Raul?" Mrs. Mason hoisted the bag to show him the dog. Joel saw it was wearing a miniature Bison jersey with a tiny number 7. "He's your brother's biggest fan."

Joel opened his mouth to say something, hesitated. "I'm sure Dylan needs all the support he can get."

"It just takes one state championship to turn a town around," Mrs. Malacek whispered.

The dog in Mrs. Mason's bag eyed the hot dog in the woman's hand. "And Heaven knows we need it—these stands are liable to rust right out from under us."

"Has Dylan told you which way the wind is blowing?" Mrs. Malacek asked Joel.

"Well, there's a storm to the southeast."

The women showed their teeth when they laughed. Mrs. Malacek said, "You always were too clever for me. His *college*, silly. We got us a pool going at the teachers' lounge. I have my money down your brother's going to pledge to Baylor University. I know he's a good Baptist boy at heart, even if this mother of yours has started dragging him around with the Methodists."

Mrs. Malacek and Mrs. Mason went very still. They fixed Joel with stares so fervid he felt a flush creep over his cheeks. He decided to test a theory. "What do you think would happen if Dylan decided he didn't want to play football in college?"

His mother's head snapped up from her phone. The two women raised their eyebrows.

"But we love Dylan too much for him to quit," Mrs. Malacek said brightly.

Mrs. Mason laughed and set Raul the terrier trembling again. "I think this town would kill him if he tried."

"Jesus," Joel said as he and his mother made their way toward their seats, leaving Mrs. Malacek and Mason to make a run on the convenience stand. "Since when did you hang out with the skinny moms?"

"Since they started calling me. Are you saying I weren't always skinny?"

Joel marveled at the people around him. Here was Mr. Lott, the cartoonish man in the overalls and bow tie who somehow still ran the county's oldest hardware store, followed by his tall wife and her permanent scowl. Here was the girl who had dropped out of Joel's class to raise the boy who now trailed behind her with a Nintendo in his face. Joel had thought more people would have left this town. He couldn't imagine what kept them here.

"How can nothing change in ten years?"

"You mean you didn't notice on the way in?" Paulette arched an eyebrow. "The old church burned down. It was the talk of the summer."

A little chill prickled in the back of his scalp. Sure enough, when Joel turned to look down the highway he saw that the electric cross of the Bentley First Baptist Church's steeple, the white cross that had once burned bright enough to be seen for miles, was gone.

"Then thank God summer's over."

His mother gave him a patient look. "I figured you'd see it as an improvement."

A roll of thunder made the pilings of the metal stands rattle. Paulette pulled two green ponchos from her bag, a bottle of water, a sack of trail mix. They made their way to the front row, where two empty spaces awaited them, not fifteen feet from the sideline.

Joel checked his phone, swiped away emails, saw he'd received a message from his brother. It was a selfie from inside the locker room—Joel would recognize those green cinder blocks anywhere—with Dylan and two other boys grinning in their pads. KILLING IT, the caption read, and nothing more.

"I thought that was you," said a voice to Joel's right, and a moment later Joel let out a laugh of surprise. It was Wesley

Mores, a man who had been a year older than Joel in school and one of the few football players who had always treated him decently.

The two men embraced. Wesley's broad back was still stiff with muscle.

"I was wondering if you'd moved back to town," Joel said.

"Back? I hardly left. I teach science at the junior high."

In the years since Joel had seen him, Wesley had suffered only a gentle retreat at his hairline. He'd gotten his teeth fixed, but now seemed shy about showing them, touching his mouth when Joel's eye ran over it. He wore a thick wooden cross around his neck.

"Science?" Joel said, his ass clenching when he took his seat on the cold bleacher. "For some reason I thought you majored in art."

Wesley smiled. "My passion is with the church. I lead the youth ministry at First Baptist."

Christ—Joel couldn't escape that place. "I just heard about the fire."

"There's a blessing in it somewhere." Wesley fixed Joel with a smile that seemed to add, *If you know what I mean.*

Joel didn't, but before he could say more the marching band launched into the opening bars of "My Herd, My Glory" and the Bison poured out of the field house. Joel rose to his feet with the rest of the town, hardly aware he was moving, and cheered wildly at the sight of his brother jogging out ahead of the others. Even under his pads, Dylan seemed to float an inch above the turf.

The Cougars' captain accepted the ball from the referee, watched his line assemble. Dylan thumped a pale Latino boy on the back and hustled to the sidelines.

"Tomas Hernandez," Wesley murmured as the Latino boy headed for the end zone. "He knows how to kick a ball when he feels like it. Your brother caused some consternation when he won the coin toss at the top of the game but deferred the kick until the second half. The Bison're an offense-heavy team. You'd think he'd want to use the o-line while they're fresh."

"Is it something to do with the weather?" Joel eyed the black sky.

"The weather?" Wesley said, and in response a strong wind kicked up from the south.

The whistle. Hernandez, the Bison's kicker, struck the ball hard and the line sprinted after it. Rattichville's offense fought a humid gust of storm wind. By the end of four quick downs, Bentley had pushed the visitors to within thirty yards of their own goal line.

Joel felt a novel twist of pride—Dylan had checked the forecast this evening. He smiled at the back of his brother's helmet. Provided the thunderhead moving into town didn't do anything erratic, Dylan had just arranged for the Bison to play the second half of the game with the wind at their backs.

Dylan made his way to the field with a chorus of cheers. A shouted play. Dylan clapped, caught the ball and lobbed it long. The wind took hold of the pass and carried it snugly into KT Staler's bony arms. The boy trotted it into the end zone with a pompous little stomp as the stands let out a roar to rival the thunder.

Through the euphoria that followed, Joel caught sight of one player who seemed unimpressed. The Bison's muscled running back accepted a squirt of water into his mouth and removed his helmet to wipe his face with the hem of his jersey. He had a stomach so grooved Joel could count his abs from yards away.

"Is that Luke Evers?" Joel asked. Luke and Dylan had once been inseparable.

"Don't mention that name when your brother's around," said Paulette, still clapping. "Pity how Luke's face turned out, no?"

Indeed. Luke had never been the cutest of boys but now his good looks started firmly below his neck. He only looked worse when Dylan finally reached the sidelines and Luke said something with a violent shake of the head like he was trying to beat an old argument back to life. Dylan waved Luke away but the muscled boy stepped forward, jabbed a finger at Dylan's chest, scowled.

"The hell is eating him?" Joel said.

"There's no telling." Paulette chewed trail mix.

"They haven't been the same since Dylan started dating Bethany Tanner," Wesley said. He nodded at a tall blonde cheerleader who was iridescent with glitter. Joel recognized the girl from his brother's Instagram but couldn't place what Wesley meant. Unless Joel was much mistaken, Bethany and Dylan had been dating for years.

Joel regarded Luke and Dylan with a touch of concern: whatever they were fighting over it seemed far more dire than an old breakup.

In the end, he said nothing.

The wind held. The Cougars were beaten back again and again. After a few long plays, someone called a time-out from the sidelines and, a moment later, Beyoncé's reliable hype belted from the speakers. Three black cheerleaders threw themselves into a hip-hop dance. Flanked by two girls, the boy in the center of the trio—the sole boy on the cheer squad, to Joel's eye—threw his hips forward and back with a flair that made Joel smile.

Wesley itched his cheek. He said out of the side of his mouth, "We've had more of that the last few years."

And just like that, all of Joel's old anger at this place came flaming up again. His mother was wrong—things were *exactly* like they'd been in his day. When the cheerleaders' routine was over, Joel realized he was the only person in the front row clapping.

Wesley flinched at the sound of Joel's applause. People stared.

Joel clapped harder. It was going to be a long weekend.

BETHANY

At the start of the fourth quarter, the Bisonette cheerleaders piled themselves into an inverted pyramid. From her place in the pyramid's center, Bethany Tanner—cheerleading captain, blonde darling, Homecoming Queen-to-be—scanned the faces in the stands for her father. If she didn't see him now, then Bethany might—just *might*—have a chance of succeeding at the weekend plans for which she'd spent an aeon preparing.

Her father wasn't here. All the fear floated free of her shoulders as she hit the crowd with her most radiant smile. That smile was a hundred percent genuine. Bethany was a very honest person.

"What's that sound?" the girls shouted to the packed stands. *"What's that noise? What's the herd with all my boys?"*

The rest of the cheer went great, just great, and by the time it was through, Bethany's head was so swollen with anticipation she almost missed her cue.

"Ready for dismount," said Kimbra Lott, one of the sturdy spotters behind the pyramid who nobody came to see.

"Ready for drop," said Jasmine Lopez, the second-prettiest girl at the school and Bethany's dearest friend, standing on the pyramid's flank.

"Bison herd!" Bethany shouted, but the boys had returned to the field and nobody was paying attention to her anymore. Which was fine. Just fine.

Bethany, Jasmine and Alisha Stinson, the girl to her other side, all raised their linked hands. The girls at Bethany's feet counted to three and heaved her up as Alisha and Jasmine flung her skyward. For one delirious second Bethany was airborne. All she could see were stars.

When she landed in the interlaced arms behind the pyramid, Bethany felt a fingernail burrow itself into the tender flesh of her knee.

"Sorry," whispered Kimbra Lott.

Bethany winced at the pain, but blessed the girl by ignoring her. Tonight was too good to spoil on someone as pedestrian as Kimbra Lott.

By the start of the fourth quarter, the Bison were sixteen points up, the wind had grown heavier and battered the visiting team every time they worked up a lick of momentum. Maybe the saying was true, Bethany thought: maybe God really did love football.

When He had a boy like Dylan Whitley playing for Him, how could He not?

Her boy, Dylan Whitley. Hers and nobody else's.

When the town stormed the field at the end of the game—the Bison had won 35–16—Dylan and Bethany posed for photos for the *Bentley Beacon*, for the school's sports blog, for underclassmen's Instagrams. Dylan's body was taut and hot and clammy where it pressed against her hip. His fingers behind her back played with the top of her bra.

At Dylan's signal, he and Bethany kissed deep. She popped one leg up behind her. When the little crowd around them went apeshit, Dylan and Bethany laughed into each other's mouths.

A troupe of grade schoolers brought out a collection of footballs for Dylan to sign. When a coordinator brought Dylan a towel, he wiped his face and offered it to the crowd with a smile. A girl from the middle school snatched it from his hand, giggling at her own courage.

"Can we have your gloves?" asked a pair of sandy-haired boys with the Bison's logo lacquered to their cheeks.

The boys' mother, a dowdy housewife in a T-shirt, looked Dylan over and whispered to Bethany, "Who gets to take home his cup?"

Bethany laughed, thanked the woman for coming. Down the line, she saw the other players and their girls holding court—much smaller court—with Sharpies and selfie sticks.

A rumble of thunder made the field lights tremble as Paulette Whitley and Dylan's brother arrived. The two boys embraced with far more enthusiasm than was strictly necessary.

Bethany tapped Dylan on the back to remind him he had one more duty to fulfill. Her man eased off his jersey with a chuckle, signed a dry spot on the back, passed it to a portly kid from the Mathletes. Bethany struck the boy's name off a list in her phone. She assured a pimply college dropout with a baby on her hip that she was absolutely scheduled to receive next week's jersey.

The portly kid took a few steps away, thinking no one would notice him, and brought the jersey to his nose.

"Y'all should raffle that shit for charity," said Dylan's brother, with what was either perplexity or disgust.

"Don't give them ideas. They'd eat me if they could," said Dylan. "How was Mexico?"

"Lots of fifty-k." The boys snickered at some private joke. "You'll have to come with me next time."

Bethany cut in to introduce herself, smiling and struggling to conceal how badly Joel Whitley perplexed her. He hardly resembled the boy she'd seen in the scandalous pictures that had caused such a stir around town years ago, the pictures Bethany had sworn to Dylan she'd never seen.

And, the pictures notwithstanding, could anyone really blame Bethany for being surprised to discover that a man with such thick arms as Joel Whitley could have such a faggy voice?

Not that there was anything wrong with that, of course. Bethany was a very modern girl.

She gave Paulette her biggest hug. "Will I be seeing you at the church service this Sunday?" Paulette asked.

"Of *course*." Bethany elbowed Dylan in the side. He laughed and squeezed her hip. She said, "At least one of us should be there this weekend."

"Are you going somewhere?" asked Joel, sounding surprised.

Dylan opened his mouth, hesitated.

Oh, Bethany thought. Joel didn't know.

"I'm just going for a little fishing trip," Dylan said after a beat. He hugged his mother without meeting Joel's eye. "KT's family got a place in G-town."

Joel looked confused.

"Galveston," KT Staler said, stepping over from the sideline with that little sneer he always wore these days. "Down at the coast?"

A flash of lightning broke through the glare of the halogen lights. Thunder followed a moment later, so close Bethany felt the field tremble beneath her feet.

Joel dug his car keys from his pocket, eyed his brother. "I was going to talk to you about something, D."

"Don't be out late, sweetheart," Paulette said, glancing at the sky. "It looks nasty tonight."

"We'll be back Sunday," Dylan told Joel. "I'll text you in the morning, yeah?"

The brothers embraced again. "Drive safe," said Joel.

Bethany almost felt bad for him.

When Joel was gone, Jamal said, "He seems chill."

The four of them started back toward the field house. KT said, "His hair's gay as fuck."

"That hair probably cost more than your house," Dylan said.

"Least my house ain't gay as fuck."

"Hey," Bethany said to KT. "Is Kimbra okay?"

KT said nothing.

Dylan passed Bethany her Sharpie. He patted her ass, murmured, "You ready for tonight?"

Her heart fluttered. She touched her tongue to her lip. "As I'll ever be."

They stopped outside the field house. Even after everything this town had put them through, after all of the tumult and tears and baring of the heart, when Bethany felt Dylan focus his full attention on her, when he rested a hand on the small of her back in that easy way of his, she still went warm.

Her boy leaned down close. He parted his lips. Slowly, softly, Dylan slipped into Bethany's ear the final words he would ever say to her.

"You're a fucking champion."

SATURDAY

SOMETHING YOU CAN'T FIX

JOEL

Friday night, the dreams began. As the storm finally burst, as the windows rattled with thunder, Joel lay in his old bed, his heart racing, his legs tangled in his bedclothes. He was running from something—something rotten, something *old*—that was chasing him through the hungry open country outside of town. He could it feel it, feel it right there behind him, snatching for his ankles, nicking the skin with a long cool nail. Getting closer. Closer.

When he awoke the next morning his mind was as cold and blank as a slab of marble. He was all but poached in sweat, one hand lost beneath his pillow, and when he checked his phone, he saw that he had slept for ten hours and was somehow more exhausted than when he'd gone to bed.

Joel struggled to recall his dream. A few vague impressions flickered, fast fading: a great black hole in the ground, a thudding in the earth. An ungodly stench.

And coursing through it all, his brother's voice, calling to him from somewhere deep in the dream, shouting something that sounded a lot like *run Joel run Joel* RUN.

Dylan. Joel sat up in bed, unlocked his phone. No calls. No messages.

Where the fuck was his brother?

Joel chewed a Xanax, cranked out a few sit-ups, but the awful anxiety that had squeezed itself around his heart refused to relent. He felt queasy, light-headed, terrified for no good reason. If he didn't move he'd be throwing up soon.

One thing at a time, Whitley. Shirt, pants, socks, sneakers, coffee. Breathe.

On his way to the front of the house, Joel stopped at his brother's room and pressed his ear against the door. He listened to the way the silence inside seemed to throb like a swollen heart—

imissedyou.

—and pulled away. He tasted dirt on his tongue.

His mother was eating at the breakfast table, her elbows propped over a plate of toast, her phone in her face.

"Has Dylan called?" Joel said, fighting a tremor in his fingers.

"He mostly texts."

Joel went to the kitchen for coffee. The mugs had moved.

"So he hasn't texted?"

"Why would he text?"

"Because he's been out all night. Because he's seventeen."

"Meaning he's asleep."

Joel slid the coffee's carafe back into the machine. "I couldn't take five steps at his age without you calling me."

"I learned a lot of lessons from you."

Joel heard the pat of soft footsteps from the hallway and looked up to see Darren, his mother's boyfriend, in a tank top stained all over with mustard. Joel had met Darren only twice, on the family's Christmas trips to the city. Like Paulette, he'd gotten older, though unlike her he'd grown narrow shouldered, paunchy, spry.

"Your mother told me you'd filled out." Darren rapped his knuckles on Joel's chest. "You must be beating off the boys up there with a stick."

"I mostly use my hands."

Darren laughed so hard he had to wipe his eyes. He'd always been alright with Joel.

"Some of us are eating," said Paulette.

"Dylan hasn't texted you, has he?" Joel said.

Darren headed for the refrigerator. "Dylan? Text me?"

"Joel's afraid the boy's dead in a pit somewhere," Paulette said.

Joel's coffee paused on its way to his lips. "What did you say?"

He caught the way her eyes narrowed, the way she looked away. Paulette delayed her answer with a bite of toast.

The dream. Joel's gut, that vaunted intuition of his, spoke clear and cold in his ear. *Did she have the same dream?*

"Ditch," she said. "Dead in a ditch. And he's not. What does it matter?"

Joel set his mug in the sink, his fingers going cold. Why was he so afraid this morning?

"I'm going for a run," he announced.

"You can leave the door unlocked." Paulette didn't look up from her phone.

"Love you," Darren called.

It was cold outside. The trees shushed one another, shook their boughs free of last night's rain. Joel tapped his Apple Watch. No messages. A cold bead of water fell from the eaves of the porch and shimmied down his neck.

He took off jogging.

Don't be afraid until you need to be afraid, he told himself (not that it did him much good.) As he rounded the corner of Gillis Street and ran on the road's shoulder—why did nobody in Texas believe in sidewalks?—Joel realized it wasn't just his dream that had set him on edge this morning. Joel had been afraid since before bed, since he'd driven around Bentley after the game and tried to assure himself that his brother's odd behavior last night was normal.

As he ran, Joel couldn't help but feel watched. He thought of those black eyes—those hungry empty eyes—in the stuffed bison he'd seen on the way into town. The thought made Joel's stomach twist. Sometimes he didn't want to know why one memory echoed with another.

Last night, in the rain, Joel had driven past the old storefronts on South Street, past the auto shop with the little Everest of stacked tires in its parking lot, past the dark splotch of the Milam Municipal Park on the west side of town. Such a runty little place, that park—a few trees, a parking circle, an overgrown gully—but they're never auspicious, are they, the places where your life is detonated?

An undignified site for an undignified arrest. An arrest which, depending on how you measured it, had been either the beginning or the end of Joel's problems.

It had certainly given the folks at Bentley First Baptist plenty to talk about, back then (though those folks were seldom at a loss for gossip.) Even with its steeple gone from the sky, Joel almost hadn't believed his mother when she'd told him last night that the church was gone. But, sure enough, he'd found a vacant lot lashed with rain on Hollis Avenue at the exact site where that old pile of red bricks and abrogation had once reigned.

That vacant lot had made Joel giddy in a way that he

doubted was entirely healthy. Back in his day, the church's brilliant white cross had loomed over every soul in Bentley like the eye of fucking Sauron. He wondered if it had been arson that had brought it down. He wondered why it had never occurred to him to burn it down himself.

Joel jogged harder.

When they'd been boys, it had always been Joel's responsibility to escort Dylan to school, to ferry his younger brother around on errands in the back of his old Civic like some rare (but uninteresting) breed of dog. For his part, Dylan had always seemed self-sufficient, enclosed, preternaturally competent—the thorough opposite of Joel in every way—and in the decade since his departure, Joel had never once experienced a moment's guilt for leaving his brother in their mother's care. Rearing the boy could hardly have taken much effort.

But last night, driving over these cracked streets, Joel realized you didn't have to be gay to feel trapped in this town. How could a kid Dylan's age look at a place with half its businesses chained shut, at a community where your every mistake was a topic of conversation, and not yearn to escape? In a way, Joel couldn't blame Dylan for taking a little trip to the coast to get away from it all. Joel only wondered how he could bear to return.

it's like i hear this town talking when i sleep.

Last night, not long after Joel had driven past the old site of the church, a massive chunk of nothing, a deeper night, had loomed up at him to the east, like he'd driven right to the edge of the earth. He'd run up against the Flats, of course, the endless miles of uninhabited countryside that brooded on the other side of the narrow highway. Shadows had formed and melted out there in the storm. Empty, hopelessly empty.

Joel had spent the past week being coy with Dylan about his exact motives for coming home, but for good reason. In

Joel's experience, the sort of money he planned to put on the table this weekend was best discussed in person. And it would be quite a sum: full tuition, an apartment, a car—whatever it took to finally be a brother to this boy that Joel, for all his intuition, had never once imagined might need him.

But at the sight of the Flats last night, at the sight of this chancre sore of a town, Joel had pulled out his phone, his palms sweating so badly he struggled to hold it. Don't worry, he'd written to Dylan, idling on the empty street. I'm getting you out of this shit hole.

He'd hit Send.

The road beneath the car had trembled, though Joel had heard no thunder.

A stoplight spilled blood over his windshield in the rain. He'd watched as his message was marked as Read by Dylan's phone.

A moment later Joel saw three little dots fill and empty on his screen, fill and empty, as Dylan typed a response.

Then the dots disappeared. No message came.

Now, twelve hours later, Joel's jog brought him to Spruce Boulevard, one of the three old thoroughfares that ran laterally across town, and he could see clear through to the Flats. Nothing moved out there. Not even a bird passed over those wastes. The Flats were just as empty this morning as they had been last night, just as *hungry*—

Joel felt a shiver creep up his arms. *Hungry?* Where had that come from?

He tapped his watch again. He wondered (hoped, to his surprise) if he would hear from Officer Clark today. It would be a welcome distraction. He thought of the indignant stare she'd fixed on him last night, those startling green eyes she'd shared with her brother Troy. An erstwhile Bison running back, a jittery has-been, missing and presumed dead, Troy

Clark was the man Joel had sworn to himself he would never allow Dylan to become.

Joel remembered Troy's eyes resting on his face in the light of a fetid summer afternoon. Joel remembered Troy nodding toward his truck's glove compartment and saying, *"Pass me those pills in there."*

Joel took a long breath. Silence blanketed Bentley.

He felt a faint pulse on his wrist.

1 New Message, his watch informed him. From Dylan.

Joel read the message. Read it again. His stomach began to burn.

He turned toward home and ran.

"My brother isn't illiterate," Joel told the large man in the rumpled blazer and jeans who had arrived from the sheriff's department. "He knows how to use an apostrophe."

The man smiled blandly, shifted himself from one large haunch to the other on the Whitley family's sofa. He had introduced himself a few minutes before as Investigator Grady Mayfield. He'd brought muscled Deputy Browder with him, the younger man reeking of body spray and chewing tobacco.

The two officers read the message that had arrived from Dylan, traded almost imperceptible shrugs.

The message was time-stamped 10:53 a.m. this morning.

joel im sorry but i cant stay in bentley right now theres something i gotta get away from somthing u cant fix dont worry im fine i will call when things r settled love u talk 2 u soon.

"He sounds bothered by something." Mayfield accepted a sweaty glass of iced tea from Paulette. Browder settled himself against the door frame and pinched his reddened eyes. "Which is a good thing."

"A good thing?"

"It means he'll calm down. Where else is he going to go but home? You folks don't have any other family, do you?"

"He's not *bothered*," Joel said. Mayfield and Browder exchanged looks again. Joel tried to calm himself: sounding like a hysterical queen wouldn't do his case any good. He cleared his throat, deepened his voice like he was back in a boardroom. "I know how my brother texts when he's upset. He gets worked up but he punctuates."

Mayfield sighed through his nose. "Are you saying that someone else texted you from your brother's phone?"

"But Dylan's never been happier," Paulette said before Joel could reply, picking at a fingernail. "Boys, they just need to stretch their legs sometimes."

Browder flipped open his notebook. Mayfield said, "Ma'am, can you give me the address of the place in Galveston where your son is staying for the weekend?"

There was a pause. "The address?"

"Yes, ma'am. Where they're staying with…"

Browder said, "KT Staler's brother."

"Thank you. With Mr. Staler's brother. That *is* where you said he was staying, yes?"

"Oh. Yes. Well—" She broke off for a moment. "It's just I never asked for the address, Investigator. I never saw any need for one. It's not like I was the one driving down there."

Joel gaped at her. Even once he'd bought his first cell phone, when he was Dylan's age, he'd never been allowed to step out the front door without telling his mother exactly where he would be, who with, the exact minute he would be home. All those precautions had done little good, of course (as Joel suspected these men from the sheriff's department knew very well), but he still couldn't believe that this was the sort of lesson his mother had learned from Joel's youth: to give a teenage boy unfettered run of the entire state of Texas.

"Of course." Mayfield smiled. "Then you'll have the phone number for Mr. Staler's brother? And a name?"

"Frank," she said.

"Floyd," Darren corrected her gently.

"Floyd. But he has a different last name, not Staler. He's a half brother." Paulette fumbled at her pockets for her phone before she caught sight of it on the edge of the wooden coffee table. "His number is—I know I had it, just a moment—"

While they waited, Mayfield turned to Joel. "I couldn't help but notice you got some real mud on the tires of that convertible out there. I assume that's yours?"

Joel considered his answer. "A rental."

"Well, she's pretty. What kept you out in that storm last night?"

Mayfield had a hard, sun-browned face, a flat nose, a tiny mouth. Joel caught the way his smile tightened, the concentration it betrayed. This investigator was only acting aloof, half-bored. There was a mind at work inside him.

Do not underestimate this man.

"I was enjoying the chance to drive. Living in the city you come to miss it."

"She can't handle nice in the rain."

"The weather must have gotten worse by the time I made it home. The car handled fine."

"And when was that, exactly?"

"I have it." Paulette flashed the screen of her phone at Mayfield. "The number. The Staler boy's number."

"Wonderful." Mayfield's smile was frigid.

Paulette read the number off her phone, went back and read it over again. "Floyd's a very nice young man," she said. "He works in construction."

"I'm glad someone from that family's made good," Mayfield said. "Your son hasn't had any problems with KT, has he?"

"Problems?"

"Excuse me," Joel said. "You've written that number down wrong."

He nodded at the notebook in Deputy Browder's hand.

Investigator Mayfield raised an eyebrow to Joel. "Is that right?"

"Look for yourself. The last digits. He's got them backward."

Browder handed Mayfield the pad. He didn't bother to suppress a scowl. "We're gonna have fun with you in town, ain't we?"

Mayfield cleared his throat. He set his glass on a table coaster, produced a pen and corrected the number himself. The investigator stood and smiled. Joel and his family rose after him. In the commotion, Joel noticed, Mayfield slid Browder's notebook into his own pocket.

"We'll get in touch with this Staler boy in the afternoon, see if we can't get Dylan on the horn for a few minutes. He might still be there, you know, at the coast. Or if he's gotten it in mind to run off, maybe he's told his friends where he's headed. Either way, y'all let us know if you hear from him in the meantime, yes?" Mayfield extended his hand to Paulette, to Darren. "I'll bet you a nickel he'll be walking through that door the moment we're walking out."

—*run Joel run Joel* RUN—

"Don't you want to see his room?" Joel said.

"No sense disturbing the boy's privacy till there's a call to." Mayfield ambled his way to the house's little parquet foyer. "Just by the by—when was it you said that you got in last night?"

Joel didn't hesitate. "Eleven o'clock. Maybe a minute past."

"Is that right?"

"Of course it is. I heard that car pull in right after the night news." Paulette's arms were barred across her chest, her chin jutted out, every inch of her suddenly ready for a fight.

The investigator said nothing more. He glanced between mother and son before letting himself out the door. The smell of Browder's cheap body spray choked the air when he was gone.

"That department always will have it out for you," Paulette told Joel with a scowl. He noticed she wouldn't meet his eye.

CLARK

When Clark arrived at Rummy's eight hours later, the only people crouched over the bar were the professional drinkers. She recognized George Mason—father to Garrett, the defensive safety—an oily man who'd once been a big deal at the power plant at the dam before the county had shut it down. Mr. Mason was flanked by a pair of former employees, all three men whiskered and humbled, clad in grease-stained jeans and fraying plaid shirts, drinking slowly with a gruff, masculine boredom. A woman with frizzled hair was making eyes with one of them. All three were making eyes at her.

Clark retreated to a booth in the back before any of the men could register her as fresh meat.

It had been an odd day, had followed an odd night. She thought again of Jason Ovelle, her old classmate she'd arrested at the field last night. She'd hoped to question him at the station after the game but Jason had been gone by the time she'd arrived.

"Full house," Deputy Jones had said. "I had to cut him loose." When Clark had taken a peek down the hall and found half of the station's holding cells empty, Deputy Jones, looming at her elbow, had said only, "A few slept it off since then."

The sheriff's station was small, it was true, but still, to let Jason go when he'd been facing a slam dunk charge of attempted burglary—it was peculiar. Deputy Jones was not a lenient man.

Joel arrived at Rummy's a few minutes after Clark, and before he noticed her, she took the opportunity to study him through the dull wall of smoke that thickened the room. She saw that Joel had corrected his teenage slouch. He now walked with an alert, entitled poise which she suspected had once been affected but was no longer. He looked cocky, careful, bored. He signaled to the barman without being spoken to.

Remarkable. How different this Joel was from the one she'd once dated. Tonight he seemed closer, indeed, to the Joel who appeared in the photographs that had arrived on Bentley's doorsteps ten years ago. That had been a nasty prank: a half-dozen loose photos of a naked Joel Whitley had been found stuffed inside the town's Sunday newspapers one weekend, hiding between the glossy Dillard's ads and the new issue of *Parade* magazine. In those photos Joel had sneered at the camera, had wielded a heft in his hand more compelling than anything he'd shown to Clark in all their fumbling efforts at fucking.

Clark had been seventeen at the time, old enough to have seen plenty, but still the pictures had shocked her. Before her father unwittingly flapped open the paper across the breakfast table that morning, Clark could never have imagined that the shy little gentleman who always asked permission to take her hand could be this same cocky provocateur with a face as brash and snide as any pinup boy.

The phone had rung not ten minutes after Clark had seen the pictures: her neighbor Miss Lydia calling to tell Clark of the rumor—the very *creditable* rumor—that Joel had been arrested with another man for indecent exposure at the park that past Friday night. Miss Lydia had called Clark to warn her. Joel's arrest—and these *strange* photographs everyone was finding—were all *anyone* could talk about.

Young Clark, to her credit, had pushed through her shock to ask Miss Lydia the smarter questions: who was this other man who had been with Joel at the park? Why had he not been arrested as well? Who had taken the photographs, xeroxed hundreds of copies, stuffed them in so many papers?

And sure enough, the sheriff's department did indeed mount an investigation into the photographs but things rapidly went nowhere, as they often did in Bentley. Who cared? The town had always known there was something *off* about that Whitley boy—really, had Clark never suspected *anything*?

Her miserable year had come to a ghastly conclusion. Six weeks after the photos had spread through town, Clark's brother, Troy, had left the little house he had shared with his girlfriend in Rockdale, an hour north of Bentley, to buy cigarettes and a case of beer at a Zippy Mart a few miles down the highway. He'd never made it. Somewhere between Troy's gravel driveway and the gas station's door he and his truck had apparently evaporated into the twilight.

It had wrenched Clark's world off its axis, broken all laws of nature as she knew them, to discover that her quiet brother with his razor wit—a boy who had once described the death of their batty, tender, financially hapless mother as simply, "The thriftiest thing that woman ever did"—could somehow slip between the cracks of the world and become abruptly, insistently absent.

Troy's girlfriend had reported him missing, another investigation had been mounted (that had been a busy year for the Pettis County Sheriff's Department), but little attention was ultimately paid to the disappearance of some old running back who had allowed something as simple as a neck injury to keep his team from reaching the championships in his high school days. The town gossips had been too busy still raging about Joel to care.

When Clark's troubled mother had died, the grief had been simple enough for Clark to handle: the woman was gone, and probably the better for it. But with Troy, Clark had long since found she could not grieve nor resent nor relinquish him. Troy, somehow, was both alive and not alive. He was baked white in the sun, delivering infants in Ecuador or, at this very moment, nursing a drink in some fuggy bar, just like the one Clark sat in now, and thinking of her.

So, despite all her furious misgivings about Joel, when Clark had received word this afternoon that Dylan Whitley had apparently decided to run away from home, she'd dug Joel's card from where she'd stuffed it in the pocket of last night's uniform. She'd texted to ask him if there was anything she could do. Who could imagine better than she the anxiety he must be going through?

She wasn't sure Joel deserved her kindness. She wasn't sure she could have treated the news any other way.

Joel made the barman pull down a full bottle of whiskey from the dusty top shelf, paid with cash, left his change. He approached her booth with the bottle and two milky shot glasses. He had spotted her after all.

"I hope you've developed a taste for rye," he said, settling into the booth.

"I'll taste whatever's liquid." She accepted a glass, let him pour her a heavy shot. "How are you holding up?"

He didn't answer her immediately. He downed a double

with a grimace, watched her in the hazy light. A runty man at the bar whose eye Clark had been avoiding sidled to the jukebox with a pout and turned on "When You Say Nothing at All."

"How much do you know?" Joel asked.

"Just that Dylan wants to stay out of town," she said truthfully.

"And won't respond to anything I write." Joel opened his phone, scrolled through it and laid a text exchange in front of her.

Dylan's most recent text read:

joel im sorry but i cant stay in bentley right now

This was followed by three messages from Joel:

Who is this?

If this is Dylan answer the phone.

Where is my brother.

"Why did you assume right away that this isn't him?" Clark said.

"Because even when he's upset he doesn't text like this. Look." Joel pulled down an earlier message, one that began, i can't quit football. "That message Sunday night is the reason I came down here in the first place—there's something wrong with my brother. Not that the investigator bothered to ask."

Clark read the message twice. "What's the Bright Lands?"

"Fuck if I know. Did anyone get hold of the guy Dylan and his friends were supposed to be staying with at the coast?"

She pushed the phone back across the table. She tried to smile. "You have to know I can't tell you that."

He nodded, played his fingers on his glass.

"Hey," Clark said. "Maybe the message this morning was just a prank— KT or Jamal got hold of Dylan's phone and decided they wanted to put you through the wringer. Boys can be like that."

"How did they get through the phone's passcode?"

"Maybe they saw Dylan type it in one time. Maybe he didn't have one."

"And Troy never sent you anything like this? Back after—everything?"

Clark wondered if Joel realized how rude he had become. She poured another shot for the both of them and said calmly, "How is New York?"

"Isn't it a hell of a coincidence?" Joel went on like he hadn't heard her. "Two football players who both run off for no obvious reason?"

"Joel, I don't quite know how to say this. The biggest game of the season is Friday. It must be plenty of pressure." She slid her glass back and forth. "People around here might say a coincidence is you turning up after ten years away and your brother running off the next morning."

He narrowed his eyes at her. "I have an alibi."

She downed the drink. "I ain't accusing you of anything. Listen—boys your brother's age do strange things. Present company included, yeah?"

He struggled to return her smile.

"You'll be happy to know the fat fucker who arrested you at the park had to go on medical retirement," she said.

"Heart attack?"

"Something more satisfying. Old Deputy Grissom was out riding his horse this summer and the damn animal spooked, fell on him, dragged him over a rock. By the time some hikers found him, he'd had so much brain bleeding he'd percolated into a vegetable."

"I'm sorry to hear that."

"You shouldn't be. Listen, Joel—" She waited for him to meet her eye. "We care, alright? The whole department, the whole town, we love Dylan. The sheriff's already gotten a call from the mayor about it, just like he has from every man in the Chamber of Commerce. If Investigator Mayfield says he's going to call KT Staler's brother then he's going to call him. But you've got to bear with us, alright? We had two officers take jobs in the city this spring. Thank God we had Browder join up because Grissom's retirement would have put us three down otherwise. It's a big county. All the usual rambunction. We got the meth crazies breaking into trucks and farms, we had someone burn down that damn church—"

"So it *was* arson?" Joel said, tilting his head. "My mother said it was an electrical fire."

Clark *tsked*. She'd forgotten how sharp Joel was. "Have a good night, Mr. Whitley."

She rose to go but he grabbed her hand. "I'm sorry," he said, and sounded like he meant it. Sounded suddenly, thoroughly defeated. "I know it sounds crazy but I was just—I woke up afraid. I spent all night dreaming about my brother."

Clark's hand lingered under his. So had she.

SUNDAY

THE SEARCH

JOEL

The whiskey pulsed in Joel's head. He shielded his eyes from the morning light, squinted at his phone through his fingers. A stone formed in his gut. A new message awaited him.

u never tried to understand me. how many years u lived in the city u nver bothered to ask am i ok is everything ok until i had 2 beg u to help its too late joel i never want 2 talk to anyone from that fucking town again. go home. u make mom sad

Fuck all of yesterday's doubts. Dear God, just let this be Dylan texting him.

Joel typed:

A ticket to NYC. No questions asked. You can stay with me or I'll get you a place. No one will know. Please Dylan, talk to me.

He rose, paced, couldn't wait.

Dylan, I'm sorry. I'm sorry. I should have done everything and I should have done it more. I know. I know. Please Dylan, please come home.

He didn't realize he was crying until he saw a tear spatter across the glass of his screen.

I never realized how much I cared.

fuck u joel. go home

He found his mother in the kitchen dressed in her church slacks, powdering her face at the table. She glanced at Joel, at the phone in his hand. "Any word?"

He fumbled for coffee. "No." Something—maybe paranoia, maybe some strange protective pride—kept him from mentioning the messages, let alone informing the police of them just yet. It persisted, no matter how hard he tried to ignore it: that gnawing suspicion that the person on the other side of these messages wasn't his brother at all.

"He must have caught a big one."

"A big what?"

"A fish." She spoke sharply, softened. "He's fishing, right?"

Joel said nothing.

Paulette untwisted her lipstick. "You can't win as a parent, Joel. I hope you remember that."

"I doubt I'll ever need to."

"Your father used to say the same thing."

Joel put down his coffee. His belligerent father used to say a lot of shitty things, the last of which (before a choked blood vessel burst in his brain) was, *"What part of headache don't you fuckers understand?"*

The man hadn't been missed. The fact that Paulette would mention him at all told Joel plenty about her current state of mind.

"Oh hell, Joel," Paulette said. "It's going to be alright, alright? Dylan's been thrilled all week to see you."

This didn't soothe him.

Darren tooted the horn of the truck outside. His mother gathered up her Bible and a little plastic carrier of muffins.

Joel, desperate for anything to say, asked, "Did Mrs. Malacek say we're Methodists now?"

His mother rolled her eyes. "We've been Methodists ever since the Baptists took an opinion on my moving Darren into the house without rings on our fingers. I swear to Jesus, Joel, some of those ladies act like God made pussy just to keep yeast in circulation."

Darren tooted the horn again. She wrapped Joel in a quick hug, kissed his cheek. He felt an anxious heartbeat in her hand. Saw, in the brisk way she twisted on her tall heel, a stubborn effort to fool the world into behaving itself.

"Dylan's fine," she said. "And if he ain't fine, you call me—I got my phone on ring."

Joel paced the empty house. He studied his brother's Instagram, spotted faces from the game on Friday, noted the ways the boys either posed in their football pads spreading their fingers into *W*'s like gang signs (it took him far too long to realize that the *W*'s stood for "win") or else leaned against truck beds and lockers with their hands cupped over their crotches, their eyes, broody and vacant, fixed to the camera. So serious, so young. What were the odds, Joel wondered, that Dylan and his friends pulled on this showy angst to conceal a truer turmoil inside?

Joel bounced around Instagram profiles. He settled on Bethany Tanner's, his brother's girlfriend, but learned little in studying it. Bethany was the sort of petite, strong-boned blonde darling Joel used to be told he should desire. He detected the glow of money in her impeccable skin and finally realized why her name was so familiar: the Tanner family owned a cattle ranch west of town. If the ranch was still running—which, judging from Bethany's gleaming Lexus, it was—those cows must be one of the few moneymaking ventures left in Pettis County.

Here Bethany stood with Dylan at the game Friday night, one leg cocked up behind her. Here she was beaming with the other cheerleaders in the high school's gym. Here she was with Dylan again, the two of them smiling in camouflage, posed in front of a deer stand with hunting rifles in their hands. Sharpest Shot In the West he calls me lol, read the caption. #girlslikegunstoo.

In her most recent picture, posted yesterday, Bethany lay resting against a pile of pillows, a sticker of a cartoon thermometer jutting from her pouting mouth. why does this never happen on school days haha #fever.

Joel wondered what the odds were that Dylan might be resting on a pillow beside her, cropped just out of the frame.

Joel made a lap around the kitchen. Another. He canceled his flight back to New York and emailed his team to tell them he would be in Texas for a few days longer.

He pushed open the door to his brother's room.

Things inside were remarkably tidy for a boy Dylan's age. Joel went to the closet, found a shirt on every hanger. He checked the drawers of the dresser and found them full of socks and underwear. His brother was traveling light.

Three posters hung on the wall: a close-up of Peyton Manning; a team photo of the Bison bearing the words STATE SEMIFINALISTS, DALLAS, TX; the back of a white jersey that read #1 CHRIST. The only other note of personality in the room Joel found resting facedown in the drawer of a small oak desk.

It was another photo, this one of a much younger Dylan—in a jersey and pads—smiling with his arm over the shoulder of Luke Evers, the muscled running back Joel had seen arguing with Dylan at the game on Friday night. *"They haven't been the same since Dylan started going out with Bethany Tanner,"* Wesley Mores had said.

Joel returned the picture to the drawer, tapped his phone. A response from work, texts from tedious men in Manhattan, but nothing from Dylan. Joel had lost count of how many times he'd called his brother's number but he called it again now. It was routed immediately to voice mail.

He dug through the other drawers of Dylan's desk but found little of interest—iPhone charger, pencils, chewing gum. One drawer contained a dusty hunting knife, his brother's initials written in Sharpie on the sheath. Joel slid the blade free. Long, serrated, perfectly clean, it clearly hadn't seen use in ages. He returned the knife to the drawer.

He rose from the desk's chair and crossed the room to check inside Dylan's bedside table. At first he saw nothing but loose change, an exhausted tube of Lubriderm.

His eye settled on something odd: a gleaming gold Movado wristwatch. Joel held the watch to the light and wondered how Dylan (who, as far as Joel knew, had never worked a day in his life) had bought it. Paulette and Darren weren't the type to give showy gifts, and even if they were, they could never have afforded a brand this expensive on their modest paychecks.

Very strange.

And then Joel spotted something far more troubling in the nightstand's drawer. From far in the back he fished out an unlabeled amber vial with a dozen yellow tablets inside.

Joel googled the imprints on the sides of the pills and let out a sigh. They were Oxycodone, a powerful painkiller, and a high dose at that. POTENTIAL FOR RECREATION/ABUSE: SIGNIFICANT, read the pills' literature.

Joel wondered what the odds were Dylan had been prescribed the pills to help with the aches and pains that must be inevitable in a game as strenuous as football. Not unlikely, but if that had been the case, then why didn't the bottle bear an official label from a pharmacy?

Something Clark had said last night flitted through Joel's

head: *"We've got all the usual meth crazies around here."* Oxycodone was a sedative, whereas methamphetamine, he knew, was a stimulant (a stimulant, Joel reminded himself, only a molecule removed from the Adderall currently pulsing in his own brain.)

Different drug classes, different effects, but the sight of the pricey watch waiting so near to these pills put an unpleasant thought in Joel's mind. A thought that Dylan might be connected to something far more dangerous than the school's athletic department.

Joel paced the room. He knew he should tell Investigator Mayfield about this discovery, should at least text Clark. Perhaps if he threw the cops a bone they would keep him abreast of the search for Dylan (assuming, of course, they were even searching at all), possibly give him some comforting news.

Joel laughed to himself. Who was he kidding? After what the Pettis County Sheriff's Department had put him through as a boy, was he really naive enough to think they would be of any use to him now? Any news Joel gave the police would become the gossip of the town. He'd never subject his brother to that sort of pain. Hadn't he come here to keep Bentley from chewing up yet another troubled boy? No, Joel would do his own digging, and he would keep any discoveries to himself.

Starting with these pills. He carried them into his room and stuffed them in his bag.

South Street resembled an old Western set left to blanch in the sun. Joel counted six businesses still in operation in the splintered wooden storefronts: the First Community Bank (GO #12 T-BAY BASKIN! read the marquee in the window), a CVS Pharmacy, Mr. Jack's Steaks, Hash and Brown's Egg House (the large fiberglass chicken suspended above the door in desperate need of a wash), Beauty Sanchez Beauty

Parlor and, all but hanging off the butt end of the street, the tall polished windows of Lott's Hardware.

Joel walked past the last store slowly, hoping he might talk to Mr. Lott—one of the few men who had been decent to Joel in the wake of the scandal—but saw instead a plain, mousy girl standing behind the counter.

When Joel stepped into the store the girl gave him only a curious glance—curious but not unkind—and looked back down at her phone.

"Excuse me," Joel said, approaching the counter. "I'm Joel Whitley—"

"I know." The girl finished typing a message, set down her phone, leaned back on her stool. Joel recognized her from the game. She was a cheerleader, and if Joel wasn't much mistaken he'd seen her posing for photos with KT Staler, Dylan's friend, in those giddy moments after the town had stormed the field.

"Are you Mr. Lott's daughter?" Joel asked, though on second glance he saw he didn't need to ask: she had her father's brows and her mother's frown. She wasn't the prettiest person he'd ever seen—he hated himself for noticing, but the girl certainly had nothing on Bethany Tanner—and judging by her faded clothes and her frizzy heap of hair it was clear her family's store was far from flush. But Kimbra had a spark in her eye, a slyness. Here was a girl who knew she was made for something more exciting than this.

"Kimbra." She extended a cool hand across the counter to him. Her handshake was firm. "Dadders is away quail hunting this weekend. Do you need him?"

Joel wasn't surprised to hear this—he'd never known Mr. and Mrs. Lott to enjoy each other's company.

"Actually I was hoping to speak to you." Joel lowered his voice. "You're dating KT Staler, yes?"

The girl glanced over Joel's shoulder at the door. A blink and her eyes had gone dark. She said softly, "Is he okay?"

"Why would KT not be okay?"

"I thought maybe Dylan called you."

"Called me about what?"

"Like an accident or something."

"He hasn't called at all. I was wondering when we could expect those guys home today."

"What's this about?"

Joel regarded her a moment. "I'm just looking forward to seeing Dylan again."

The girl didn't blink. "Aren't we all?"

Joel stopped by the CVS to ascertain something he'd already guessed: his brother didn't have a prescription at the pharmacy, and, after a little wheedling ("Are you sure? My mother swears it's here for him") discovered that Dylan had never filled a prescription for Oxycodone, or any other medication for that matter.

Joel sat in a creaking wooden booth at Hash and Brown's Egg House for the better part of an hour, drinking coffee and skimming the pages of the *Bentley Beacon*. There was a breathless write-up of the game on Friday (DYLAN WHITLEY AND BISON CONTINUE CHARGE… TO STATE FINALS?) and small ads for VOTE MAYOR MALACEK, COUNTY ATTORNEY BOONE, SHERIFF LOPEZ— FOR A CLEAN RECORD.

A waitress came to refill his coffee, but when Joel raised his head to thank her, her eyes widened in recognition. Joel knew that look well. Bethany Tanner had given him one just like it at the game: this waitress was comparing the man in front of her to the boy she had no doubt seen brandishing himself at a camera when she was a girl.

Joel had forgotten just how long this town's memory could be.

He handed her a twenty and didn't wait for his change. As he returned to his car, he felt eyes on him from all directions.

He came to a decision. If he wanted to learn what was wrong with his brother he would need a friend in Bentley, someone the place still treated as a local. Clark—*Deputy* Clark—was out. Paulette was too close to give Joel impartial help. What few buddies he'd hung around with in high school had all distanced themselves after his little scandal.

No, he thought. *Not quite all.*

"Those boys are fine," Wesley shouted from the kitchen. "Most of them, I mean. Do you want a beer?"

Joel caught the bright tang of onions striking oil. The size of the house had surprised him: it was an ugly mishmash of tall windows and peaked gables that sat alone at the heart of a new (and apparently abandoned) subdevelopment, its neighbors nothing but bare studs, empty window sockets, drywall swaddled in tattered Tyvek sheeting.

Inside, Wesley had clearly struggled to fill the place. A muted TV rested far enough away from the sofa Joel could hardly read the names of the men in their boxy suits discussing a football game. A little drinks cart rested in a distant corner. A massive iron cross hung above Joel's head, an outline of the state of Texas inscribed on its heart.

Joel agreed to the beer. "Are you the only person on this block?"

"Only person for miles," Wesley called. He returned to the living room with two sweating bottles of Corona. "I got this house off the Evers family for a song a few years back. Mrs. Evers got a little carried away with her redevelopment plans and had to unload fast."

Joel took a long pull of the cold beer. He knew the sort of property developments Wesley was talking about—fat bubbles of speculation slippery with enthusiasm—and had counseled plenty of investors against them in the course of his career.

"This is the same Evers family as Luke, the running back?"

"The very ones. His family owns half the town these days, runs the Chamber of Commerce, such as it is. Did you ever go in the back room of the steak house on South Street? Mr. Evers is like a king in there these days, smoking and talking with the other men, scheming how to get us back in the black. Not that it does him much good at the moment. Football's the only business still going around here."

"You don't say," Joel said, as casually as he could. "Were any of your kids at the youth group talking about the fight Luke and Dylan had at the game?"

"That's all for appearances. Those boys have to keep up a rivalry, you know. Your brother stole Luke's girl back in middle school so now they have parts to play."

"Luke and Bethany Tanner used to be an item?"

"I think their parents still wish they were. Evers and Tanner would be worth a small fortune if they got together."

"But instead she chose my family."

Wesley laughed. "Bethany and Dylan seem like the real deal."

"She certainly loves the attention. Mind if we lay into something stronger?"

Joel was halfway to the drinks cart by the time Wesley told him to help himself.

Joel plucked a whiskey at random from a thicket of bottles and poured himself a double. He drank it down fast, poured another for himself and Wesley. For a man with a cross in his living room, this youth minister possessed quite an array of booze.

"Does KT Staler ever come to church with my brother?" Joel shouted toward the kitchen.

"You mean Mister Powerball? He's a cat, he comes and goes. His sister, Savannah, was in your class at school, no?"

"The one who went to jail?" Joel faintly remembered Savannah Staler, a cheerleader rumored to have a hole in her nose from all the powder she snorted.

"The very same. She used to date Jason Ovelle."

"I saw that guy getting loaded into a cruiser Friday night," Joel said, with a faint odd blush of nostalgia. Jason had been a bully, and a savage one at that, but Joel had once had quite the locker room crush on him (and on all that he'd once kept, barely concealed, beneath his towel). "What did Jason do at the game to get arrested for?"

"What *hasn't* he done? It's a sadness, how that guy's turned out. And his buddy Ranger Mason is hardly any better. He lost most of his hand in Afghanistan."

Now *there* was a name with no pleasant memories tethered to it. Joel felt his heart shrink, felt a sudden need to pull his mind away from everything the thought of Ranger brought back to him. He opened his phone. He logged on to Grindr, smiled at the number of men who had messaged him since his arrival in town. Just like that, and he was desirable. He was worth something again, whatever Ranger Mason might once have said.

Joel took a sip of his whiskey. With a grin, he had a sudden recollection of Dylan at the field, smiling as the town laid itself at his feet.

They had something in common, the two brothers: they both loved attention from people they never wanted to know.

"My mother says KT and Dylan are very close," Joel said.

"They are. Dylan was real concerned for KT over the summer. Staler got into some kind of trouble."

"With drugs?"

Wesley poked his head out of the kitchen. Joel felt him glance at the open phone and quickly concealed it. If Wesley recognized what he saw on the screen, however, he gave no sign of it. "What makes you say that?"

"Dylan and KT went to the coast a few times this summer, no?"

Wesley accepted his drink. "Every few weekends. Your brother isn't much of a churchgoer either way. Why do you ask?"

Joel almost mentioned something Investigator Mayfield had said yesterday—*"The Staler boy hasn't given Dylan any trouble?"*—but caught himself. Just like he had with Kimbra Lott at the hardware store, Joel was leery of giving this man ideas.

Joel realized that Wesley had held his eye all this time. He cleared his throat and rose from the couch. "Can I use your bathroom?"

Wesley blinked. "Straight down the hall."

On Grindr, a grid of men's online profiles covered his screen. Most of the profiles, Joel saw, lacked any photo of their owner, which was unsurprising considering this corner of the country. A man's faceless gray silhouette, the app's placeholder image to conceal those users too cautious to even hint at their identity, repeated itself twenty times before Joel spotted an actual profile photo. A tight torso was posed in the mirror of an elegant bedroom so softly lit Joel doubted it could be found anywhere in Pettis County; good taste like this didn't seem to exist outside of cities. This user, he suspected, was using someone else's photographs.

Whoever they were, they had sent him a message:
omg ur the brother!!

Joel glanced at the man's profile: no height listed, no weight, no age, no name. Who was this?

Am I? Joel wrote.

The user sent him an emoji with hearts for eyes.

Joel responded:
How old are you?

Joel stepped into a bedroom large enough to house a small

plane and found little inside but hideous oak furniture and a sprawling painting of a cattle range.

15...y???

Jesus Christ. Joel tapped BLOCK. The profile vanished from his screen without a sound.

Another cross awaited Joel over the toilet in the master suite's bathroom. As he relieved himself, he wondered what sort of life he had escaped in his exile from this town.

He almost didn't feel his watch tremble with a message on his wrist.

It was Dylan.

im sorry, came first. Then, after a pause:

i loved you too.

Why did this bring Joel no comfort? He flushed the toilet, splashed water on his face, fumbled with a branded Bison hand towel—he'd somehow gotten hammered on a glass of whiskey. Or was it three?

call me D. Lets fixx this.

A metallic glint caught his eye on the dresser as he made his way back across the bedroom: a gold medal embossed with a footballer. Joel, drunk as he was, could just make out the words MOST VALUABLE PLAYER on the back.

"I'm still repping," Wesley said from the bedroom door, nodding at the medal and sounding abashed.

"I didn't know you were MVP."

"Oh, you know me." Wesley stepped close. He took hold of the medal still dangling between Joel's fingers on its crisp blue ribbon. "Mister Glory Days."

Something curious happened: Wesley let the motion of grabbing the little gold disk carry him forward, like he'd drunkenly lost his balance, and a moment later his head had come to rest on Joel's shoulder, his chest against Joel's chest, his free hand—calloused and dry and very hot—cupped loosely around Joel's bicep.

Their faces were close. Joel, somehow, always forgot just how shockingly right another man's body felt against his own, even when it was this unwelcome. He always forgot the heat of another man's throat.

"We've had more of that the last few years."

Joel's stomach turned. He stepped away quickly. Wesley gave him a pained pout, smoothed his shirt and tucked the golden medal in his pocket with a chuckle. "Sorry about that," he said. "Whiskey's too much of a blessing sometimes. Do you like mayonnaise with your burger?"

"I think I've lost my appetite," Joel replied. He fumbled for his keys, though he knew he shouldn't be driving with all the booze in his blood. A car wreck would still be better than whatever sad accidents Wesley had in store for him here.

But as he reached the front door, the fog of alcohol lifted long enough for him to notice the obvious.

i loved u too, his brother's message had read.

Loved. Past tense.

MONDAY

BLOOD

CLARK

When the call finally came, the one she had been dreading all weekend, Clark had been dreaming (like she had all weekend) of Dylan Whitley.

She was asleep in her childhood bedroom—the room down the hall, in fact, the one which she now used to lodge exercise equipment—and while her dream-self knew that she had come to bed alone a few hours before, she had stirred, in the deep dark, and realized abruptly that there was a man standing just past the corner of her bed, dripping water onto her floor.

"Troy?"

A silence. In the far distance, beyond the man in the dark, she heard a thick insect drone, the faint rumble of a large engine.

"No," the man said, and she recognized the voice as Dylan Whitley's, though it lacked all of his Friday swagger. Instead he spoke almost in a whisper. "There's not much time. You need to be ready, Officer. Both of you need to be ready."

Odd, she thought—her eyes refused to adjust to the blackness that surrounded her.

"Ready for what?" she said.

"The big game."

She heard her phone ringing, chirpy and distant, and a single strand of white Christmas lights stuttered to life above her bed. They revealed that she wasn't in her childhood room after all. She had somehow been dropped into a black box with nails jutting from its walls, pale floorboards, a little kitchen. She recognized the droning. A mass of writhing flies glittered above her, gleaming like the garnet shawls her mother had always worn.

Clark went cold at a sight past the end of her bed. She and Dylan weren't alone. There, in a dark corner, she could make out the leathery shape of another man. A man, but not a man: its fingers too long, its arms bent with too many joints. The man-shape, a blackness where its face should be, was coiled in a ball on the floor and rubbing itself, slowly.

Clark didn't dare to move. She'd seen this shape's work before but never the shape itself. It was death, she thought at first. Death, pleasuring itself with a little whimper.

No, her dream-self said. It was something much worse than death.

"Dylan," she whispered, because now Dylan Whitley, standing at the end of her bed, had turned to study the thing with her. "Dylan, what is that?"

The droning mass of flies above them began to cheer, the engine outside sputtered and when the black man-shape in the corner rose to its feet, a stench of rot filled the room: a smell that was putrid and sour and *old*. A low whisper escaped the void of the thing's face.

Dylan Whitley smiled at her. Where his right arm should

have been there was nothing but a single piece of collarbone jutting from his jersey, the wound weeping blood onto her floor.

"That's only the best years of my life right there, Officer," he said with a laugh, and the man-shape forced its hand inside the boy's open mouth.

She startled awake. The phone stopped ringing the moment she grabbed hold of it: 6:02 a.m. The smell of rot lingered in her dark room. After some of the things her crazy mother had told her as a girl, Clark couldn't help but crawl to the end of her bed where Dylan had been standing in the dream and reach out to ensure that her floor was dry.

The phone began to ring again. Investigator Mayfield.

She was at the intersection of South Street and the highway when she heard a siren behind her. Deputy Jones pulled into the oncoming lane and rolled down his window.

"Stay close," he shouted.

Clark nodded. She leaned on the gas, eased the clutch.

Go.

To the left they passed the school, the bar, the sheriff's station. To their right, the empty eastern Flats flew by, the shaggy scrub and wild grass burning in the dawn. Soon they were passing the football field. Its rows of dead lights all cupped the crimson sun.

Only the best years of my life.

She debated calling Joel Whitley and decided against it. Let him sleep, if he was sleeping. If her suspicions were correct he wasn't about to get much rest for a while.

The two deputies made it almost thirty miles north of town at top speed before Jones began to tap his brakes. Clark followed him around a tight turn, her shocks letting up a moan of protest.

Pebbles scattered as they bustled down what looked to be

a private drive. Clark lowered her visor against the molten sun. Soon she caught the shape of a wooden fence, a wooden house in the distance, a scattering of outbuildings: a toolshed, a chicken coop, a horse stall.

A semitruck loomed over three SUVs and a Dodge Ram. Three men were smoking in the shade of the tall truck's cab. Clark recognized Sheriff Lopez, Investigator Mayfield and Jack Spearson, the owner of the semi.

Jones and Clark clambered out and gave the men hollow little nods. Lopez gestured the two deputies closer.

"You don't spook easy, do you, Clark?"

A bird whistled from among the leathery leaves of a nearby pecan. A woman's face watched her from the house's screen door.

"I don't believe so, sir."

Lopez glanced at Mayfield as if for his assent. The investigator nodded.

"The ATV don't seat but four," Spearson said. His eyes were glassy, like he was coming off stimulants. "One of y'alls could stand on the fender but—"

Jones said, "I'm fine right here."

Spearson led them to a rusted red ATV. Clark sat in the back, next to Mayfield, and they went bounding around the house. There was nothing awaiting them on the other side but open country.

"It weren't nothing but luck," Spearson shouted over the whining motor. "All this here is Evers land these last few years. Mrs. Evers, she bought it out from me when the stocks went all to shit in oh-eight. But she kept me on as a groundskeeper, see."

Clark bounced in her seat. She gripped the cool metal bar of the ATV's frame to steady herself.

"I drives around once a week for her, the Evers lady, to look see has any vagrants set up camp, any of them tweakers cooking up that meth crank out here. I drives armed—I won't make no secret of that."

Spearson gunned the gas and soon the little house was only a fleck of black on the gold horizon behind them. Ahead of them, as far as Clark could see, was nothing.

"I got in from my haul late last night, maybe near past midnight, but I couldn't sleep for shit—pardon, Officer, ma'am—on accounts I got the cedar allergies something bad, so rights around four thirty I say to hell with it, I'll just make my rounds in the dark. This little guy's got him the new lights on him, after all, and it were a clear morning."

They bounced over a nest of small stones. In the very far distance Clark could make out a few spindly trees cutting a ragged lateral line across the country ahead of them.

"Now, normally, I start by heading out down to the south, at the property line, thens I cut across and head north up along Balton Creek till I hit the other line and come back around home. The creek is the eastern dividing line, see, between here and the far property."

The ground sloped softly downward. Clark caught a faint tang of water in the air. Spearson banked to the left.

"But see, this morning, I thought I heard me a cayote up there northaways so when I set out I started off that direction first. I didn't find no cayote but I still set off to the east till I ran up on the creek. And if I hadn't gone that way I would have drove right past it." A pause. "I would have drove right past it."

The ATV began to slow. Clark's feet had gone numb on the quaking metal floor. Spearson brought them to within twenty yards of a creek bed and stopped. Under the whiny click of the motor, Clark could hear the faint babble of slow water.

She saw a teeming cloud of flies.

Spearson nodded past the hood of the ATV. "It's just there."

Dry grass crunched under Clark's boots. Cicadas droned.

The iron smell of water grew stronger. The mass of flies pitched and reared. They didn't disperse when the officers reached the edge of the creek.

The boy was stretched out on his belly, his feet bare, one arm flung out, the other folded beneath him. One side of his face was sunk in the shallow water. The other was turned up to greet them.

His cheeks were battered blue. His hands were a stark, cold white. He wore only a pair of dark jeans and a green Bison leather jacket. The jacket rode up around his hips. He wore no shirt underneath. On the side of his ridged stomach Clark saw the unmistakable dash of a knife wound. She noted, with a sudden irrational relief, that both of his arms were attached to his body. Instead, something horrible spread open on the boy's throat.

And, of course, Clark saw the name branded across the back of the jacket, stitched just above the leaping Bison logo.

WHITLEY.

Only the best years of my life.

They stood in silence, watching the shallow water skitter over Dylan's open eye. Finally Lopez stepped back, turned to Spearson and said, "Who have you told about this, Jack?"

"Just y'all. Not even my wife."

Lopez nodded. In a low voice he said to Mayfield, "Get to that school. The boy's friends, the ones he went to the coast with, did they make it back last night?"

Mayfield gave a careful shrug.

"Find out. Shake them a bit. I'll wait here for the pathologist. Tell Jones to notify the family. Now. No sense waiting till we've got the body at the funeral parlor—we won't be able to keep the lid on this long anyhow."

Mayfield turned to Clark. "Did you bring the change of clothes I asked you to?"

"They're in my truck, sir."

"You can change at the school, then."

"The school, sir?"

Mayfield headed back to the ATV. "You think I'd trust Browder to assist with this?"

Clark looked to Lopez. The sheriff nodded. "Talk to the kids. Get their confidence before they button up each other's stories. Someone on that team knows something."

She thought of Joel. "Everyone's a suspect right now, aren't they?"

"You know what kind of forensics you get off a wet corpse?"

She knew that well enough. Zero.

Stepping back to the ATV, Clark asked Mr. Spearson, "You said all this here is Evers property?"

"Everything on this side of the creek, ma'am."

She turned to the sun climbing over the open Flats. "And what about out there?"

"Out there?" Spearson lowered his head like he was afraid to look at it. "There ain't nothing out there to own."

KIMBRA

Kimbra Lott was not the richest of the Bisonette cheerleaders, nor the tallest, nor the prettiest. Despite her best efforts, she had the sort of chunky thighs that were made to hold up pyramids and catch the glamorous girls, holes in her jeans that weren't there when she bought them, acne along the crest of her brow.

She wasn't pretty, but she was smart—the cleverest girl in her class—and so when Alisha Stinson, one of the lithe fliers who stood on Kimbra's shoulders at the games, texted the Bisonette's group chat to say that Dylan isn't at practice this morning wtf, Kimbra knew that something this past weekend had gone awry.

Bethany Tanner, the girls' captain and the pyramid's peak—not to mention Dylan's bae—responded to the message in a matter of seconds:

Jasmine have you heard about this?

Jasmine Lopez, another middle-runger like Alisha, was the sheriff's daughter and their surest source of solid news. She texted the group a minute later:

dad got a call super early. he's been gone all morning.

what the fuck? wrote Nivea Poler. Aside from throwing people in the air, Nivea wasn't good for very much.

Alisha wrote:

bethany are you feeling any better btw?

what the fuck?? Nivea wrote.

Bethany texted:

Kimbra, what time did KT get back from the coast last night?

Kimbra wiped her burning eyes—for the third night in a row she'd hardly slept, beset again by a dream which she refused now to even consider. Bethany, Kimbra noted with some interest, hadn't answered Alisha's question.

Kimbra typed a long response and deleted it. She realized that she might soon be asked to tell some very complicated lies. In the end she texted only, idk. late.

Where's Dylan's brother? asked Jasmine.

the gay one? wrote Alisha.

I saw him downtown on Sunday!! wrote April Sparks, one of Kimbra's friends. April wore black nail polish that she buffed off every Friday afternoon to replace with glittery green, right around the same time she slipped off her nose ring and contoured her cheeks and replaced her grungy self, for a few hours, with a dazzling little Bisonette. April's family, like Kimbra's, always lived a tenuous step above broke. She asked:

Joel was at the hardware store wasn't he K??

Thanks, April. Kimbra typed fast.

He just wanted to know when the guys would be back.

And then, to keep the conversation from lingering somewhere she couldn't afford it to, Kimbra wrote:

Has anyone heard from Jamal Reynolds?

She exited the chat, opened the thread she shared with her boyfriend. Call me, she wrote to KT Staler. Now.

But he didn't call. He didn't pick up *her* calls. All the way to school, as the Bisonette's group chat sizzled and snapped, Kimbra's astute mind studied and prodded and resigned itself to a simple fact: her boyfriend might be hiding even more from her than she suspected.

KT Staler, bless his heart, really was not as clever as he thought he was, but Kimbra had always loved that about him. Unlike Bethany Tanner, Kimbra Lott knew her boyfriend lied to her on a daily basis. KT's deception, in some odd way, was almost part of his charm. It was charming because Kimbra had a pretty clear idea of the sort of work he did on those weekend trips he took to the coast with Dylan Whitley. KT always thought he was fooling her. It had been adorable until today.

She skimmed through all the messages from the Bitchettes, began to type, and then there was her man, slipping through the door of the geography room with a heavy bag on his shoulder and black circles around his eyes. KT walked with a slouch to the back of the room, refusing to look up when she called his name.

the cops are here, wrote Alisha.

the fuck?!

omg omg omg

Kimbra went very cold. Before she could stand up and drag her boyfriend outside and twist his arm until he came *very* damn clean about what the *fuck* he had actually been up to this weekend, the bell rang. Mrs. Sparrows rose from her seat and even the wildest of students came to attention. None of them wanted to risk the wrath of Mrs. Sparrows on a Monday morning.

Which made Lady Cop all the more impressive. Stepping through the class's door without a knock a few minutes later, taking in all of their frightened faces, Lady Cop said, "I need to speak with Kyler Thomas, please."

Kimbra heard Bethany suck in a little gasp three rows away, felt her captain (*Oh captain, my stupid captain*) turn to stare at the side of Kimbra's face.

"Class just began," Mrs. Sparrows said, but KT had already pushed back his chair.

"It's KT," he said, and trudged to the door.

"Officer," said Jasmine Lopez. "Is Dylan alright?"

Lady Cop didn't blink. She didn't say a word. She led KT out into the hall and left Kimbra staring at the door, her heart in her throat, her clever mind briefly gone truant.

CLARK

KT followed Clark down the hall without a word. She led him to the vacant classroom where Mayfield was waiting. He thanked the boy for coming, said, "I hear your sister's doing well."

KT folded his bony frame into his seat. A patchy stretch of stubble climbed his neck. His small eyes were sunk in their sockets. He looked tired, irritated, but relatively calm. He did not look, as far as Clark could tell, like a young man hoping to conceal a murder.

"If this is about Dylan I ain't got no idea where he is," KT said. "He told me he never wanted to come back to this shitty town again and he was going to drive till he found a new place he wanted to be. I was like whatever. Jamal and me drove back from G-town last night and I ain't heard from D since."

Mayfield tilted his head. His considerable gut was creased

over the edge of the table. "You're answering a question I don't recall asking."

"That's what this about, right?" KT said. "The wonder boy don't show up to practice and now the school's bugging?"

Clark hoped her nerves didn't show. Her experience with interviews had, until now, been limited to drunks, meth heads driving cars with hot plates, battered spouses and their battering spouses. She had never worked a murder, and the wounds on Dylan's body left little doubt that they were dealing with a homicide, making his the first violent death reported in Pettis County in years.

Clark felt far out of her depth. She knew that these initial interviews were precious to the investigation, that Dylan's friends and schoolmates would likely never be more honest than they were now—or more apt to fumble some unpracticed lie—and she was terrified of squandering the moment.

"Just treat this like talk," Mayfield had told her when they'd arrived at the school. *"If they've got something to hide they'll do all the work for you."*

"Maybe we could back up a little," Clark said to KT now. "What exactly did the three of you do in Galveston over the weekend?"

KT rolled his eyes. "We fished."

Mayfield cocked his head. "You fished for two days straight?"

No, KT explained, *of course* they hadn't. The three of them— Dylan, KT and Jamal—had left town straight after the game Friday night, getting into Galveston around 1:00 a.m. Dylan seemed weird from the minute they arrived, KT said, distant and moody, and had gone straight to sleep. They got up around ten the next morning, ate some breakfast with KT's half brother, Floyd, and then took a little putter boat out into the Gulf to fish all day.

Clark jotted all of this down. "And was Dylan still acting moody when you got out on the water?"

"He's was a fucking pain is what he was," KT said. All day long Dylan talked about how shitty a place Bentley was for a guy who wanted any kind of future, how the only thing anybody cared about was a game that gave you brain damage, blah blah blah. By Sunday afternoon, KT had had enough. "We was out on the water again, nothing biting, and still he's just going on and on about how he had *dreams*, how he wants to have a *future*. So finally—it must have been like around six I guess—I say, 'Bro, if you hate that place so much, how come you don't just leave?' So he got real quiet, didn't say much till we docked that night, and then he just got out of the boat, grabbed his keys and was like 'Peace.' He got in his truck, headed out and that was the last I heard from him."

"That's it?" Clark asked. "He just up and left?"

"Yes, ma'am."

"Did he have a change of clothes with him? Money to live off of?"

KT's eyes narrowed. "If he did, he didn't tell me nothing about it. He uses his momma's credit card. That boy never has no paper."

"He also doesn't have any other family that we know of," Mayfield said. "Meaning he has no one to stay with."

KT glanced over his shoulder, lowered his voice. "You want my opinion, Dylan's got some girl on the side somewhere. You find her and you'll find him with a finger in her."

Mayfield, sounding as if he hadn't heard any of this, said, "Did Dylan mention his brother at all?"

"The queer one?"

"Does he have another?" Clark said.

"You're the detective, lady. Dylan maybe said something to Jamal about him, but to me—"

"How exactly did the three of you get to Galveston on Friday night?" Clark said. "Did you all take your own cars?"

"Nah, lady." KT scratched at the strap of stubble along his chin. The condescension in his voice was starting to rankle her. "Jamal's ride been fucked all semester. Alternator shit, you know. If he takes it more than a few miles a day it'll be dead in the morning."

Clark and Mayfield said nothing. The boy looked between the two of them, frowned.

"So what you wanna know? Dylan took his ride, Jamal and me rode in mine's. It weren't no thing."

Something occurred to Clark. "You and Jamal drove in your green Tacoma truck, yes?"

"That's me, yeah."

"Do you make a habit of leaving your car door unlocked, Mr. Staler?"

"What? No. Never." Then, after a pause, "I mean, maybe once or twice, but—"

"A man named Jason Ovelle was arrested on Friday night for breaking into a player's truck. Are you familiar with him?"

KT's eyes widened. "Who?"

"It was *your* truck he broke into. Jason was stopped before he could get into your belongings. This looks like news to you." Clark shrugged. "Well, how could anyone tell you—you were gone the minute you were out of your pads. But didn't your sister date Jason Ovelle in high school? Weren't they arrested together back in the day?"

A muscle in KT's jaw was throbbing. The room smelled of dust and sweat and hot metal from the window blinds beaten by the sun.

"I never heard of that Jason guy."

"You said it was your brother, Floyd, you stayed with in Galveston," Mayfield said smoothly. "I've worked in this town my whole life and I never met a Staler by that name, son."

"He ain't a Staler. He's my half brother."

"Last name?" Clark said.

"Tillery." KT spelled it.

"Phone number?"

KT pulled out his phone, read her a number, gave an address.

Clark jotted all this down. She noted that his story about the trip, at least, more or less aligned with what she knew so far. Before they began the interview Mayfield had brought her up to speed on the work he'd done to track down Dylan over the weekend. Paulette Whitley had given Mayfield the same name for this mysterious half brother during the investigator's interview with Joel's family on Saturday, had given the same phone number. There was, Clark knew, just one problem.

"Well, that is unusual," said Mayfield. "I spent all weekend calling that number. Never once did it answer."

KT's face darkened. "We must of been on the water."

"You'd have to have been miles out to sea for cell service not to reach you. Radio waves fly farther out there, you know."

KT studied them, perfectly still but for the vein pulsing in his jaw.

"You should call Floyd today," KT finally said.

"You said Dylan left on Sunday evening," said Mayfield. "Last night."

"He did."

"Then why did he text his brother on Saturday morning saying he was running away from Bentley?"

That rattled the boy. After a long pause he said, "He did?"

Mayfield said quickly, "So when did you and Jamal get back to town yesterday?"

KT told them nine o'clock. He dropped Jamal at his house and was home himself by nine twenty. No, he didn't hear from Dylan in the evening, nor this morning.

"So Dylan doesn't have any family that could take him in. Who's this other girl you mentioned? You're saying she might have feelings for him enough to let him stay on her couch?"

"Not on her couch." KT smirked. "It was just—Dylan, he's always texting somebody, trying to hide it from Bethany, you know. Real covert. But I see it."

"And you've never seen a picture of this girl? Never caught a name?" Mayfield said.

"Nah, man. Dylan can be real secret if he wants to. He want to hide something from you, you ain't *never* gonna know it."

Mayfield and Clark exchanged bored little frowns.

"I put out an APB for Dylan's truck on Saturday afternoon," said Mayfield. "That's an All-Points Bulletin, son, a request for every cop from here to Atlanta to keep an eye out for a sky-blue Chevy with a Bison bumper sticker. If Dylan left out of Galveston Sunday night, *someone* should have seen him by now."

KT shrugged again. He was beginning to look irritated. "That ain't my problem."

"You don't seem especially concerned about finding your friend."

"He's a grown man, ain't he? He got a right to his privacy."

"He's dead, son."

The news hit KT like scalding water. He pushed back in the chair, stared from Mayfield to Clark and back again.

"You're fucking with me."

"I'm afraid not," Clark said.

"He was discovered early this morning," Mayfield told KT.

KT blinked. Tears had sprung up. "How?" he tried to say, but his voice cracked.

"Dylan Whitley was murdered," Mayfield said. "Past that we ain't at liberty to say."

KT stared at Clark, stared through her. He opened his

mouth to speak, closed it, opened it again. "But Dylan was with me all weekend."

"Fishing?"

"Yes!"

"So why did Dylan come all the way back to Bentley last night just to get himself killed?" Mayfield said.

"Man, you're the fucking cop!" KT shouted. Clark saw the anger return to his eyes. She saw fear as well. Fear for himself, she wondered, or for his friend? "I don't know why the fuck he'd come back. He just kept talking about how he couldn't handle it here no more. He said he ain't got no future but for football and he's sick of the way people make him like some fucking king. Ever since he told them over the summer he wanted to quit he—"

KT broke off. The boy seemed taken aback by his own words, like he'd said too much and knew it.

Clark cut in fast. "Dylan threatened to quit the team?"

"It weren't no threat." KT shook his head. His nose had begun to run. He struck the desk with his fist and said, "Fuck. *Fuck.* It's fucking stupid."

Mayfield deftly tugged a small packet of Kleenex from his pocket and pushed it across the table. He itched his ear when KT's face was buried in a tissue. Clark caught the signal.

"KT," she said, suddenly speaking in her warmest voice. "What happened when Dylan tried to quit the Bison this summer?"

KT pressed the tissue to his eyes. He wiped his nose. He sniffled. "You can't tell nobody I told you this."

"Of course," Clark said. "We ain't here to spread gossip."

KT took a deep breath. He looked between the two of them with raw red eyes and started to talk.

When Clark led Jamal Reynolds into the room fifteen minutes later the backup quarterback was shaking.

If Mayfield was at all unsettled by what he'd just heard from KT, he gave no sign of it. "We're sorry to drag you out of class like this," the investigator said, rising to shake Jamal's hand. "I'm sure you'd much rather be learning about—what class did we drag you out of?"

Jamal stared at the packet of tissues on the table. "He ain't dead, is he?"

Mayfield glanced at Clark. She nodded.

"He is, son. I'm very sorry."

The news knocked something loose in Jamal. He didn't look up, but he seemed to sit deeper in his seat. His breathing grew heavy. "An accident?"

Clark and Mayfield exchanged glances again.

"No, Mr. Reynolds." Clark pushed the tissues toward him. "It looks like homicide."

Jamal shook all over but he didn't cry. After a long minute of silence he said, "He was fine on Friday."

"Friday?" Mayfield said gently. "Or do you mean yesterday?"

"What?" Jamal looked between the two of them blankly. "Oh. Yeah. Yesterday."

"Were you and Dylan alone at the coast?" Mayfield said.

A long pause. "KT was with us too. At his brother's place."

"What was that guy's name again? KT's brother?" Clark said.

Jamal shot a look at the blank notepad in front of her as if hoping to find a hint there.

"I didn't really talk to the brother much," Jamal said. When the cops didn't break their silence, Jamal looked up and added, "I think it was… Tommy?"

He watched Clark's face as he said it. The boy was clearly hoping she'd give him some little tell: warmer, colder. He was out of luck.

Instead, it was Jamal's panicked eyes that betrayed him. He'd never met KT's half brother in his life.

"What time did you last see Dylan, Jamal?" Mayfield said.

"Why you asking me this?"

"Answer the question please, Mr. Reynolds."

Jamal took a tissue and pressed it to his eyes. "Jesus, help me."

Mayfield's voice never wavered. "It's a simple question, Jamal. When did you last see Dylan Whitley?"

"Sunday."

"At what time?"

"Late."

"When Dylan drove you back from Galveston?"

"Yeah."

Clark and Mayfield glanced at each other again.

"And what time did you return to town?" Mayfield said.

"Eight. No. Nine."

"Which is it?"

"Nine."

Mayfield frowned. Clark felt it too: one of these boys was lying, no question, but here, at least, their stories matched, just barely. KT too had said that he and Jamal had returned to town last night around nine o'clock.

"So Dylan dropped you off at your house around nine. He drove you because your car's having alternator trouble?"

Jamal nodded his head yes.

"And did KT drive back by himself?"

Jamal flinched. Clark would bet money the boy had just realized he'd made a serious mistake.

"KT stayed in Galveston, I think. I don't really know. He's been a dick lately."

Mayfield cocked his head. "Is that right? I understand you boys all went to Galveston a lot this summer."

"Them two did. I hadn't never been before. That's why we went. So I could come."

"KT told us it was your idea to go with them this time, Jamal," Mayfield said, which was the truth: KT had divulged it at the end of his interview. Revealed that, and plenty else. "Is he correct?"

Jamal blinked. He toyed with the tissue in his fingers. "I guess."

"Why did you want to join?" Mayfield said.

Jamal shrugged. "It seemed fun, I guess."

Mayfield adjusted his shirt's collar.

Clark spoke gently, as if this were just a simple mistake to clarify. "Jamal, why would KT tell us that *he* drove you home from Galveston last night, not Dylan?"

From somewhere outside, a door burst open and a moment later another door slammed. In the space between, a girl was screaming.

Jamal stared at the wall. "That sounded like Bethany."

When the young man's back was turned, Mayfield gave Clark a shake of his head. Jamal was shutting down on them.

"Jamal," Clark said calmly. "Jamal, look at me, please. Is it true that Dylan talked about quitting the football program over the summer?"

Reynolds glanced at her. "He what?"

Clark said nothing.

"Why the fuck would Dylan want to quit?" Jamal sniffed. "What's that even matter now?"

"Right now, Jamal, everything matters."

The bell rang, a worried hum of voices flooded the hall-way. Faces stopped to stare through the door's window until Clark taped it shut with a sheet of paper.

Jamal said when she sat back down, "All I remember is back, back in June, D said he's gonna get me more field time this season."

"Is it possible that Dylan did more than talk about that?" Mayfield asked.

"He wasn't shouting it."

"Mr. Staler said that Dylan told you two he was quitting in June, but then the very next day he came around and said he'd changed his mind. Is that true?"

"I don't know nothing about that."

"How's practice going for you, Jamal?" Mayfield asked.

Jamal clenched his hands into fists.

"I imagine you'll be starting for us on Friday, won't you?"

"What?"

"That must be exciting."

"Man, the fuck are you saying?"

Very calmly, Mayfield laid out KT's most damning allegation. "Mr. Staler told us *you* were the one pushing Dylan to quit the team in the first place. He says you've wanted to be a starter for years. He says you finally got Dylan to agree to quit only for him to back out at the last minute and keep playing. KT says you were livid, Jamal. He says—"

"That's a fucking lie!" Jamal shouted. "Why the fuck would Dylan want to quit?"

Mayfield's voice never wavered. "You mean to tell me a talented player like yourself wouldn't want a piece of the spotlight while he had the chance?"

Jamal opened his mouth but no words came. Tears glistened on his cheeks.

"You didn't want to spend your last year with the team cooling on the bench, did you, Reynolds?" Mayfield toyed with his pen. "You never went to the coast—your story's got more holes in it than a bum's shorts."

"That's a lie, KT's telling lies—"

"You asked Dylan if you could tag along on this trip, asked him for a ride, tricked him out into the middle of nowhere where you didn't think a soul would ever find him."

"Oh fuck. Oh my fucking God."

"You dumped the body. You walked home, made your folks promise to say you'd been gone all weekend."

Jamal started shaking.

"And then all you had to do was tell people that Dylan had run away. No one ever had to be the wiser. It was just dumb luck that body was even found." The table groaned as Mayfield leaned forward. His voice softened. "Let's end this now, son. Nice and easy."

Jamal pressed his hands to his face and tears dripped through his fingers. He let out a low, pained whine.

Clark had misgivings. Mayfield's theory had plenty of faults, but it had a sort of logic. If Jamal was going to confess to something, he would do it now.

But instead the young man said, through a barrage of sobs, "I'd never hurt D. He was my fucking brother."

Mayfield pressed Jamal for a few minutes more but could get nothing else out of him. The young man was still shaking when they released him.

"Christ, I miss smoking." Mayfield paced the stuffy room.

"If nothing else, KT and Jamal agree on one thing." Clark popped the soles of her feet free of her heavy heels—the only pair she owned—which she'd dug from behind the boots in her closet early this morning at Mayfield's request. She wondered if the street clothes she was wearing made her look less intimidating than if she were in her deputy's uniform, as the investigator had said, or if she just looked like she was too uncomfortable to be any sort of threat. "Both of those boys say they got home around nine."

Mayfield fumbled with the air-conditioner only to find it was dead. "And what does that tell you?"

Clark hesitated. "That they had a story planned out in advance. Maybe."

"Maybe. They sure didn't plan it well." Mayfield looked at her again. "You've got a knack for this, you know."

Clark looked down at her notes. The interviews had made her heart race worse than a brawl in the dirt, but they'd also made her giddy in a way that was almost embarrassing. She had always suspected she would be good at investigative work; she prayed Mayfield didn't notice the little smile his words had sent over her face.

"We're fortunate they're both eighteen," Clark said. "Should we care that they didn't ask for attorneys?"

"I'd have been more suspicious if they *had*. Try calling that number the Staler boy gave you, the one supposed to belong to this mystery brother of his. I bet you a dime KT himself will answer it with a sock stuffed in his mouth."

Clark reached for her phone. She'd half expected to see a message from Joel—saying what, she couldn't guess—but instead there was only the daily email from her father's nursing home, checking in to say that yesterday he enjoyed pea soup and asked his nurse why the lights outside were so funny.

Clark filed the email, punched in the number KT had given them, listened to it ring.

There was a knock at the door. Coach Parter slipped his considerable bulk through a surprisingly narrow crack. For a time he only stared at Mayfield, patting his forehead with a handkerchief.

"Lord, Grady, you might have warned us." Parter leaned against the door frame, wiping sweat from his meaty arms. "Principal Mathers is beside himself. I'm sweating enough to salt a fish—you know how I sweat at bad news."

"It's a bad situation."

"Christ almighty, the Whitley boy. And just five days before the Stallions game."

Mayfield narrowed his eyes. "I'm sure the team will find a way to carry on."

To Clark's surprise, a man picked up her call. She turned away from the men and introduced herself.

As she spoke into the phone, Parter shook his head, said to Mayfield, "I come to say they're canceling class today. They'll announce it soon. You need to talk with the team, I'm assuming?"

Mayfield said, "We'll talk to the boys today, yes. We'd also like to speak to Bethany Tanner, Mr. Whitley's girlfriend."

"Bethany?" Parter looked up. "I heard one of her friends took her home. The news hit that girl awful hard. You won't turn the boys' screws today, will you, Grady?"

Mayfield picked at a nail. "I'm sure we'll just have a chat."

Parter looked dubious but seemed to realize there was little he could do. He promised to gather the team, shimmied back into the hall. Clark lowered the phone, more puzzled than when she had picked it up a moment ago.

"*Somebody* lives at that address in Galveston," she said to Mayfield. "He says his name is Floyd Tillery and he wants to know—are we free to come see him tomorrow morning?"

JOEL

Joel sank into a padded chair in the funeral parlor's lobby. He stared at a painting of an incandescent Jesus looming over a man sliding out from beneath a rusted truck.

He thought of the jersey that hung on his brother's wall: #1 CHRIST.

At the thought of his brother, he craved pills.

Joel had given his statement twice at the station, once directly to the sheriff and the county attorney and again to Mayfield and Clark, a plate of untouched sandwiches resting between them on a sticky table. In each instance, Joel repeated exactly what he had told Mayfield on Saturday: he had last seen Dylan at the football field.

Joel did not tell the police about the painkillers he had discovered in Dylan's room.

He had been asked, twice, if he could imagine a connection between his own return to Bentley and his brother's death. Joel had thought Mayfield was joking the first time he asked. No, Joel had told the investigator, he couldn't, and finally Mayfield had seemed satisfied with his answer, or had at least let it go.

Joel had not let it go.

Because there was a memory he couldn't escape. Because that rainy night after the game, when he had texted Dylan, *Don't worry, I'm getting you out of this shit hole*, his brother had begun to type a response he'd never finished. Joel remembered those three little dots on his screen filling and emptying, filling and emptying. Remembered the fear that had roiled his gut at the sight of them. That fear returned to him now, even though—he thought—the worst had already happened.

A door opened and Mr. Ortiz, the town's mortician, stepped soundlessly into the little lobby, followed by Mayfield and Clark. The mortician gave Joel a well-practiced, sympathetic nod and ushered him toward another, more discreet door, half-hidden by a fern.

The back of the funeral home had a chill that settled fast into the bones. A line of humming fluorescent lights ran above a cavernous room lined with pumps and tubes. A dozen wigs in every shade of brown. A grinning Bison bobblehead perched atop a refrigerator.

A table draped by a white sheet.

A shape under the sheet about six feet long.

Mr. Ortiz asked Joel to attest to being Dylan's brother, made him sign here and here and here.

They approached the body.

"In the city you would do this on a TV monitor in the other room," said Mr. Ortiz, one hand poised over the sheet, sounding suddenly as if he'd lost his nerve. "We would understand if you'd rather wait until he might be moved."

Joel shook his head, and the mortician folded down a portion of the sheet.

His brother had died afraid. Dylan's mouth was locked open

in a gasp. Dull brown bruises covered both sides of his face. One blow had ripped open the skin above the left eye. Another had turned his temple into a single wide scab. Joel noticed there was no blood on the face. Where it wasn't bruised the skin was a marbled white.

Two red bricks were positioned to either side of the head. The sheet had been folded back to rest on Dylan's chin. "Why did you stop the sheet there?" Joel asked.

The mortician shot a quick, panicked glance at the deputies. Mayfield said, "The boy was in the water for a while, son."

Joel didn't move. He pointed at the bricks. "Why is his head like this?"

Mayfield let out a long sigh.

Clark said, "Don't do this to yourself, Joel."

"Fold it down."

"Joel—"

"Fold it down."

Mayfield gave Mr. Ortiz a little nod of assent. The sheet sighed as it was raised.

A wide wound to the neck exposing a dull mass of private flesh. Fibers of muscle, the severed cords of the vein and the artery. A dark cavity at the core, which even the whining lights above couldn't penetrate.

Joel stared at the wound until the logic of his mind threatened to break down. He saw a hole that refused to be seen. He heard the whispers of dreams, the whisper of a voice hissing through static and doors:

imissedyou.

Joel noted every detail one final time. He nodded to Mr. Ortiz, to the police. He thanked them in a voice that didn't sound like his own.

Joel returned home to the silence of a house in grief. He brought inside the first of many flowers deposited on the porch. The lights all off inside, the tactless sun beaming through the open windows.

Joel could feel his mother asleep down the hall—he had loaded her down with enough Xanax and Ambien to knock out a horse. Darren stepped out from the kitchen.

"You were always good to him," Darren said. "You always took care of him."

Joel didn't have the words to answer this.

"It was good of you to send him that money. I know it meant so much to him."

"Money?"

"That two thousand you sent him, back over the summer, to get him some savings started. I saw him counting it in his room but I never told nothing to Paulette about it, of course. He said the two of you wanted to keep it private." Darren caught himself, teetered on the edge of tears. "I took him to the bank to open his account and put in two thousand of my own money. Though I don't guess he'll be needing it now."

The two men embraced for so long they forgot they were doing it. Darren held on for his own reasons. Joel was too preoccupied to manage the effort of letting go. A single fact tumbled and tumbled through his head.

He had never sent his brother a dime.

TUESDAY

THE HOUSE AT THE COAST

CLARK

They drove through a clutch of little towns that looked just like Bentley. The same cramped businesses and towering churches, the same empty streets and dangling stoplights. After leaving high school, Clark had spent a brief, ugly marriage in Waco, a hundred miles away. Since returning to Pettis County three years ago with a criminal justice diploma, she'd felt a quiet pride in knowing that she had become one of the guardians of her hometown, one of the quiet few who kept the fires lit. Bentley's streets, its flat horizons, had comforted her upon her return in a way they never had in school. Had been blessedly familiar. Stable.

Why, then, did the sight of these other tiny towns on the highway fill her with nothing but dread? As Mayfield rocketed past diners and feed stores, Clark felt the eyes of people on the other side of their dark windows wishing her away, wishing her to tend to her own town's secrets.

Dylan's body had been discovered in a creek, on an unseasonably cool day, and those forces together had acted as a refrigerant, slowing the process of decay and making it difficult to determine a time of death. An autopsy was scheduled for this afternoon, which would hopefully shed more light on the matter. *"But don't get your hopes up,"* the medical examiner had said. *"You may as well have tucked this boy in a deep freeze."*

Meaning Dylan Whitley could have died anytime between Friday evening and Sunday night. Meaning that Clark and Mayfield were on their way to Galveston to visit KT Staler's half brother, the man who swore on the phone with Clark yesterday that the three boys had stayed with him over the weekend.

"Can I say something?" Clark asked Mayfield.

"I should hope so. It's a long ride."

"I have real issues with the story KT told us about Dylan running away Sunday night."

"Go on."

Clark muffled a yawn before she could begin. She felt as if she had slept—if that was even the word for it—at the sheriff's department. Upon their return from the funeral home yesterday afternoon, Clark and Mayfield had been greeted by the mayor and the sheriff and the sheriff's boss, County Attorney Harlan Boone.

Mr. Boone was a squat, polished man, sixty but blessed with a glow of youth: full head of hair, taut skin, a nervy edge in his every word. He was partial to turquoise bolo ties, pointed cowboy boots, gleaming diesel trucks he replaced every year. He had always struck Clark as vain and vaguely useless. Her experience with him yesterday had not altered her opinion.

"The mayor and I have never had more faith in this department than we do tonight," Mr. Boone had said. "I've assured my lovely wife—and I'm sure by now she's assured every lady in town—that you will bring this case to a swift and firm conclusion."

Boone drove his fist into his palm for emphasis. Mayor Malacek nodded a dignified assent. Clark had looked over her shoulder to be sure the county attorney wasn't speaking to an audience of reporters that had somehow sneaked its way into the station behind her.

Now, on the road, she forced down some brackish truck stop coffee and struggled to sort her thoughts. "It's just, I keep coming back to the text message that Joel Whitley received on *Saturday*. Why would Dylan send a message in which he sounds like he'd already run away but then wait to leave his buddies until over twenty-four hours later?"

"Waited to tell KT he was leaving, at least," Mayfield said.

"You mean you don't think Jamal ever came here with them?"

"I don't know. I *do* know that Reynolds didn't even know the name of this mysterious Tillery man."

"Then why go to the trouble of leaving with his friends at the game Friday night if he wasn't going to the coast with them?"

Mayfield shrugged. He seemed just as disappointed by their interviews with the rest of the team yesterday as she did. Other than confirming the fact that Dylan, KT and Jamal had all three left together on Friday night, Clark and Mayfield had learned little else from the Bison.

"Let's play with hypotheticals," Mayfield said. "Maybe all three boys came down here after all, and Jamal somehow forgot Floyd's every detail. Maybe Dylan was upset when he texted his brother on Saturday morning but then he calmed down and didn't leave." Mayfield reached for his coffee. "Jamal said Dylan had been acting hot and cold since the start of the summer. Maybe something set him off Sunday, and this time he was upset enough to go through with it."

"'Go through with it.' Like suicide," Clark said and, not for the first time since Saturday at the bar with Joel, she thought of her brother. Suicide had long since become the popular theory to explain Troy's disappearance. There was enough empty country in Pettis County a man could drive twenty minutes in any direction and put a gun in his mouth and run good odds of never being found. A search for Troy in the Flats east of Bentley had been mounted a decade ago—Clark remembered that much, though the search party had somehow gotten turned around and returned to town almost without realizing it, empty-handed and unsettled. A second search had not been mounted.

"Not suicide. Dylan Whitley couldn't have cut his own throat so deep on his own," Mayfield said, steering their car around a rickety horse trailer. "But making the choice to run away from home with just the clothes on your back ain't much more reasonable than the choice to kill yourself."

"Fair enough. But then what? Dylan leaves out of Galveston at six, changes his mind *again*, turns around, comes back to Bentley, drives twenty miles north of town to a spit of empty land and gets his throat cut? What happened to his truck? What—"

Something occurred to her. She flipped through the case file until she found the page she wanted. "Listen to this: Dylan was found wearing 'one pair of Levi's jeans (heavily blood-stained), no underwear, one leather belt and one Bentley Bison synthetic leather team jacket (also bloodstained).' What happened to his shoes and his socks? His shirt? Hell, why wasn't he wearing *underwear*?"

Mayfield made a satisfied little noise. "Why indeed?"

Clark read over the notes again to be certain her memory was correct. It was. A forensics search of the area in which Dylan's body was discovered had not been fruitful. There was no trace of blood, no boot prints or tire tracks, no signs of a struggle. Deputies Jones and Browder had not discovered a scrap of clothing.

"Reynolds is lying about something. But if he killed Dylan for a piece of the spotlight, why would Whitley be half-naked when his throat was cut?" Clark said.

Mayfield said nothing.

"Sir—" Clark looked at the map on her phone's screen, at the little red pin on the coast toward which she and Mayfield were crawling, one little town at a time. "What the hell happened at this house?"

BETHANY

Bethany Tanner, the team captain of the Bisonettes and Dylan Whitley's erstwhile ride-or-die, awoke beneath stars and a hard sliver of moon. She was stretched in the dirt, her hair in her face, her shorts riding high in her crotch. When she pushed her hair aside, she saw the body beside her.

She recoiled, scrambling to her feet, but some cold survival instinct stopped her as she turned to run. There was no ground behind her. She stumbled, screamed and very nearly pitched herself over the edge of a great black pit: a perfect circle of nothing, a wound in the earth. Past the circle, all around her, there was only the countryside: flat night sky, inky empty prairie.

No escape. No safety.

With a *shush* of falling dirt, the pit opened wider. Her head turned over her shoulder, Bethany took a few clumsy steps away but found she could go no farther. She was paralyzed by the sight. Her throat prickled with cold. She heard a distant, high screech from deep inside the dark and realized that something was moving down there, watching her.

The pit crept open wider and Bethany realized that what she'd heard was not falling dirt but a voice—a real voice, an *old* voice—whispering words that wound their way up her mouth and down her ears and around the inside of her skull, oily and almandine as the coiled meats that spilled from the stomach of a deer when the knife did its work.

bosheth

the voice said, and the wall around Bethany's mind collapsed.

The faceless body slipped into the pit without a sound. A joyous smell of rot rose up to greet it.

The ground beneath her feet disappeared.

"Bethany? Bethany? Jesus Christ, girl, breathe."

Bethany awoke with a gasp, scrambled away from the body in her bed and got tangled in her sodden sheets. Her heart beat so hard she thought her veins would burst.

"Bethany, it's me. It's Jasmine."

Jasmine. Not a faceless corpse but Jasmine Lopez, the second-prettiest girl on the squad.

Bethany breathed. The panic faded. Her bedroom seemed to form itself around her: her massive bed, her tall dresser, the frilly lounging sofa she'd taken from her mother's room after the divorce. Sunlight prodded at the curtains. In the distance Bethany could hear the cows lowing on the ranch behind her property.

The whispering voice—the *old* voice—went silent in her head.

"Fuck my cunt," Bethany said with a sigh. "I've been having these dreams."

Bethany caught something on Jasmine's face in the dim light, a hesitation.

"How about you? Did you sleep okay?"

Jasmine sat up and stretched, fluffed out her hair. "I can't believe any of this is real."

Bethany's phone began to chime its alarm. She reached over Jasmine to silence it, checked her messages, felt a dull ache of loss replacing the fear around her heart. Dylan was dead. Finally, after everything they'd been through, Dylan was dead.

And Jasmine hadn't answered her question.

Before she could press her friend, Bethany caught the rattle of the garage door rising beneath her. She scrambled for a shirt, for eyeliner.

"Is that your dad?" Jasmine asked, her nails clicking on her phone.

Bethany fumbled with the light in her bathroom. "I can't let him see me like this."

Russ Tanner had just steered his suitcase into their sprawling kitchen when Bethany and Jasmine reached the foot of the stairs. Her father was like many men around town, a towering former lineman who'd gone to seed. The last five years had added several inches to his waist and a jiggle to his chest. His embrace had grown no weaker, however. Bethany felt the air deflate from her lungs as he wrapped his arms around her, squeezing like he wanted to break her back.

"Oh, Spud," he murmured into Bethany's hair. "You must be a wreck."

"I was yesterday," Bethany replied in her calmest voice.

"I came back as soon as I heard." He ignored Jasmine completely. "Have you talked to the police yet?"

"They were at school yesterday but I left early. Why?"

Her father dropped a coffee pod into their gleaming new Keurig machine, dug a bottle of bourbon from behind the cereal—it was never too early for Russ Tanner. "You just tell me when the cops come to see you," he said. "I don't want you talking to them alone."

"I wouldn't have anything to say. I was sick in bed all weekend."

Her father appraised her. "It took the fried chicken off your legs."

Bethany felt Jasmine hold in a shudder.

"We've got to run," Bethany said.

Her father spiked his coffee and took a long sip. "You won't talk to the police alone," he repeated.

"I'll call you if they come for me." She kissed her father on the cheek. "Which they won't."

She and Jasmine were halfway up the stairs when he stopped her. "You were in bed all weekend."

It wasn't a question.

"I'm just wondering," he continued. "You had the strength to clean the garage when you were sick?"

Oh fuck. Oh fuck.

"I told Maria to hose it out yesterday," Bethany said, praying her voice didn't betray the panic in her chest. "Some mud got under the door in the storm."

From the stairs she watched her father take another long slurp of his coffee. He nodded at her, pulled loose his phone. "I heard that rain was wild."

CLARK

When they'd finally pushed their way through Houston, Mayfield rolled down the windows and soon Clark could smell the sea. Her phone steered them off the interstate and onto a winding highway. The water appeared on the horizon, dull and flat as tin.

"It doesn't quite square, does it?" she said, glancing through the case file again. "Mrs. Spearson, the wife of the man who found the body, said she was home most of the weekend and didn't hear any cars on the road outside the house. She said she was quote 'ninety-seven percent certain that no vehicle was on our road from Friday night to Monday morning' other than her husband's rig. Theirs is the only road in that area for miles."

"Which tells us what?"

The longer Clark sat in this car, the more keenly did she recognize how underqualified she was to handle a murder case. The worry that had gripped her yesterday, in her interview with KT Staler, had only intensified.

"It tells us that either Mrs. Spearson is mistaken or whoever dumped the body didn't take her road."

"Or she's concealing something," Mayfield said.

Clark scanned the crime scene photos. Something in them was staring her in the face. "Does the lady have any motive for that? She's not related to any of these boys."

"Motive matters less than you think," Mayfield said. "Half the time people don't even know why they done something once they've done it. But. No—I don't take Mrs. Spearson for a liar."

"But that means the killer—"

"Killers. Possibly. Plural."

"Killer or killers—if they murdered Dylan Whitley in Galveston that means they drove three hours with a corpse in their car to deposit it in the middle of absolute nowhere. Why? There's a thousand places you could leave a body between Bentley and the coast."

"Why drive the body back from the coast at all and risk its being found by some kid on the Highway Patrol pulling you over to fill up his quota?" asked Mayfield.

"And why would Dylan take off his shirt but still keep on his jacket?" Clark said.

Soon they were on a gravel road that ran straight along an ugly patch of hard coast. The waves were loud. The few small houses were battened up with storm shutters.

A prickling heat spread between the hairs of Clark's scalp. This shoreline looked abandoned. It was easy to imagine that a murder committed in one of these boarded-up houses would never be heard.

Her phone spoke. "Your destination is on the right."

The house at the address Floyd Tillery had given them was sided with ragged wood shingles, a yellow VW Bug turning to rust in the sandy grass. Someone had formed large peace signs over the windows with masking tape. "In case the wind cracks them?" Clark wondered aloud.

"Keep your weapon handy, Deputy."

They went around back—Mayfield leading, Clark keeping an eye on the road. They saw nothing behind the house but ocean, pebbly sand and a little pier, barely more than a stick of wood jutting into the water. A fishing putter was lashed to the pier's side. Was that a hole in its rusted hull or a trick of the light?

The prickling heat spread down her neck.

Mayfield knocked at the back door, one hand over his holstered gun. He knocked again. "Mr. Tillery?" he called. His voice was swallowed by the waves.

Clark peered through a grimy window. She saw nothing but a rattan rug, dust.

"Sir," she began, but Mayfield busted the window in with his elbow, reached in to unlatch the door. Wiped the knob with a handkerchief.

Clark didn't ask questions.

They stepped into the dim house. The rug was stained with years of damp, as were the collapsed remains of a couch.

The prickling heat spread over Clark's entire body. She'd never felt anything like it before—exhilaration, fear, a very bad vibe. She followed Mayfield down the dim hallway, briefly certain that they were about to push open a door and discover bloody walls, a knife abandoned in a grisly sink. Evidence.

And then she noticed that theirs were the first footsteps to disturb the dust on these floors in years.

A few minutes later and they were sure of it: the house was empty. Clark and Mayfield visited the five neighboring homes, all of which were shuttered for winter. No signs of forced entry anywhere, nor of any sort of entry at all. If Dylan and Jamal and KT had come to Galveston on Friday night, they hadn't stayed in these houses.

No. Clark shook her head at the empty coast, realized what that tingling heat had been telling her all along. Those boys had never come to the coast at all.

KIMBRA

Kimbra could barely walk by the time she made it to the school's bathroom, she was so shaky with exhaustion. She looked at her phone and wondered how her interview with the police could have lasted only thirty minutes. She'd never realized how much effort it took to prop up a lie under pressure.

Bethany Tanner was at the bathroom's sink, touching up her face in the chipped mirror. Her eyes settled on Kimbra with a chill. Bethany dropped her lipstick into her bag and said, "You must be worried sick."

Kimbra hesitated. Too late to turn back now. She approached the sink next to Bethany, cupped her hands under the water. "I'm sure he's fine."

Kimbra had awoken this morning to the news that KT had failed to make it to practice. She had just spent the last half hour telling Lady Cop and spooky-eyed Investigator Mayfield that she had called and texted KT all day and gotten no response. She'd told the police she had no idea where KT had gone, which was the truth, impossible and bewildering as it was.

She hadn't been entirely truthful about much else.

Bethany lined her brow with a pencil. "I thought my man was fine too."

Kimbra's stomach turned. She said nothing.

"Staler knows something," Bethany continued. A toilet flushed in the stall behind them.

"If he does then he didn't tell me."

The stall behind them opened. Jasmine Lopez, Bethany's bony sidekick, washed her hands without a word.

Kimbra knew that Bethany was fucking with her, that the girl had to torment someone because she was too superior to be humbled by grief, but still Kimbra didn't let her guard down. "Do *you* know something I don't?" she said.

"I'm not the one dating the meth addict."

Kimbra took a long breath. That one hurt. "You know every boy on that team is a liar, right? It's the only thing they're good at."

"Not mine." Bethany snapped her bag closed. "My boy was perfectly honest. Maybe if he'd listened to me and cut *yours* loose he'd still be here."

"Oh, fuck off." Kimbra rolled her eyes. She couldn't take Bethany seriously sometimes. "If you knew half the shit KT told me about Dylan you'd—"

Jasmine had Kimbra pinned by the arms before she could say another word. Kimbra struggled but Jasmine only gripped her harder. Mother*fucker*, the skinny bitch had some strength in her.

Bethany came to stand within an inch of Kimbra's face. She spoke very calmly. "What did you just say?"

Kimbra couldn't help but smile at the thought of how KT would laugh when she told him this story. Bethany didn't scare her. Nobody in this town did. Give Kimbra six more months and she'd never see any of these bitches again.

"The fuck are you smiling for?" Bethany said.

Jasmine gave her a shake. "She asked you a question."

Kimbra chuckled. "I just thought it was funny, you know? The way you happened to get sick the weekend your boyfriend disappeared." A thought occurred to Kimbra. "And didn't you tell Alisha your dad was going out of town Friday night? You must have been so lonely, sick in that big house all weekend."

A look of pure fury ruined Bethany's pretty face. Her eyes, bloodshot though they had been a moment before, all but turned black now. The change in her was startling, if unsurprising. Kimbra had always suspected someone as perfect as Bethany Tanner must have an animal in her somewhere.

"Ladies!" called a clipped voice from the restroom door.

Jasmine let Kimbra go. They turned to see Coach Rushing, the dour bull mama of the Bisonettes.

"The police are ready for you, Tanner," Rushing said. "Come with me."

The rage that had consumed Bethany was just as quickly bottled up again.

"Yes, ma'am."

Well then, Kimbra thought, watching Bentley's blonde darling and her skinny attack dog follow Coach Rushing into the hallway. She rubbed the burn Jasmine's hands had left on her arms. She wondered how much trouble a girl could get into with a house to herself all weekend.

Well then.

CLARK

Clark spotted the poster when she raised herself from the school's water fountain. MEMORIAL SERVICE 2NITE FOR THE BEST DAMN QB WE EVER SAW it read over a blurry picture of Dylan's smiling face. BRING CANDLES.

"Officer?" said a boy's voice at her shoulder. She turned and saw Benny Garcia, one of the backbenchers, standing at her elbow with an anxious frown on his pockmarked face. "Exc-c-cuse me, Officer. C-c-can I speak t-to you?"

"Of course."

The halls were glutted with students after the final bell. He leaned in and said quietly, "It's about F-F-Friday night."

"Would you like to step—"

The boy seemed not to notice the attention they were drawing. "You know J-Jamal? It's j-j-just that he s-s-said s-something weird at h-h-halftime. At the g-g-game."

"In the locker room?"

"Y-yeah. H-h-he asked me if I had a c-c-condom."

Clark blinked. She saw Benny's eyes track a cluster of Bison players as they filed down the hall, their gym bags slapping their hips. Saw the way Garrett Mason, the team's hulking defensive safety, caught Benny's eye and held it for a long, charged second.

Clark frowned. This didn't feel right. "Jamal asked you for a what?"

Benny nodded. "I d-d-didn't have one, of c-course. B-b-but it's w-weird, right?"

Before she could thank Benny for his time, the scrawny boy had slipped away to catch up with the bigger Bison who'd passed them earlier. He said something to Garrett Mason as they rounded a corner and Mason responded with a single, curt nod.

That nod bothered her. She'd always imagined that some foundation of discreet loyalty underpinned the team—an impression which her interviews with the players yesterday morning had only strengthened—but Benny didn't look at all bothered by what he had just told her. *Strange*, she thought. To whom was that loyalty extended? To whom was it withheld?

Bethany Tanner was already seated in the interview room with Mayfield when Clark arrived.

"Sorry for the wait," Clark said. They had decided on the way back from Galveston that she would take the lead with the girls this afternoon. Her interview with Kimbra Lott had been smooth, if uninformative. Kimbra had been weirdly inscrutable, clearly concerned about KT's whereabouts, generous in her answers but seemingly unaware of anything that failed to occur outside her line of sight.

Bethany Tanner studied Clark with an elevated air, her face a perfect balance of grief and boredom. Something about the girl put Clark on edge.

"Thank you for coming, Bethany. I imagine this must be difficult for you."

The girl gave her a sad little smile. "Of course."

"We won't keep you long. But firstly, wouldn't you like an adult sitting with you? You are under eighteen, yes?"

"I'm eighteen next month," Bethany said, as if that settled it.

"Sure. But this is a murder investigation. What you say here you might be called on to repeat in court. It's customary for a minor to have—"

"I don't have anything to hide." The girl cut her off smoothly, toying with an expensive-looking silver bracelet on her wrist. "But I do have to get to practice."

"You'll be performing at halftime this Friday?" Mayfield asked.

"Of course. Dylan wouldn't want us to stop. There's still the championship to think about."

"Alright, then," Clark said, already anxious to get away from this girl. "To start, can you tell me if Dylan kept a lock on his cell phone?"

Bethany had clearly not expected this. "He used the thumb-print scanner. Why?"

Clark nodded as if this was merely some trivial detail when Bethany had, in fact, just solved one small mystery for them. Clark had tested it herself this morning: all the killer would have needed to open Dylan's phone and reset his security settings was a single press of the boy's finger. Once the security was reset the killer could do anything with that phone—send messages to the victim's brother, for example.

The finger didn't have to be warm.

"Can you tell us when you last saw Dylan?"

Bethany seemed much more confident answering this. She'd last seen Dylan when he and the other boys left the game to head for the coast on Friday night, Bethany told her, some-time around ten thirty. Dylan left alone in his truck while

Jamal hitched a ride with KT Staler. The last Bethany saw of Dylan, she said, he was heading up the highway.

"Up?" Clark said. "As in north?"

The girl hesitated. "I think so."

This interview was proving productive. On the way back to Bentley this afternoon, Clark had finally seen what had nagged at her in the crime scene photographs. The boot prints of the officers working the scene were clearly visible in the mud. So where were the tracks left by the person (or persons) who had dumped the body? Upon closer inspection, she'd seen that several pictures revealed a muddy patch near the bank of the creek in which Dylan's body had been discovered.

"I think this muddy smudge on the other side of the creek is our tire track," Clark had said to Mayfield. *"No one ever took the Spearsons's road. Someone brought a truck in over the Flats on Friday night, during that storm. They stopped at the side of the creek, dumped the body and then let the rain wash away the tracks where their wheels had pulled up the grass."*

Galveston was two hundred miles *south* of Bentley, but according to Bethany, Dylan had last been heading in the opposite direction. The girl had just cleared any doubt for Clark and Mayfield: wherever Dylan had been murdered, he'd never had any intention of going to the coast before he got there.

"And when did these trips to the coast begin?" Clark said.

"Back in May." Bethany gave her an elegant shrug. "Right around the start of the summer games, I remember that. I didn't pay them much mind."

"You wouldn't happen to know the exact dates of these trips, would you?" Clark said, and to her surprise Bethany opened her phone and read aloud a list of dates from her calendar. Clark was further surprised when she realized just how often these trips to the coast had been: Dylan Whitley had left town with KT Staler almost every other weekend during the summer, departing late if there was an off-season game on a Friday night and leaving early if not. He had spent the last three consecutive weekends away. A total of ten trips, over twenty days of unaccounted time.

The best years of my life.

Clark, jotting down the last date, pushing the voice of her dream away, asked Bethany, "You recorded when Dylan was out of town even though you didn't pay the trips any mind?"

"So I'd know when I had the weekend to spend with my girls." Bethany stared at her like the answer was obvious. "I'm a very organized person."

"Did Dylan and KT travel separately when they left town over the summer?" Mayfield asked.

"No. They took Dylan's truck. KT's Tacoma's barely safer than Jamal's Explorer—it leaks oil like a motherfucker. They had to take extra last weekend to be safe."

"Then why not all go together in Dylan's truck?"

Bethany chuckled. "Because it doesn't have a back seat. Can you imagine one of those guys riding bitch for three hours?"

"But, Bethany, *why* did Dylan make all these trips in the first place?" Clark said, waving this away. "You must have been curious."

She didn't answer immediately. She returned her phone to her bag, pushed back a strand of hair, regarded Clark and Mayfield with a piteous frown.

"Being quarterback is very stressful, you know." The girl spoke as if she were explaining this to a child. "People around here *worship* Dylan—they stop him at the gas station and the Egg House, they always want something from him. After we made it to the semifinals it was batshit around here. He *had* to get away. To clear his head. He said he'd forget who he was otherwise."

Clark opened her mouth, hesitated. Kimbra Lott had given her basically the same answer to the same question. And, unless Clark were much mistaken, her brother, Troy, had once told her the same thing about being a successful running back, long before the neck injury in his senior year had brought out an uglier side of the town's devotion. She supposed, in some strange way, it was a blessing to Dylan that he'd died beloved.

Clark noticed, also, that Bethany was speaking about Dylan as if he were still alive.

"I think I understand," Clark said. "But, Bethany—why wouldn't Dylan take you with him?"

"My dad would never let me."

"You must have missed your boy, though."

"It's not like that."

"Not like what?"

The briefest glimpse of a scowl crossed Bethany's face. "Dylan didn't have anything to hide from me."

Clark frowned. That wasn't what she'd asked.

Mayfield cleared his throat. "Dylan never went alone?"

"No. He and KT are good friends."

"But this was the first weekend all three of the boys went together," Clark said. "Dylan, KT and Jamal?"

It was, Bethany said.

"And whose idea was it to bring Jamal?" Clark asked.

"It was Dylan's. They'd always wanted to bring him but Jamal's dad is real strict. It took some convincing him."

"And what did Jamal do on those weekends over the summer when his friends left him here?"

Bethany shrugged. He spent the time with his family, she guessed. Jamal was single, Bethany said, and had been so since spring. Past that, she swore she didn't know a great deal about him. "Dylan has his friends," Bethany said. "And I have mine."

"Be that as it may—" Clark made a show of turning over a page in her notebook. "You must be worried about KT Staler. We hear he never made it to class today."

At that, Bethany very clearly frowned. "You should ask Kimbra about him. Staler and I were never close."

"Was there any particular reason for that?"

Bethany shrugged, glanced at the blinded window. "His family's garbage."

"They've had their troubles." Clark arched an eyebrow. "Did you ever get the impression KT took after his siblings?"

"You mean did I think he was on drugs?" Bethany said, meeting Clark's eye. "No."

Clark's mind returned to KT's insistence yesterday that Dylan had had a girl on the side. Clark wondered how Bethany would react to such a claim. Did this girl with the perfect skin and the sheet of golden hair have it in her to kill her boyfriend and dump his body in a creek?

Watching the way Bethany smoothed the hem of her sleeve with a muted precision, the same precision with which she appeared to smooth down every inch of herself, Clark's answer was obvious.

Of course.

"It must have been difficult to watch your man get so much attention," Clark said. "I bet there's plenty of girls hoping to catch his eye."

Bethany gave Clark a quizzical look. "They might have hoped. Dylan had his priorities straight."

"Really? A boy his age? A boy that handsome?"

"Really." Bethany chuckled, shook her head. "Dylan and I had something real. We—"

"You never had reason to suspect there was another girl in his life?"

Bethany refused to be flustered. "No."

Mayfield scratched at his cuff. If Bethany knew anything else, she wasn't going to reveal it today.

Clark smiled, clicked shut her pen, closed her notebook. "Thank you for your time, Miss Tanner."

Something curious happened as Bethany readied herself to go. A long, painful-looking yawn brought tears to her eyes, a little tremor to her fingers. For the first time since she walked through the door, the girl looked unguarded. Off balance. Scared.

Clark couldn't have chosen a better moment to ask her final question.

"You said you last saw Dylan leave the game at ten thirty Friday night, yes? What did you do with yourself for the rest of the weekend?"

"Me?"

"Yes. I just need something to put in the notes."

"I went home by myself." The girl sounded distracted when she said it, preoccupied by something else in her head—grief? pyramid drills?—but the moment the words were out of her mouth Bethany went very tense. Clark would have sworn she saw a flash of panic across her eyes.

"Your father wasn't with you?"

A long pause. "No. He had business in Dallas."

"Did he make it back that night?"

A tight smile. A green nail playing on the table. "No."

"So you were home all weekend? Alone?" Mayfield said.

"I was sick."

An idea occurred to Clark. "Your house doesn't have a security system, does it? Cameras on the fences, maybe watching the doors?"

That green Bisonette nail on the table: *tap-tap-tap.* "You'd have to ask Dad."

WEDNESDAY

PATTERNS

JOEL

Lying in his room, a thin square of hot sunlight burning his thigh, Joel felt unmoored. He had a body of sorts, an impossible heavy thing, but he had no conscious will, no desire to eat or drink, no idea how he had ever done anything as strenuous as walk or bathe or breathe. He had heard of people being broken by grief, consumed by it, but he had never realized before that so much of grief was guilt: guilt for not doing more (not doing *anything*) to help the people who needed you, back when helping could have been done. Guilt, and beneath it, a sadness at realizing you were more alone than you had been before. And then fresh guilt, for thinking of yourself and your own sorrows when someone else was dead on a slab.

He found himself slipping, quite unwillingly, into a memory he thought he had dammed and drained and forgotten. Apparently not. A decade wasn't long enough to obliterate the sort of summer he'd had back when he was Dylan's age:

the delirious hot afternoons, the bitter fall that followed. How hopeless, how embarrassing, to think he could ever put those days behind him.

There was that guilt again, reminding him how he only ever thought of himself. Perhaps. But anything was better than thinking of the present.

The announcement had come in early June, a few months before the start of Joel's senior year. In addition to their summer practices, the Bison would now play exhibition games to raise money for the football program. The team, still suffering after the injury and then graduation of Troy Clark—their once-brilliant star of a running back—had failed to even qualify for play-offs in the past season, but the town was enthusiastic about these new games. Maybe, the men at the bar murmured, playing in the heat would put some spine in those soft boys.

Joel had worked for two seasons as an athletic assistant on the football team—one of the gangly nerds who'd picked up towels and squirted water into players' mouths on the sidelines—but he had retired before the start of his junior year. He wanted to devote more time to his tennis game, Joel had told the coaches, but this excuse had sounded flimsy even to his own ears: tennis practice began in the spring, long after the end of the football season.

The fact that Troy Clark had graduated the spring before Joel quit the team was definitely, certainly, *entirely* coincidental. Never mind that from Joel's two seasons on the sidelines he remembered Troy's every *"Thanks,"* and *"More water,"* and once (miraculously) *"Can you get the knot out of these laces?"* Never mind that Joel remembered every time Troy's startling green eyes had settled on his own, every glimpse of the soft brown hairs of his thigh when Troy had stepped from the showers.

Surely, Joel assured himself, other boys felt a similar thrill in moments like these. Surely there was nothing wrong with him.

Now, if Joel could only feel those same thrills when he was with his girlfriend then they'd really be in business.

His girlfriend, who through coincidence (*pure* coincidence) happened to be Troy's sister. Practical, hardy Starsha Clark. Because surely the relation was a coincidence. Joel hadn't seen Troy in a year but he was still dating *her* so obviously he loved her. Obviously.

By the night of the Bison's first off-season game, Troy was (according to Clark) living in Rockdale, an hour away, with a scrawny beautician who wasn't good enough for him but who was apparently as good as he was going to get. *No hope of seeing him at the game, then?* Joel had almost asked her, stopping himself just in time.

The turnout at the game was larger than anyone had expected. The people of Bentley arrived with a display of spirit that dwarfed the baffled contingent from Franklin who had come to watch their own boys, the Hornets, pummel the Bison from the first whistle. Seated in the stands, Clark slipped her hand from Joel's to cup her palms around her mouth and bellow "*Defense*, goddammit!" in a hoarse voice that drew more than a few stares. He dispensed apologetic smiles on her behalf.

This was romance, he supposed. Three years together, and Joel and Clark were made for each other. They'd both lost a parent. They both loved tennis. The fact they never touched above the wrists simply spoke to the purity of their devotion.

In the second quarter, Joel made his way to the bathroom. He spotted his brother and Luke Evers ignoring the game and pacing the edges of the end zone. How small Dylan had been in those days. How his head had barely fit his Bison cap.

Joel was nearly to the cinder block toilet when a cackling laugh reached him from inside. Joel froze, hesitated, but it was too late. Ranger Mason, the old bane of Bentley High, emerged with a crooked smile on his chapped mouth.

Ranger was a loathsome young man. He had been a Bison himself, had graduated in the same class as Troy Clark but, unlike Troy, Joel seemed to see him everywhere. Ranger Mason wasn't as big as his younger brother, Garrett, would become a decade later but he was still menacing enough that evening to send a squelch of bile up Joel's gullet. Ranger was dressed in one of his seven shredded Slipknot T-shirts that reeked of sweat and stale smoke. Joel spotted a new tattoo on his neck: a raw red snake winding down his jugular.

Next to Ranger stood feral little Jason Ovelle, looking much the same as he would a decade later, when Joel would watch him get arrested in this very same parking lot. A wispy mustache, thin arms, teeth all crowded in the front of his mouth like a muskrat's. His face lit up at the sight of Joel. He knew there was about to be a show.

"Whitley!" Ranger shouted. "We was just thinking about you."

Joel took a step back. Was there anything more terrifying than the thought that these two might have been discussing him?

"Where's your team spirit, son?" Jason asked.

"I'm giving the team room to grieve. They're going through a tragedy."

"Ain't you clever tonight?" Ranger's smile revealed a dry gum. He scrutinized Joel for a final second, glanced at Jason. The boys exchanged subtle, almost imperceptible nods: they'd come to some consensus. Joel's stomach tightened.

"Speaking of tragic, Whitley," Ranger said, turning back. "How is Miss Clark doing?"

"We hear she's real lonely these days," said Jason.

Joel felt a sudden flush of panic. "She can take care of herself," he said, and regretted it immediately.

The two boys guffawed. "She must be doing that a lot, dating you."

Jason took a step forward. "Is it true you used to sniff our straps after the games?"

"That's disgusting," said Joel, who had.

"That's what we said when we heard about it." Ranger shook his head. "You need help, Whitley."

Ranger reached out a hand to stroke Joel's cheek. Joel flinched. "You need to get out of my fucking face," Joel said, and heard his voice crack.

He backed away. They followed him. Why weren't they letting this go like they usually did? What had he done to bring this on?

"Listen, Whitley," Ranger said, all tender sympathy. "We're progressed around here, ain't we?"

"We's in the new millennium," Jason agreed.

"Exactly. The millennium. So we don't give two fucks how you get your rocks off. But we got some goddamn standards in Bentley, alright? We've got rules of *comportment*." Ranger drew himself up to his full height, puffed out his chest. His nipple peeked through a hole in his shirt. "You keep your private life private around here, you hear me? Because, Whitley, I saw you at your job the other day and I got to tell you— you're starting to show."

Joel didn't think about what he was doing. Looking back a decade later he suspected he could have saved himself a great deal of hurt if he'd just taken a breath and walked away. If he had brushed Ranger off, let the man grow into the tragic fuckup he was destined to be.

Instead Joel succumbed to a lifetime of fear. It was rage, he told himself later, indignity, but deep down, he knew the truth. Not that it did him any good.

That evening at the stands, Joel took a step forward, drew

back his fist and swung it at Ranger's face, all because Ranger was right about him. Pity.

The blow hardly connected—Ranger was already turning back to snicker at Jason when Joel began to swing and so his nose avoided what would have been a nasty break. But Joel's knuckle still cracked against Ranger's cheek, tore loose a piece of skin. No one had warned Joel the pain in his knuckles would bite like a bear.

Ranger staggered back. He pulled up his own fist.

A pair of kids from Franklin High started to cackle in the shadow of the stands. Jason, suddenly looking panicked, murmured something urgent in Ranger's ear.

Ranger spat out a mouthful of blood. He all but shimmered with rage. He whispered something to Jason, and the smaller boy took off jogging. Already Joel was realizing the magnitude of his mistake.

In a soft voice, with something approaching tenderness, Ranger said, "You are going to regret that, you little fucking faggot."

Joel didn't weep—he remembered that much. He remembered the way his knuckles throbbed, the way the crowd of feet visible beneath the walls of his toilet stall had swollen throughout halftime, remembered the grumbles as people tugged at the stall's locked door. He ignored them. He couldn't face another soul.

All his hard work—the twang he'd wrestled onto his voice, the stiff gait he'd spent hours practicing in front of the mirror to keep his hips from betraying him—had it accomplished nothing? What sort of future could possibly await him?

Slowly, as the little crowd shuffled out of the restroom at the start of the second half, as the sun began its endless descent and the toilet began to swell with the hot last light of the summer day, Joel forced his fear down his throat. He would have to try harder. What choice did he have? This would be his life, he realized: trapdoors, tripwires. He would always be a little frightened and a little angry, would always be conscious of the eyes appraising his every move. The men at the Egg House, the women at church, his classmates at school: he had so many people to fool if he wanted to be safe in this town. If he wanted to retain a little dignity, a little decency. If he had any hope of being loved.

He didn't think about Ranger's promise of revenge. He thought only of Dylan and Clark and his mother, of the people he held dearest, and of the pain they would feel if they ever were to learn how extensive his lies had always been, how crooked his heart. How humiliated they would be to have wasted so much time believing in a boy so broken. *Do you love me?* Clark always asked on the phone, every night before bed. *More and more every day.*

He rubbed his knuckles. He would have to be more careful in the future. He couldn't risk losing control like that again.

Though God in heaven, some days all Joel wanted was an excuse to lose control.

And then Joel opened the door of the stall and saw a man standing alone at the urinal, his profile trembling in the brassy light. It was none other than Troy Clark.

CLARK

Twelve hours later, Clark stifled a yawn in the hot cruiser and wondered what armless Dylan Whitley had tried to tell her last night when he'd led her to the edge of a black hole in the ground and showed her... What? The other details of the dream had evaporated when she awoke, leaving behind nothing but a cool dread in her chest.

What was it her crazy mother used to say? *"Dreams are just our souls going for a swim at night." Jesus, Mom.* If that was true, what the hell had happened to the swimming hole this week?

Mayfield caught Clark's yawn and pressed a fist to his own mouth. "Lordy," he said. "I ain't slept this bad since *I* was coming to this school."

Clark paused, a hand on her lighter. "Are you having dreams too?"

"They'll pass," he said, and handed her a thick file without another word.

Clark studied the autopsy photos inside. She could handle the gore well enough; she'd seen her share of suicides and traffic pileups and had never been much bothered by them. What hurt were the little details: chewed nails, streaks from an inexpert fade in the hair. The soles of Dylan's feet, calloused from a life spent in cleats.

Time of death was still difficult to determine, even after the autopsy, but Clark and Mayfield had settled on sometime between ten thirty Friday, when Dylan and his friends were seen leaving the game, and two o'clock Saturday morning when the storm had stopped, after which there would have been tracks near the creek where the body was found. The ME had seemed satisfied with this.

It confirmed, at least, Joel Whitley's suspicion: whoever had texted him Saturday morning hadn't been his brother.

The cause of death had been simple enough to establish: a blade, serrated, between four and six inches long, had opened the carotid artery. A hunting knife, most likely, which hardly narrowed it down: there were three of those in every truck and closet in Pettis County.

"Russ Tanner, the cheerleader's dad, was apparently at some cattle function when Jones went by to confirm his daughter's story yesterday," said Mayfield. "We'll try and get hold of him again this afternoon."

Clark thought of the nervous way Bethany's green nail had *tap-tap-tap*ped the table at the end of her interview. She made a note to drive by the Tanner ranch herself, see if its gate was monitored by a camera and, if so, figure out how she could obtain that camera's footage from Friday night. She was curious to know when precisely Bethany had gotten home after the game.

There was a whistle on the practice field, and the Bison threw themselves at each other with a clatter. Clark watched as Jamal Reynolds was brought down hard by Garrett Mason, the team's enormous defensive safety. It took Reynolds a very long time to return to his feet.

"They're beating the shit out of that kid," Clark said.

"It's like they already made up their mind about him."

"A little quickly, no?"

She'd been saying it all day and she'd say it again. Her logic was simple: Jamal's potential motives for killing Dylan didn't make any sense under scrutiny. The fact that Dylan had been discovered without a shirt or underwear perhaps suggested that he had been partially undressed at the time of the murder. This, combined with KT Staler's suggestion that Dylan had a girl on the side, had brought the detectives, tenuously, to some idea that Jamal might have killed Dylan out of jealousy for this girl. A love triangle gone sour, maybe. Perhaps—*perhaps*—this explained the condom that Jamal had apparently asked stuttering Benny Garcia for at halftime on Friday, though Mayfield had found that tip more than a little dubious. The whole theory was built on a shaky heap of assumptions.

Putting aside the mysterious side-girl for a moment, Clark thought even less of the idea that Jamal might have killed his close friend for the chance to steal some glory for himself. Even in a town that worshipped its quarterbacks, this felt like a stretch. For one thing, the other boys on the team had all stated that Jamal and Dylan were fast friends, hanging out often and studying together on school nights. Paulette Whitley had attested to this. Jamal's parents had attested to this. And Jamal was a senior—he had only a handful of football games in his future. Would he really kill a close friend—not mention risk the death penalty—for a few hours of field time?

Clark didn't buy either theory. From the moment they'd told Jamal that Dylan was dead he'd been shocked, disgusted, bereft—but he hadn't betrayed a moment's concern for his own safety until Mayfield started putting the screws to him. Clark didn't buy this boy as a killer.

Dylan's other friend, however, she had trouble with.

"You do realize that both of the possible motives we've given to Jamal come from statements made by KT Staler, a boy who's now conveniently vanished to leave his friend in the soup."

Mayfield shrugged. "Sometimes these things are easy."

"Would it be so easy if the roles were reversed?" she said. "If KT were stuck here and Jamal had disappeared?"

"I'm not sure what you're implying, Deputy."

"What if Jamal's skin was a little lighter? KT's a little darker?"

"You're going to stop that kind of talk right now." Mayfield twisted slowly in his seat to fix her eye. "The fact stands that every other boy on the team but Reynolds and Staler has himself an alibi for Friday night. Furthermore, Joel Whitley was spotted by a half-dozen people in town right after the game. He's got a nosy old crow of a neighbor who swears Joel woke her up when he pulled in just after eleven. The mother's boyfriend, Darren, he woke the lady up again at two fifteen, and we've got *him* on a video at a gas station in College Station an hour before, driving back from working on an oil rig in Corpus Christi. Maybe there's a hole in that man's story somewhere but I don't see it. So the family's out. The team is out. We've got an APB in every station looking for KT Staler's teal-green Tacoma but that's about all the resources we can give that boy. You can't follow every lead in a case like this, Deputy. He'll turn up if he turns up."

"But he's our prime suspect."

"Correction—that would be Reynolds, the only boy— white or black—left in town without an alibi," Mayfield said. "For what it's worth, Mr. Boone says the county attorney's office is going to file subpoenas for KT Staler's phone records to help us track him down."

"If he's alive," Clark said. "I still don't like the fact that

Jason Ovelle was rooting around in Staler's truck. He said something about KT owing him money."

"Ovelle's got holes in his brain from all the tweak he's cooked. Funny you mention him, though. Browder swung by his old room in that rat's nest motel down the highway and apparently nobody's seen Ovelle since Friday. God willing, we never will again." Mayfield studied a printout from a stack of folders.

"Go back. Nobody's seen Ovelle since Friday night? The night Whitley was murdered?"

"No, they haven't, but before you ask I already have the APBs filed for *him* too. Like I said, you chase one bird at a time." Mayfield studied the field. "And when you have it in your hand, you squeeze it till it chirps."

Clark followed his eyes, noted the tall Turner twins and pale little Tomas Hernandez studying Jamal as their new quarterback struggled again to his feet. They shook their heads and turned away.

She said, "What if we're looking at killers. Plural. Like you said yesterday. I'm thinking about the phone."

"The phone?"

"Dylan died in a nasty fight—look at these bruises. If you've just beat a boy black-and-blue and cut his throat deep enough to slice the vocal cords then you're going to be high as a kite on adrenaline. You ain't going to have the sense to take the boy's phone and unlock it with his thumb so you can start covering your tracks the next day. You need a cool head for that sort of forward planning. Someone to look at what you've done and see a way out."

"Hence why we wait for Jamal to crack. If he and Staler were in it together, he'll lead us to him, one way or the other. Dead or alive."

Clark spotted something in one of the autopsy photographs. "What's that?" she asked, pointing.

A thin, pale mark ran straight across the back of Dylan's left thigh. It looked like an old scar, but Clark couldn't imagine what sort of accident could produce such a clean, even line.

Mayfield studied the photo. "Any record of a surgery?"

"None that I'm aware of."

"A play of the light," the investigator said, sounding unconvinced. They were hitting a wall.

"Have you ever investigated a murder before?" Clark asked.

"Open-and-shuts." Mayfield shrugged. "An ugly bar fight. A man beat his wife with her own iron for burning his shirt. Only a few real mysteries. A disappearance. As you remember."

Mayfield let the word hang in the car's hot air. She knew perfectly well what he meant.

Clark watched as the players on the field lined up to throw themselves at each other again. Big Coach Parter himself stood at the thirty yard line, bellowing something to Jamal—"No strength in your goddamn legs, Reynolds!"—his mouth inches from the boy's helmet grill. Clark wasn't sure she'd ever seen the school's athletic director actually coach. With a player like Dylan on the team, he'd probably never had to.

"You must have wanted to ask," Mayfield said. "Don't tell me you didn't print off your brother's case the first day you had a password to the computers here."

He was right, of course. "Possibly," she said.

"And you remember it was me who came around looking for Troy back in the day," Mayfield said. Clark nodded with a bemused smile—her first meeting with Investigator Mayfield years ago had not been a pleasant one. "Be honest now. Was all that business with your brother the reason you wanted to join up with the sheriff's in the first place?"

"You mean did I spend three years in school so I could print off case notes from a missing person's report?"

Mayfield shrugged. "Folks have done more for less."

Clark considered this with an odd mixture of pain and frustration. She'd asked herself the same question many times since her return to Bentley and had yet to arrive at a convincing answer.

She only trusted herself enough to say, "Maybe. In some tricksy way."

Mayfield seemed satisfied. "Well, you've got a good career ahead of you. You're made for more than speeding tickets."

Clark lit a cigarette. His praise felt coarser this afternoon than it had yesterday: appeasing, cheap. She couldn't shake the feeling that his single-minded interest in Jamal Reynolds had an air of expediency to it, as if Mayfield weren't looking for Dylan's murderer but rather for the boy the town would most willingly believe fit the role. From their theories about the crime to Mayfield's encouragement, everything today was coming just a little too easy.

"You know," Mayfield added. "There was some things we kept out of your brother's file."

JOEL

Joel wasn't certain how much more sympathy he could tolerate. Darren, with no little misgiving, had left town again that morning to work on his oil rig outside Corpus Christi—considering the tenuous state of the oil economy these days he could hardly be blamed for working when there was work. Joel had somehow dragged himself out of bed and tended to his mother, sat with her through endless courses of coffee and pity and fretful murmurs about the team's new chances at the play-offs.

Mrs. Mason and Mrs. Malacek, his mother's friends, had turned up an hour ago with casserole and cake and showed no signs of leaving anytime soon.

"It's hard to believe what they're saying," Mrs. Malacek said, after sitting through another of Paulette's long silences. "I'd have never thought the Reynolds boy had it in him."

Joel and his mother both snapped to attention.

"You mean Jamal?" Paulette said.

The two ladies shook their heads. Mrs. Mason stifled a yawn before saying, "No alibi, apparently. The police went down to that house on the coast and—well. It seems the boys weren't there after all."

"What?" said Joel. His mind wrestled with the effects of the Xanax he'd sneaked into his mouth when the ladies arrived. "How can the cops be certain about that?"

Mrs. Malacek shook her head, not a strand of golden hair stirring. "My Peter won't tell me another word about it, just that the alibis ain't any good."

"But Dylan and Kyler Thomas went to that house a dozen times this summer," Paulette said. A cookie crumbled between her fingers. "They can't seriously say—"

Mrs. Mason laid a hand on Raul the terrier's quivering head and said, "My brother, George, tells me the gossip down at the bar is the same. Men there're saying the cops just need one good piece of evidence to pin on Reynolds. That's all it'll take."

"But that's absurd," Paulette said. "Jamal's the gentlest soul on this earth. Dylan told me so himself."

"What about KT Staler?" Joel said.

"Oh, he's running scared of Reynolds." Mrs. Malacek spoke almost in a whisper. "The Chamber of Commerce has been chewing on it all week—Mr. Evers told my Peter that if *his* guess is right, the Staler boy knows enough to get out of town while he can. All the evidence adds up, the Chamber says."

Joel and his mother exchanged baffled glances.

"I heard—" Mrs. Mason began, but was racked again by a long yawn.

"Are you having trouble sleeping?" Joel asked her, something stirring in his foggy mind.

Now it was the women's turns to exchange looks. "Sometimes the lights are just wrong," Mrs. Mason said, shrugging as if this made perfect sense.

Before Joel could ask her what she meant, Mrs. Malacek cut in with a nod. "The whole town is grieving."

Joel helped Paulette gather the coffee things onto a tray. He couldn't keep from noticing that the ladies who were so concerned for his mother's well-being hadn't bothered to tidy up their mess.

"You realize when Mrs. Malacek says 'her Peter' she's talking about the mayor, don't you, Joel?"

"'The gentlest soul on earth.' Dylan really said that about Jamal?"

"To that effect. Christ, the sheriff's department is hopeless. That fat deputy who arrested you fell off a horse so well it turned him from a pig into a vegetable—did you hear that?"

Joel's stomach turned over at the thought of Deputy Grissom. "I heard."

"The sheriffs must be up a real creek if they're trying to hang this on Jamal goddamn Reynolds."

Paulette made to lift the tray from the table but it slipped from her fingers. Cups scattered. Coffee threw itself over the carpet. Joel's mother took one look at the mess and dropped herself to the sofa with a little wail of fury.

He took her hand in both of his. He sat with her a long time while she trembled all over. He was surprised to see that for the third day his mother still refused to weep.

A few words finally escaped her.

"You were right, you know. Years ago. There's something wrong with this place."

Joel watched her face, said nothing. He had a feeling of what was coming.

Paulette turned her eyes from the coffee at her feet to the

son in front of her. She laced her fingers through his so hard he thought the knuckles might snap loose.

"Promise me you'll fix this, Joel," she whispered. "Don't let them do to Dylan what they did to you."

Joel met her eye. The truth was she didn't even need to ask. Joel knew he wouldn't be going back to New York anytime soon. He'd grieve later. Call it guilt, call it revenge, call it settling old debts: Joel had unfinished business in this town.

"Whoever it is." Joel wiped a strand of hair from his mother's face. He said, very softly, "Whatever it takes."

CLARK

She couldn't believe what she was hearing.

"This case today ain't nothing like Troy's," Mayfield said. "I know it may look that way on the surface but it ain't. Troy never sent no messages to his girlfriend saying he was fine, the way Dylan did with his brother. And Dylan, far as we know, didn't disappear holding the bag on eight grand of drug money."

The ash fell from her cigarette. "He what?"

Mayfield sighed. "Eight-thou-oh-five, if memory serves. You didn't realize? Troy was in the meth game bad, Deputy. Using *and* selling. We found out pretty quick that he was stuck in the loop, borrowing money to buy product but only ever paying back the interest. Getting high on his supply, the works. Apparently Troy decided to use his last loan to buy himself a full tank of gas and split."

Mayfield rubbed at a stain on his collar, pursing his lips at a sour memory. Clark couldn't speak.

"Old Mr. Boone, the county attorney, he asked that we keep that little detail out of the files," Mayfield added. "Boone figured—understandably, knowing the way this department leaks—that there wasn't no point in besmirching your brother's name. It wouldn't do anyone any—"

"My brother owed a cartel eight thousand dollars for meth?" The words were so absurd they all but gagged her coming up.

"Not the cartel directly. One of their businessmen. Troy owed it to Benicio Dos, you remember him? Honest to God, Clark, we thought for sure your brother would come back any minute after they finally arrested that greasy fucker a few years back. The fact that Troy didn't come home when the coast was clear makes us wonder if someone else found him first. I'm sorry about the whole business, I truly am."

Clark's back went stiff. She stared at the man. Her brother, a drug addict. A drug *dealer*? A man on the run from a Mexican cartel? She couldn't imagine it. Troy had struggled with life after high school, she remembered that well enough— had drunk even more than their father in his prime—but by the summer of 2007 he had seemed to stabilize. He'd been living in Rockdale with his quiet girlfriend—a bland beautician named Hannah Szilack—for over a year. He'd gotten a welding license. He'd been talking about starting a family.

"You should have put that in the report," Clark said.

Mayfield shrugged. "Maybe so. But really, what good would it have done? The money was gone. The man was gone. There weren't no drug soldiers on our turf looking for him and we figured that was a blessing in itself. Mr. Boone's shrewd like that, Clark. He may not seem like much but he is."

Clark pushed open her door. A shrill whistle rose up from the field and the boys began to jog inside.

Mayfield said, "Where are you going?"

"Scratching an itch."

"Deputy," Mayfield said, leaning over in his seat to hold her eye. "We inherited this town. We all did. That don't mean we have to love everything about it. I hope you can remember that."

"I've got police work to do," she said, and set off toward the school.

JOEL

Fifteen minutes later and Joel was behind the wheel of the convertible, already wondering how he could keep his absurd promise to his mother. He didn't know the first thing about investigating a murder. He was hopeless at everything beyond reading Excel spreadsheets and fighting hangovers and executing dead lifts.

All this grief and anger—it was a little pathetic, wasn't it? He'd barely paid Dylan a thought in a decade. Upon learning last Sunday that his little brother had problems, an inner life of any kind, Joel had secretly delighted in how noble it would be to save him, how easily he could make a permanent friend of Dylan with just a little lazy largesse.

And now? Now Joel craved one of his signature Manhattan benders. He wanted bottle service, hard drugs, a handgun in his mouth. He wanted anything that would take his mind off the fact that beneath his cultivated body and his boutique

T-shirts Joel Whitley was nothing more than a scrawny fag who'd been too weak to protect the one person in his life who had ever needed him.

He settled for Adderall, and motion.

As Joel drove he dialed Wesley Mores, the Baptist Church's youth minister. Joel remembered something Wesley had mentioned Sunday night: how KT Staler had gotten into trouble over the summer and Dylan had been concerned about it.

The phone rang and rang. The voice of Darren, Paulette's boyfriend, flitted now through Joel's head: *"I put in two thousand of my own money."*

Joel thought about the expensive Sonos soundbar he'd noticed on Dylan's dresser, the pricey watch Joel had found in Dylan's nightstand drawer, right alongside a bottle of painkillers (*POTENTIAL FOR RECREATION/ABUSE: HIGH*). Paulette had told Joel that the soundbar and the watch were gifts from Bethany Tanner. Joel couldn't quite believe this.

Investigator Mayfield had asked Joel if KT Staler had given Dylan *"any trouble."* KT's sister, Joel remembered, had been arrested for concealing meth in the shells of hollowed-out Nokia phones. It wasn't much of a stretch to imagine that KT might have gotten involved in some shady business through her. Perhaps Dylan had gotten sucked in as well.

And now, apparently, KT Staler had gone missing. Joel wondered if Wesley Mores might have any theories why.

The call went to voice mail.

Fine.

He drove to the bank to inquire about his brother's account and was told that it contained two thousand dollars, not four. *"I put in two thousand of my own money,"* Darren had said. So where had the other two thousand gone? Despite his best efforts, the girl behind the counter at the bank would tell Joel nothing more.

Joel stopped when he reached an empty spot in front of Lott's Hardware. Inside, gnomish Mr. Lott, a man Joel had hoped to speak to since his return on Friday, gave him a sad little wave through the store's front window.

The sight of this bald, small man with his bushy mustache, his shirt and bow tie and starched overalls, brought back a memory to Joel like a knife through the chest. Ten years ago, Joel had been inside that store, hiding inside a pair of headphones in the wake of his arrest, sent by his mother to buy something his house didn't need—paint thinner? a torpedo level?—in the hopes of getting him out of bed. At the counter, Mr. Lott had made no effort to ring up his purchase. Lott had motioned for Joel to take the headphones off, which he did, reluctantly. Braced for some fresh humiliation, Joel had instead heard the first kind words an adult had spoken to him since those photos had appeared in everyone's paper the week before.

As Joel stepped inside the store today, the bell chimed brightly, as if even it too was grateful to see him again.

"Dear God, Joel," Mr. Lott said, embracing him. "Am I ever sorry."

Déjà vu. He had said exactly the same thing to Joel ten years ago.

Joel composed himself enough to say, "I'm glad this place still exists. I heard they opened a Walmart down the highway."

Lott waved this off. "Forget the Walmart. Joel Whitley, how the hell are you walking?"

"I'm not entirely certain." Joel glanced around at the empty shop. "I don't want to keep you—is your daughter here?"

"Kimbra? She mentioned you were looking for me Sunday. She's probably at the Egg House with a few of the girls. I try not to make her work on the weeknights. God knows we hardly have the business."

Lott's eyes seemed to follow Joel's around the shop, taking in with him the faded deals, the ersatz stack of wheelbarrow tires and, on almost every vertical surface, Bentley Bison merchandise. There were pennants, commemorative calendars dating back decades, framed jerseys of yesterday's golden boys: BROADLOCK, STEELE, CLARK.

TOBIAS LOTT, BOOSTER CLUB CHAIR, read a nameplate mounted on the store's wooden counter. A pristine replica of the State Semifinals trophy from the year before sat next to the paint-speckled cash register.

Joel spotted a picture of his beaming brother mounted next to an official portrait of the president. The president's photo was smaller.

"It's nice to see you haven't changed," Joel said.

Lott tried to smile. "Should I be concerned about your designs on my daughter?"

"It's her boyfriend I'm worried about," Joel said, and Mr. Lott's face darkened. "Has KT ever made any trouble for Kimbra?"

"There's always going to be someone else you'd wish would take a shine to your little girl."

Joel noticed something odd on the wall. "Did they not have a team picture in '75?"

Lott seemed happy to change the subject. "That's the only one I'm missing. Nobody held on to it. I have a few with your brother, though. They're yours if you want them."

Joel demurred. He turned to go, hesitated and looked back at Mr. Lott to say, "Do you remember what you told me that afternoon? The week after everything happened?"

"I've said a lot in my time."

"It was just a few words—" Joel began, but Lott cut him off.

"I'm sure I meant every one of them."

For years, though he had no interest in returning to Bentley, Joel sometimes imagined coming home, thanking this funny little man for saying exactly what he'd needed to hear at exactly the right moment.

"You're too good for this town," Lott had said back then. Simple, and yet it had saved Joel as surely as a flare fired in heavy fog. It had pointed toward a future. It had given him a reason to live: to see what life was like elsewhere.

"When you told me to get out of Bentley I think you kept me alive, Mr. Lott. That's all."

"When I told you what?" Lott said. The man rubbed at his mustache and looked acutely embarrassed.

"Never mind," Joel said, after a long hesitation. He took one last look at all this Bison bric-a-brac. "Good luck to the boys on Friday."

CLARK

She found Wesley Mores seated behind a desk in the middle school, sunk in a snowbank of papers. He jumped a mile when she rapped on his door.

"Clark," he said. "I apologize. I'm a little on edge today."

"We all are."

A banner of the solar system hung above Wesley's head, though she noticed the school's budget was so tight that poor diminutive Pluto had been X'd over with a Sharpie. Looking at this plain man in front of her who had once been noteworthy, Clark realized that a similar demotion had been visited on Wesley: Bentley Bison, the moment they graduated, stepped down into being nothing more than men.

"Is the investigation going well, Officer?"

"It's proceeding." At the sight of the cross around Wesley's neck an idea occurred to her. "Have any of the boys in your youth group given any indication that something dirty might be going on around town? It could just be something small, something gossipy. They do talk to you, yes?"

Wesley gave a little laugh. Unless Clark was much mistaken, he sounded relieved. "They do talk to me, yes, but never about anything serious."

"No trouble they want to keep quiet? Any rumors of infidelity?"

"'Infidelity'?" Wesley laughed again. "They talk about football and more football. But it's funny—I think Joel Whitley was curious about the same sort of thing."

"Is that right?"

Mores shrugged. "If I had to guess I'd say that gossip's the only reason he came over for dinner on Sunday. He's a funny guy. Troubled, you know."

Clark made a *hmm*. She studied Wesley—stubble on his cheek, eyes sunken from lack of sleep. Something odd about him. Something off. "And what did you tell Joel?"

"What I just told you." Mores laughed again. "Those boys only talk about the game. Some might talk about some porn they've googled, you know. Garden variety stuff."

"The porn is garden variety?"

Wesley blushed. "I can't say much."

"You can't say much about the things they tell you? So they *do* tell you things?"

A silence. "I'm not sure what to tell *you*." Wesley held up his hands and said pointedly, "While you're here, can I ask you if there's been any progress with the fire?"

"You mean at First Baptist?" Clark rose to go. "Electrical miswiring in the steeple, last I heard."

"Funny. That cross had been burning fine for twenty years."

Clark thought of Mayfield, wondered how many details had been left out of how many files. She shrugged to Wesley and headed for the door.

"So Joel Whitley was at your house on Sunday night?" she said before stepping into the hall.

"He was."

"And what were you up to Friday?"

Wesley blinked at her before turning his attention to his desk. He sighed.

"I went home to get out of the storm. And grade papers. If you'll excuse me, Officer—they laid off all the teacher's aides to buy the boys new uniforms and I'm already a week behind."

JOEL

A gang of boys in blue leather Perlin High jackets were sprawled across a corner of the Egg House, looking eager to take offense. No one sat near them. The other diners ate all huddled together, relative strangers sharing tables like they were back in school themselves, all eating their sandwiches and sipping their iced tea as if there were nothing at all unusual about leaving half of a restaurant abandoned.

Joel found Kimbra Lott in a booth, seated near the back between Dashandre, the lone boy from the cheer squad (*"We've had more of that the last few years"*) and a girl with a lip piercing and bright black nails. Seated across from them were two boys, one a portly red-faced ginger and the other a handsome black kid, both of them footballers Joel recognized but couldn't name.

Kimbra, Dashandre and April were all three cramped around Kimbra's phone, struggling to hold a smile for a selfie.

When Kimbra lowered the phone, they looked dissatisfied with the results.

"If I might make a suggestion," Joel said gently, and the five of them flinched. "Your natural light is actually that way."

"Boy, we ain't trying to be a supermodel like you." Dashandre scowled, though Joel noticed the way he shot a look across the table, like he was hoping to make the players smile.

But the boys were too distracted introducing themselves, the portly ginger rising to shake Joel's hand with both of his. "Mr. Whitley, good to finally meet you. Whiskey Brazos, starting center. Your brother was a brother to us."

The other player leaned around Whiskey to say, "Tyrone Baskin. Defensive captain. Call me T-Bay."

Joel was more than a little taken aback by this courtesy—he'd long since assumed every boy in town found him contemptuous. He said something about Dylan having nothing but respect for all of them.

The girl with the black nails toyed with her ketchup. When Whiskey introduced her as his girlfriend, April, she said, "The hell dragged you back here from New York?"

"I've asked myself that question a lot. Do y'all mind if I speak to Kimbra?"

The Perlin High boys let out a booming parody of the Bentley cheer from the other side of the diner: *"Bison Turd!"* The residents of Bentley, refusing to indulge them, intensified their polite discussion of the weather.

Kimbra studied Joel before giving a little shrug, sipping her iced tea.

"The cops should be looking at those Perlin guys," she said in a low voice once she and Joel were alone. "The Stallions haven't won a Stable Shootout since your brother made quarterback."

Suddenly the presence of the blue-jacketed boys made sense: the game against the Perlin Stallions was the event of the season. They always came around town to stir shit the week before—it was as much a tradition as the smack-talking soap signs (WE MAKE GLUE W/ STALLIONS) Joel had started seeing in car windows this morning.

"I'm sure the cops have their own priorities. I was wondering if you'd heard from your boyfriend."

"Didn't we have this conversation on Sunday?"

"We did. Boys seem to evaporate in this town."

"You're telling me." Kimbra frowned. He had the distinct impression she was sizing him up for some private purpose. "Have you ever been to Los Angeles?"

"Unfortunately yes."

"People say California's beautiful."

He smiled. "You want to be in the movies?"

"I want to be somewhere people want to be."

"Are you and KT getting out of here together?"

She froze, her straw between her fingers. "How did you know that?"

Joel smiled wider, trying to calm the panic he saw in her eye. "Because I used to live here."

Kimbra lapsed into silence. Her eyes were swollen and weighed down with bags. She hadn't straightened her hair in several days, Joel saw. Frizzy split ends tickled her neck.

"KT and I are leaving in the spring, the day after Finals," Kimbra said. "Just get in a car. Head west. We've been talking about it since we were kids."

Joel nodded, waited.

"Do you think he's okay?" she said.

"I really don't know. He hasn't spoken to you?"

"No. Nobody's seen him since school on Monday." She paused. Her voice cracked. "You don't think he might have been—it's just, he wouldn't *know* anything to get killed over. He's stupid. Really. I love him but he's not very smart."

"Maybe he got spooked," Joel said. "Needs a chance to calm down."

"I heard Dylan sent you a text saying the same thing." She bit her straw.

Joel felt the Adderall ticking in his brain. He played with a fork. "Is it true that KT got in some trouble over the summer?"

"Trouble?" Her surprise looked genuine. "What trouble?"

"I don't know. With the cops? At home?"

"His mom's always trouble," Kimbra said. "But summer was mellow."

Joel readied himself to go. It had been worth a shot. He pulled a card from his pocket and slipped it across the table. "Listen, if KT gets in touch with you, maybe I can help."

"Help how?"

"Depends on the situation."

Kimbra gave him a last long look, pulled a little notebook from her backpack and jotted down a number. Her eyes shot around the diner before she passed it to Joel.

"That's me," she said. "If I can do anything to help find him—"

The diner door clanged open.

"Here comes trouble," she murmured.

Mitchell Malacek and Garrett Mason had arrived. The Perlin boys let out another fake cheer. They started bawling like cows, began to sing a rendition of the Bison fight song so vulgar it made even Joel raise an eyebrow. Garrett Mason flipped them a finger.

Mitchell Malacek had the same golden hair as his father, the mayor, which he wore long and pulled back in a mussy bun. Garrett, though far heavier than his older brother, still held the same permanent, spiteful light in his eyes as Ranger used to wield. Joel recalled something Wesley had said on Sunday, a mention of Ranger being hurt in Afghanistan.

An idea struck.

"Excuse me," he said to Garrett, and when the younger Mason fixed him with his hard brown eyes Joel felt the same cold twist in his gut as he'd experienced ten years ago, the moment Ranger had emerged from the football field's toilets. Joel forced himself to smile. "I was wondering if your brother was around."

"Unless you grown a pussy you ain't his type," Garrett said and turned away. Mitchell snickered and shook his head. The Perlin boys let out a whoop.

"I just had a few questions for Ranger, some sympathy. I heard he got hurt." Joel refused to be shaken off so easily (though Garrett and Mitchell were intimidating in more ways than he'd anticipated—up close, both boys were jarringly handsome). "Maybe talk about the old days."

Garrett looked back at him, his tongue running over his teeth in a gesture Joel recognized. "Is that right?"

"You'll never learn," Mitchell Malacek said. "Maybe if you'd minded your business in New York your brother'd be alive."

Joel felt the air rush out of his chest. He struggled to say, "Excuse me?"

"That's fucking unfair, bro." Whiskey Brazos appeared at his side, T-Bay a few steps behind him.

The diner went very quiet. Even the Perlin boys hushed. Joel had the distinct impression he'd somehow stumbled into a rift within the team: Garrett and Mitchell sneering from one side, Whiskey and T-Bay on the other.

What, Joel wondered, had Dylan thought of his arrogant teammates? And what had they thought of him?

The silence was broken when the waitress emerged from the back with two heavy to-go bags for Mitchell. He took them with a perfect political smile, a distant air of superior gratitude.

"Keep your head down, Mr. Whitley." Garrett said, before

following Mitchell out the door: "Plenty of folks 'round here wouldn't mind you got yourself hurt."

Joel emerged from the diner a few minutes later, his hands trembling. Whiskey and T-Bay had apologized for their teammates' behavior, seeming genuinely aghast, and even the Perlin Stallions, perhaps out of sympathy, had begun joking loudly about their food.

Mitchell had just been trying to fuck with him—he was ninety percent certain of it—but still Joel felt as if he'd been mowed down by a truck.

Joel was so preoccupied that when he saw the young boy standing under the eave of the diner in a Bison ball cap too large for his head he at first mistook him for Dylan, looking just as Joel remembered him as a boy. The sensation lasted precisely long enough to be painful.

As Joel made to open the door to the convertible, the boy called to him.

"How kem you ain't got Snapchat?" The kid's accent was so thick Joel struggled for a moment to understand him. He had a pinched face, a bad overbite, wore a T-shirt of a grinning Mario leaping toward a mushroom just out of reach.

Joel stopped. "Excuse me?"

"Some'un wanna talk tee ye." From a pocket of his cargo shorts the boy withdrew a folded slip of paper and held it out for Joel. He made no effort to come closer.

Joel looked both ways up the street. They were alone. Joel accepted the paper, and without another word the boy set off running.

Seated in his car, Joel saw one word when he unfolded the note. He presumed the word was a screen name: BBison50k. Staring at it, Joel felt his fingers start shaking again.

He logged into Snapchat—an app he had installed years before and promptly ignored—and fumbled with an interface that appeared designed to bewilder anyone with a living memory of the Clinton administration. The search bar for new friends was concealed, bafflingly, near what appeared to be an options menu with no options.

He typed BBison50k into the search bar. His phone buzzed seconds after he hit Add Friend. The user had been waiting for him.

Is this Joel?

Yes.

I need to talk to you.

Would you like my number?

There was a pause. Joel accidentally backed out of the chat and when he opened a new message from BBison50k he saw that the previous messages in the conversation had evaporated. This person didn't want to leave a trace. *Clever*, Joel thought.

Or dangerous.

BBison50k wrote:

In person would be better.

Joel could still hear Garrett Mason in his head: *"Plenty of folks 'round here wouldn't mind you got yourself hurt."* Joel didn't doubt it.

He chewed an Adderall and typed:

Where works for you?

LUKE

Far to the southeast of town, Luke Evers, the Bison's muscled running back, loaded two shells into a shotgun. He brought the gun to his shoulder, trained it on the wild expanse of open country behind Coach Parter's property and shouted "Pull!" The Turner twins released a pair of clay birds. Luke held his breath, cleared his mind of everything but the sights of the gun, waited.

The first bird exploded. The second. The twins cheered. They wore a pair of matching Ray-Ban sunglasses that Luke would never have thought their poor parents could afford.

Tomas Hernandez, the Bison's pale kicker, took the gun from Luke and socked him on the shoulder. He made a show of wincing. "You're like hitting a rock."

"Don't wear out that arm now," shouted Coach Parter, ambling down from the house, followed a few steps behind by Garrett Mason and Mitchell Malacek. Bringing up the rear, somehow carrying a large case of Bud Light in both hands while to-go bags from the Egg House dangled on her wrists, was Coach Parter's wife. Luke struggled to remember her name: Juney? Junelle? Whatever it was, Luke's father would have pronounced it (and her) to be "low-rent." Luke thought she was nice.

Mrs. Parter eased the beer onto a spindly little table, unhooked all the food with a wince. "Anything else, dear?" she asked, laying a plump hand on the coach's shoulder. He dismissed her with a coy squeeze of the thigh.

"Joel Whitley was asking questions at the diner," Garrett said, and a hush fell over Tomas and the twins. They all took their seats at the table, the metal shedding rust on their fingers like pollen.

Luke accepted a beer from Parter, trying to look as concerned about this news as the other boys. Today was getting stranger and stranger. Luke Evers had few friends on the football team (he had few friends at all, for that matter). Mitchell and Garrett, Tomas and the Turner twins, they had always formed a tight little knot at the heart of the Bison. Luke had often seen them together with Dylan and KT Staler, hanging around after practice in the locker room and laughing with their voices low, disappearing after games, tearing through town at night with their trucks' mufflers pierced and bellowing. Years ago, the boys had made it very clear to Luke that they had no room for him in their gang.

But now here Luke was, at their invitation, and here they were, kind as country, and Luke was too flattered by their sudden interest in him to acknowledge any misgiving.

Coach Parter took a long pull from his beer. He was a big man, pelted with wiry hair from the chin down but curiously beardless. A faded sailor's tattoo of an anchor and a cross was sketched over his meaty forearm. He wore a tight watch around which sweat always seemed to pucker.

"We hear we might be needing a new quarterback soon, Mr. Evers," Parter said.

Luke's heart stuttered. He sipped the beer and suddenly it was all he could do not to gag. He'd never actually drunk beer before. He'd never had anyone to drink it with.

Luke forced himself to swallow. "Is that right?"

"Did D never tell you?" said Ricky Turner. "You was first pick to be quarterback back in the day."

"I was what?"

"It's true." Mitchell Malacek smiled with those perfect teeth of his. "Dylan only got the spot 'cause the team was desperate for a running back that year and he couldn't catch for shit. Ain't that right, Coach?"

Parter nodded. "It is, indeed. I always wondered what would have changed had things gone the other way. If we might not have got us a fatter trophy last year."

Luke couldn't believe what he was hearing. Football tryouts in the summer before freshman year had pretty much ended his childhood friendship with Dylan. Luke had wanted to be quarterback more than he had ever wanted anything in his life. Dylan, on the other hand, had never wanted much of anything and somehow always got everything.

And look at them now.

"There's more to the job than just throwing balls and calling plays, you know," Tomas said.

"We might need your help with little things here and there sometimes." Garrett Mason wore no shirt, and in the falling sunlight Luke saw a strange scar on the boy's pec that he'd never noticed in the locker rooms: a tidy white dash, running just beneath the nipple. "The *town* might need your help. Do you understand?"

A thick, sudden silence sprang up, broken only by the drone of insects. Luke had no idea what they were talking about.

"Of course," he replied.

The boys laughed, sounding excited, relieved. Luke laughed as well, though he felt the strangest sensation, like he had just swum into a cold current in a still lake. What exactly had he signed himself up for?

"Very good, Mr. Evers," Coach said. His lazy smile reappeared. "Now—I believe you boys have work to do."

JOEL

Parked on the curb of Hollis Avenue at the north edge of town, Joel wolfed down a burger and waited in front of the empty lot where Bentley First Baptist and its inescapable eye of a steeple had once stood. Yet again, he felt a touch of envy at whoever had burned the place down. After the way the congregation there had treated his family—well. His mother was right. He couldn't help but see these weeds and this charred oak tree and the Evers Realty sign as anything but an improvement.

Ready, wrote BBison50k.

With the church gone there was little left open on Hollis Avenue but the dingy storefront that was Bentley First Baptist's temporary home; a faded painting of a cross hung in its window. Even through the store's closed doors, Joel could hear the music of the church's Wednesday night youth service. He wondered what Wesley Mores would say were Joel to wander inside tonight with a Bible in hand.

Joel steered his convertible around the store to a smaller parking lot behind the building and idled in the shadow of a tree turning inky in the sunset. The clock on his radio read 7:27 p.m. Right on time. Ready, he wrote.

He flipped on the radio. It was tuned to static. He listened for a time, remembering the night he'd arrived and the way he'd been certain—almost certain—that he'd heard a voice slithering out of his speakers the moment he first caught sight of Bentley on the horizon.

imissedyou

Dumb dreams. Bad dreams.

i fucking hate football

it's like i hear this town talking when i sleep.

The back door of the building cracked open. Joel switched off the radio.

The girl strode briskly to the car, a little too confident. She climbed into shotgun and lowered herself until she was practically flat on her back.

Bethany Tanner said to him, "Do you remember how to get to the dam?"

When he turned onto the industrial road southwest of town, she risked a glimpse out the rear window and flinched when a car zoomed past.

"I'm starting to worry I shouldn't be seen with you," Joel said.

"What? Why? Take a left."

"You mean onto the road buried in weeds?"

"Trust me."

The car bucked over a stone in the overgrown road. Joel shot the girl a look.

"It's just through there," she said, rising up again to point.

A line of cedar trees, their crowns all weighted down with streamers of poison oak, stretched ahead of them. A single black bird watched their approach from a low branch, almost invisible in the long shadows of the sunset. Its tiny head cocked one way, then the other.

Joel steered them toward a rough path and flipped on the headlights.

"My dad tracks my mileage," Bethany said flatly. "He'd know if I came here in my own car."

"I remember hearing some scary stories about your father." Russ Tanner, Joel recalled, was big, red-faced, loudly rich, somehow connected to Mr. Evers, who was president of the Chamber of Commerce. Powerful. Angry.

"You don't have to worry about me. Jasmine's covering. My dad thinks I'm sleeping at her place."

Joel eased the convertible down the path. He considered reminding Bethany that Dylan and his friends had tried the same sort of story last weekend with mixed results, but he decided against it. Branches snapped beneath the tires. Something whispered as it ran along the doors.

"Nobody comes out here anymore since the cops started patrolling it," Bethany said.

"Nobody except the cops."

"The cops don't bother Dylan. They don't bother me."

"Who was that kid? The one at the diner?"

"If I started naming everyone at school who owed me a favor, we'd never have time to talk."

"You said you had something to show me."

She bit her lip. "You're friends with the lady officer, right?"

"You mean Clark?" Joel wasn't sure what he and Clark were to each other. "We're cordial."

"Do you think you could tell her something for me? But, like, quietly? So nobody would know it but her?"

"I could try. Is that what you brought me here to see?"

The trees ended at a tall chain fence enclosing the town's abandoned dam. The dam had once housed a power plant, up until fracking in North Texas had undercut the energy market with natural gas and made hydropower a luxury only the rich, liberal cities could afford. Joel knew: he'd written a report recommending his company's clients divest from water. He'd never once considered how such an opinion might have affected his hometown.

Bethany climbed from the car without answering him.

She strode through the undergrowth and stopped at a weathered green ribbon (identical to the one she wore in her hair) tethered to a post. She pushed gently against the links of the fence. They had been snipped sometime before.

"You came to get Dylan out of this town, didn't you?" she said.

They slipped through the hole in the fence and started up the steps of the dam.

"How'd you guess?"

"I'm a very perceptive person."

Joel wasn't sure what to say to that.

A narrow walkway ran for nearly a half mile across the middle of the dam, a long plummet into the water only prevented by a single narrow handrail to either side. Joel spotted two rusted lawn chairs in the distance, a red plastic ice chest, a scattering of cigarette packs and glass.

"You're awfully trusting," he told her. "Not a lot of girls would come out here alone with a stranger."

"Dylan always said you were alright."

"Dylan told me he hated football."

Bethany turned. "Are you sure you were talking to the right Dylan?"

She settled into one of the chairs, folded one bronzed leg atop the other.

"Did you ever give Dylan a golden watch?" Joel said, settling into the seat beside her.

Bethany scoffed. She raised a bright silver bracelet to the failing light. "Dylan gave *me* gifts."

"With what money?"

"With the money you sent him. What else?"

Joel looked over the railing. God, he wished he *had* sent Dylan money. He couldn't shake the feeling (though he prayed it was just guilt) that much of this could have been averted with a few real contributions to his brother's savings account.

The chairs afforded them a striking view of the winding river, the barren countryside, the upper rim of the trembling sulfur sun. Litter surrounded their feet—twisted burn papers, the faded blue foil of a condom wrapper. Joel was struck, suddenly, with a vivid image of his brother seated here, in this very chair, sucking on a blunt as he reached a finger toward the perfect silky arc of this girl's thigh. The thought filled Joel with a strange, sad sort of envy. What had his brother gotten himself into?

And then Joel caught sight of the lines cut into the concrete beside his chair—three grooves, worn smooth in the stone, spelling *50K*—and a sudden sob caught in his throat. He stared at the etchings, at the rusted screwdriver left under the chair that had no doubt been used to carve them.

50K. An old private joke. Dylan had sat here, fidgety and bored, and he had thought of Joel.

He was never coming back.

"That's what I wanted to show you," Bethany said, nodding at the etching. "What does it mean? He'd never tell me."

Joel stared at it till his eyes burned. "I'll have to get back to you."

"You want a cigarette?"

Joel shook his head. Bethany raised the top of the red cooler and withdrew a pack of Camels, sealed inside a Ziploc bag. Joel felt his mind coming back to him.

He studied Bethany's face in the flare of her lighter and was struck again by the firm line of her cheekbones, the elegant point of her nose. She took an expert drag of the cigarette and breathed out smoke in a long sigh.

"Dad broke my mom's jaw over a jar of mayonnaise. It's why she left. Mayonnaise." Bethany's nails clacked on the arms of her chair. "Have you ever heard of the Southern Heritage Preservation League?"

"I've always been dubious about my heritage."

"They're racist as fuck. All the places he sends money to are. All the men here treat my dad like he's just the bestest goddamn old boy in town, but he'd join the Klan if they had a club here." She tapped ash between her feet. "Maybe those guys wouldn't care."

Joel ran some odds in his head. He had a pretty good idea what this was about.

"Was Jamal Reynolds at your house on Friday night?"

She let out a harsh laugh. "You want to know what's funny? What's so stupid about this whole fucking situation? Jamal and I didn't even do anything. We planned everything out so fucking careful for a month and then when I finally get him into the house that night we stopped messing around after five seconds. It was too weird."

"You want me to tell the police that Jamal's innocent?"

"Dylan always said you were smart." Bethany spat tobacco over the railing. Her father, she explained, had been out of town on business last weekend. Before the game, the boys had stashed Jamal's Explorer in a stand of trees north of town—"I know the ones," Joel said—so afterward everyone would say he and KT left together for the coast when, in fact, KT dropped him off and Jamal took the back roads to Bethany's house, meeting her at the corner of her road so he could follow her Lexus through the property's gate.

"It wasn't even supposed to be a big thing," Bethany said. But of course, once they'd realized the chemistry was off, Jamal couldn't leave and risk being seen around town—he was supposed to be in Galveston until Sunday. So he and Bethany had idled away the weekend awkwardly, often not seeing one another for hours on end inside Bethany's enormous home. Jamal had gotten paranoid, became convinced one of the Tanners' ranch hands could see him from the backyard. Bethany had told Jamal not to be silly. The hand whose job it was to watch her was away that weekend—she'd made sure of it.

Sunday evening came and neither Bethany nor Jamal had heard from KT or Dylan. They weren't sure when the others would be home but they couldn't tolerate their confinement any longer. When it got late, Bethany had texted her father to tell him she'd been ill all weekend but was feeling well enough to go and get some food. She did this because Mr. Tanner received an alert on his phone every time the gate on the property was opened. Bethany knew from experience that if her father wasn't kept abreast of her plans he would keep an eye on her through his security app.

"And then yesterday I fucked up," Bethany said. The pitch of her voice crept higher and higher. "I haven't been sleeping right and when I do— Listen, yesterday, it was like my mind just stopped for a second. I'd made up a whole story about having Jasmine and Alisha over for the weekend but I was so damn tired that when the lady cop asked me what I did after the game I forgot everything, the whole story. I panicked. I said I was alone. It was the first thing I could think of."

Joel swallowed.

"I can't have the cops asking my dad for the security footage from the gate's cameras that night."

"I'll see what I can do," he said. His eyes had started to

ache, though whether from grief or exhaustion he wasn't sure. After five nights without rest, he was beginning to forget what real sleep felt like.

For a long time neither of them spoke. Stars appeared.

"Don't get the wrong idea—I'm not the sort of girl who's about saving it until marriage, okay?" Bethany spoke sternly, as if to correct some snide comment Joel hadn't made. "Dylan got that shit out of me when we were kids. It's why I broke up with Luke Evers, you know. He was a real church boy back then."

Joel thought of Luke's photo buried in his brother's desk, the argument he'd witnessed between the two boys on Friday night at the game. "How did Luke feel about your decision to leave him?"

"He never liked Dylan after that. Who would? But before you ask, no, I don't think Luke could have killed Dylan. His mom's almost as bad as my dad. Everyone knows Luke has to go straight home after games."

"And where's KT Staler gone to?"

"Somewhere there's drugs. He's trash. His trouble started with his mom and worked its way down. I always told Dylan hanging around that boy would get him in trouble and here we are. I'm a very prescient person, you know." She pronounced it *present*.

"You're saying Dylan died because he was wrapped up in drugs?" Joel thought again of the two thousand dollars his brother had been caught counting in his room, of the gold watch and silver bracelet, of the unmarked bottle of painkillers.

"Dylan? No—KT was the drug addict. Families like his are a menace to society." Bethany lit another cigarette, the flame shaking in her hands. "My dad will kill me if this gets out, you know, really he will. He'd kill Jamal and me and fuck, maybe kill you, just for knowing."

Joel would like to see him try. "Where did KT and Dylan go last Friday night?"

"They left like always."

"And went where?"

"Dylan went to the coast," Bethany said, sounding just a little too certain.

"But why did Dylan have to leave so often? Bethany, from where I'm sitting he looks like a guy leaving town to scratch an itch. Like a guy with a habit. You have to see that."

"I had *total* trust in Dylan. We were very honest with each other." Joel heard a rustling sound as Bethany adjusted her hair in the dark. There was something nervous in the sound. The girl added vaguely, "We were made for each other. Mostly."

Joel took a cigarette from the baggie. Lighting it, he felt a sudden lightness in his chest. Somewhere, somehow, they had just moved in a strange new direction.

Bethany was saying, "Of course all I could think about when I was with Jamal was how I'd rather have just been with Dylan, like we were in the old days. Which is of course *exactly* what he told me *not* to do. We would sneak into the house sometimes, Dylan and I, even when Dad was there, and—"

"What Jamal told you not to do?"

"No—Dylan. The whole fucking mess was Dylan's idea in the first place." She sucked her cigarette till the filter smoldered. "Dylan always used to say the point of being this young is to fuck up and get away with it. So when he said, 'How 'bout you and Jamal give things a shot,' I thought fuck it. Jamal's hot. He's nice. He's been single ever since that Shanice girl moved away. Why not?"

"But Dylan wasn't with you last weekend. That wasn't the idea—the three of you together?"

"I just told you Dylan was at the *coast*," Bethany snapped. "Dylan set things up between Jamal and me because he felt guilty we weren't fucking anymore."

"You and Dylan had stopped sleeping together?"

"Of course we had. I mean, we tried to keep it up for a while. *I* tried. But you can't fix it, can you? You can kick and scream and say it isn't fair or you can live with it, right? That's what the women around *here* have always done. It's a goddamn way of life for these bitches—acting like you can't see what's right in front of your goddamn face."

Joel blinked at the night, at the shallow river puddled with stars.

"Bethany," he said. "What did you accept?"

"You mean—but Dylan said you must have known. Dylan always said you must have known about him because he always knew about you."

CLARK

On the edge of town, long past dark, Clark was dozing fitfully at her kitchen table when she heard the sound of tires
on the gravel outside. By the time a car door slammed, she
was pressed against the front wall of her living room, her
truck's keys in her pocket and her father's old revolver in her
hand. Her heart was thudding, her mouth was dry, but she
was frightened of more than just an unexpected guest. She'd
been briefly certain, the moment she'd awoken, that someone
outside had been watching her sleep.

There was a brisk knock at the door.

She eased back the hammer of the revolver. "Who is it?"

"Just me," shouted young Deputy Browder, their brash
man-child with two nice arms and half a brain. "Don't you
ever check your phone?"

Clark cracked open the door on its chain. He looked like a

Boy Scout come to sell her coupon books. He held up a brown bottle of rum. He was alone. "A nightcap?"

It would do. She unlatched the door.

Browder stepped inside, taking in her small front room, her kitchen scattered with papers, the gun in her hand. He smelled of sweat and boot polish, a blend Clark was surprised to discover she didn't entirely dislike.

"Are they helping you sleep?" Browder asked.

She folded up the case files on her kitchen table. "If by 'they' you mean 'these,' then no." She grabbed two glasses from the cabinet by the fridge. She said, "Just one drink, yeah?"

"Long as it's a double."

Browder filled the glasses to their rims, propped himself against her counter. "Drink," he said. "Be merry."

The neat rum tasted wrong on her tongue, too jaunty for a week so somber. She drank more. "It's quiet on patrol tonight?"

Browder shrugged. "Jones is running the squawk box. I ain't heard nothing in hours."

The squawk box was the department's name for the software that forwarded any local 911 calls to an officer on duty. In the wake of the town's latest budget cut they couldn't afford a dedicated dispatcher.

"No sign of KT Staler, I take it?" he said.

"He'd have to walk through the door for us to find him, it seems. I can't help but wonder if—"

"What?"

"It's nothing."

"You mean you can't help but wonder why no one seems too worried about chasing a white boy with no alibi?"

She smiled, though there was nothing good about it. "Something like that."

They sipped their drinks. Browder's eye settled on a file. "'Troy Clark,'" he read aloud. "That was your brother's name, no?"

When Clark had returned home from the station this evening she hadn't been able to help herself. She'd pulled her brother's file from her closet and scoured the thin record of his missing person's investigation for any sign of the eight-thousand-dollar debt Mayfield had told her about this afternoon and, just like the investigator had said, she'd found no trace of it. No record of drug use, no mention of known drug users in the few skimpy interviews that had been conducted with Hannah Szilack, the girlfriend who had reported Troy missing, nor in the interviews that had been conducted with Clark's father or herself.

"It still *is* his name, as far as I'm aware," Clark said.

"Sorry." Browder pulled his eyes up from the file. "He was really something till he hurt his neck. Did they ever talk to any of the guys who was on the team with him?"

"Not that I know of. He hadn't played for a few years by the time he disappeared." Clark leaned back to check her phone, saw that it really had died. She plugged it into a charger by her toaster.

Browder chuckled. "It probably wouldn't have done no good. They say girls is secretive, but shit—some of the Bison I played with had more tricks than a deck of cards."

"I think the same's true today." Clark frowned. "How do I talk to those kids, Browder? How do I make them open up?"

The deputy gave her an exaggerated shrug. "Torture? I don't know, man. If those boys know anything about what happened to Dylan they're probably settling their own scores."

"I'll keep that in mind." Clark finished her rum.

Browder refilled her glass before she could stop him. A funny look came into his eye as he filled his own. "I'm thinking of getting another tattoo," he said abruptly, and he eased the shirt of his uniform up from beneath his belt to reveal a pale, firm stretch of stomach. He indicated the band of muscle that ran along his hip. "I want it to say Lead the Charge. Like inside of a football, maybe? Or is that corny?"

Eyeing all the tattoos already visible on his arms and torso— lots of birds and crosses and Chinese script—Clark said, "Why not just a Bison or something?"

"I already got two of them."

She looked him up and down, arched an eyebrow. "Where?"

Browder undid his belt buckle.

"Oh God." Clark held up a hand, laughed. "I don't want to see this."

"Too late," the deputy said, and when Clark peeked between her fingers she saw Browder's bare ass, where two green Bentley Bison charged toward one another from either cheek. Two scrolls floated above them, ornate and frilled like the garland of some ludicrous ceremony, reading *2008* and *2012*.

Clark couldn't hold back a guffaw. "Put it away! Put it away!"

"I'm taking your mind off the situation," Browder said over his shoulder. With a touch of disappointment he added, "You don't like it?"

She laughed harder. "Not in my kitchen I don't."

Browder tugged his pants back up. He blushed. "It was my graduation gift to myself."

"Money well spent."

The radio on Browder's shoulder sputtered. It was Jones, calling in a report of illegal fireworks being shot off FM 217. Browder copied him. Clark finished her second glass of rum in one long gulp. Her phone buzzed.

Browder thanked her for the drink before remembering he'd brought it himself. He hesitated at her open door.

"That was inappropriate," he said. "I'm sorry."

"I'm not filing a complaint."

"I just feel so useless out here sometimes. Like I can't do nothing to stop the shit people keep doing to each other."

Clark squeezed the young deputy's shoulder. "You're keeping the peace."

"Just don't go easy on them. Whoever did this fucking thing. Don't let them get away like they always do."

She didn't know what to say to that. She watched him until his taillights flared and disappeared down her road.

When Clark closed the door again she heard the old windows of the house rattle in their frames. She checked the latches, carried the empty glasses to the sink. Browder was right. People sure seemed to get away with a lot around here.

the best years

She thought about missing case notes. She thought about dreams.

Only the best years of my life

She stared out at the night, half expecting some black shape to detach itself from the horizon and come shambling across the Flats toward her house.

But nothing moved, of course. She was totally, hopelessly alone.

For the second time that day, Clark thought of her mother. Margo Clark, née Delbardo, remained the strangest woman Starsha had ever met in her life, even after three years in law enforcement. Margo had lived in Pettis County from the day she was born but never did she seem at home here. She had once—somehow—been a cheerleader as a girl but, as an adult, had grown into something of a hippy, or perhaps just a watered-down Texas mystic (though she'd have no doubt resented the description, much as she resented everything). She was prone to wearing beaded garnet shawls and turquoise headscarves and talking, whenever she was overcome by her drunk husband's antics, about a spirit that had visited her in high school and revealed to her the exact date of her death.

Margo used to explain away all her mistakes with superstitions she had failed to heed or rituals she had failed to properly execute—the floors of Clark's house had always been gritty with salt—and the woman could say something like, "Dreams are just our souls going for a swim at night," with all the calm, bored confidence of a woman describing the laundry.

It had been Margo who'd instilled in Clark a lifelong aversion to the Flats outside the family's house. Other children grew up with Bigfoot in the woods and the bogeyman under the bed, but not Clark. She'd been told stories since she was in diapers about a monster that slept in a trench under the Flats, coiled and lethal as a snake in a toilet's U-bend. "The thing out there's got long whiskers like a catfish," Margo used to tell her daughter. "And nails as long as the school bus and two black iguana eyes that're as big as your face."

Looking back, Clark always thought that the monster had been a brilliant tool for a mother with a useless husband and two wild children to corral. The creature drank little girls' tears, for one thing ("So quit your bawling unless you want him to come say hello") and kept Clark well on her mother's side of the property line. "Don't you dare go over that fence, Starsha Marilynn Clark. Ain't nobody goes out there in the Flats don't get lost on the way back. And that's how he gets you."

The monster even had a name, though it was something so bizarre and alien it had always struck Clark as far too peculiar for her mother—a woman who was rather prosaic, under all the crazy—to have invented herself. Clark struggled now to remember that name, feeling suddenly as if it were a vital thing to know, though why on earth she suddenly cared after twenty years was beyond her. The name had sounded like something she'd find in the Old Testament, she remembered that much. "Botox," Troy had called it once. "Bullshit."

Margo hadn't cared for that. "You just wait till you feel it moving in your sleep," she'd told him. "Just you wait till he makes your nightmares go woolly—then you'll know he's took a shine to you."

When Clark had discovered, much to her surprise, that none of the other children in her kindergarten had ever heard of a monster that slept under the Flats, her mother's stories had quickly lost their power. But now that Clark, with more than a little fear, was approaching what she was certain would be a sixth night of troubled sleep, she couldn't help but wish her mother were here with her tattered tarot deck and her prayer beads. Because Margo had been right about one thing: one afternoon, when her mother picked Clark up from the middle school, she'd greeted her by saying, "Next Tuesday's the day."

And sure enough, late on the morning of the following Tuesday—April 6, 2004—a pickup truck from Denton, Texas, had come roaring down the highway with Margo's name all but written in blood on the front fender.

Clark turned away from the dark Flats outside her window with a shudder. She rinsed out the glasses in the sink and told herself she didn't see a pair of brilliant black iguana eyes out there, staring back at her from just across her fence.

Her phone buzzed again on the counter. She ignored it. All her fear had knocked loose a thought. Browder had even mentioned it: rifling through her brother's file, Clark saw that none of Troy's old teammates had been interviewed after his disappearance.

Something else occurred to her. It was in her own interview with the police ten years ago—an interview conducted, she remembered, at this very table—during which she had told a much younger Detective Mayfield that she had no idea where Troy had gone but that her brother might have said something about his plans to Joel Whitley.

Yes, *that* Joel Whitley, she had told the detectives. By the time of the interview it had be almost two months since Joel's arrest but the sound of his name had still sent a tremor through the room. Joel and Troy had hung out on a few occasions over the summer, she'd explained to Detective Mayfield, usually on weekends when Troy was back in town.

And yet there was no mention of Joel in the notes of her interview. There was no mention of him anywhere in the report.

Was it a clerical error, she wondered, or another deliberate omission, just like the drug money?

"Mr. Boone asked that we keep that little detail out of the files."

A heavy, painful memory fell unbidden into her mind and began unwrapping itself before she could stop it: late fall, midway through a chilly football season, a few weeks before everything started to come apart. Clark and Joel had never been better. Clark and her father had been a different story.

The old man had been out of work for weeks (again) living half in a bottle and pawning whatever he could carry out of the house. Clark had returned home from school one afternoon to find her father, chisel in hand, working to open the padlock she used to seal her bedroom shut against him. In a fury, Clark had wrenched her father away from the bedroom door and all but thrown him down the hall. She spotted the revolver he'd been using as a hammer a moment later.

She got out of the house before he could get his wits about him. At gossipy old Miss Lydia's house a mile down the road she'd called Troy, had told him that he needed to come *now*, and then spent the last hours of the day in Miss Lydia's kitchen, eating stale Fig Newtons and suffering through recorded episodes of *The Price Is Right*. "If you play them back you can guess the answers," the lady had explained. No shit.

She saw her brother's truck pass Miss Lydia's windows just after dark. She set off after him on foot, the first few stars appearing above her, and when the coast sounded clear she made her way into the house just in time to find Troy emerging from their father's room bearing an armload of empty bottles, a box of ammunition and the old revolver, his finger rogu-ishly hooked around the trigger guard.

"Is that all of it?" she said, nodding at the ammo.

Troy dropped the bottles in the sink with a clatter. He wiped sweat from his brow, eyes wide with adrenaline (*or*, she wondered now, *with something harder?*) and said, "The man's room's a rat's nest."

In those days, Clark had still been sore that Troy, the only person on the planet who could calm their father, had moved away. "Took you enough time to get here," she had said. "The highway from Rockdale get longer this afternoon?"

At first she'd thought Troy hadn't heard her. He seemed interested only in studying the sprawling Flats outside the window.

"I have to tread so careful around here, Star," he said at last.

She had not taken that well. She had not taken that well at all. *He* had to tread careful? *He* had not been the one living alone with a drunken animal for a year. *He* had not been the one with the gun pointed in his face that fucking afternoon.

He was not the one who, despite every achievement, was perpetually known as "Troy Clark's sister."

No. She ran Troy from the house that evening and told him to tread his careful way home. She had spat on his truck. Hell, she shouted, if it were such a strain then maybe he should never come back at all.

It was the last time she ever saw him. She hadn't expected him to take her seriously, but there you go.

But what did any of that matter now? Why did that mem-ory come back to her, why those words specifically—*"I have to tread so careful"*?

"If you play them back you can guess the answers."

Her phone buzzed. She snatched it off the counter.

"Christ, Clark, I've been trying to reach you for an hour." It was Joel. He was driving somewhere, by the sound of it.

"I was sleeping," she lied, not caring for his sharp tone. "You might try it."

"I envy you. I've been trying to sleep for days."

Clark felt that prickling heat in her scalp again. "Have you been having strange dreams?"

"It sounds like everyone has," he said, sounding annoyed she would mention it. "Clark, listen to me, that's not why I called. I think whatever happened to Troy happened to Dylan—"

"Joel, I've been over all this with Investigator Mayfield—"

"They were gay, Clark."

The sound of Joel's car seemed to fade in her ear. The table grew distant. Her brother's face appeared briefly in front of her kitchen window as Joel Whitley, very distantly, said, "Troy and Dylan, they were both gay."

THURSDAY

SMOKE

JAMAL

Jamal's mother pulled up to the front of the school. "Your father and I gave you too much rope."

"It'll be fine," Jamal said, and told himself he meant it.

His mother said nothing as he climbed down from her car. He would learn later that her next stop was a lawyer's office.

He pushed open the school's front doors and stepped into a trembling tunnel of green and yellow crepe. The cheerleaders had arrived early, he saw, and thrown themselves into the spirit of the biggest game of the season. He shouldn't be surprised. This town would never allow something as trivial as a homicide to stop the Bison herd.

Hand-painted posters covered every wall. Bison stickers clogged the lockers. No wonder the school didn't have the money to bring in grief counselors, Jamal thought. The cost of all this green tinsel alone would have paid for his lunch for a month.

The door of Dylan's locker was so loaded down with ribbons and pennants and bouquets of flowers it almost seemed to be gloating. His photo, the one you saw everywhere around town, was stuck in the center, and beneath it was printed "RIP Leading the Big Herd in the Sky."

Jesus. Dylan. One of the few guys on the team who'd ever been decent to Jamal had been reduced to a poster as sweet and sad as flat soda.

Wait: someone already scrawled a line of graffiti on a corner of Dylan's photo. Could nothing in life stay good anymore?

Jamal leaned in, squinted at the words.

help it feeds help

The fuck?

Jamal's locker stood almost bare beside Dylan's, untouched but for the words WE BELIEVE IN YOU scrawled across the metal in green Sharpie. It was nice to know someone did. The sloping handwriting, he recognized, with a little smile, was Kimbra Lott's.

His body ached from the pummeling he'd taken all week at practice—that fat fuck Parter had made a special project of Jamal. Never mind that a good quarterback behind a solid line is only sacked a handful of times in a season. For the last two days, Parter had sent his heaviest tackles after his new QB at every opportunity until Jamal was now half-certain the man had broken something in his brain.

How else could Jamal explain everything he saw when he slept?

He felt a fist strike his shoulder. Garrett and Mitchell ambled by, laughing to themselves. For the hundredth time this week, Garrett asked, a little singsong lilt in his voice, "Where were you last weekend, Reynolds?"

Jamal massaged the pain flaring down his arm. He wondered how much more of this treatment he could take.

He thought (as he'd been thinking all week) of Bethany, and immediately he was livid. *"You should go for it, bro,"* Dylan had said last month. *"I think she's really into you."*

"I'd never!" Jamal had protested, his face flushing, his heart in his throat. *"I'd never do that to you, D."*

"Please, it's nothing. My girl and me, we've got an understanding."

"You what?"

"Go for it, seriously." Dylan had laughed, then gotten mock serious, the Grand King of the Gridiron, joking in the way he did when he wanted something. *"You have my blessing, Reynolds."*

So Jamal had finally responded to Bethany's unanswered text messages:

OK. Let's do it.

And yet when they'd finally gotten down to business Friday night she'd called the whole thing off the second his hand had touched her chest. She'd said she had a headache. Maybe it was her period coming on, she wondered.

Hell, Jamal had thought bitterly. Maybe it was Ebola. The girl had been made of excuses.

Jamal was, at heart, a decent man. He didn't believe girls owed him a thing—least of all sex—but considering all the shit he was now mired in, he vaguely wished he had more to show for last weekend than a couple awkward moments with a small boob, a microwaved pizza and ten hours of good TV. At least, he thought—always looking on the bright side of things, even in the face of a capital murder charge—Bethany's house got HBO.

The bell rang. He thought back to Friday's game, back when he had been so excited to put their plan into motion (excited if only because he knew how pleased it seemed to make Dylan.)

At the thought of the game, something came back to him.

"Yo, G," Jamal called down the hall. Garrett turned back. "Tell me, Mason—what was you and the other boys looking at during halftime?"

The bell rang again. Students hastened into class. A weak breeze struggled through the hall's open windows.

"The fuck did you just say?"

Garrett started toward him, Mitchell following a step behind.

"It's an easy question," Jamal said, holding his ground as the massive boy came close. "You and KT and Mitchell, all the boys in your little squad, you was all looking at something on your phones, being all clandestine and shit. You gotta remember. You sure thought it was amazing."

Garrett's cheeks had turned purple. Jamal could smell the rage on him, a mustardy scent that reminded him vaguely of Frito pie. He couldn't help but be startled. Garrett was hardly a mild man but Jamal had never seen him tweaked like this before.

"If you say one more fucking word I will kill you, Reynolds."

"You can try," Jamal said. He smiled.

Garrett brought up his fist to strike Jamal; Mitchell grabbed his arm to hold him back; Bethany's voice shouted their names down the hall. She was hustling in their direction, wearing pants and a sweater despite the heat of the morning.

"You remember what I fucking told you," Garrett said. He stormed away.

"Are you alright?" Bethany said.

"No." He turned his attention to her, adrenaline still racing through his brain. "Where the fuck did Dylan go last weekend?"

She frowned. "He was at the *coast*, Jamal, how many times do I have to tell you people?"

"'You people'?"

"Forget Dylan—you have to go, Jamal. You have to go *now*. My dad knows."

Jamal blinked. "What?"

"He found me at Jasmine's this morning. It was that fucking *fence*. I texted Dad when you were leaving Sunday night to say I was going to get food but the fucking fence never opened again for me to come back. He finally put it together. Jamal, he has cameras in the house, places he never told me about. They were recording everything. The whole time."

The bottom fell out of Jamal's stomach. "But we didn't do anything."

She pulled back the sleeve of her sweater. Her arm was a vivid purple-brown.

"You have to go somewhere, Jamal. He's going to do something crazy."

At the sight of the bruises, Jamal slung his bag over his shoulder with a strange cold calm. Fine, he thought. Running seemed to be working fine for KT. Bentley could keep its dreams and its nightmares. Jamal had never much liked it here anyway.

Only when he reached the parking lot did Jamal remember that his Explorer was still at the auto shop—the trip to Bethany's place this weekend had finally overtaxed his SUV's spotty alternator and the part was, of course, on back order.

He started dialing his mother out of habit. He stopped. What would he say? *Can you drive me to the airport and buy me a ticket to Colombia?* Why, he wondered now, had he never thought to get a passport?

A moment later he heard the sirens, saw the flashing lights flying down the highway. The cars headed straight for him. Some distant sense of self-preservation made Jamal replace the phone in his pocket so no one could imagine it was a gun.

He supposed, in the end, he had dug this hole himself.

CLARK

Ten minutes earlier, Clark had been on her way to the station, so jittery she could barely drive. She and Joel hadn't even bothered trying to sleep the night before. They'd stayed up comparing notes over the phone, and by the time Joel had finished telling her his side of Dylan's story Clark's tired mind had been kicked into overdrive.

"They were gay," Joel had said, and Clark had sunk into her chair.

Dylan had set up Bethany with Jamal because he hadn't slept with her in months. It made a sort of sense to Clark. Bethany, Joel said, had had suspicions about Dylan for years, had wondered if Dylan might not be something the girl called "bisexual-ish," but, last May, Dylan had come to her and said he couldn't pretend anymore: he loved her, but he was hopelessly, "totally gay."

"I have to tread so careful around here, Star."

"And Troy?" she'd asked.

The line went silent. Joel finally said, "You mean you never guessed about all those afternoons?"

"Was that the only reason you dated me? To get near my brother?" She was surprised to hear how coolly she asked it. How little it had even upset her to consider the question. Maybe it was all the rum.

"I don't think so. I'd had a crush on him for ages but— Listen, can we talk about this later?"

"Did Troy take those pictures of you?"

"No."

"Was he the other man at the park? The one that got away?"

Joel had hesitated, but Clark had been willing to wait all night for his answer. The identity of "the other man" had long been a subject of speculation in Bentley. Deputy Grissom, the officer who'd arrested Joel, had stated repeatedly that Joel had been "in the act" when he was discovered but the other man involved had escaped before Grissom could get a good look at him.

Finally, Joel said only, "No."

"Joel, I don't mean to sound closed-minded but if that wasn't Troy in those bushes how many queers do we have here in Pettis County?"

"Look, I need your help." The anxiety in his voice was unmistakable—she let her question pass. "This can't be a co-incidence, Clark. Two Bentley Bison, both closeted gays, both vanish. One turns up dead, the other's still missing a decade later. Be honest—does the sheriff's department actually have any evidence against Jamal Reynolds?"

"Are you suggesting we're railroading him?" she said, as if she hadn't been asking the same thing all day yesterday.

"I'm suggesting this investigation is a lot more complicated than you thought. If news of my brother gets out nobody will care what happened to him. It'll be just like the pictures of me all over again. I was *seventeen*, Clark—those photos were child pornography and the department hardly even acknowledged they existed. There must have been witnesses—you can't stick photos inside two hundred newspapers and not leave some kind of evidence. But it went nowhere. All anybody cares about here is something to gossip over. Clark, are you—"

"After my brother disappeared, did the cops ever come to talk to you?" She couldn't stop thinking of her interview with Mayfield at her kitchen table a decade ago.

"What are you talking about? Of course they didn't."

"You can't follow every lead in a case like this," Mayfield had said yesterday afternoon in the car, justifying the baffling fact he wasn't pursuing the missing KT Staler more aggressively even though the boy's disappearance set off every obvious alarm in a case like this. Why hadn't Mayfield followed up the obvious lead that Clark had given him in the wake of her brother's disappearance: *"You could ask Joel Whitley about Troy."*

Clark suspected that Mayfield was going to regret telling her she had a knack for this work.

"Okay," Clark said, her scalp tingling.

She wasn't certain she agreed with every step in Joel's logic, wasn't certain he'd even told her the entire truth about that night in the park, but it was enough for now. She wanted to find Dylan's killer, of course she did, but Clark was wise enough to know her motives weren't entirely altruistic. If Joel was right and Dylan's death *was* connected to Troy's disappearance then maybe—*maybe*—she would find something in Dylan's case she could use to finally staple closed her brother's. She was willing to try.

"Okay," Joel said.

Driving now to the sheriff's station, Clark walked herself through what she knew. Jamal Reynolds was likely innocent, just as she'd always suspected, though she wasn't sure how exactly she could help him. She doubted she could confirm

Bethany's story about sneaking Reynolds into her house without in turn alerting the girl's father that something was amiss, but Clark figured she could do her best.

The fact that Dylan had possessed a bottle of painkillers, apparently without a prescription, was not, on its own, especially damning. The fact that he'd been seen counting two thousand dollars in his room, cash about which he'd lied and said was from his brother, might even have had an innocuous explanation. But when Clark held the two facts together—along with the mysterious gold wristwatch in Dylan's bedside table, or Bethany Tanner's expensive bracelet—Clark came to the same conclusion as Joel: it looked like Dylan Whitley had gotten himself tangled up in the drug business.

Just like Troy.

Clark had a theory that went a long way toward explaining the "weekends at the coast." If Dylan had gotten involved in the drugs through KT Staler—and if ever a boy came from a family with a disposition toward narcotics it was KT Staler—then it stood to reason the two boys might have left town to move their product, perhaps at someone's behest. She'd told Joel how Jason Ovelle, at the game on Friday, had been caught searching KT's Tacoma, with Jason insisting KT owed him money. Just a few minutes before, on the sidelines, she'd noticed that KT had lost several pounds in just a week, which was a textbook consequence of consuming methamphetamine. Most meth dealers, in Clark's experience, tended to be addicts themselves, addicts with an unfortunate tendency to dip into the product they were supposed to be selling.

"Those trips would be a perfect chance to scratch an itch," Joel had said.

And the fact that Dylan was gay? Well, she told Joel, the boy sure seemed to spend an awful lot of time with KT. It wouldn't be the first time a pair of young lovers had gone into some sort of business together.

A few things still concerned her. For one, the drug game today was different than it had been in Troy's time. Back then, as Mayfield had mentioned, a cartel representative named Benicio Dos had controlled most of the supplies of meth and opioids sold in central Texas. Benicio, to put it bluntly, had been a very bad man, rumored to have killed an informant by injecting radiator fluid into the woman's brain stem.

But Benicio had been arrested by the Feds three years ago. Clark remembered the day of the arrest well—it had come during her first week on the job. An air of relief had filled the department for a few months as drug arrests finally trended down.

Yet lately things had started to change. Over the last nine months or so Clark had discovered more and more baggies of ice and handfuls of pills while making traffic stops and house calls. Someone new had taken up shop.

Clark's stomach turned. If her brother had stolen money from Benicio, could it possibly follow that Dylan had gotten involved with whatever reprobate had replaced Señor Dos? She'd taken an Introduction to Forensic Accounting course in school, passed it by the skin of her teeth and brought home only one lesson: drug money had a habit of turning up in even the most dignified of pockets.

Clark's truck began to buck and she realized with a jolt of panic that she'd somehow veered onto the rough shoulder—when had she started to drift? She jerked the wheel, returned to the highway, let out a shaky breath. Had she just fallen asleep with her eyes open? Did that really happen to people?

"These dreams, they started the night your brother died," she'd said as a flat yellow dawn had teased the Flats through her kitchen window. "Don't that seem odd?"

"They're dreams, Clark. You think the government's putting them in our head?"

"My mom used to talk about stuff like this. She used to say there was a monster that gave us nightmares when it moved."

"Your mother also thought the Pope was sending her messages in the Dillard's catalogue."

She'd also correctly predicted the day of her own death, but Clark wasn't sure that would hold much water with Joel. It was true, Margo had believed in a number of strange things; perhaps with enough predictions and assertions you were bound to get lucky and have one pay off eventually (if you could call a head-on collision with a hay truck lucky). Stopped clocks are right morning and night, et cetera, et cetera.

Clark had let it go. Or, rather, she hadn't fully acknowledged, to either Joel or herself, what she'd become so frightened of last night before he'd called: an awful suspicion that whether they were talking about drugs or secret gay affairs or boys dumped in creeks, something far uglier was at work here than either of them was quite prepared to accept.

She was a half mile from the school when she saw the flashing lights. She heard the sirens a moment later. She picked up speed, saw a cruiser and two unmarked cars screaming in her direction. One of those cars, if she wasn't much mistaken, belonged to Investigator Mayfield.

The three cars swerved toward the school's parking lot. She followed them to the front door, her pulse thudding in her ears.

Jamal Reynolds stood frozen on the curb a few yards away.

As Clark sped across the lot, she saw Investigator Mayfield, Sheriff Lopez and County Attorney Boone stepping out of their vehicles.

And Jones, climbing out of the flashing cruiser with his gun drawn.

"Hands in the air!" Jones bellowed. When Jamal only stared at him, wide-eyed, mouth agape, Jones shouted it again.

Clark parked behind the cruiser, threw herself from her

truck without killing the ignition. Jamal Reynolds raised his hands. Mayfield turned back to give her a quick blank look and started toward Jamal.

"Mr. Reynolds," Investigator Mayfield shouted. He held a plastic bag in his hand. "Are you the owner of a red Ford Explorer SUV?"

"What?"

"A red Ford, Mr. Reynolds. Currently being serviced at Sparks's Auto Body?"

"That's mine, but—"

"You have the right to remain silent, Mr. Reynolds," Mayfield said, and rattled off the rest of it. As the investigator spoke, Jones made his way across the lot, pushed the boy to his knees, cuffed him.

Bethany Tanner burst from the front door of the school, her blond hair flying. "Stop!" she shouted. "He was with me!"

"That's enough, darling," said Mr. Boone sharply.

"But it's true!" Bethany shouted. Clark saw faces in the classroom windows watching them, saw sashes sliding up so the folks inside could listen. Bethany repeated, "Jamal was with me all weekend!"

"Mayfield, what the fuck is this?" asked Clark. "Why didn't you call me?"

Without a word, Mayfield tossed her the bag in his hand.

It was an evidence bag, she saw. Her first thought was of protocol: why was there evidence floating out here in the wild and not locked up, logged and tagged, in the station? Then she saw what was inside.

A sock, so stained with blood Clark thought at first the fabric had been brown when it was bought. Only the upper hem of the sock remained white. Written along the hem in black marker were the initials DW.

JOEL

He'd fallen asleep—no, that wasn't the word for it, in sleep you got *rest*—sitting in a stiff chair in his old bedroom. He awoke to the sound of his phone ringing. His back hurt and his neck hurt and his nose was filled with the smell of clay, blood, decay.

"Joel," Clark said when he answered the phone. "They've arrested Jamal."

Joel struggled to his feet. His body was weak, his mind sluggish. "What? How?"

"Reynolds's Explorer has had alternator trouble. It's been in the shop since Monday. Early this morning one of the mechanics started to clean it as a courtesy for keeping the car so long and they found a bloody sock wedged in the fold of the back seat." Clark hesitated. "It had your brother's initials."

Clark had told him last night that Dylan's body had been

found without a shirt or socks. It didn't matter. Joel tasted bullshit.

"One sock? It's just been sitting there this entire time?"

"Exactly. They were in such a rush to arrest the kid they didn't even bother to log the evidence at the station before they cuffed him. They're only now typing the arrest warrant. It's fucked, Joel. It's fucked."

Joel fumbled with his bottle of Adderall, fished out a pill and chewed it. He'd never taken one this early but he knew a cup of coffee could do nothing to fight the fog that still floated in his head. After a second's hesitation he chewed another.

"A wound like Dylan's must have drained blood for ages, right?" Joel said. "If Jamal transported the body in the back of his car, would he even be able to clean it all up?"

"That much blood would have got into the carpet's padding. A car in a hot mechanic's bay would have started to stink something awful. They'd have noticed it days ago."

"And why the hell would he take off a dead person's socks? It's the perfect piece of evidence to incriminate you."

Clark whistled. "Exactly. Portable. Blood soaked. Easily identifiable. Whoever was smart enough to unlock Dylan's phone with his thumb on the night of the murder planning to contact you the next day…is it a stretch to think that same person would have taken the bloody socks off the boy's corpse in the hopes of pinning the murder on someone?"

Joel paced his room. "I take it this hasn't been a topic of conversation at the station."

Clark hesitated. "Mayfield says Jamal must have been in a hurry, panicked and realized he had the sock still in his possession after he dumped the body so he stuffed it in the seat and forgot it. But shit, Joel—why would he even leave it in his car at all? Why not burn the fucking thing?"

Joel wished the Adderall would hurry up and kick in. "Who's this mechanic?"

"Alan Sparks owns the place, he's alright. But the kid who found the sock is named Waley Cabe—he's got a sheet of priors as long as my arm. He just got let out for assault a few months back."

"Maybe I should pay him a visit."

"I wouldn't recommend it. If Cabe's doing somebody's dirty work you might just make more trouble for yourself. And it gets worse." Clark sighed. "Bethany Tanner came running to stop us this morning, screaming her story for the whole school to hear, not that the men paid her any mind. I just spoke with her father about it and he told me she's delusional or else covering up for her friend Jamal. When I asked him about the cameras on his property he said the security footage is only saved for three days because he don't want to pay extra. He's just trying to keep her nose out of things, I'm sure of it."

"That's ridiculous," Joel said, his fingers tapping on his knee. "And even if *he* doesn't have it, is it possible the security company keeps it on their servers for a few weeks?"

"I was thinking the same thing. Maybe I can get Mr. Boone to subpoena them. If we can place Jamal at the house all weekend…" She broke off, sounding dubious. "I'm going to put out a new APB on KT Staler's Tacoma. I might add a few shades of green to the description and see what happens."

"Can you talk to Jamal yourself? Privately? Maybe he knows something about KT and Dylan that he wanted to keep quiet before. I doubt Jamal would be willing to cover up dirt for KT much longer now that the kid's story's gotten him arrested."

There was a long silence. When Clark came back on her voice was lower. "Sorry, I thought someone was coming in the women's toilet. I'll work on Jamal as long as they don't make the kid confess. What about you?"

Joel chewed his lip. He struggled to recall what he'd been thinking about last night before he fell asleep. The Adderall had gone from not working to suddenly working too well—he never could find a balance in life.

"Jason Ovelle," he finally said. "He feels like a missing link here. Wasn't he arrested years ago with Savannah Staler, KT's older sister?"

"A week apart actually, but yes. Meth on both counts. Jason and Savannah, they were dating at the same time they were dealing. The rumor's always been that she turned state's witness to rat Jason out but she's been such a bad apple down in lockup they keep denying her parole."

"Well, maybe Jason doesn't know that. Maybe he met KT through Savannah and they've gone into business together. And Jason Ovelle was younger than Troy but they were on the Bison at the same time for a year—I remember that well enough. If Jason was doing business with Troy back then and dealing with KT now, then maybe by extension he was doing business with Dylan."

"It's a stretch."

"I know. But if Jason can help us pin down what exactly Dylan and KT were up to when they said they were at the coast, it'd be a start."

"Jones cut Jason loose on Friday night. He wasn't even booked. Mayfield told me the other day Ovelle left town again and there's APBs out on him but—still."

"Mayfield's said a lot of things."

"Exactly. You think you can find Jason?"

Joel figured that if he kept burning through his Adderall at this rate he might be needing Ovelle's services soon anyway. "I'll certainly try."

"Start at the Varsity Motel—it's a little dump on the highway south of town. Jason used to stay there. Are you alright? You sound…"

"Never better."

There was a knock on Joel's door. He said goodbye to Clark,

stumbled as he crossed the room. His drugged mind was racing but his body was heavy as a stone. Joel suspected he was pushing very close to the limits of absolute exhaustion.

It was Darren. His face was troubled. "You get run over last night?"

"I wish I knew." Joel propped himself against the door frame. "Are you alright?"

Darren frowned. "Something you might want to see out front."

Joel's sleek black convertible was parked on the street. Standing on the house's porch, he had no difficulty reading the words that had been etched into the paint.

GET OUT NOW FAG.

The last word had been repeated across the hood of the car. The cloth hood had been shredded down the middle and lay sunken inside, draped over the seats like a pair of wilted petals.

Joel regarded the car a long time. Regarded the street that must have seen something, heard something last night, just as it must have noticed something ten years ago when pictures were being slipped into papers all over town. No one had said anything then. They would say nothing now. If anything, Joel suspected the folks behind those closed curtains would wish the same thing as his car did: that he would leave, now, and never come back.

"There's not a gun in the house, is there?" Joel said.

Darren shook his head no.

Joel said nothing more. He stepped into his brother's room and shut the door. He pushed a hot tear from his eye. He pulled open a drawer of Dylan's desk, removed what was inside.

A hunting knife. From tip to tip it ran just over half the length of Joel's forearm. A strap attached to the sheath allowed the weapon, Joel assumed, to be carried over the ankle.

Joel slid the blade free, regarded the keen edge, balanced the knife in his hands. Saw the initials DW on the hilt.

If someone thought this fag would give up so easily, they were sorely mistaken.

CLARK

Clark paced behind the interview room's one-way glass, straining to hear the conversation piped through the shitty speakers on the wall above her head.

"What did you need the condom for, Jamal?" Mayfield's voice came through as a whisper, half his words lost to the pop and hiss of the department's ancient wiring.

"I didn't say shit about that…"

The one-way glass gave the interview room a strange silver sheen, as if Clark were watching not an interrogation but a scene in some classic movie. It *all* felt too classic, clichéd even, watching the two big cops sweat the young black kid: smacking the table, pacing, sneering like bad actors overplaying their parts. *"Clichés have to come from someplace,"* Mayfield had told her coolly this morning when they'd returned to the station with Jamal, the only words the investigator had directed her way since the school's parking lot. She'd caught the little flicker of hesitation in his eye, however. This mysterious sock was incriminating—it was enough for an arrest warrant, at least—but it wasn't enough for an easy conviction in court. Mayfield and Lopez needed Jamal to crack and confess.

Clark only prayed the boy could hold out.

"Is that condom how Dylan learned you and Bethany were sleeping together?" Lopez's voice dipped and warbled through the speakers. "Dylan got angry, didn't he? He tried to stop you from meeting her."

"It was his idea in the first place!"

Through the glass, Mayfield and Lopez shared a bemused silence, like this was too absurd to even credit.

"And why would he do that?" said Mayfield.

After a long silence, Jamal said with a scowl, "You wouldn't believe…" The volume fell so low Clark had to watch his lips to understand him.

If Jamal knew that Dylan was gay, he had just declined a golden opportunity to out his dead friend and possibly help his own case. Clark tucked this away to chew on later.

Mr. Boone, standing in the little anteroom with Clark, was fussing with his bolo tie.

"We can subpoena Russ Tanner's security company, can't we?" Clark asked the county attorney. "We can see if Jamal really was at Bethany's house all weekend like he said."

"Hypothetically we can, yes."

"Just like we can subpoena Facebook and Apple and all of them. Snapchat. That's where the proof will be, you know—in all the messages these kids send."

"I imagine you're right."

"We haven't heard back about none of the subpoenas you've already filed?"

"You're as dedicated as my wife." He chuckled. "That's a compliment, truly."

Clark said nothing.

"It's a complicated matter, Deputy. The legal departments at those technology companies are quite qualified."

She couldn't help but laugh. "Well, hell, that's what you're here for."

"There's a question of budget as well. Processing fees. Court fees. You wouldn't believe the fees they charge in the California courts."

She felt a thread of assumptions snap.

"You haven't filed those subpoenas."

The county attorney turned back to the glass. "Yet, Officer. Not yet. It'll be easy when we have a fuller picture of what to request. Those judges are butchers. They prefer you file in bulk."

Clark didn't bother to mask her disgust. Fine. She would be happy to write Boone off—the man was, at very best, useless to her. If she and Joel were going to get to the bottom of this case, they would have do it without the help of a legal department.

Mayfield and Lopez stood. Mayfield pushed a legal pad toward Jamal, a pen riding atop the paper. "Just write the truth, son. Make it easier."

Jamal made no move to pick up the pen. Good. The two older men left the room with somber faces, letting the door latch behind them, but by the time they made it to the anteroom Mayfield had grown affable, almost giddy. He ignored Clark.

"Just a few more hours," the investigator said. "It's simple, really. We were looking at this the wrong way all along. We thought Dylan had a girl on the side but it was Bethany who had a boy. She and Jamal were carrying on. Dylan got wind of it, tried to stop them, the end. Jamal's gonna crack by sundown."

"If he doesn't get a lawyer soon," said Boone.

"He won't ask for a lawyer—he's too afraid of looking

guilty," Lopez said. "He's got balls, though. He might just lock down on us."

Clark wasn't certain she agreed with Joel: closed-minded as she knew Bentley was, she struggled to believe that the simple fact Dylan Whitley was queer would motivate the sheriff's department to drop an investigation of his murder in exactly the same way it had abandoned its investigation into Joel's very public shaming.

But there were more factors at play here than simply Jamal's race (though that, she knew, was no small consideration). She had no doubt that Investigator Mayfield had scuttled the investigation into her brother's disappearance and he seemed more than ready to ruin another.

"I got more good news today, actually," Mayfield said. "Old Deputy Grissom's recovered enough to start talking again."

An odd look crossed Lopez's face.

"Is that right?" Mr. Boone said. "I thought the doctors told us that with the horse breaking his spine—"

"They did. But he is." Mayfield smiled. "His day nurse called saying she couldn't believe her ears."

A piercing chime rang through the speakers when Jamal adjusted the handcuff on his wrist. The men flinched. An idea struck Clark.

"Can I speak to Jamal?" she said, hoping to God she sounded nervous, harmless, female. "Maybe he'd open up to someone a little closer to his own age."

Mr. Boone frowned. "Does she even have interviewing experience?" he asked Lopez.

But Mayfield grinned to her, smug as a cat. "I don't see it could do any harm."

Clark thanked him. She'd see about that.

She stepped into the interview room a few minutes later with two bottles of water, a handful of mints stuffed in her pocket, a gentle smile. Jamal hardly looked at her. The room was thick with silence. No air-conditioning. No vents. Clark sat across from him, her back to the one-way glass.

"If nothing else you should have a drink."

Jamal stared at the blank pad of paper in front of him.

She retrieved a mint and took her time pulling the candy from its plastic.

"Do you love Bethany, Jamal?"

He stared at the table. "It weren't like that."

She sucked at the mint. She pulled another from her pocket and passed it to him.

She shot a quick glance at the dusty microphone bolted to the side of the table. After a moment she set his mint on the pad of paper, making sure it rustled. Clark propped her arm casually on the table's edge. She held her mint's empty plastic wrapper a few inches from the microphone.

Feeling the eyes of the men in the other room burning against the back of her head, Clark crinkled the plastic wrapper a few times between her fingers and prayed that the sound washed out their speakers. She said softly through the noise, "Then tell me how it really was."

Jamal didn't seem to understand. "Don't I get a lawyer?"

"Do you feel you need a lawyer?" She shot an urgent look at the microphone. *Crinkle crinkle.*

Please God, she thought, *make this boy understand.* "Or would you rather talk to me first?"

Jamal's eyes lit up. To Clark's relief he covered it fast. He pulled on a scowl, shook his head, said, "D had his own thing going on."

"You mean on the weekends with KT?" Clark said loudly, hoping to throw the men off the scent.

"I don't know *what* the fuck those two were doing."

She crushed the wrapper, said softly, "Something with drugs?"

"Maybe you should figure out why D hung out with that guy."

The skeptical tone returned to Clark's voice. "You're saying KT wasn't a good influence?"

"None of those guys were."

"Which other guys?"

"KT, Garrett, Mitchell, all those fuckers. They weren't never my friends."

They sat in silence a moment. Clark strained to hear anything from the little room behind her.

Jamal held her eye. He took a water bottle, unscrewed it clumsily with his free hand and drained it in one long gulp. Bringing the bottle down he crushed it loudly. "On their phones," he murmured.

Clark cocked her head. "What?"

He squeezed the bottle tighter. "Something on their phones. At halftime."

Clark heard the sound of a door slamming, the click of shoes in the hall. Shit. It had been worth a shot.

She leaned forward, whispered fast, "What was it, Jamal?"

"I don't fucking know. I think something bad. Garrett almost killed me when I asked—"

The door to the interview room swung open and a small black man in a baggy blazer and brilliant shoes strode inside, bringing with him a sudden scent of cinnamon. Clark recognized the man (and his cologne) with a mixture of resignation and relief. At least Jamal finally had a lawyer.

"Not another word, son." Mr. Irons spoke with a voice far deeper than his little frame looked capable of containing. The man ran an eye over the blank pad of paper Mayfield had left on the table, the empty bottle of water. "Did you drink from that?"

Jamal nodded.

County Attorney Boone appeared at last, followed by the

sheriff. They both gave Clark a dubious look—she prayed they only thought her incompetent, not complicit—and a moment later Boone and Jamal's new attorney were embroiled in dense legal talk. She knew she'd never get another unguarded word with Jamal now.

She thought about what sort of secrets players could pass around on their phones at halftime. A halftime a few hours before one of those players turned up dead.

She'd need help from someone else at that school. Rising from the table she gave Jamal a curt nod. He stared through her, the way you would a stranger.

KIMBRA

Kimbra Lott was in the cafeteria when her phone buzzed. Dashandre, sorting through his little fuchsia cooler, shot a look at the contents of her lunch box and said, "Is that supposed to be spaghetti?"

April Sparks said with her usual fake disinterest, "I hear Mrs. Sanchez from the beauty parlor fell asleep at her stove this morning and caught her robe on fire. They say it's *very* serious."

"You really give a shit about that?" Dashandre said. "You miss the part where the cops arrested an innocent motherfucker?"

Kimbra hardly heard this. She couldn't think of much except the message that had just arrived on her phone from Joel Whitley.

Are you still willing to help find KT?

She sighed through her nose. She would be an idiot to help

this buff guy with the whiny voice. Hell, word had already spread through the school that Joel had been asking her questions at the diner yesterday. But the fact remained that her boyfriend was still missing despite all she'd done in the last two years to protect him. That he'd been hiding something from her before he disappeared. That he might be hurt. That this town could go fuck itself.

She typed, what do you need?

As Kimbra waited for Joel to reply, she spotted something unusual across the cafeteria. Luke Evers was seated near the head of the Bison table, flanked by Garrett and Mitchell, Tomas and the Turner twins, the six of them laughing violently at something Tomas had just said. It was strange. Every day for years Dylan had sat exactly where Luke was sitting now.

"They're saying Luke's going to be quarterback tomorrow," April said.

"It's like they don't even know Jamal's in jail." Dashandre deftly flayed an orange with his thumb.

"And now people are saying Bethany made up all that shit about her and Jamal," April said. "But *other* people are saying she actually did something *much* worse."

"She's been getting that dark chocolate to melt in her mouth," Dashandre said.

At the cheerleaders' table Bethany sat carefully chewing a salad, looking more guarded behind her eye shadow and her contoured cheeks than Kimbra had ever seen her before. Guarded and exhausted. The news of her alleged weekend with Jamal—news spread first by the students who'd opened their classroom windows this morning and heard every word she'd shouted to the police in the parking lot—had already done its damage. Kimbra suspected that Bethany's position at the top of the school's pyramid was in danger of toppling.

Joel wrote:

I've heard that the footballers were showing each other something secret on their phones Friday night at halftime. Did KT mention anything?

no, Kimbra wrote, which was the truth. She felt April watching her quizzically and ignored her. She texted Joel:

want me to see what I can find out?

Please. Also is there any chance Dylan and KT might have been involved?

involved?

Romantically?

lololol i'll ask around abt that half-time thing.

She looked up. She frowned. She realized he wasn't joking. wait—what?

She found Whiskey Brazos, the team's portly center, seated at a table in the school's small library after lunch, exactly where his girlfriend April had said he would be. He held a book splayed open in front of him, his mouth screwed up in concentration.

"Is this seat taken?" Kimbra asked.

Whiskey shuddered. "You scared the shit out of me."

She took that as a no. "Jumpy?"

Kimbra had always liked Whiskey: his harmless face, his country manners, his decency with April, who could be—to put it mildly—difficult. He always wore one of the same five plaid button-ups with the sleeves cut away at the shoulder, always had a fishhook slipped over the brim of his ball caps in case a desperate need for a bass ever presented itself. He asked her now, with what sounded like genuine concern, "Don't you have class?"

"Depends who you ask. What're you reading?"

He tilted up the spine of his book to reveal the cover: it displayed an airbrushed quarterback, his teeth a shade of white commonly known as "wealthy," promising down-to-earth advice. "Dylan said I should read it."

"That's deep," Kimbra said, wondering if Dylan had been as distracted by the handsome face on the cover as she was, and a second later she had to suppress the incredulous whistle that the thought had brought to her lips. Jesus Christ: Dylan Whitley, queer? When Joel had casually answered her question at lunch—I have it on good authority Dylan was gay. Did nobody know?—she had almost spilled spaghetti down her top.

Imagine the damage news like that could cause in this backward shit hole. Kimbra had been around football long enough to understand that its players weren't just boys throwing a ball: they were everything the men of this town used to be, or never were, the walking realization of every frustrated hope and squandered opportunity and dream.

The men of Bentley would bulldoze their football field before they let a homo quarterback stand in for them under those Friday night lights. And their wives would be relieved.

Whiskey Brazos also regarded the book's cover. He said, "I wonder if D ever could have had a shot at pro."

"At least now he'll never be disappointed." Kimbra shrugged, and when Whiskey winced she added quickly, "Hey, did you see that thing on Friday night?"

"What thing?"

Scooting forward in her seat, Kimbra whispered, "KT wouldn't tell me what it is. You know—that thing on your phone."

"KT told you about that?" said a voice from the stacks of books, and a moment later T-Bay Baskin emerged. T-Bay, the son of the manager of the First Community Bank, was an oddity in Bentley: namely, a rich and black kid. Kimbra had mixed feelings about him. Like her, he acted as if he too were made of some finer substance than this town could appreciate. Unlike her, he never had to wonder how he'd leave.

She held his eye. "He did. But he didn't say what it was. And now he's gone."

The two boys exchanged looks.

"I didn't send that to *nobody*," Whiskey said.

"Who's asking?" T-Bay asked Kimbra.

"Nobody but me."

T-Bay raised an eyebrow. "Then what did Joel Whitley want to know at the diner yesterday?"

"Nothing." She blinked. "Just where KT had gone."

"I mean it had to have been a joke, right?" said Whiskey, sounding a little pathetic. "Those pictures."

"You mean the ones of Joel back in the day?" Kimbra said.

The two boys looked at each other again. "You might as well show her," T-Bay said.

Whiskey hesitated before he pulled his phone from his pocket.

"It's some racist shit anyway," T-Bay said. "Jamal's not the only guy on the team without an alibi."

Kimbra felt her phone buzz again. She didn't move. "What?"

"Can't nobody know that came from us," Whiskey said, locking his own phone and gathering up his book.

Kimbra opened the message she'd just received. At first it wasn't as bad as she thought. Then she clicked the link, let her browser load and gasped. She looked up at the two boys. "Who sent you this?"

T-Bay narrowed his eyes. "It doesn't matter. If you're talking to Joel there's something else he needs to know."

JOEL

The morning had been a wash. The employees at Sparks's Auto Body had refused to talk to Joel about the discovery of the bloody sock in Jamal's Ford Explorer. A grungy man with an ugly dash of a scar under one eye had asked him, "You want us to buff them words off your door?" Joel had declined.

He drove to the Varsity Motel, a peeling cinder block horseshoe south of town on the highway, and asked after Jason Ovelle, just as Clark had recommended. The woman behind the counter said she didn't know a man by that name. Joel slid her two twenties and she told him she hadn't seen him all week. Joel asked to see Ovelle's room, hoping to discover some trace of where he might have gone, but the woman said that it had been rented to another party. When Joel pointed out that his was the only car in the parking lot, the lady only shrugged and turned back to her magazine.

On South Street, Joel passed Mrs. Mason, his mother's

friend, walking out of the bank with her terrier in her purse. She did a bad job of hiding her surprise at seeing him. When he asked her how her nephews Garrett and Ranger were doing these days, she invented a hair appointment in Temple and climbed into her car.

He went to the diner. Waiting for a fried sandwich—years of self-deprivation, and all it took was some violent grief to finally forget about his abs—he overheard a man in the booth behind him say, "It all feels a little familiar, don't it?"

"You mean like it was with the Clark boy?" replied a second man.

"No, like—" The first man lowered his voice; Joel would swear he'd heard him shiver. "I ain't been right at night. I ain't felt like this since our school days, since with Broadlock and all."

"*There's* a name that's bad for your health."

"But that voice, Phil—you heard it yourself."

A lady cut in. "This ain't nothing like back then. This here all starts with the mother. She teaches a boy she can move a man into her home without a lick of ceremony then how's the boy supposed to know smart from hazardous? I ask you. It's the breakdown of tradition is what it is."

Joel refused to be baited. He strode out of the diner as the waitress brought the sandwich to his table.

Now he drove his ruined car up the highway and pulled onto the shoulder at the little stand of trees that sat two miles north of the football field. According to Bethany, it was here that the boys had hidden Jamal's SUV before the game and dropped him off to retrieve it. Joel saw no reason to doubt her; the plan was so elaborate and superfluous it could only be invented by a group of teenage celebrities who had to make their own entertainment. The trees, just as Joel remembered, sat on the west side of the highway, opposite the eastern copper Flats, and were still packed in so tight together that from the road you'd never guess you could fit a car between them.

Ten years ago, back when he would meet Troy here, he had always seen the First Baptist Church's steeple in his rear-view mirror, watching him from back in town. Now, with the church gone, there was nothing on the horizon but the football field's tall halogen field lights. They seemed to follow him wherever he went.

Joel wondered if they might not have been the steeples of this town's true religion all along.

He eased over the shoulder and found the space on the western edge of the trees where, by the luck of nature, two shedding cedars had decided to grow a few extra feet apart from one another.

Joel climbed from the car and found himself back in the small clearing he remembered intimately from when he'd been Dylan's age. Roughly ten yards long and five wide, the clearing was blanketed with strips of cedar bark, a few cigarette butts. Joel spotted a dark stain in a patch of dirt and realized with a start that this place might be the site of his brother's murder—it was north of town, after all, in the direction Dylan had been last seen going, and God knew it was plenty private. But when Joel pressed his finger to the dark patch and brought them to his nose he found that the stain was only engine oil. Jamal's SUV must have had a drip.

The scent brought on an overwhelming stab of nostalgia—Troy had always smelled of grease, sweat, welder's smoke—and when the moment passed Joel realized he was in danger of losing his balance. He caught hold of a branch and awoke to the sound of his heart racing in his ears. He'd fallen asleep on his feet.

He shook himself, rubbed his face. Chewed an Adderall. Paced the clearing. There was something important here, a vital question his intuition was struggling to ask him. Something to do with the fact that it had been Joel who had once mentioned this secret place to Dylan years ago, and Troy who had shown it to Joel.

If nothing else, Joel supposed he could only hope that Dylan had enjoyed as happy a summer this year as Joel had enjoyed a decade before. Because at this point it seemed clear that those few months Joel had spent with Troy, whatever their consequences, would go down as the happiest of his life. There had been many trips to this very clearing, long sticky hours spent parked in the cab of Troy's truck or pressed against the shedding trunk of a cedar or standing to discover the fallen bark's mahogany stains lingering on the knees of their jeans. Things he hadn't been brave enough to tell Clark last night.

The night of the Bison's first summer game, the night that he had struck Ranger Mason with the first and only punch he'd ever thrown, Joel had emerged from his toilet stall to see Troy at the urinal. Troy had grown slimmer since Joel had last seen him a year before, wiry with muscle, an unkempt patch of stubble spreading down his neck. He still had the same bony wrists a little too big for his arms, still had his sister's brilliant emerald eyes, and those eyes had fixed on Joel that night with an attention, an interest, they'd never betrayed before. An attention that was thrilling, but not entirely kind.

Troy had said more to Joel in five minutes in the toilets than he had in the two years they'd spent on the team together. Looking back, Joel realized now that Troy had been appraising him. When Troy asked Joel if things between him and his sister were well, Joel had hesitated, and Troy had seemed relieved.

A week later, a half hour late—he was always late—Troy picked Joel up and they headed to the muddy country northwest of town. Troy's truck smelled of spearmint gum and cheap body spray and nicotine. Troy filled the silences with clumsy small talk, telling Joel about a 7-Eleven in Rockdale that would sell you beer without asking for ID if you paid twenty percent extra—*"You know how to calculate that, right?"*—about how Joel should never play football if he could help it (as if Joel, soon to be a senior, hadn't already missed that train by years), about the importance in a man's life of one day buying property.

At Troy's request, Joel had opened the glove box to retrieve a bottle of pills and found them resting atop a handgun. The gun's small black mouth was aimed straight at Joel's chest. *"Bandits and thieves,"* was all Troy would say in explanation, snickering, as he swallowed three tablets dry.

Pills, Joel thought now, recalling all that Clark had told him about Troy's debt, the bottle of Oxy in Dylan's room. *Pills. Of course.*

Troy and Joel had driven, whooping and laughing, through the wet country west of town, until mud had covered their windows and the engine started to smell. Troy parked in the shadow of a spindly tree to let the truck cool down. A tenuous silence settled between them. They looked at each other, at the patch of sky visible through the filthy windshield. An opportunity had presented itself—they both felt it, just as they both felt they were about to squander it if they didn't move fast.

Troy abandoned subtlety. He grabbed Joel's hand and pressed it to the hard weight in his lap.

When they were through, Troy had turned on the truck's wipers and said, "Sorry about that," as if he had just spilled ketchup on Joel's shirt (years later, Joel would hear the same words coming from Wesley Mores, spoken in the exact same tone).

Joel, finding nowhere to spit, only swallowed.

He wanted to weep. He had just learned that there was nothing more debasing, more perfectly disappointing, than getting exactly what you wanted: whatever Joel might have imagined in his wildest fantasies, Troy had ultimately tasted as bland as a short, salty finger. What had Joel just spent to discover that? What black mark had he just set permanently against his manhood? Against his soul?

When he felt a faint tremble rise through the ground and quake in his seat, he knew, without question, that it was just the Lord God, turning His eye on him in shock and shame.

Troy felt it too. He went still. He pushed sweat from his forehead and started to drive. He was so jumpy the truck nearly stalled.

The two boys were silent on the way home. Joel was almost too ashamed to breathe. He sometimes forgot, ten years later, just how religious he had once been, how the sight of Bentley First Baptist's cross had made him so fearful: the God of First Baptist was not a merciful God. Joel nearly barfed up all that Troy had spat inside him.

The guilt and the horror were all so awful Joel would have gladly let that afternoon be the end of it, would have never spoken to Troy again (imagine the shape his future might have taken), if something remarkable hadn't happened.

Troy seemed to calm when they reached the highway. His jitters faded. And when he moved the truck up from second gear to third to fourth, Troy let his hand fall from the gearshift and come to rest on Joel's thigh. He kept it there the entire way home.

Their arrangement went on like that all summer. Troy would make plans on some pretense every few weeks to come to town and would drive them somewhere remote or arrange a meeting in secret. When they were through they would study the ground, wipe their chins. And then they would let a thigh rest against a thigh, or an arm rest over a shoulder, and they would return to the real world like wounded soldiers, leaning against each other on the way back to their lonely trenches.

Joel had learned another lesson that summer, in those moments of fulfilled, defiant happiness: that shame and love, while one might breed the other, could never truly be felt at the same time. For a few brief miles on the way back to Bentley, before the disgust and the fear and the cunning set in again, Joel would feel happier with Troy, *righter*, than he had ever felt in his life.

He doubted now that Troy's feelings had been anywhere near as ecstatic. Apparently the man had had much larger concerns that summer than some rough head in a stand of trees (Joel supposed a drug habit explained the permanent sheen of sweat that seemed to cover Troy's copper skin under even the coldest air-conditioning). Troy had certainly abandoned Joel easily enough: in the wake of all that happened in the park, all that had happened with Deputy Grissom and Joel's arrest, Troy had cut off all contact, had let Joel sink like an anchor cut loose from its tether.

When Joel had heard, two months after his world had imploded, that Troy had gone missing, he hadn't allowed himself to be worried. He'd forced himself not to care. After that final betrayal, Troy had taught Joel a second lesson that summer. He had taught Joel how to cauterize his heart.

As Joel's phone began to buzz, the question finally popped into his head: why had Troy not asked Joel to meet him *here*, in this clearing, that night when Joel was arrested? The two of them had never once gone to the public park together, and for good reason.

Kimbra Lott had texted him.

hey. there's some things you should know.

I'm listening.

There was a pause.

Luke Evers doesn't have an alibi for Friday night.

Joel let out a little whistle. A manic grin tightened his face. He began to type a response but Kimbra cut him off.

there's more.

CLARK

At 2:04 that afternoon a woman named Patsy Boyd Vaughn, a forty-one-year-old mother of three, made a left onto South Street from the highway going fifty-five miles an hour. She was speeding, though this was hardly unusual in Bentley— South Street was all but abandoned in the midafternoon and was often treated as an extension of the highway. That morning, however, Patsy had complained to her husband that she hadn't slept well since Friday night.

At 2:04 she was asleep at the wheel, and by 2:05 was lying dead against it.

She lost consciousness somewhere in the middle of the turn. Her foot came to rest on the accelerator. Her restored lime-green Cadillac, a lavish birthday gift from her husband as an apology for an affair, carried on at fifty-five miles an hour and fishtailed into the first building at the intersection of South Street and Highway 77.

Emily Bunner, a bored girl with a husband (still) in Iraq, was the sole teller that afternoon at First Community Bank, and she didn't look up from her phone until Mrs. Vaughn's Cadillac came flying through the bank's front windows. Emily leaped out of the way, though she lost her leg in the subsequent collision. Ironic, folks said later, that Emily's husband had made it through three tours of IEDs and ISIS unscathed, but it was she who would be the amputee.

Jamal was still in the interview room, speaking to his lawyer. Clark was seated in the sheriff's department bull pen. Mayfield was seated at the desk across from her, filling out paperwork, treating her just as he had all day: as if she weren't there at all.

Mayfield's phone began to ring. Clark's curiosity was piqued when she heard the way the investigator said, "You're shitting me? On I-35?"

Still listening to Mayfield's conversation, Clark began running searches through the department's system. She pressed Enter and discovered there was no official record of any kind regarding KT Staler, whom Wesley Mores had told Joel *"got into some kind of trouble"* over the summer. No arrests, no tickets, not even a citation.

She discovered a moment later that there was no record of any investigation into the distribution of those dirty photographs of Joel ten years ago, the investigation the Whitley family had been promised was still ongoing.

Out of curiosity (Clark was long past caring that all of these searches were tracked), she pulled the record of Joel's arrest in 2007 and discovered it was so thinly written it was almost laughable. Old Officer Grissom had written:

Two men interrupted at Milam Municipal park in midst of sexual act…unidentified man between 5'8 and 6'2 (*re-*

ally?) fled the scene… Whitley, nude, produced wallet from pants on the ground stating quote "we can figure something out" end quote but…

Clark found all of this doubtful. She struggled to imagine Joel Whitley, aged seventeen (and no doubt terrified), possessing the wherewithal to offer a uniformed sheriff's deputy a bribe to avoid arrest. For that matter, she struggled to imagine fat, fidgety Officer Grissom turning the money down: before his accident this past summer, Grissom had possessed a reputation for being almost endearingly corrupt.

But it begged the question: why would dirty Officer Grissom write a false report? To cover for the other man, the one who had allegedly escaped unidentified?

"That was the Dallas PD," Mayfield said, hanging up the phone at his desk. "They arrested KT Staler for drug possession at a traffic stop on Tuesday night. Apparently they received some new APB this morning describing his Tacoma as 'aquamarine' and it flagged him in the system." Mayfield raised an eyebrow. "I'd have thought 'green' would have covered all our bases."

Clark's heart fluttered. That had been her APB.

"They say KT's ours for the taking if we want him. The new mayor up there put in a catch-and-release policy for the possession charges. They was about to cut him loose again."

Clark reached for her keys. "Are we going now?"

"You're going over to South Street," said Sheriff Lopez. Clark spun in her chair. She hadn't heard him stepping up behind her.

"But, sir—"

"But nothing. A car just drove into the bank and cracked open the vault."

Clark stood. "Sir, with all due respect, we have a suspect in custody in—"

"Indeed we do. In our station." Lopez narrowed his eyes at her computer screen. "If Mayfield wants to be a good Samaritan and bring Mr. Staler home, that's his prerogative. We're considering the Whitley case as good as closed, Deputy. And you're out of line."

Clark's cell buzzed. She slipped it far enough from her pocket to see the name on the screen. She swallowed her anger. "Excuse me, Sheriff," she said. "It's my father's home."

It was Joel. She stepped into the woman's restroom.

"Luke Evers wasn't home Friday night." Joel didn't bother with hello. "Where did he say he was?"

Clark ran her mind over all the alibis the boys had given them on Tuesday. "He went home to his mother straight after the game. We followed up with her—she said he was in by ten forty."

"T-Bay Baskin, the tall kid on the defensive line—you know him?"

"Of course. He was at home on Friday night too. We checked."

"Precisely. Which is how he knows that Luke Evers *wasn't*." Earlier this morning Clark had heard a calm in Joel's voice she didn't trust, the quiet of a coiled spring. It had gotten tighter. "T-Bay's family, apparently they live down the street from the Evers place—the guy can see Luke's driveway from his upstairs window. T-Bay told Kimbra Lott he was up late with Whiskey Brazos on the Xbox and by the time they fell asleep at four o'clock Luke's truck still wasn't parked at his family's house. T-Bay said he noticed because Luke's mother is so 'psycho'—his word, *not* mine—she never lets Luke stay out late. T-Bay even mentioned to Whiskey that Luke would have hell to pay when he came home. Luke lied to you, Clark. And his family fucking covered for him."

"Or T-Bay lied to get Luke in the shitter."

"Why would he lie?"

"Why would Luke kill Dylan?"

"You saw how the two of them were fighting at the game. Those kids had bad blood."

"They could have been disagreeing on a play."

"Can you talk to Luke? Shake him a little?"

"I'm not shaking anybody," she said, then added, "They're putting me back on street duty. It's a wild day over here."

Joel was silent for a moment. "Then I'll talk to him."

"No!" She nearly shouted it. "Christ, Joel, that kid's parents are richer than God. Do you have any idea what his father would do if he heard you came near his boy?"

"It would just be a conversation. Nothing scandalous."

Clark did not care for Joel's tone of voice at all. She also doubted she could stop him if he set his mind to something crazy. She made a decision. "Give me a couple hours. Let me settle things here. We'll figure out a way I can talk to Luke, somewhere private where he won't feel any pressure."

"Fine."

Clark made to hang up, but something in the silence on the line made her stop.

"Is there something else?"

"I wish there wasn't."

"What's that supposed to mean?"

"I found out what the Bison were passing around at halftime."

Her phone buzzed against her ear. She put Joel on hold, opened the message he'd sent, paused. It was a URL with a name she vaguely recognized. She opened it.

The link led to an escorting website. Across the top of the page was the profile name REALTXQB99. Beneath the name were all the tedious statistics.

6'1. 185 lbs.

8 inches cut.

$200/hour. Your place.

I'm a fucking horny Texas Teen who loves to FUCK and SER-VICE mature men.

Happy to serve the Dallas/Austin/Houston areas.

Available most weekends just give me heads-up.

And there, right in the center, was Dylan Whitley, shirt-less, chiseled, smiling with his hand disappearing into a thick darkness at the bottom edge of a bathroom mirror.

JOEL

Milam Municipal Park was a glorified ditch. There was a strip of road to park your car, some rough-hewn steps cut into limestone, but there was nothing at the bottom of those steps but wild holly and poison oak all running tangled through a gully.

At nine o'clock, well past dark, Joel took four steps down the side of the ditch and refused to take another. The night breeze, warm with the last traces of summer, stirred a heap of dead leaves. This was possibly the last place in Bentley he wanted to be. If you walked all the way to the bottom of those steps you could find the exact location he'd been standing when the photos had been taken ten years ago. This gully could be a landmark in Pettis County.

Clark texted him:

I just want you there in case he tries to run. Stay out of sight.

Joel's mind was not well. He was so strung out after a week of no sleep he believed—really believed—that he could feel a single thought as it dragged itself sluggishly from one synapse to another. He'd spent a long afternoon spinning his wheels about the escorting ad. He had lost count of the Adderall tablets he'd eaten today. Blood beat against the back of his eyes.

$200/hour. Your place.

He considered telling Clark that if Luke tried to escape from her down these steps, the boy would have nowhere to run once he reached the gully, as Joel's arrest record could attest. Instead he wrote back, I'm covert af.

AF?

Kimbra texted Joel:

Luke says he's fifteen minutes away. I told him to please hurry I really need to see him etc etc.

Meeting here at the park had been Clark's idea but it was Kimbra who had made it possible: the girl had devised (with enthusiasm and few questions) some story to lure Luke here. She was remarkably crafty. She'd told Joel that Evers was so desperate for friends he'd show up anywhere someone promised him a secret.

Joel had yet to tell the girl that KT had been found, safe and dubiously sound. He didn't want her getting second thoughts.

Clark texted Joel: I'm 10 min away.

Joel glanced at the brambles that overgrew the gully. There was nothing but danger down there.

He typed, Hurry.

He touched his brother's knife, strapped to his ankle above his jeans. Just to be safe.

I'm a fucking horny Texas Teen who loves to FUCK and SERVICE mature men, the ad read. Could his brother have really written that? Could it explain the Oxy in his room? Had Dylan popped those pills to forget all the things he had let these mature men do to him? Or, instead, had he done all of those things to afford all of those pills?

Had Dylan worn this knife for his safety on his weekend trips to the coast?

Joel hadn't been able to look at the ad for long. Here was a photo of Dylan in football pads that Joel recognized from Instagram. Here were half a dozen nudes: dimly lit backside, hard penis, ridged stomach. How brazen had Dylan become with his local fame to think he could get away with posting his face on something so salacious? How naive did you have to be to think that nobody in your hometown would find you out, eventually?

I put in two thousand of my own money.

i fucking hate football

dumb dreams. bad dreams.

What dreams, Dylan? What did you need so badly you would sell your body when a brother with a limitless credit card was a phone call away?

it's like i hear this town talking when i sleep.

Imagine if Dylan had called and told Joel everything. Imagine all that Joel could have shown him in the city, all the pleasures that would have been open to his handsome, masculine brother with his deep voice and easy charm. Dylan now would never walk into a bar and watch the sea of men around him ripple with attention at the sight of his smile. Would never walk down the street and feel a pair of eyes rove his body from his hair to his brilliant new white shoes. Dylan, dying here, had never been allowed to be himself.

God have mercy on whoever denied him that.

Joel wouldn't.

Hey, Kimbra Lott texted. Joel heard tires approaching through the quiet night. The girl wrote, I just remembered something. Ask Luke about the White Lands. KT said once he was gonna hang out with his White Lands boys but idk what that means and he never would tell.

Headlights washed over the trees of the park. They threw

the same shadows Joel had seen ten years before. His body shuddered as a memory—the bad memory, the worst memory—tried to climb his spine. His screen was replaced with the notice of an incoming call. It was Clark.

"Call it off," she said. Joel heard sirens blaring. "Christ in the shitter, I got a fire. A bad one."

"Send somebody else to deal with it."

"There *ain't* nobody else. Browder's got a man over in Rockdale who's gone crazy waving his gun in the street. Jones's posted up at the bank all night making sure nobody walks into the goddamn vault because nobody knows where to take the goddamn money and Mayfield just dropped off KT Staler because of course the goddamn kid's in the clear facing no goddamn charges—this goddamn fire, it's an officer's house, Joel, it's—"

"Luke's here," Joel said. "I'll call you later."

"Joel—"

He slipped the phone back into his pocket. A heavy truck lumbered to a stop on the road above him. It was, indeed, Luke Evers. He was bigger than Joel remembered from the game (did boys his age use steroids?) with a pillar of a neck and bulbous biceps and legs that looked ready to burst from their jeans. His face was even uglier than Joel had recalled.

"Where's Kimbra?" Luke asked. "She said she had something for me."

"Down here. She's waiting." Joel gestured to the stairs.

"Where's her car?" Luke squinted at him. "Where's *your* car?"

He wasn't an idiot, then. Joel smiled. "Where were you on Friday night, Luke?"

The boy froze. "What are you talking about?"

"You weren't at home—I know that much. Your mother lied to the police—I know that too—but it's not surprising, is it? Big shots like your family, of course their son's going to get out of trouble."

"How the fuck—"

Joel stepped forward. "Did you ever forgive Dylan for stealing your girl?"

"Bethany didn't give him a choice."

"How underwater is your family right now? Your parents own half the town, sure, but what's to own? Everything's closing. That big new subdevelopment's empty."

Luke narrowed his eyes.

"How bad does your family need the football program to keep going strong? Get new families moving in and sending their kids to Bentley High, buying houses, opening stores? How bad would it hurt y'all if my brother decided he hated football after all?"

"Dylan would never quit." Luke almost laughed. "He needed the attention too much."

"And what if he wasn't who this town thought he was?"

Bull's-eye. Luke all but recoiled from the question.

"Who told you that?"

Joel's rage mounted.

"Who sent you the ad, Luke?" Joel was frightened by the calm in his own voice. A voice that no longer felt entirely his own. "Who told you the golden boy wasn't very golden?"

"You watch too much TV, man."

Liar! his intuition shouted.

"Whoever it is," he'd promised his mother. *"Whatever it takes."*

"I'm going to ask you one more time." Joel took two long steps forward, bringing the boy within arm's reach. "Where did you go after the game on Friday?"

"Fuck you, man." Luke seemed to briefly consider throwing a punch at Joel with one of those big arms—*Just try*, the animal inside Joel pleaded, *just fucking try*—but instead the boy only turned away with a shake of his head. "I wasn't hurting anybody."

The moment Luke's back was turned Joel's vision went black. He felt the rage and the horror and the shame—the shame, always and forever the *shame*—tighten his heart. And Joel didn't want to fight it any longer. He let his mind slip free and let the darkness take control and bent down to grab the blade on his ankle and all he could hear was *endthis*—the blood in his ears whispering pleading demanding—*endhimendyouendthis*.

He had forgotten to undo the safety strap holding the knife in its sheath. He fumbled with it for a moment, just long enough for Luke to take a step away.

The strap popped free. Joel took hold of the knife's handle.

And then the back window of the truck lowered and a young boy shouted, "Luke!" and Joel shot to his feet empty-handed and felt his brain stutter and crash and refuse to start up again.

Luke was a brother too. How had he forgotten? Luke was an older brother, just like him.

Evers turned back, shook his head at Joel.

"And I thought Dylan was the crazy one," he said.

When Luke reached the truck he tousled the young boy's hair and climbed into the cab and left Joel standing alone in the dark.

With all the amphetamine in his system it took ages for the adrenaline to wear off. Light eventually began to creep through cracks in his vision where a moment before only darkness had been. He marveled at how easily he had surrendered himself to all of the violence and rage and despair that had climbed up from the pit of his mind.

Marveled at the way some of that darkness felt as if it had come from somewhere else. Somewhere not inside him.

Perhaps Clark had been right last night when she'd started talking about her kooky mother. The nightmares Joel had experienced since Dylan's murder—they didn't feel like normal dreams. That hadn't felt like normal rage. And while Margo Clark had seemed utterly bonkers, if she really had been in touch with some force or energy or occult magic, well: who could blame her for coming a little loose at the hinges?

After all, something had just come knocking at Joel's own head. Something rotten. Something *old*.

With a twist of guilt he remembered that Clark had been called away to an emergency of her own. He texted her:

Everything ok?

He texted Kimbra:

I've learned that KT was brought home this evening. He'd been arrested in Dallas.

Kimbra responded: Oh.

Sorry about that, Joel thought. Add it to the pile of things to feel awful over.

Joel walked until he caught a glint of moonlight on his black convertible parked in the distance, on the highway's dark shoulder. He toggled his phone over to the escorting ad and found he could still only study it for a few seconds. Looking now at his brother's grinning face, his shirtless body, Joel saw it in a new light.

Didn't the ad feel a little absurd, like a bad joke? Indeed, some of the Bison, according to Kimbra, had apparently considered it a prank when they saw it. But Joel wasn't stupid. There must have been plenty of Bentley boys who did not find it funny, who might even have taken it seriously, considered it evidence of his brother's deviance. Would it be such a stretch to imagine that the ad could have outed Dylan, however inadvertently? All it might have taken was one person spreading this URL to put the boy in terrible danger.

His brother's murder might have been a hate crime. The thought was too banal, too appalling, to fathom.

Whether the ad was genuine or not, it raised another question. Why had Dylan never told Joel that he was gay? Surely he must have known that Joel would treat the news with nothing but love and discretion. Dylan had always laughed when Joel described the absurdities of the city's gay scene, had always taken a good-natured interest in Joel's trips to bars and beaches, had never betrayed a hint of homophobia.

That old joke—50K—Dylan had carved into the concrete of the dam, had started back when Joel was fresh in Manhattan. One weekend, he had met a lavishly drunk man at a bar in Chelsea who had clung to Joel's elbow and insisted, endlessly, that he had a "fifty-karat cock." When Joel had told that story to his brother, Dylan had been aghast and delighted by the phrase in the way only teenage boys can be. It had passed into their limited private lexicon: "Yo, J—you found any more of that fifty-k?"

Maybe there was an answer in that, he realized. Maybe Joel had been so busy bringing word of the modern world to his simple backwoods brother he'd never bothered to learn if there was any news at home.

The dirty ad was featured on the escorting site's listings for Dallas, Houston and Austin. Joel wondered what kind of offers his dead brother's digital self was receiving at this very moment. He played with a hypothetical: suppose someone in Bentley had been planning a trip out of town one weekend, and while browsing the pages of the escorting website, looking to set up a little fun while they were in the city, they had happened to find Dylan's ad. Long odds, Joel's analytical mind told him, but still—stranger things have happened.

As he approached his car, he felt a spark in his ragged brain. Wasn't this ad of his brother's—with all of its lurid pictures—

uncannily similar to the photos that had been spread of Joel ten years before? Wasn't it—

There was someone seated in his convertible.

Joel stopped. He had lowered the convertible's ruined cloth hood this morning and so had no difficulty seeing the man sitting in the driver's seat, staring forward out the windshield. Sitting very still.

imissedyou.

The man's head began to turn, very slowly. Joel saw that it wasn't a man.

It was a boy. It was his brother.

Dylan stared at him with one eye. The other eye was so badly bruised it had swollen shut.

Dylan opened the car door.

Joel's brother wore a green Bison jacket and a pair of pants that glistened silver in the moonlight. His bare chest was the same cold white Joel had seen at the morgue. Dylan's bruised face was drawn into a grimace of pain.

Dylan took one faltering step out of the car. Another. His bloody bare feet sent up a whisper as they kicked the gravel. *imissedyou.* Joel clenched his fist around his phone, felt the useless knife on his ankle. He willed his legs to run. Every raw synapse in his brain willed his legs to run.

Dylan opened his mouth. His voice came out tight, twisted.

"You have to go."

Dylan took another step.

"You have to go tonight."

Joel opened his mouth to scream. No sound came.

"Run, Joel."

Dylan stopped. He stood a few inches away, giving off an awful stench of rot and mildew and clay. The wound in the boy's throat was a black pit into which no moonlight penetrated. It stared back at Joel like a reptile's eye.

"If you don't go tonight there's no escape."

A truck's horn blared behind Joel. A pair of headlights washed over Dylan and by the time they passed he was gone, his body vanishing in their glare.

The truck roved on down the road. Joel wondered if perhaps its driver had seen nothing more serious than a lone man on the side of the highway losing what was left of his mind.

Except the door of Joel's car was still open.

A few steps later, he stared down at the exposed driver's seat. Something dark clung to the leather. He reached out a hand to touch it, bring it to his nose.

It was clay—sour and rotten and *old*.

Joel knew that smell. He'd awoken to find it caught in his throat every morning this week.

LUKE

Luke pulled up to the curb. "Don't tell Mom about all that."

Timothy, his gangly little brother, glanced at him in the mirror. "I thought you were in trouble."

"Trouble? Me?" Luke pushed Tim on the knee. "Never. Sorry you're late."

His brother opened his mouth to say something but thought better of it. He gathered up the bags at his feet. "You want me to use your lucky rag?"

"Only on my helmet." Luke produced a scrap of old denim. "Don't go spreading that luck around."

"Why don't the school just pay people to do this? They act like they don't got stacks."

"It's tradition. Get the hell out of here."

Luke waited at the curb until his brother's friend let him into a little house north of town. Through the front door Luke could see that a few other middle schoolers were already hard at work inside. Forty helmets, forty pairs of sneakers, were spread down a long dining table, all waiting to be shined to a high gloss for the game tomorrow night.

Luke knew it was no good trying to pretend that a sight like this didn't make him a little tipsy with pride. Unlike Dylan Whitley, Luke had always cared for traditions, ceremony, heritage. Ironic maybe, considering the direction in which his heart had always pointed, but Luke was a Texas boy through and through.

Strange, he thought, that Joel hadn't asked him the obvious questions.

Fuck that guy for wasting his time. Luke was impatient to taste some of this town's devotion for himself. He was ready to awaken in the mornings to find messages waiting on his phone. The second the front door of the house closed Luke's hands began to shake on the wheel.

He texted Garrett Mason: Ready.

JOEL

Wesley Mores opened the door of his sprawling, lonely house with bourbon on his breath. He gasped at the sight of Joel's car.

"I think I hit a dog," Joel said, his voice shaky enough to make Wesley take a step back—the youth minister was quite drunk. Joel let himself in.

"I need to wash my hands."

"You can use the guest bathroom," Wesley said, a slur in his voice.

"This is fine, thank you." Joel was already halfway down the hall to the master suite, the minister hurrying after him. He gave Wesley an exhausted smile and closed the bedroom door in his face.

The little lock in the doorknob turned without a sound. Joel waited a moment, just to be certain Wesley wouldn't try to break in, and went into the adjoining bathroom. He turned on the tap, left the water running.

Back in the bedroom, Joel saw that Wesley had tidied up the massive oak dresser. It now held only a little dish of loose change, a Bentley Bison class ring—the year *2006* engraved along the top—and a wallet. Joel eased open a drawer: loose boxers. Gym shorts. Undershirts.

Wesley knocked on the door. "Are you alright in there?" He sounded tipsy, anxious.

Joel didn't bother answering. The door's knob jiggled.

"Joel?"

He saw a closet, a big TV stand.

"Joel, what are you doing in there?"

His eyes settled on a little nightstand with a big iron key-hole in the drawer. Antique, or trying to look like it. When Joel tugged on the drawer, he felt a latch hold it shut. Barely.

Wesley went quiet in the hall. Joel suspected he'd begun to look for the same thing as him: a tool to pry open a lock.

Joel found his first. He pulled his brother's knife free from its sheath and wedged the blade into the drawer. He heard Wesley hurrying up the hallway.

"I'm calling the police, Joel." *Pohleessh. Jull.*

The drawer began to give. Joel leaned on the blade. "That's a bad idea, Wesley."

"You have no right to come into my house like this, Joel, to—"

The drawer came open with a loud snap and a little puff of sawdust. Its contents clattered to the floor: a pocket Bible, a tacky old necklace with a dubious stone in the center, a credit card.

And, tucked in amid the clutter, was a small golden disk hooked to a wide blue ribbon. Joel pulled the medal free. He saw on it just what he thought he would, what he had been too drunk to recognize when he saw it on Sunday night. The letters MVP were embossed on the front.

And written across the back: STATE SEMIFINALS 2016.

Joel smiled. He thought of Clark asking him, *"How many queers do we have in Pettis County?"*

Standing on the side of the road a few minutes before, the adrenaline finally fading from his head, he'd finally stopped to think about what Luke had told him at the park. *"I wasn't hurting anyone."*

It was a stretch, but it was worth a shot.

Joel opened the bedroom door. Wesley stood on the other side with his phone in his hand, a finger poised over the screen, but at the sight of the medal he slid the phone slowly into his pocket and took a step away as if Joel had made to strike him with it.

"Just what were you and Luke Evers up to on Friday night, Mr. Mores?"

"I don't like your tone."

Joel did his best to sound bemused. "You must have shown that kid a hell of a time to deserve a gold medal."

"He's not a kid!" The burly man took another stumbling step back, hiccuped. Wesley was not—Joel was relieved to see—the sort of man whose drunkenness dissipated when shit hit the fan. He stumbled again, shook his head, stared at Joel like he wanted his forgiveness, but said only, "I—I have no idea what you're talking about."

Joel studied the medal. A careful, conspiratorial hesitation. "Do you want to sit down?"

In the living room, Joel dropped his phone casually on the arm of the sofa, went to the drinks cart to pour Wesley a whiskey. The man accepted it without a word.

"I'm trying to help you here, Wes." Joel sat down close, a hand on Wesley's massive thigh. He thought of that clumsy stumble Sunday night when the minister had fallen against his chest just for the chance to touch him. How many sad accidents had this man survived on? "The cops know Luke wasn't home Friday night. They haven't spoken to him yet."

"But you have."

"He told me he was here."

"Consent in Texas is seventeen."

"But Luke was still one of your pupils at the church, wasn't he?"

"He's a Methodist."

Joel gave him a muted shrug.

"What's the point?" Wesley sighed into his glass. "Luke was caught sleeping with some boy over in Rockdale. In a parking lot. A parking lot! His mother—I hope you never meet that woman—she and I'd been friendly since I bought this house. She came to me for help, asked me to give the boy some private guidance. How could I say no?"

The minister raised a toast to the TV.

"Luke was a lot less confused about himself than his mother thought," Wesley said. And, the minister went on, Luke didn't waste any time. When things started, Wesley and the boy would meet for lunch at a chain restaurant in Waco, a ninety-minute drive away, and over enchiladas Wesley would try to talk about the Lord, about the value He places on keeping one's body pure, about all the old promises of retribution for those folks who failed to follow some simple commandments. "He seemed receptive," Wesley said.

I bet, Joel thought.

Wesley said it was all so quotidian. Things took a turn. Their sessions grew longer, more personal.

Soon Luke was giving the minister little gifts as thank-yous for making so much time for him—a small cross he'd carved at home, a chunk of quartz he'd discovered on a hike with his brother. That was when he'd given Wesley the medal. "He said he remembered how well I played in my day. He said Troy Clark didn't deserve all the love he got."

Of course, Luke knew that Wesley was the only person living on this stretch of the Evers family's subdevelopment. Last Friday, things finally came to a head. Luke had texted Wesley Friday night after the game was over and said he had something he couldn't wait to ask the minister about.

Joel couldn't help but say, "And you were shocked when he came over with more than Jesus on his mind?"

Wesley closed his eyes. "You don't know what it's like here, Joel."

"You could leave."

"Right. Of course. And have you found someone special in the city? Someone to wake up for?"

After a moment, Joel said, "No."

Wesley gave him a tight-lipped smile: spiteful, and yet with a strange air of relief, like he'd just heard confirmation that he'd made a wise choice back at some difficult time. Joel would never forgive him for that smile. "I'm glad to hear it."

"Did Luke mention the ad on Friday night?" Joel said.

"What ad?"

"The one the players were passing around at halftime."

"The boy doesn't have friends. It's why we got along so well." Wesley gave a tipsy burp. He rounded on Joel, jabbed a finger in the air, suddenly all anger and self-justification. "What we did was *nothing* compared to the shit that goes on in this town, you know."

Just as he had last night at the dam, Joel felt something large looming in the air, waiting to be said.

"What sort of shit, Wesley?"

"You remember."

"Let's say I don't."

Rage overcame Wesley. He stared at Joel, eyes black and narrow, and said, "You're as bad as your fucking brother, you know that? You fucking sanctimonious shit. Who do you think burned down my church? Some meth addicts? No, you fucking idiot, it was your brother and those boys, those goddamn footballers who can get away with anything. They've been a terror for years because they know the cops won't touch them."

Wesley's voice grew louder. Here was a man, Joel thought, who could fill a pulpit.

"Most of them are happy to rip off someone's stereo or a wallet but your brother decided he wanted to save the fucking world and torch a church. Dylan only ever showed up at the service to sit next to Bethany Tanner and keep this town thinking he was their damned heart and soul. Luke figured it out easy."

Wesley paused to give his lip an angry bite.

"When that mother of y'all's moved a man into her house over the summer there was a little perplexity why those two couldn't follow basic protocol. There was talk."

"Dylan burned down a church because people were gossiping about our mother?"

"He didn't even bother lying when Luke spotted the kerosene cans in his truck."

Joel let a long silence settle before he said, "What else was Dylan doing? Where did he and KT go on the weekends?"

Wesley gave an indignant little shrug. "How the hell should I know? They never talked to me."

This sounded genuine to Joel's ears. He let it go for now. Something Wesley had said a moment before echoed with something Bethany had told him yesterday: *"The cops never bothered Dylan."*

"So Dylan was immune to police investigation? Why isn't Jamal? He's on the team too, backup or not."

"It's not the entire team that's safe." Wesley was beginning to sound exhausted. He rose and headed for the drinks cart. With a shaky hand he filled his glass. "There was always a clique. A little band of golden boys no one could touch."

"Was Troy Clark one of those boys?"

Wesley emptied the glass in one gulp. "Of course he was. He and Ranger Mason, Jason Ovelle, a few others."

Joel's stomach turned at the thought of Ranger Mason. Of Ranger's bloody mouth.

"Is that why Troy Clark was selling drugs around here? Because he knew he was immune from the law?"

"How should I know? I wasn't one of them."

"And what about Dylan? Was he one of the untouchable boys today?"

"You have to ask?"

"Who else?"

"Not Luke, I'll tell you that. Joel, this can't be hard to figure out. Look at this town. Look at who walks around like they own it." For the first time since he spotted the medal dangling from Joel's fingers in the hallway a look of fear came over Wesley's face. "I don't want to talk about this."

"One of those untouchables killed my brother, didn't he? It's why the whole damn town is trying to cover it up by framing Jamal Reynolds."

"I wouldn't know."

"KT Staler got mixed up in trouble over the summer. You said it yourself. But his girlfriend knew nothing about it. There's no record of anything in the sheriff's department's system. Wesley—what did KT do?"

"I can't talk about that place, Joel."

"What place?"

Wesley splashed bourbon somewhere in the vicinity of his glass. His face had gone white.

Joel studied the fear in the man's sunken eyes. The exhaustion.

Joel said, "You're dreaming about it too."

Wesley stood so still Joel thought the man had stopped breathing. "I don't know what you're talking about."

KT told me once he was gonna hang out with his White Lands boys.

Joel said softly, "You can't remember them well, can you? The dreams. They chase you all night and then you wake up shaking and stare at the ceiling and ask yourself, 'What the hell has got me so scared?'"

i can't go to the bright lands it's not the same no more.

The bourbon sloshed in the minister's glass.

"Wesley," Joel said. "What are the Bright Lands?"

Mores laughed abruptly, a violent reflex, the second the words were out of Joel's mouth, knocking his hip into the bar cart and making the bottles titter. Yet when Wesley regained control of himself all he said was, "I don't know. I was never invited."

I was never invited.

The memory came rushing up at that: the bad memory, the *worst* memory. Joel felt a coarse thumb press itself against his asshole. He heard a man say, *"Cheer up, son. I weren't ever—"*

As the memory of fat deputy Grissom filled his mind Joel dug his nails into the leather of the couch. If Joel thought about it, if he let himself remember, he was certain he would go falling backward, be lost permanently in the dark folds of the past.

Pulling himself into the present, Joel stared at Wesley and said, "What does the Bright Lands have to do with my brother?"

A little echo of the laugh rose from the other man's chest. He shook his head. "You just can't help yourself, can you?"

Joel felt another question forming, but a moment later Wesley's attention fell across something on the floor near the kitchen.

The phone, Joel's gut asked him. *Where's your phone?*

"You son of a bitch," Wesley said.

Joel spotted it a few feet away—he must have knocked it from the sofa's arm a moment ago. A little red square was blinking on the phone's screen, the universal sign for RE-CORDING.

Joel looked up, saw the fury in Wesley's eyes.

The man's heavy glass came flying toward Joel's face.

LUKE

Driving, Luke recounted to Garrett and the Turner twins his bizarre meeting with Joel Whitley at the park that evening. Garrett, with a thin smile, said only, "He's on the list for tomorrow. Kill the lights."

They parked outside a sagging two-story house on the northern edge of town. The house, like the neighborhood around it, let off a sour scent of decay. Luke had never actually seen the Staler house before. He wished he weren't seeing it now.

"Didn't KT run off?" Luke said.

The twins chuckled in the back seat of Luke's truck. "He tried," said Stevey.

"He couldn't even do that right," said Ricky.

A strange stasis descended in the cab. The fetid breeze, the creak of old vinyl siding. Luke's mind turned briefly back to

Joel. He almost couldn't believe the man still hadn't figured it out.

Love wasn't the word for what Dylan and Luke had shared as boys. Not love, but a few years of confidence, of mutual discovery. Or, in Luke's case, years filled with an uncanny sense of reacquaintance. It was enough to make a person believe in past lives. Those pleasures he and Dylan had found when clinging sweaty to each other beneath their pillow forts, behind the shed of practice equipment in Luke's yard—those things which had been revelations to Dylan—had never felt to Luke all that profound. Even as a young boy they'd felt like old memories, half-forgotten, that had needed only a sudden touch to swell with life again.

But it had never been love. Dylan had never allowed it to be love.

And what about these old friends of Dylan's sitting now in Luke's truck? What had Dylan been to them?

"Hey," Luke said, eyeing KT's dark house. "Why did y'all need a ride to Sparks's Auto Body last night?"

The Turner twins went very still. Garrett turned to Luke. "You want what Dylan had, yeah?"

Yes. Yes, oh yes God, Luke wanted to be needed.

"I guess," Luke said.

"Then drink your beer."

After a last moment's hesitation, Luke brought his bottle to his lips, and with one swift motion Garrett tilted the bottle upward. Luke struggled not to choke as the beer drained down his throat.

"Good," Garrett said. "Let's go."

Insects thrummed in the balmy night. Luke, still fighting a retch, followed the three boys across the house's overgrown yard. Garrett rapped on the front door.

A woman answered, wearing nothing but a bathrobe. Half her face still bore the lines of a corduroy cushion. Luke had heard stories about KT's mother. He was surprised to see that most of them were true.

"Excuse us, Mrs. Staler," Garrett said, still smiling, the picture of courtesy. He held Luke's empty beer bottle behind his back. "Is Kyler Thomas home?"

Mrs. Staler seemed too exhausted to stand. She propped herself against the door frame and said, "Ain't nobody come in this house."

"What is it, Garrett?"

KT appeared on a dim staircase behind his mother, dressed in basketball shorts and a baggy shirt that read MAKING MONEY MOVES. He carried himself down the steps the way Luke had seen boys drag themselves from the field with broken wrists, shoulders popped loose like cherry pits.

"KT!" Garrett said brightly. "We missed you, brother. Want to throw a few?"

Stevey Turner held up a football he'd brought with him. Luke did his best to smile at this bony boy who bore only a passing resemblance to the KT who'd been at school four days before.

"Just a few passes," said Stevey.

Garrett caught the ball. "For old time's sake."

"I ain't playing no more," KT said.

"Get these boys *out* of my face." Mrs. Staler groaned, blocking the door with her arms.

There was no fence to stop them. They found KT standing on a wide porch around back the house, surrounded by bright plastic toys, faded folding chairs, a grill so rusted thorny creeper had twisted itself up through a hole in the lid. A single bare bulb screwed into the porch's overhang did its best to light a yard that had gone badly to seed.

Garrett and Luke and the twins stood in the yard and gestured for KT to join them. "Come here, son," Garrett said. "We was worried shitless for you."

Ricky Turner tossed Luke the ball. Luke caught it at the last moment, hesitated, took a few steps back and tossed it into Stevey's waiting hands. The narrow scar over Stevey's brow gleamed where it caught the moonlight.

"I didn't tell them nothing," KT said.

Luke felt the grass around his ankles tremble, heard a faint *shh* rise up from the dirt. Was this what the start of an earthquake felt like? He opened his mouth to say something but saw that none of the other boys seemed to notice. Luke told himself he was imagining things.

Even when it happened again.

Garrett said cheerfully to KT, "We had an agreement, man."

"It ain't my fault I'm back."

Stevey jogged to the side of the yard and caught the ball from his brother.

Garrett bent to run his hand through the grass. "Yet here you are."

"The charges in Dallas is getting dropped," KT said. "Soon as that's done I'll have my car back and I'll go. You ain't never seeing me—"

"That wasn't the deal," Garrett said.

Ricky threw a zip pass to Stevey.

"What was the deal, KT? Say it."

"I know what it was."

"Say it."

"Fuck you, Garrett."

Stevey heaved the ball hard into the back of KT's head. It struck him with a loud thud. KT staggered forward, almost losing his balance, and Garrett pulled the empty beer bottle from behind his back and shattered it over KT's skull.

KT fell to his knees. The twins worked fast. Stevey hustled to the side of the house to keep lookout. Ricky flipped KT onto his back, stretched out his wrists, pinned him to the dirt.

Garrett turned to Luke. "Grab his feet."

Luke took a step away. "The fuck are you doing?"

"I said grab his feet."

KT groaned.

"Think fast, Evers," Garrett said. "You're either a brother or an enemy to us. Everybody is. You hear me? You grab his fucking feet and you're a brother for life."

"Isn't KT your brother?" Luke said, thinking of all the times he had seen KT running with these boys.

"This fucker? KT's the reason Dylan's dead, Evers. We've had to go through a lot of trouble for this little cunt."

KT's head lolled from one side to the other, eyes fluttering.

"You're made for glory, Evers," said Garrett. "Dylan may have got there first but I'm giving you the chance now. I'm giving you the chance to have the best year of your fucking life. Twenty-four hours from now you are going to be so goddamn grateful you did what I say. Grab his fucking feet."

Luke grabbed KT's feet.

Garrett brought all two hundred and forty pounds of his weight onto KT's sternum. He slapped KT twice, hard, until the boy came to with a gasp and thrashed his legs.

"Listen to me, Kyler Thomas. Listen very fucking carefully. I have this from on high. We promised you freedom. We promised not to come looking for you. But in exchange you promised to never come back to this town. You broke that promise, just like Jason broke it. But for you we'll be merciful. You leave tomorrow. Don't matter how you do it, don't matter where you go. But, Kyler—Kyler Thomas, goddammit you never listen to me."

KT gasped. "That thing out there will kill you, you know."

The ground shook again. A breeze rose and carried the distant roar of a cheering crowd with it. Was gone.

Garrett punched KT so hard Luke felt the force of it in the boy's ankles. "If I ever see you again *I* will fucking kill you,"

Garrett said, and for a moment it sounded like he was holding back a sob.

They left KT in the grass. On their way back to the truck, Garrett wrapped his big arm around Luke, pulled him tight, suddenly all smiles. "I'll let the others know," he said, lips brushing Luke's ear. "Tomorrow, after the game—you're in."

JOEL

Sitting on Wesley's couch, the blood from his busted lip spilling onto the bright leather, Joel struggled to stay conscious. A satin blackness, cool and supple, wrapped itself over his eyes. There, peeking through the fibers, what did he see but the past, catching up to him at last? What did he see but everything he had worked his entire life to forget?

Ranger Mason had enlisted in the army shortly after the Bison's first summer game ten years ago. Joel and Starsha continued as always. His shame was such that when Joel made her happy he felt wretched. When he made her sad he thought to himself, *Well, at least she doesn't know.*

One evening that summer, Joel had discovered an issue of *Playgirl* waiting in his house's mailbox, the naked men on its pages smeared with cow shit. A few weeks later, Joel had taken a job as a carhop at the Sonic Drive-In and one afternoon had brought an order for four fudge milk shakes to a car full of footballers who'd never once given Joel any trouble. A few seconds later he'd been covered head to toe in liquid chocolate. "Ranger says hello from Baghdad," said the boy behind the wheel, all of them cackling on their way out of the drive-in.

Joel never told his girlfriend about the punch he'd thrown at the game, nor any of the harassment that punch had apparently brought to bear on him. When he mentioned the chocolate incident to her brother during their next round of mudding, Troy had replied offhandedly, "Oh, fuck 'em." After a beat he'd turned to Joel with a clumsy smile and added, "But, you know, it might hurt my feelings."

Joel had laughed, his heart in his mouth. It had been so thrilling, so distressing, to finally flirt like he meant it.

If only Troy had always been so kind. As the summer cooled and coppered into fall, his calls to Joel had become more infrequent, their time together briefer. He was always chewing pills when Joel saw him, always rubbing his neck and grumbling about the sprain he'd experienced years before, as if Joel could do anything but fret for him. Troy was always hurrying off early from their meetings or arriving hours late. Daily, hourly, Joel suffered violent fits of jealousy.

Not that Joel possessed the strength to do anything about it.

"I want you tonight," Troy had whispered into the phone, on that final November afternoon.

"Where have you been?"

A pause. A heavy breath. "Meet me tonight? I'm seeing the game. I'll come find you after, down at the park?"

"The public park?"

"I want you," Troy said again in a whisper.

Joel had only hesitated for a moment. He didn't see that he had a choice. "Of course."

It was well past dark by the time Joel arrived, and a cold wind had harried the town all day. He listened to the Bison lose their game and snapped off the radio. He sat a long time in his car, his headlights illuminating the plain stone steps descending into the dark. He took a long breath.

As he reached out a hand to kill the engine he stopped when he heard static come leaking from the radio, a low, expectant *shh*, even though the little light above the speaker was a dead red. Was there another car here? A radio playing down in the gully below? But no: Joel brought his ear to the grille of the speaker and heard a faint pop from inside, a rattle, something that sounded an awful lot like a distant groan.

He told himself not to be crazy. The radio was old. Speakers got weird when they got old. That was all. That was all.

He wrenched his keys free from the ignition and hustled from the car.

Joel let his eyes adjust to the dark. The bed of the gully was thick with dead leaves that crept up his legs. He turned and spotted a little nook in the gully and took up position there. He stuck a hand down his pants to keep it warm.

The cold came rolling down the rock. The temperature was falling fast. With the game over, he estimated it would take Troy fifteen minutes to make it here from the field (though after all of Troy's imprecations against football, Joel wondered vaguely—jealously—what could have inspired him to go to the game tonight in the first place).

Half an hour passed. Joel couldn't pretend to be surprised. Troy was always late.

Sounds played funny against the walls of the gully: the whisper of the leaves at his feet echoed with every fresh breeze. He looked at his watch, buried his numb hand back in his underwear, then wrenched it out, sensing suddenly that he wasn't alone. He squinted at the thicket of brambles and thorns a few yards away. That thicket was as tall as a person and tangled tight as a wall. There was no way anyone could conceal themselves in that overgrowth, Joel told himself. There was no way a person could be down here watching him, whatever the hairs on the back of his arms might say.

He sure was having to tell himself a lot this evening.

With a warm flood of relief, Joel heard the sound of tires creaking over the blacktop above him. But when the light of the car's headlamps spilled, briefly, down into the gully, all that relief drained out of him. He held in a scream. He felt his knees struggle to hold him upright. He saw in those brambles at the end of the gully something he spent years telling himself he'd never seen.

He saw a pair of glassy black eyes watching him between the thorns and creeper. Saw them shine in the light with the ancient smug intelligence of an iguana, of a creature from the dark deep dreaming its way up to the surface, hungry for a show. Joel would have sworn—if his mind hadn't teetered right on the absolute edge of oblivion—that those eyes, those *big* eyes had a smile in their shine.

And then something else registered in his panicking brain. The car above him had come to a stop but the engine hadn't cut out.

That wasn't Troy's engine.

The car door swung open. Footsteps on the gravel. The headlights dimmed as someone passed in front of them. A pause. The person started down the steps.

It wasn't Troy. The person was wheezy with the effort of the stairs, and by the time they were halfway down the side of the gully Joel was eyeing the sheer walls around him for handholds, sturdy roots, any possible escape.

There was none. Just as Joel decided to take his chances with the thicket, he saw those black eyes watching him again, saw them blink (*imissedyou*) and the thorns rattled in a shudder: the thing inside was stirring, settling itself in. Joel caught a smell of rot on the breeze, felt his bladder threaten to fail.

A large man, bald-headed and thick-necked, stopped at the

bottom of the stairs. The man jingled with keys and some other metal sound Joel couldn't place. Then he saw the hand-cuffs.

It was Sheriff's Deputy Grissom, a man so corrupt he was practically a town joke. He had no neck, and a head all out of proportion with his body—long and narrow and raw with eczema—so that his face resembled nothing so much as a red pushpin pressed into fold upon dark fold of sweaty khaki. You could always avoid a ticket from Grissom, joked folks at the Egg House, if you just paid him in cash half of what the county would cite you. When Joel had started driving, Pau-lette had even given him a few twenties to keep in the glove box of his car, just in case, she said—*"Better to grease the deputy than have the points on your license."*

Joel realized with a shiver that he'd spent that money weeks ago.

Grissom burped into his fist, rubbed the backs of his hands together in some weird private gesture, peered into the bram-bles that blocked the northern end of the gully as if he knew precisely what he was looking for. He reached for the flash-light on his belt.

Joel held his breath.

The deputy took a few heavy steps through the leaves, playing the beam of his flashlight ahead of him through the overgrowth, but there was nothing there. Where had those eyes gone? How could something so big—it would have to be big: those eyes had been the size of hubcaps, those thorns had been quaking—how could it have just slithered away without a sound?

But no, they weren't gone. Joel felt that scrutiny, that hun-gry smile, watching him as his knees shook, as a single tear ran down his cheek. He had never been so afraid in his life, had never been so ashamed—of the stupidity and the hunger and the desperate love that had brought him here—and now, as he suspected that all of the summer's happiness might be about to ruin him, Joel felt he had no one to blame but himself.

Those eyes, wherever they'd gotten to, were enjoying this.

Deputy Grissom swung around on his heel. Joel pressed himself against the rocky wall, squeezed his eyes shut. He was trapped.

There was a high whine of delight in Grissom's voice when the beam settled on Joel. "Well—ain't this a sight."

Joel couldn't speak.

"Don't you know the park closes at dark, son?"

Grissom lowered the flashlight. Joel saw that the man was standing between him and the stairs, blocking him in.

"I didn't see a sign, sir." Joel's teeth were chattering. "I'm sorry."

"If only ignorance was an excuse. The hell are you doing out here anyway?" (*And here, with a cold jolt, Joel remembered something else he'd forgotten for a decade.*) "Why ain't you out there with the other boys?"

"I was taking a walk, sir."

Above them, another car pulled into the park. Grissom heard it too. He flicked off the light.

It was Troy. At last. Joel had spent enough hours in that truck to know the sound of its engine even with panic ringing in his ears. The truck rumbled to a stop above them, idled for a moment—just long enough, Joel later thought, for Troy to recognize what was happening in the gully beneath his headlights—and turned away.

The noise of the truck's tires seemed to recede for an age.

The deputy clicked on the light again and laughed. "You must be so *lonely* out here all on your own."

Joel struggled to breathe. He heard the roar of Troy's engine when it returned to the highway, its eager rattle as Troy climbed from second gear to third to fourth. Joel thought of

Troy's hand falling from the truck's stick and coming to rest on his thigh.

The engine fading, endlessly fading.

"I was actually about to leave, Officer."

Joel took a step forward. Grissom held up a pale, fleshy palm. "You're in quite a hurry."

"It's cold, sir."

"Hence my confusion as to why you're down here." The man's nose flared. "Are you familiar with the concept of loitering with intent?"

"No, sir."

"It's an arrestable offense."

"But I haven't hurt anyone."

"Well, you've certainly inconvenienced me." Grissom sucked spit between his teeth, deliberated. He lowered his voice. "Perhaps we could come to an understanding, you and me. An exchange. Would you like that, son?"

"I—I left my wallet in the car." Leaving aside the fact he was broke, Joel wasn't sure if this was how adults negotiated a bribe. Was there some sort of signal, something he should be doing with his eyes?

But Grissom only shook his head. "I don't want your *money*, son."

Time thickened and stopped and started sluggishly again.

The deputy stood there a long time, blocking the stairs, muttering something to himself, a whole little conversation Joel couldn't catch. Finally Grissom straightened his uniform, nodded to Joel and said very calmly, "If you move one step they'll find you in five pieces."

Grissom hustled up the steps. When he reached the top, Joel heard the sound of a car's trunk opening, a distant rustle of fabric, a zipper unfastening. Joel stared across the gully at the thorns that blocked the path out of there. They whispered in the dark.

Like a tape rewinding, all the sounds from above played back in reverse. The fat deputy returned to where he'd stood a moment before. He held a boxy camera in one hand. His other hand was draped over the gun on his hip.

"I think we might have a solution here for all parties involved." Grissom adjusted the camera, raised it to his eye, clicked the shutter. Joel was blinded, briefly, by the flash. "Take off your shirt."

Joel was certain he'd misheard him. "Sir?"

"I said take off your fucking shirt."

So, Joel thought: this was how they happened, the stories you always hear about on the news. He fumbled at the hem of his shirt. His fingers had gone numb.

Flash.

Grissom shook his head. "No, no. Look like you want it."

Joel didn't have to ask the man what he meant. He didn't hesitate. Joel thought, at that moment, that he would do anything he was asked if it meant he could make it out of this gully alive. He swallowed a retch, poked out his mouth in a pout. He made the face that would later fall out of newspapers all over town.

Flash.

"Better. Now your belt."

Flash.

"Now the pants. All the way. Over the shoes, goddammit."

Flash.

"Give me that face again. Perfect."

Flash.

"Now the briefs."

"Please, sir—"

"Now."

Joel pulled down his briefs. A cold breeze ran through his bare legs.

"Pull them loose." Grissom moved his free hand from his gun to the front of his pants. He squeezed. *Flash*.

Joel tugged down his frigid balls.

"If you start crying you're a dead man. Get it hard. Christ, boy, look like you want it."

Joel wondered if there was something in store for him tonight that might be worse than death. In his head he could still hear Troy's truck, rumbling away.

"Turn around. Hands on the wall. Bend over."

Flash. Flash. Flash. Grissom approached and lowered himself on his haunches. Joel could feel the man's wet breath on the cheeks of his ass. He shuddered when he felt Grissom's thumb rest, briefly, in their cleft.

"That one's a beauty," Grissom said, his voice trembling with something like awe. "Like the button on a navel orange."

Joel heard something spatter across the leaves between his feet.

Grissom stayed crouched behind him a long time. Joel stood perfectly still. He didn't dare to breathe.

Finally Grissom cleared his throat, rose, zipped up his fly.

"Hands behind your back, son."

Joel didn't move.

"I said give me your fucking hands."

"Why?"

"Because I have a goldarn arrest to make, that's why. Lordy, just look at the sight of you." Grissom laughed. He leaned his bulky frame against Joel's bare back to grab the boy's wrists.

"We had a deal!"

"A what?" The cuffs bit Joel's skin. Grissom gave them a tug. "Let's get you to the station—are you gonna walk or do I need to drag you?"

Joel stumbled on the way up the stairs—had the ground quaked or had his mind just departed his body?—and nearly fell back into the dark. He couldn't help it. He was crying so hard he could hardly see.

His tears all but choked him when he was pressed naked into the squad car, when the door was slammed, when Grissom lowered his bulk into the seat ahead of him with a spicy burp. Joel couldn't stop shaking on the cold vinyl seat. He saw eyes in the trees, watching him with a smile.

His mind shorted out.

Was it any wonder that Joel forgot what Grissom said next? That it had taken him ten years and a blow to the head to finally see what his vaunted fucking intuition had been trying to show him all this time? To recall the way Grissom *pops loose the camera's memory card and tucks it into the shirt pocket of his uniform shakes his head shifts his cruiser into Reverse speaks with a tenderness that's almost worse than all he's said before:*

"Cheer up, son. I weren't ever invited out there, either."

By the time Clark arrived Wesley was long gone. The fight for Joel's phone (and the recording of Wesley's confession that rested on it) had been brief. Wesley had heaved the heavy glass of bourbon. Joel had already reached his phone by the time the glass exploded against the wall. Wesley took a second too long to cross the cavernous living room: Joel had his phone jammed into his pocket by the time Wesley threw his first punch. Joel stumbled back, dodged it.

He wasn't so lucky a second time. Wesley's fist (and the force of all his old football muscle) had crashed into Joel's jaw, sent his head into the little wooden end table beside the couch. Joel's brain had flickered, his mind struggled to process the complex task of breathing, blinking, pulling loose the knife at his ankle.

But then there it was, in his hand, the blade's tip shaking in the air.

A moment later and Wesley was heading for the hall with

a sob in his throat. Joel, crouched on all fours, vomit in his mouth, watched as Wesley stumbled out the front door a minute later with his keys and a green backpack.

"Joel?" Clark was here. A half hour had passed. He thought he had hallucinated calling her.

Rising from the couch, the memory of his arrest still echoing in his brain, Joel recoiled when he saw the state she was in.

Clark was covered in ash. It powdered her hair, smudged her cheeks like theater paint. Her eyes were a violent red. When he told her that Wesley's house was empty, she brushed glass from the sofa and dropped heavily into the seat beside him. A chalky ghost remained, briefly, suspended in the air above her.

"Are you alright?" he asked, rising to get her a drink before she could tell him otherwise.

"Have you ever seen what an oxygen tank does to someone when it explodes next to their bed?"

Joel handed her a whiskey.

She said nothing. Joel poured himself a drink and considered his approach. Clark was clearly exhausted, but he needed her now more than ever. He needed to move while the memory was still fresh. Joel needed to know what that fat fucker of a cop, like Wesley, had never been invited to.

"I have to speak to Grissom," Joel said. "Do you know where he lives?"

Clark stared at Joel as if to confirm he wasn't joking. She exploded with a violent spasm of laughter. Little wisps of ash drifted off her quaking body and rose through the air like she was smoldering herself.

"I was just at his house," she said. "There's not much of him left."

FRIDAY

THE BRIGHT LANDS

JAMAL

"We need to talk." Jamal awoke to the sound of his lawyer rapping on the bars of his cell. Mr. Irons was dressed in a sharp suit and tie, smelled of leather and cinnamon. "But you got a visitor. Hurry now, I have an appointment at the federal courthouse."

Jamal dragged himself up from the hard cot. He had finally slept last night, had suffered no dreams, but after a week of terrible nights it felt almost more exhausting to be rested.

He said to Mr. Irons, "I can't shower or nothing first?"

"They're transporting you to the jail in Austin tomorrow. They have showers there." Irons dug into his suit pocket. "I brought you these."

Jamal accepted a pack of wet towelettes his lawyer passed through the bars.

He let the deputy cuff him and lead him down the hall past

a drunk who had screamed half the night and a woman curled in the corner of her cell. She raised her gray head as he passed.

"It's back," she said, staring Jamal straight in the eye. "It never left."

Jamal stepped into the interview room and saw Kimbra Lott and for a moment he was happier than he'd been in weeks. She had straightened her hair and made up her face and painted her nails a bright Bison green. Of course. The Stable Shootout was tonight.

A foil packet waited for him on the table. Jamal slid out the cookies he knew awaited him inside—he noticed that someone at the department had already opened them for him—and tried to laugh at the name written in icing across their crust: KT.

"Don't mind the name," Kimbra said. "I figure you deserve them more."

"Did your dad make these?" Jamal asked. Mr. Lott was famous for his Bison spirit.

"The man can't help himself."

A brief silence came over them. Jamal took a bite of the cookie: he hadn't eaten anything decent since his breakfast yesterday at home.

He waited a moment to raise the cookie and asked, "Has anyone heard from KT?"

Kimbra glanced back at the one-way glass. Jamal wondered if Mr. Irons had warned her about the men who would be listening on the other side. If he had, her face betrayed no concern. She said only, "I hear he got home last night."

"He did? Where was he?"

"Dallas, I think."

"He hasn't texted you?"

She shrugged.

Jamal pushed the cookie aside. "That guy treats you like shit, you know."

Kimbra only shrugged again. "What can you do?"

God, Jamal thought, and not for the first time: if only he had spent last weekend with Kimbra instead of Bethany. He'd always had a soft spot for the girl, for her sly little smiles and the eyes that said she was too smart for you but she'd politely endure your company anyway. The fact she had come here just to bring him a pack of cookies was perhaps the kindest thing anyone had ever done for him. Jamal fought a sudden, foreign urge to weep.

"Hey," Kimbra said softly. "Have you been having weird dreams?"

It feeds

Jamal flinched. For some reason he thought of the words he'd seen scribbled beneath Dylan's face yesterday. "Sometimes."

"I think everybody has. You heard what happened at the bank yesterday, right? And some guy's house blew up. Of course everyone's fronting like there's nothing wrong. Like we always do here." Kimbra hesitated. "What's in yours?"

"My what?" he said, though he knew what she meant.

Kimbra only cocked her head.

Jamal toyed with his cookie. A cold slick of sweat ran down his neck. "Lights. Just…lights. Way out in the dark."

"Not a woman with long hair, watching you from a window?"

"What? No."

Kimbra let out a relieved little sigh. "Thank God. April swears we've all been dreaming the same thing."

"But they started Friday night, didn't they?"

The girl's attention had already moved on. She glanced at the one-way glass again, at the microphone bolted to the table. She lowered her voice. "Have you ever heard of the Bright Lands?"

Yes. Oh yes. "Is that what you came here to ask me?"

"I brought you a snack." She narrowed her eyes. "Is that a yes?"

"I didn't say that."

"But you—"

"It's stupid. Don't ask about that."

Mr. Irons opened the door of the little room. "That's all we have time for today."

"Is it a place you go to? Or just some kind of party?" Kimbra made no move to rise.

Jamal stared at the table.

"They didn't talk about it in the locker room or anything?"

"Thank you, young lady," Irons said. "You can leave now."

Jamal stared at Kimbra. She was too clever to bullshit. Clever enough to get herself hurt.

"Just—don't ask people about that," Jamal said in a low voice. The big deputy hooked a hand under Kimbra's elbow. "Don't let those guys fuck you up."

But Kimbra had stopped listening. She didn't say goodbye. She shook off the deputy and stepped through a door where nothing awaited *but a black night, an empty sky, an awful dome of lights—bad lights,* wrong *lights—trembling on the far horizon. The girl takes a step toward the lights, stops, turns back to give him a quizzical look and—*

A blink of the eye and the sight was gone, the sheriff station's hallway returned to its proper place outside the door, and Jamal could only give Kimbra a little wave and watch her go. No big deal. His dream hadn't left him, after all. It had only followed him into his waking life.

CLARK

Clark passed Kimbra Lott coming out of the sheriff's station. They nodded to each other, said nothing.

Deputy Jones emerged from the holding cells. Clark avoided him. It had occurred to her last night that Jones was the last man to see Jason Ovelle, alive or dead.

Mayfield, standing at the coffeemaker, looked like he had slept in his shirt. He called for Clark as she made her way across the bull pen toward the sheriff's office. Something in his voice made her stop.

By the time the volunteer fire department had extinguished the blaze of Officer Grissom's house last night, the former deputy had been cooked a brilliant black, his polyester bed-sheets melted into a shell around him like the egg of some forgotten reptile. Mayfield had identified Grissom by a tattoo on his left arm. The arm must have been stretched out toward the oxygen tank when it exploded because they found it outside, through the window, surrounded by its charred fingers.

"Cigarette filters," Mayfield said when Clark reached him at the coffee machine. "Under the window. Three of them."

"He fell asleep smoking?" Clark said cautiously. Mayfield made her very nervous lately.

"He hadn't smoked since the accident. He couldn't. The oxygen tank was because the horse crushed his lungs when it fell on him."

"Where was his home nurse?"

"She'd left already. The overnight girl apparently quit a few weeks back. He was by himself from eleven to seven."

Clark considered what Joel Whitley had told her about Officer Grissom. Considered what Grissom had said (and, dear Jesus, *done*) to Whitley ten years ago.

"He had that horseback accident the last week of July, right?" Clark said.

Mayfield nodded. "A Saturday. The twenty-ninth. According to the dates Bethany Tanner gave us, Dylan and KT weren't in town that weekend."

Clark wondered why Mayfield's mind had made the same connection as her own. "You mentioned yesterday that Grissom had regained the ability to speak some."

Mayfield gave her a long stare. "I only said that to the sheriff."

Before she had the chance to lose her nerve, Clark turned and headed into Lopez's office.

She knocked and stepped inside without waiting for an answer. Lopez and Boone were seated on either side of the large desk, looking through the photographs Mayfield had made of the fire. Lopez grimaced when Clark stepped inside. Boone rose politely to shake her hand.

"Officer," the county attorney said. "You're here early."

Clark ignored him. She said to Lopez, "I'm here to request immediate leave."

"Denied." Lopez gave her an incredulous look. "We're a man short as it is—Jones has to replace Browder at lunch to watch that damn bank all night. Who do you expect to patrol the streets, the fire department?"

"Sir, by my count I have three weeks of unused vacation, five days of sick pay and three Jewish holidays I could find a reason to celebrate. I'm prepared to file a complaint against the department for unfair labor practices if I'm denied the chance to use them."

"As I said, you are *just* like my wife." Boone chuckled. "I will always admire your spirit, Deputy."

"It's out of the question," Lopez said, but before he could say another word a voice came from the open door.

"I'll work her shift."

The three of them turned to see Mayfield holding a steaming cup of coffee.

"You're joking," said Lopez.

"Why not?" Mayfield said. "My old khakis still fit. Mostly."

"We need you both working today," Lopez said. "We've got a dead officer on our hands, for Christ's sake."

"And I'll be here at my desk till four." Mayfield chuckled. "I was working doubles when you were still at the academy, Lopez. Clark did good work this week. Get out of here, Officer. Enjoy your weekend."

"I don't recall you being the sheriff at this station." Lopez's face was darkening.

"And I recall you owing me quite a few favors." Mayfield motioned Clark out the door. "I'll just call my wife and have her swing by with my uniform."

Clark slipped back into the bull pen, too stunned to speak. She had already reached her desk by the time Mayfield caught up with her. "You deserve the time." His eyes lingered on something over her shoulder, on something she'd already noticed on the way over: a sheet of paper had materialized on her keyboard since she'd passed it on the way into the office a minute before.

Clark turned to flip the paper over, read three words, stopped. She folded the paper and slid it quickly into her pocket. She stared at Mayfield, her mouth slack.

"Get the fuck out of here." Mayfield added softly, "Don't let me down."

Clark didn't have to be told twice. A few seconds later she was climbing into her truck.

Joel, his face a map of bruises, was seated in the passenger seat.

Clark passed him the paper. "Let's go."

JOEL

ARREST RECORD 82234
7/15/17
OFFICER GRISSOM REPORTING:

...At 2330 yesterday (7/14/17) while acting on existing suspicions (see attached notes 7/2/17) I approached the Little River Marina in an unmarked vehicle. Upon arrival I discovered three young men I recognized by sight: Kyler Thomas (KT) Staler, Garrett Mason and Jason Ovelle. The three men appeared to be in some kind of altercation/argument. As the marina is abandoned and Ovelle is a known distributor of narcotics I considered this probable cause to detain all three suspects while searching their vehicles and possessions.

I discovered in the course of search: approx 1 oz of methamphetamine in trunk of Ovelle's vehicle (Honda Civic, red) as well as approx 3 oz of marijuana, approx 30 unidentified tab-

lets and 3 small bottles of VHS video head cleaner known for
"huffing"/inhalation.

I discovered in searching Garrett Mason's and KT Staler's
person $500 in mixed bills. I was informed by Ovelle (whom
I believed to be intoxicated) that Staler/Mason were attempt-
ing to "stiff" him on a prearranged agreement. Staler possessed
approx 1/6 oz of methamphetamine in his pocket. Mason pos-
sessed approx 20 mixed pills.

I formally arrested all 3 men. After being read his rights Gar-
rett Mason said quote "You will fucking regret this" end quote.

END OF REPORT

Joel read the report aloud to Clark, twice, and choked down
some coffee, praying it would start to work. He'd flushed his
Adderall that morning, still appalled at how he had treated
Luke Evers last night: those amphetamine jitters had made it
just a little too easy to listen to whatever force had come calling on him at the park. Had made the thought of homicide
just a little too appealing.

"That report was written two weeks before Grissom's accident," Clark said.

"I think we just found the trouble KT got himself into over
the summer." Joel regarded the arrest record. "The thing Wesley Mores said Dylan was so concerned about."

"And it was just like Wesley told you last night—two untouchable footballers get arrested and the record of it disappeared."

"Then we were right about something," Joel said. "KT *was*
working with drugs."

"Hold on." Clark flicked through her notebook with one
hand. "If KT was arrested here at the marina the weekend
of July thirteenth then he and Dylan must have split up on
the weekends they were supposed to be at the coast. Bethany

told us that the boys were out of town the twelfth through the fourteenth."

"Meaning that if Dylan was in the city that weekend and—" he cleared his throat "—*occupied* on the night of KT's arrest, then does this drug shit have anything to do with him at all?"

They reached the highway, waited at the light even though no cars were coming. "There's a lot of money floating around, isn't there?" said Clark. "KT arrested with five hundred in mixed bills. Dylan counting two grand in his bedroom."

"Money that he apparently took out before he died," Joel said. "The bank told me on Wednesday that his account only had two grand, which I'm guessing was the money my mother's boyfriend gave him."

They drank their coffee. The Flats were turning hard and bronze in the sun. "If Dylan wasn't involved with drugs, why would he be turning tricks in the first place? Can you think of another way a kid could rack up a debt so bad he had to sell his body to pay it off?" Joel added.

"Maybe he needed the money for something other than a debt. Maybe he just liked having cash around." Clark tapped her thumbnail on her tooth. "If we say Dylan wasn't connected to the drug business, and if he didn't owe a large debt to a dangerous person, where does it leave the idea that his death is connected to Troy's disappearance? What parallels do we still see?"

The light changed. Clark didn't turn immediately.

"They were both Bison," Joel said.

"And they were both gay."

Joel sighed. "Does that put us back at a hate crime? The escorting ad might have been a bad joke, but it could have also gotten guys asking questions about Dylan, making assumptions that weren't entirely wrong."

The light turned yellow.

Joel continued. "Dylan apparently burned down a church

and got away with it the first week of June. He must have thought he was untouchable. If the ad was real, why else would he be brave enough to put his face up on that site?"

"Do guys even put their faces on ads like that?" Clark said.

"The professionals do. Why wouldn't they?"

She raised an eyebrow. "I suppose that's city life."

"The city, exactly. So if it was posted in Dallas and Houston, who *here* found the ad?"

Clark turned the truck. "And who did they tell about it?"

CLARK

Clark estimated she had maybe five minutes before word got around that she'd arrived at the school.

She spotted Garrett Mason seated in the back of a classroom, dressed in his football jersey. She opened the door, ignoring frigid Mrs. Sparrows. "I need you for a moment, Mr. Mason."

He was in the hallway a moment later, looking stunned and sullen.

"July fourteenth. The marina. Were you buying or selling, Garrett?"

Garrett turned to Joel, standing just behind Clark. "The fuck happened to him?"

"That doesn't matter, Garrett. You and KT Staler and Jason Ovelle were all arrested that night. It may not have gotten around but we keep records, son. We can go to court with them."

"I was at home that night. With my girl, Jasmine. Watching fucking Netflix. Just ask her. That fat cop's full of shit."

JOHN FRAM

"Which cop would that be?" Clark smiled.

Garrett realized his mistake. He rubbed his hand and said nothing more.

"That's a nasty bruise," she said, looking down at his knuckles.

"I dropped a weight on them."

"Starsha Clark. Joel Whitley," called a voice behind them. "This is a blast from the past."

Shit. It was Coach Parter, ambling up the festooned hallway as proud and lazy as a bull at a county fair. He'd certainly found them fast.

"It's Officer Clark," she told Parter. "And this is police business."

"And Lord knows Mr. Mason has had plenty of business with the police." Stepping around her, Parter draped a big arm over Garrett's wide shoulders. "But surely this can wait until after the game tonight, Officer?"

Clark was ready to fight but Joel shot her a quick look: *Drop it.*

"Just one question, Garrett," Joel said as the boy started toward the classroom. "What exactly *are* the Bright Lands?"

Garrett scowled. Parter narrowed his eyes.

"The what?" the coach said, a cool warning in his lazy drawl. They didn't bother asking again.

JOEL

KT's house seemed to blacken in the late morning sun. Haggard Mrs. Staler took an age to open the front door. "I don't allow nobody in this house," the woman said, twice, before Joel produced a pair of twenties and a small light came into her eye.

"Sorry, sir." The woman gestured to her wild hair, the dried spit on her chin. As if it explained everything she said, "Oxycodone the only way I sleep these days."

They found KT in a small bedroom on the second floor, seated atop his bedcovers, an ancient laptop unfolded in his lap.

"Kyler Thomas," Clark said gently, noticing the vivid bruise on his face. "May we come inside?"

The glow of the computer screen was the only light in the room. Heavy curtains covered the windows. The floor was buried under unwashed clothes, bags of chips.

They came to stand at the edge of the bed.

"That's an ugly bruise," Joel said. Under the purple and brown spread across his cheeks, KT was still strikingly handsome, more so than Joel remembered from the game—all cheekbones and full lips and soft lashes—yet the sly light Joel had seen in the boy's eyes on Friday night had gone out.

"Garrett Mason's got a bruise just like it on his hand." Clark smiled. "You two make quite a pair."

KT's eyes widened, briefly, at Garrett's name.

"Whose idea was it to meet at the marina in July?" Joel said.

Nothing.

"Jason Ovelle was out of town for a time," Clark said. "And then he turned up Friday looking for something in your truck. Where'd he go once our deputy turned him loose after the game, KT?"

Nothing.

Clark leaned forward, hardened her voice. She was good at this. "You got arrested again this week. They found a quarter ounce of meth on you in Dallas, KT. Did you buy it from Jason or did you have another source?"

Nothing.

"Garrett stopped by last night to make sure you stayed quiet about the drugs, didn't he?" Clark indicated the bruise on KT's cheek. "The two of you's been in the business since you figured out you could get away with anything in this town."

KT turned to her finally. "It weren't my idea. It was Garrett's brother. The one who lives out on 270 past the water towers, has all the signs in his yard. He was the one introduced us to Jason. I didn't do shit."

Clark glanced back at Joel. Ranger Mason. Of course.

"And how did Dylan get involved?" Clark said.

KT scowled at her. "Dylan was too busy for us."

"Too busy working in the cities?"

The boy squirmed beneath the laptop before setting it beside him on the bed and letting its screen rest against the wall. He stared at the door and said nothing.

Joel looked at the light the computer threw across his lap. It was enough.

He opened his phone and found the photograph he wanted, passed the phone to Clark.

After a long moment she nodded and passed the phone back.

"Those are your naked photos on Dylan's ad, aren't they?" Joel said.

The boy didn't answer. He only let his head fall into his hands. Of course.

It would have been obvious from the start if Joel had only made himself study the ad with a cool head. There was a door just barely visible in the murky background of the nude pictures. In Dylan's room that door was nowhere near the bed.

Joel hadn't put it together until he saw the way KT's laptop, its lid propped against the wall, threw its light across the boy's lap. No doubt KT rested the laptop there often, a habit, and had done so the night he took the pictures of himself, the screen's light throwing his cock's shadow straight to the left of the frame.

"It was easy to do," Joel said. "Make a fake profile on the site, pull a few pictures from Dylan's Instagram and mix it with a few nudes of your own. Type it up to make him sound as pathetic as possible. Send it out."

KT tightened a hand over his eyes.

"So if Dylan wasn't escorting or doing drugs," Clark said, "why did he have two thousand dollars in cash this summer?"

"It were mine. I made it working with Garrett. I made Dylan hold it for me awhile—my mom stole my whole stash right after school let out and I had to keep the new shit somewhere. After that Darren guy saw him with it Dylan made me take it back."

Joel nodded. It made a kind of sense, though he wondered

why his brother would agree to something so shady. Loyalty, maybe? Or had a threat been involved?

Clark said, "Does your girlfriend know you were dealing drugs?"

"She thinks I drive."

"For what? Uber?" Joel asked.

"Dylan didn't have to do shit, of course," KT said, ignoring him. "D just got to run off with his boy every weekend."

"You mean you and Dylan weren't an item?" Joel said.

"I'm not fucking gay, you idiot." KT scoffed.

"If you weren't sleeping with Dylan then who was?"

A look of sudden, palpable fear crossed KT's face. He said nothing.

"So you faked the escorting ad," said Clark. "Then what? Who did you send it to? Garrett?"

KT shook his head. He was slipping away from them again.

"Why do it, KT?" Clark said. "Why go to all the fucking trouble to make it look like Dylan was turning tricks?"

KT began to rock forward and back. "D never should have took me."

"Took you where?" Clark said.

Joel stepped forward. He felt something else struggling to click into place. "To the Bright Lands?"

The boy groaned. He pushed himself into the corner where the bed met the wall. His body began to shake. He raised his voice. "Get the fuck out."

A baby—how in the world was there a baby in this house?—began to squall down the hall. KT's mother shouted something.

Joel felt a new theory forming in his mind. He thought of Wesley's untouchables, the fear Joel used to see in Troy's eyes whenever the two of them used to pass the football field ten years ago, Garrett Mason's sneer at the diner.

"Was Dylan sleeping with one of the Bright Lands boys, KT?" Joel said, raising his voice above the din.

But KT hardly seemed to hear him. He was muttering rapidly, shaking his head like a wild man arguing with a bus seat.

"Kyler Thomas," Clark said, putting a hand on his arm. "The Bright Lands boys. The ones you mentioned to your girlfriend. Who are they? What did they do?"

"I did not Bosheth did not say a word did not—"

Bosheth. Bosheth. Clark and Joel exchanged glances. How did he know that word?

"It's not my fault he's awake now," KT said. And then he started to laugh.

CLARK

"My mother used to talk about that thing," Clark said when they climbed into her truck. "Bosheth."

Joel wiped sweat from his forehead, looked back at the dark house behind them. In a voice she'd never from him before—cowed, incredulous, scared—he asked, "What did she say about it?"

Clark keyed the ignition, hesitated. She struggled to bring back the stories that she'd spent so long ignoring. She suspected she should have been talking about them from day one.

"Mom said that Bosheth came to town when she was in high school but he was already old by then. Very old. He swam here from somewhere else, came through a trench underground. He sleeps under Bentley now. Or maybe under the Flats—she used to call them 'Bosheth's house.'" She felt absurd saying all this, embarrassed at how quickly she'd abandoned logic and deduction for a story told to her by a woman who'd once spent a week speaking in nothing but Kabbalah predictions, and yet Clark couldn't help but notice that her fingers had gone numb. "And he drinks tears."

She could see Joel struggling to process this, could see him weighing how seriously he wanted to take any sort of superstition. She couldn't blame his confusion. Ten minutes ago, they'd both thought his brother was involved in the drug trade. And now?

"Does he also eat young men?" Joel said, sounding faintly astonished at himself for asking.

"I don't know. But he spreads nightmares when he moves—she said that."

"Here's what confuses me. The week before I got here, were you having those crazy dreams?"

"Not like the ones we've been having. Why?"

"Because I think Dylan was. That Sunday he texted me, he said he couldn't sleep, said something about hearing the town talking in his dreams. Why was Dylan having the nightmares when no one else was?"

Something occurred to Clark. "My mom once told Troy that if your dreams went woolly it meant Bosheth had taken a shine to you."

"A shine? It's a monster that has crushes on young boys?"

"I—"

Clark's phone buzzed. She read the name on the screen, cursed. "I have to take this."

She stepped outside of the truck, brought the phone to her ear. She had a feeling she wouldn't like what she was about to hear. "Hello?" she said, and a moment later she was pinching the bridge of her nose and holding in an angry, tired sob.

She hung up the phone after saying only a few words. Climbed back into the cab. "It's my father." she said. "He's in trouble."

JOEL

Two hot hours later, Joel was thoroughly lost in the country-side. KT had only mentioned in passing that Garrett's brother lived "out on 270 past the water towers," and while Joel had had no issue finding the water towers west of town—they stood weeping rust onto a cow pasture long since abandoned—he soon discovered that County Road 270 in fact terminated a few miles past them. Road 270 split into two new roads, both of which unwound and eventually split again themselves. Joel passed small houses with black scabby windows, ancient trucks parked in their yards, and yet he hadn't seen another soul for miles. Driving with the convertible's ruined top folded down he soon felt the sun searing his hands to the wheel.

Google Maps was little help to him. Some of these roads didn't even appear on the screen, and those that did refused all analysis. There was no Street View. The overlay of a satellite image simply revealed what he already knew: he was nowhere. He wandered a road until he reached a dead end, doubled back, tried again. No wonder people never went into the Flats east of Bentley. He could only imagine how maddening it would be to traverse this much emptiness without even a gravel road to make you feel tethered, however tenuously, to some more ordered world.

A text message arrived from Clark: Still driving.

He responded: Same.

Joel thought about Clark's mom, about the time the woman had told him to kiss a piece of gold—*"Real gold,"* Margo had insisted. *"Not that cheap shit your mother drags out on game nights"*—to keep the devil away. What a strange world that lady must have lived in if the devil himself was only ever a few steps down the hall.

And what a world Joel lived in now. Her world. Because when he considered the eyes that had watched him at the park ten years ago, when he thought of whatever had stepped out of his car last night, when he took stock of all that he'd seen and heard this week, what answer was he left with?

That Margo might have been right all along.

Another message came from Kimbra Lott:

no word on that bright lands place—been keeping it low-key but so far nobody knows shit (which is maybe weird by itself??) will keep you posted.

When Joel had texted her late last night to ask Kimbra about the "White Lands boys" that she'd mentioned earlier in the evening, the girl had said yes, she'd probably misheard KT when he'd mentioned them over the summer. Last night, Kimbra had sounded eager to continue helping Joel, even though KT had already been found, safe and somewhat sound in Dallas, and for the life of him Joel still couldn't guess why.

Not for the first time he felt apprehensive about asking Kimbra to play spy for him. If his suspicions were correct and this secret place—whatever it was—had something to do with

Dylan's death, then there was no reason someone might not kill again to keep it hidden.

Joel wrote:

Saw KT. He's ok, not very talkative. I think you should stop asking around about this. Something bad is going on.

The unmarked road on which he'd been traveling petered out at a muddy pond. A thin band of gravel led to the southwest, off into more nowhere. To the north, however, far in the distance, Joel spotted something odd shimmering in the heat: a dense vivid block of red and green.

A few minutes later, he saw that it was a little shack tucked into a thicket of red, white and green signs. Even from yards away he knew what those signs would say. He'd seen them around town all week.

There were signs in the grass and signs in the windows, signs on the doors and pasted over the roof. MY HERD MY GLORY declared the green ones. The red ones were predictable, political, frightfully mundane. Who these signs were hoping to persuade Joel couldn't imagine. The shack looked to be the only building for miles.

Joel parked well away, idled for a long time. Nothing moved. He dug a finger beneath the sheath of the knife on his ankle, scraping at a nasty itch that had spread since last night. Clark had offered him a gun earlier and he'd declined it, certain he would be more likely to shoot himself than someone else. Now that he'd arrived here he wished he'd taken his chances.

A breeze rustled the signs in the yard. He felt a faint, silent tremor rise from the dirt road and shake the wheel of the convertible.

Enough screen had fallen from the door's outer frame Joel needed only to reach through and knock. A Bison sign was hung there, and in the Bison's eye a small circle had been cut to keep the door's peephole uncovered. Joel knocked again.

The Bison's eye darkened to study him.

A moment later, Ranger Mason was standing a few inches and a lifetime away from Joel.

"You."

"Me," Joel agreed.

Ranger had withered. A stained green jersey hung from his bony frame. The snake tattoo on his neck now ended abruptly at his Adam's apple. Nobody had told Joel that the bomb Ranger had fallen on in Iraq had peeled off most of his face in addition to taking off half his hand. A hollow socket stared back at Joel from deep inside the old scars.

"If I'd known you was coming I'd have put my eye in," Ranger said.

"You're a hard guy to find."

"That's intentional." A pause. "Well, shit. We're air-conditioning the outdoors."

Joel followed him into the shack. Inside it reeked of chili and stale cigarettes and some sweet pallid primal stink. The shack was nothing but a single room: a grimy kitchenette to one end, a rumpled daybed on the other, a wide TV on the wall catching a choppy satellite signal. There was a door in the back that looked to lead outside and another to the side that Joel assumed concealed a bathroom. He thought of his own apartment with its marble counters, its Italian furniture. He'd never felt so cultivated, which was saying something.

Ranger muted the television as he walked by. On it, Joel spotted the Bison field, saw people already claiming seats five hours before the game. The man opened a rusted refrigerator and removed two beers.

"You can push that shit to the floor," Ranger said, indicating a sunken easy chair, its seat covered in a heap of green jerseys identical to the one that dangled over his gaunt shoulders.

"Cheers." Ranger passed Joel a tepid beer. "The hell happened to your face?"

"Wesley Mores."

Ranger threw his head back and laughed. He reached out his gnarled half hand to pat Joel on the shoulder—Joel couldn't help but flinch at the touch—and said, "Thank you, Whitley. I needed that."

The man dragged over the solid oak daybed with his good arm and sat. He held his bottle between his legs and wrenched off the cap with the claw of his ruined hand. He drank most of the bottle in a single pull.

Joel sat. He sipped his beer and readied himself. He wondered how exactly you were supposed to ask a man what he had come here to ask.

Before Joel could say a word, Ranger burped and told him, "Jason Ovelle is dead. I'm sure he's involved in this somehow."

Joel blinked.

"They found him on Tuesday, in a motel up outside that town Mexia. You know the place?"

"A couple of hours north. What was he doing up there?"

"Precisely. His mother knew how to find me. She asked me to go identify him. As a friend of the family."

"An overdose?"

"That's what they told her. Oxy. Oxycodone. You know what it is?"

Oh, did Joel ever. A breeze stirred an army blanket that had been nailed over a busted window. Joel thought of the bottle of pills he'd discovered in his brother's nightstand, wondered if he and Clark had been too hasty to assume Dylan hadn't been involved in drugs after all. "It's a painkiller."

"Makes you loopier than morphine, yeah. But downers like Oxy was never Jason's style," Ranger said. "He might have got a little wired on ice every now and then but lately he hadn't even been using that. He said he was clean the last time I saw him."

"I'm sorry."

"Don't feel bad for the man, that game had already ruined

him. The busted ankle he had? Nobody likes to remember he got that at the play-offs. If he'd been any use to the team the school wouldn't have given two shits about his grades, but after that injury—" Ranger snickered his old snicker. "You want to know the sorry part? Jason been allergic all his life to that sticky shit on the back of tape. Glue. What's the word?"

"Adhesive?"

"Bless you. Adhesive. That shit so much as grazed him, Jason got himself these awful red hives all on his skin. I'd seen it before."

Ranger drank.

"The cops up in Mexia say it must have been suicide, all the pills he took. But I want to know why he would have taped over his own mouth once he'd swallowed the damn bottle. Because sure enough he had them hives all the way around his cheeks. They let me see his wrists. His ankles. Same thing. Somebody had trussed him up like a pig and tore all the tape off when they was done, Whitley. I'm sure it were an accident."

Joel said, "There's been a lot of those lately. Officer Grissom suddenly took up smoking last night and forgot to turn off his oxygen."

"Hmph."

"I know that Grissom arrested your brother in July for dealing drugs with KT Staler. The deputy had an accident on his horse a few weeks later. And then last night, after he started talking again, his house burns down. Am I crazy for wondering if these aren't quite coincidences?"

"I'll never understand that Grissom. He knew better."

"Knew better than to arrest one of the golden boys?"

A grackle squawked outside. The drone of cicadas resonated in the small crevices of Joel's ears. The only decoration Joel saw anywhere in the shack was a long shelf of football trophies that had gone dull with age. One had lost its arm.

"Wesley said you were one of them," Joel said.

"Mores was fruitier than banana bread." Ranger spat a glob of snot into a tissue and dropped it to his feet. He watched it fall. "There's some boys in Pettis County you just don't touch, Whitley. As you discovered."

On the television, a reporter on assignment from the city, a woman with better skin than anyone in miles, was interviewing a little cluster of men standing around a portable grill near the football field's end zone. Despite all the chaos of yesterday, despite the fact that the team's quarterback had died on Monday and another had been arrested on felony murder charges, the headline at the bottom of the screen read 5 TIPS FOR PERFECT "BISON" BURGERS.

"Everything that happened to me in the park with Grissom—did you have some hand in that? Was that the price I paid for throwing a punch at you?"

"I hated you something awful." Ranger looked exhausted, like he'd spent a decade kicking through sleepless nights. "I shouldn't be talking about this."

"Why? Why protect these people?" Joel made a show of appraising the filthy kitchen, the bed. "They've clearly taken such good care of you."

A long silence. The TV flickering blue and white.

Ranger's scarred face took on an eerie sheen when he smiled. He made a noise that could have been a chuckle. "Hell with it—what sort of fucks do I give now? Ten years ago, I had Jason take care of things for me while I was overseas. I knew that Troy was digging himself a hole of debt the size of Mexico with all the tweak he was using and he was eyeing an exit. Jason and me, we knew where to get some money to pay off Troy's debt—somebody big owed us a fortune, you wouldn't want to hear why. And to top it all off, I knew a deputy who would just *love* to hear a tip about a young boy waiting all alone in a shady park. It worked out well for all parties involved. Present company excluded of course."

"And the pictures?"

"Whitley, it was all just meanness." Ranger flipped his mangled hand. "We used to run this town, Jason and me. Not that it's done me any good."

Joel rested his beer on the ground. He couldn't drink any more. "Then what happened to Troy?"

"He left town that Friday, the night you was arrested. That was our deal. God only knows why his girl didn't report him missing for so long. He was out of work, they was separated, maybe she didn't know he'd left. Tell me something, Joel. I've always wondered—did Troy come to the park that night after all?"

Joel remembered the sound of tires pulling away. "He did. He must have seen Grissom's cruiser and known it was too late."

"Troy cared for you, you know. He didn't want to do any of it, he was crackling on a bad connection from the other side of the world saying, 'Can't we come to some other terms?'" Ranger rose, headed for the kitchen. "But I had him by the balls and he knew it. I wanted your head on a silver platter."

Joel caught something in Ranger's voice. A small piece clicked into place. "You were jealous of us. You knew we were happy."

Ranger stopped, his arm inside the rusted fridge.

"He's dead, irregardless," Ranger said. "Jason and the others made to pay back the Mexicans but the money was way overdue. Benicio had done took care of your boy already."

The smell of this cramped, sweaty shack was making Joel nauseous. He hadn't come here to learn any of this. He would have been happier not knowing.

If you don't go tonight there's no stopping it.

Joel cleared his throat. "KT Staler said selling drugs around here was your idea."

Ranger scoffed. "The drugs have been going on for ages. It's simple—just use some of that golden boy immunity to sell product the cops won't hassle you for. After Troy went away,

Jason thought it was a brilliant idea and started selling with the Staler boy's sister—that crazy bitch, Savannah—until the two of thems got busted on the other side of the county line, where they wasn't safe. Fast forward nine years, Jason gets out of Huntsville, comes back to town, finds out pretty quick KT's looking for money to move away and somehow KT roped Garrett into selling with him. Jason didn't tell the boys how things had ended up with Troy, of course. I told all three of them it was about the dumbest idea a man could ask for, but the money was too damn good, I guess. Jason said they'd be cleverer than last time, they wouldn't get their product from the Mexicans. He'd heard all about this new thing when he was locked up. You can buy drugs off the internet now—did you know that? They call it the *dark web*.

"Those little bag boys always work the same. KT would get the product delivered off the internet to somewhere here in town. He and Garrett picked it up. Garrett sold some to folks around the county and kept some for their little gang. KT would drive a chunk of it up to Dallas and hand it off to some hotshot he knew up there—KT must have a stack of money the size of a house. Jason skipped town after the three of them got busted by Grissom in July but the arrest didn't stop the younger boys. Jason was turning over a new leaf in Austin. He was out a few grand worth of product before the arrest so I guess he finally got desperate enough. He must have thought he could sneak into town during Friday's game and make off with some money while they was playing. Fucking idiot." Ranger pointed a scarred finger at Joel as if this were his fault. "Jason *knew* the old boys had gotten tired of him. He'd outspent his loyalty, you know."

Joel struggled to make sense of this. "And you think Jason was killed for *that*? Just for coming back to town?"

Ranger burped. "This place is old, Whitley. It has rules."

Joel's eyes drifted to the TV screen, where the reporter

with the perfect skin was talking to a man in a cowboy hat that shaded his face. The man was stationed near the football stands, a meat smoker belching beside him. Standing behind the smoker, staring at the camera with its glassy black eyes, was the stuffed bison Joel had seen on the highway last Friday as he'd made his way into town.

imissedyou.

Joel went very still when he looked at Ranger again. He was smiling, but there was no joy in it. Something had come loose inside the man. No light from the TV could penetrate the hole where his eye should be.

"Ranger—" Joel heard anxiety thrumming in his voice: he needed to get out of this house. "How does Dylan fit into all of this?"

"You really ain't asking the right questions here, Whitley. Why ain't you asking what broke me? Who killed that friend of Parter's? Who invited Troy—"

"Parter?" Joel leaned back. "Coach Parter? A friend of his died?"

Ranger laughed. He sounded incredulous. "You mean you never heard of Corwin Broadlock? I thought all that business with him is what started you down this road in the first place. The boy was just like your brother."

At the sound of Broadlock's name, static began to creep through the TV's muted speakers in a long, mad whisper, the radio-whisper, the dream-whisper—*imissedyou*—and it set to work inside Joel's skull.

On the television the stuffed bison seemed to cock its head at him like a bird.

KIMBRA

Heading 2 uncle jarvis's house early (store slow!!) will see
you Sun

Kimbra was so surprised by her father's message she forgot to slip her phone back into the top of her cheerleader's
uniform. She stood, stiff and silent, as the Bison team burst
through a panel of painted paper spread across the cafeteria's
exit and the other cheerleaders screamed and the band played
and the students lining the hallway shouted themselves hoarse.
The Bison Stampede, another ancient ritual for the Perlin
game, and Kimbra had forgotten how to cheer.

She, Dashandre and April had been stationed by the doors of
the cafeteria, meaning that by the time the Bison's starting line
had reached the gym at the other end of the school the three
of them were still stuck clapping for the backbenchers whose
names people barely remembered. This would have bothered
Kimbra enormously last year, back when she still cared about

this school and this town, back before her boyfriend started keeping Real Secrets from her and she had Real Life Problems. Now she was too preoccupied. Her father's message was just the latest strange turn in a day that had already made her tipsy with unease.

Even knowing that KT had been returned home, Kimbra had awoken this morning desperate to know what it was the boy had been hiding from her all this time. She had been eager to help Joel Whitley, certain—for reasons she couldn't quite define—that these Bright Lands he'd asked about were the key to the great mystery that had grown up around her.

Yet Whiskey and T-Bay, so helpful yesterday, had ignored her after first period. A few of the girls on the squad had shrugged when Kimbra had murmured a simple question— "Have you ever heard of some place some of the boys go? Somewhere they don't talk about?"—and given her blank looks that she took to be genuine.

Despite all her care and discretion, Garrett Mason had caught her eye in biology, had brought a bruised finger to his lips without a word. *Shh.*

Then, at lunch, KT had texted, his first message to her since last Friday, and all he wrote was lets leave now. She hadn't responded, even when he'd started blowing up her phone.

And now here was this odd message from her father. He always went quail hunting on the weekends, leaving town after the game so he could be at her uncle Jarvis's house outside Sprickstown in time to sleep and still be up well before dawn, when the quail started to rouse. Yet today he had apparently decided to miss the game altogether.

Her father never missed a game.

Something bad is going on

"Yo, K-K-Kimbra. You got a second?"

It was Benny Garcia, the backbencher's backbencher, standing like a dwarf in his oversize pads and fussing with his gloves.

The opening bars of the pep rally's warm-up number were already echoing from the gym.

"What is it?" Kimbra said.

Benny only nodded at the empty cafeteria. She studied his big green eyes through the grill of his helmet. He looked like he had something important to tell her.

She made a motion for Dashandre and April to go on to the gym without her, followed Benny through the scraps of paper that still hung from the cafeteria's doorway. Information—like money—was irresistible to her.

"Has your d-d-dad s-said anything about it this w-week?" Benny said.

"About quail hunting?"

"N-n-no. Ab-b-bout the B-B-Bright Lands." When B-B-Benny tried to whisper, spittle flew from his lips, clung to the bars of his helmet's grill. "G-Garrett said if I t-told the c-cops Jamal wanted a c-c-condom at the game then they'd t-t-take me there tonight."

Kimbra struggled to see what this had to do with her father. Nothing, she insisted. Nothing. "So?"

"They're t-t-taking Luke! Luke!" Benny pointed down the empty hallway. "B-But I h-heard it was your d-d-dad runs that p-party. He m-must have t-told you wh-where t-to find it, right?"

Down the hall the pep rally's warm-up number repeated: they were waiting for her.

Kimbra hardly heard it. She didn't care. Suddenly she didn't care about much of anything.

Benny took an anxious step away from her, another. "F-forget I said it," he said, and jogged down the hall.

Go. Go now.

Don't think. Don't ask.

"Don't let those guys fuck you up."

Something bad is going on

Heading 2 uncle jarvis's house early
Go.
She didn't bother to change out of her cheer uniform. She took off down the hall, pulled loose her phone, texted KT:
Let's do it.
u mean now?
now.
u ok?
you want to do this or not?
A pause. He wrote:
Gimme 30 min. i gotta say bye 2 mommers.
I'll get the money.
She reached her locker, pulled out her backpack and gym bag, looked for anything she might need. She grabbed an extra lip balm. A pack of gum. She would ask KT everything when they were safely across the county line, she told herself. Maybe when they hit New Mexico. Maybe never.
She shut her locker and saw Bethany Tanner standing a few feet away, watching her with an ugly mix of anger and concern. Sweet fuck, the girl looked so exhausted even the sequins of her singlet seemed to have dulled. Bethany had spent every minute since her loud confession in the parking lot yesterday morning doing her best to preserve her reputation. Considering the fact she was walking the halls alone, without Jasmine, her trusty sidekick, Kimbra suspected Bethany's efforts hadn't been successful. Things at the top of the pyramid didn't look good.
"We're waiting for you," Bethany said.
Kimbra tossed her lock into her bag. "I'm leaving."
"Leaving?" Bethany took a step forward. "You can't *leave.* This is the biggest day of the fucking season."
"Watch me."
Kimbra didn't have time for Bethany anymore. If she wanted to dance and cheer while boys were getting killed

and running away and telling lies about her father then Bethany could—

She grabbed Kimbra's arm.

"You have a *job* to do."

Jesus Christ. Kimbra dropped her bag and brought her heel down on Bethany's foot, twisted when the girl squealed and tossed her into a locker. The metal boomed through the empty hall. Bethany released her.

It was almost satisfying—Kimbra had wanted to give Bethany Tanner a nice shiner for years. She took a quick step away, out of Bethany's reach, but Tanner made no move to grab her again. The girl only stared at Kimbra, rubbed the back of her head. For the first time in her life, Kimbra saw Bethany on the verge of tears.

B-B-Benny spoke briefly in her mind. Fine. Kimbra would be a good person. "If you want to be useful for once in your life, tell Luke Evers not to go tonight, wherever he's going," she told Bethany. "Tell him it's dangerous."

And with that, Kimbra turned on her heel and strode away. For once, finally, she had had the last word.

JOEL

He retraced his route toward town and checked his phone for news from Clark. No messages, no service. Fifteen minutes earlier, Ranger had refused to say another word. Whatever had motivated him to reveal so much to Joel—spite or revenge against this town or a desire to see justice done for Jason—had run dry as abruptly as it had sprung up. The man had screwed his mouth shut, stared at the television, played with his beer, not even glancing up when Joel had slipped from the shack without saying goodbye.

So where did that leave him? He had gone to Ranger's to discover one thing: whether KT had been lying and Dylan had been involved in drugs after all. Joel had harbored a long shot theory that perhaps, if Dylan had been murdered because of KT's involvement with narcotics, then Garrett Mason, KT's apparent business partner, might have been involved in the murder—that boy with his big bruised fist sure seemed to have plenty to hide. Perhaps, Joel had thought, Garrett Mason might even have been the boy KT had spoken of Dylan traveling to the coast with; it sounded absurd, certainly, but what else did he have to go on?

A rabbit darted across the road. Joel slapped his forehead with his palm. It was right there: KT had told Clark and Joel this morning that Dylan and his boy had gone away on their weekends together. But Garrett had been arrested with KT *in Bentley* on a weekend that KT and Dylan were both supposed to be out of town.

Joel sighed. Another theory for the scrap pile.

He tapped out a quick note to Clark on his phone, hit Send, wondered if it would ever reach her.

He thought of Dylan, of his brother telling Joel five days before his murder that he couldn't sleep. Dylan had added that he couldn't *go to the bright lands* anymore. And yet had Dylan gone to them regardless, whatever they were, the night he died?

"What we did was nothing *compared to the shit that goes on in this town,"* Wesley had said.

it's like i hear this town talking when i sleep.

Broken men and frightened men. A missing shirt, a bloody jacket, a bloody sock. Escort ads and drugs and dick pics, oh my. Bag boys, old boys, golden boys, gone. A hate crime or a love crime. A shallow creek, an iron slab, a pit.

A warning etched with the point of a knife: GET OUT NOW FAG.

He drove until he found cell service and called Clark. The call went to voice mail. For the first time that day, Joel wondered just how powerful this darkness from the pit really was. Had it done something to Clark's father so it could get her out of town? To get Joel alone, just like this?

Nothing seemed impossible anymore. If Clark's mom was to

be believed then they were dealing with a force a lot older than Bentley or Pettis County or this whole prejudiced country.

"This place is old, Whitley. It has rules."

Joel googled Corwin Broadlock, the name Ranger had mentioned before abruptly shutting down. His phone's browser choked and stuttered on the tenuous connection that reached him in the open country.

He was nearly back to town by the time he found the old newspaper article.

STAR PLAYER'S WHEREABOUTS REMAIN UNKNOWN.

Joel read the story—it was little more than a blurry scan of an old page on the Waco *Tribune-Herald*'s website—and his heartbeat quickened.

On April 5th, 1976, Corwin Broadlock, the wide-receiver who brought the small town of Bentley such pride in their first championship game, ran away from home without warning. Mr. Broadlock has not been seen since.

The story stated that Broadlock's parents had received a letter one month after his disappearance, urging them not to worry about his whereabouts. The letter bore a Miami postmark, but no trace of the boy had been found there. Corwin's parents insisted that the content and tone of the letter sounded nothing like their son but there was little the police could do.

"It's an absolute shock," says Mr. Broadlock's former teammate Grady Mayfield. Close friend Tom Parter adds, "I thought these were the best years of our lives. I can only hope Corwin's found whatever he needs wherever he went."

joel im sorry but i cant stay in bentley right now

At the bottom of the article was a faded photo of the full Bentley Bison team and cheer squad, circa 1975. The picture was all orange light and seeping green jerseys. Joel pulled the convertible to the side of the road, pinched his screen to zoom in. He identified Corwin from the names at the bottom of the photo: a very tall boy with a brilliant smile that cut through forty years of deteriorating film stock. Gorgeous. Happy. Just like Dylan. Blond, not brown haired, and taller, sure, but possessing the same persuasive glee, an obvious pleasure with his casual power.

Next to him, arm over Corwin's shoulder, was a young Coach Parter, hair down to his ears, burly even at eighteen. And smiling from Broadlock's other side was Mr. Harlan Boone, today's county attorney, already standing (even as a teenager) with the straighter back of a man deigning to submit to public service. The three boys—Boone and Broadlock and Parter—were clearly tight. They held themselves apart from the rest of the team, a trio of golden boys.

Son of a bitch. Son of a bitch.

Farther down the line of players Joel spotted "former teammate" Grady Mayfield—a man who had told Clark he *"hadn't had dreams like this"* since he was in school—giving the camera a thumbs-up. A few players away stood young Keith *"I weren't ever invited in my day either"* Grissom, a scowl on his thin lips, already looking mean and permanently disappointed. Among the cheerleaders standing in the photo's wings, Joel spotted a luminous girl who could have been the Starsha he'd dated ten years ago (if that Starsha had ever bothered with her hair): MARGO DELBARDO, the citation read. Joel marveled at her. What had happened to Clark's mother to make her the nervous, limpid woman he'd always known growing up?

Joel's eye fell across a short, scrawny boy with a wispy mustache standing alone at the end of the Bison's line, so shy he seemed to shrink in front of the camera. TOBY LOTT, the caption read.

Mr. Lott. The friendly cartoon man who had been the sole source of decency to Joel in the wake of the scandal ten years ago. The only man in town who hadn't flinched at the sight of Joel upon his return. How had Joel never thought to ask Mr. Lott about any of this?

He loaded Google Maps, intending to call the hardware store, but his service had died again. *Fuck it.* He was only a few miles from Bentley. Joel tapped out another quick message to Clark, dropped his phone between his legs and sped toward town.

KIMBRA

A steady stream of cars passed her in the highway's other lane, all of them heading for the field as she drove toward South Street. Her Bisonette singlet pinched her tits like it always did but for once Kimbra didn't mind. It was hard to believe that after three years on the squad (and after misplacing God knew how many uniforms) this was the last time she would ever be seen so spangly and green.

Because she suspected she wouldn't have much cause to wear a beaded singlet in Hollywood. She ran a thumb along a seam. Maybe she would become a costume designer, she thought, a stylist, one of those people who hide halfway down the movie credits. She saw them on Instagram. They seemed to make okay money.

God knew she'd need it.

Goodbye, creepy Flats, she thought. *Goodbye, vacant lot where the church used to be. Goodbye, Bentley.*

Four hours before kickoff and already South Street was deserted. The parking spaces were all empty. Signs hung in the windows of the Egg House, of Mr. Jack's Steaks: CLOSED FOR GAME. She flinched when the deputy guarding the ruined bank waved at her from the mouth of the busted vault. She prayed he didn't try to stop her.

She parked in front of the hardware store and looked through the front windows. Crazy. No lights from the back, no movement. Her father really was gone.

And yet even without him here, even with the deputy's back to her, why did Kimbra feel like she was being watched?

She didn't want an explanation. She hurried down the alleyway to the back door and punched the code into the beeping alarm, left the door ajar—she wouldn't be here long. She flipped on the lights, scanned the top shelves of the old paint corner in the stockroom. She spotted Canary Yellow #65, just a little too far back on the shelf for her father to reach it easily. Right where she'd left it.

Kimbra retrieved the squeaky little stepladder and pulled down the can that contained close to twelve thousand dollars in cash.

She popped the lid loose and took a long smell of the fragrant money inside. God almighty, did she love it. After years of growing up just this side of bankrupt—her father may have been winning the battle against Walmart but Bentley had already lost the war with globalization or global warming or whatever had taken all the jobs away—Kimbra loved her money just like this: tucked together into little folds, growing like a green sea creature she fed with her time and her care and her savvy. Loved money not to spend, not to display, but to *have*.

The cash had been hard earned. It represented every dollar her father had paid her to work at the store, plus KT's eight trips to Dallas over the summer, minus the money his mother had stolen in the spring, and minus also the outlay for fresh product. Asking Dylan to hold the cash for a time had been Kimbra's idea after KT's mom stole the first couple thousand. When Dylan bugged out because that Darren guy saw him with the cash, this paint can too had been Kimbra's idea. The trips to the coast, the invented half brother, Floyd Tillery, even the fake address that KT's guy in Dallas had given to Officer Clark on Monday: they had all been Kimbra's ideas. Because she—*they*—had to get out of this place.

Twelve thousand dollars. Kimbra had wanted to leave town with more, had wanted enough to walk into a car dealership and pull out a stack of bills and buy herself a vehicle that would never break down, that would get them out west with no fear of failure.

Well. She and KT would have to take their chances in her creaking Pontiac. If things got tight on the road to Los Angeles, Kimbra supposed he could do some of the work she had long suspected he'd gotten up to in Dallas.

The girl wasn't an idiot. Every weekend when KT went on a business trip, he'd left Bentley with the same amount of product, taken it to a guy he said he'd met online—Kimbra didn't know who, nor did she want to. Then, after hanging in the city for the weekend to keep up the front that he was at the coast, KT would return Sunday evening. The only problem? He always left with the same amount of product, but returned with different sums of cash.

He'd explained this away by saying that sometimes his guy was a little short of money, and then sometimes he was paying him back what he owed, but Kimbra had never quite bought this. When KT had first come to her with his plan he'd sworn—sworn up and down—that he wasn't actually *dealing* drugs like Garrett, just *carrying* them to someone in the city who wanted a steady, white-skinned supplier who could carry a large amount of product unmolested up the highway.

"When was the last time I got pulled over?" KT had told her with a laugh. *"You know how special I am to them?"*

So if this guy in Dallas was such a big shot, such a sure thing, how come he never had their pre-agreed amount?

Kimbra knew that KT left Bentley with the same amount of product on every trip because she had been the one to unpack it. Every other week a plain brown box arrived at the hardware store with a return address in Seattle. Her father never unpacked any boxes, thank God. If he did, he might have discovered a vacuum-sealed foil bag that weighed a little under two ounces and bore the cryptic words SEALED FOR MY FRESHNESS.

Kimbra had never opened a single pouch. She didn't want to know what was inside. When KT had come to her in the spring with a half-formed plan he had hatched with Garrett Mason, that had been her one stipulation: she never wanted to see whatever it was they were moving.

So if KT had driven to Dallas with the same amount of product on Fridays and returned with different sums of money on Sundays, Kimbra knew that in between KT hadn't just been "waiting for his guy to sell our shit," as he'd told her. No. KT was earning extra on top. The sight of the escorting ad that Whiskey Brazos sent her yesterday had solved a number of suspicions. Kimbra would recognize that dick anywhere. *Ah well.*

She wasn't certain how she felt, knowing her man had been turning tricks. She told herself she should be bothered by it, should be worried about STDs and the cops, should be consumed with fear at the knowledge that her man might not be as straight as she'd always assumed, but in all honesty she felt nothing but gratitude. He'd made her more money; it might be the most selfless thing (perhaps the *only* selfless thing) he'd ever done for her. Escorting, to Kimbra's mind, was crafty, dangerous, stupid and useful: did any four words better summarize the love of her life?

She wondered how it had started, wondered how her man had first discovered he could stomach whatever it was he had done for this money. Even if he was some kind of queer (difficult as that was for her to imagine), wouldn't it take a special sort of damage for a boy like KT to perform the things promised in that ad she'd sent to Joel Whitley? She couldn't imagine it was easy on the body or the brain. Had he gotten practice, she wondered, somewhere close to home?

Which led her to another question: if the escorting ad she'd seen was KT's (again, she would know that dick anywhere), why had KT put Dylan's face on his own listing? It smacked of some sort of revenge, but what could Dylan have done to deserve it? She wondered if that vengeance had anything to do with the fact KT had been snorting up half of his product all summer. Because thieving mothers or not, there should have been *much* more money in this can than twelve grand.

All week long, Kimbra had thought she wanted to know what secrets were eating her poor beautiful boyfriend so badly he'd started using (again). She'd been certain that if she knew, she might be able to help him, like always. She'd thought she could find a solution to it the way she had found the paint can and the half brother and every other answer she'd come up with when KT had come running to her, crying because the world was so hard.

It was confounding, the loathsome gravity at work in her heart. Kimbra knew that she was clever, reasonable, cautious, and yet against this one footballer with the little freckle on his upper lip, his careful hands, the glimpses she sometimes caught of the better, gentler boy who lived inside him, none of Kimbra's caution did her a bit of good. Look at them, the girl with the bankrupt family and the eighteen-year-old footballer with the drug habit and a sideline servicing men for money. The town's tabloid sweethearts, Dylan Whitley and Bethany Tanner, seen through a busted filter. With some mixture of relief and resignation, Kimbra had lately begun to tell herself that she and KT were made for each other. A part of her—a grotesque, powerful part—would always be the plain girl who had been stunned two years ago when that handsome, funny, dangerous boy had first privileged her with his attention.

Kimbra sealed the paint can shut, readied herself to go. A thought finally occurred to her: maybe she had other options. Look at all she'd uncovered by herself this week. Think of all she could accomplish without a man dragging her down. Of how much further a single person could stretch twelve thousand dollars in sunny California.

Maybe—maybe—when she reached the turnoff for KT's house Kimbra would carry straight on.

But at that moment she noticed something glinting behind an old can of spray paint deep in the back of the shelf.

Because she noticed the glinting thing, Kimbra didn't hear the faint sound of the door opening wider behind her.

The top shelf was very deep. She balanced carefully on the tips of her sneakers, braced one hand on the lip of the shelf and was just able to grab the little glimmer of green that rested against the far wall.

It was a Bisonette's singlet, just like the one she was wearing now. Just like the ones she was always misplacing.

Kimbra turned the singlet over. Sure enough, the name LOTT was printed on the back.

How on earth had it wound up here, covered in dust? The singlet had been in a pile near the wall, like it had been tossed atop the shelf and forgotten. But who would have stolen one of her singlets and misplaced it way up here?

Who else had access to this room?

B-B-Benny Garcia stuttered in her head: *"I h-heard it was your d-d-dad runs that p-party."*

Kimbra didn't want to know what this was about. There were some rumors she didn't want confirmed.

She turned.

She saw the man waiting behind her.

JOEL

His jaw throbbed where Wesley Mores had struck it last night. His head ached in the heat. And, worst of all, the skin of his ankle burned where the knife had been strapped all day. He wondered if it was some kind of allergic reaction, something his sweat had drawn out of the Velcro. Maybe a response to adhesive, just like Jason Ovelle had suffered.

By the time he reached Lott's Hardware he was still clawing at the skin through his sock. He tugged loose the strap of the knife, just for a moment.

The store, Joel saw, was already closed. Of course. The president of the booster club would leave for the field hours before the start of the game. GO BISON GOOD LUCK EVERS read a handwritten sign in the window. Joel climbed from the car, pressed his hands to the door's glass, saw a little strip of light way in the back of the store.

South Street was silent. No cars, no music leaking through

cracked windows. From the ruined bank came the steady drip of a busted pipe. Joel's feet made the old wooden boards of the storefront's porch pop.

He saw light spilling through an open door in the alley. A man emerged from the back of the hardware store, a man whom Joel had no reason to suspect of anything.

The man looked panicked. He shouted, "The girl! She's bleeding bad."

"What? Who?"

"Kimbra! Hurry, please, she's—"

But Joel was already running, fueled by a sudden swell of guilt and shame. He'd put her in danger, just as he'd feared.

Out on the quiet street, there was only a soft thump when Joel was struck on the back of the head. Another thump when he hit the ground. The boards of the storefronts rattled and squeaked when the ground shifted, when something beneath them rose a little closer to the surface, let out a rumble of what just might have been satisfaction at these fresh drops of blood, at this sudden splash of fear.

And then silence again.

LUKE

Luke had never heard anything so loud. The drums rattled the lights of the field house. The roar of the crowd floated, trapped, in his open locker like the ocean in a shell. His ears still rang from the screams that had gone up when he'd correctly called heads at the coin toss. All of last night's misgivings had left him when that coin had slapped the ref's palm. Luke could see the future: glory, state championships, his face tagged in other people's Instagram feeds. Friends.

The hip-hop on the field house's soundbar was cranked down. Coach Wesford and Coach Ruiz shouted their speeches, and now big Coach Parter stood in the center of a ring of boys and said, "I ain't a man to tell you what Jesus wants. I'm a man to tell you what *I* want and what *I* want is for you to take these goddamn Stallions to the grass and *keep* them in the grass."

"Yes, sir!"

"Put 'em in the fucking hospital!"

"Yes, sir!"

All eyes on Parter, wide pupils, Adderall and Oxy, their hands squeezed in their gloves, black paint dulling their cheeks.

"Because this is the only goddamn game you've got. You ain't got school—school we'll take care of. A job? That's later. You boys, all you boys have is this."

The boys piled out of the field house and corralled beneath the goal. The Bisonettes, stacked atop each other's shoulders, had formed a wall to conceal them. Two pairs of girls—Bethany and Alisha, Jasmine and April (where, Luke wondered, was Kimbra Lott?)—held up the wide swathe of painted paper the team would tear through. A tall ghostly Bison was all that stood between them and the field.

The marching band caught someone's signal. A moment later everyone in the Bentley stands was singing.

"My herd, my glory; my autumn years, my rightful story."

And suddenly all forty Bison were staring at him. Staring at Luke. Of course. Somehow, without realizing it, Luke had been brought right to the front edge of their scrum, just where Dylan had always stood. And what would Dylan say now?

Dylan would say, *What are you doing, Luke?*

Garrett nodded to him. Mitchell. Tomas. The Turner twins. His boys. His brothers.

"Don't fuck up!" Luke shouted.

"Hallelujah!" the Bison shouted back.

Luke turned to the shaky wall of paper, bent low and let out a roar.

JAMAL

Outside Jamal's cell, Buddy "The Real Voice of Central Texas Sports" Laurie sputtered and popped through a tiny radio one of the deputies had brought in earlier and left on the hallway's floor. The deputy, Jamal had noted at the time, hadn't brought the radio close enough to the cell's bars for him to adjust the signal. Or use it as a weapon.

"And it looks like Evers is still struggling to make good on that extraordinary rush the Bison enjoyed at kickoff," Buddy said. "We're closing in on the end of the first quarter and the Bison have yet to put a point on the board."

The door at the end of the hallway opened with a squeal. Jamal recognized the smell of cinnamon cologne and rose from his cot. It was Mr. Irons, a bulging brown bag in his hand, followed by Deputy Jones.

Jones dialed down the radio, unlocked Jamal's cell without a word.

Irons stepped inside and pushed the bag into Jamal's hands. "Get dressed."

Jamal stared at the unlocked door. He opened the bag wide enough to see inside it the clothes he'd been wearing at his arrest: leather jacket, jeans, Bison T-shirt.

"You can lace up your shoes in the car," Irons said. "Hurry now. There's no telling when the word will reach them."

"Word about what?"

"Just hustle, will you?"

Jamal eyed the blinking security camera in the hall. A muted cheer came from the radio—Perlin had scored another touchdown.

"They won't just let me leave," he said, but already Jones was stepping away, taking a sudden interest in his boots.

"They don't have a choice," Irons huffed, handed Jamal a sheaf of paper. The words *ARREST WARRANT* were written fat and curly across the top. Below it read:

To any sheriff or officer of police, you are hereby commanded to arrest: JANAL WILLIAM REYNOLDS and bring him before…

"My middle name's Davis," Jamal said, blinking slowly at Irons. Only a day in a holding cell and already his mind had gone gummy. "And my name's spelled—"

"You think I've been at the country club all day?" Irons pulled the jeans from the bag Jamal had dropped. "Hurry now. The judge in Austin only owes me the one favor. Boone will file a corrected warrant the second he gets the news. I plan to have you halfway to Georgia by then."

With a sudden, violent lurch Jamal felt the gears in his head catch, the lights flicker back on. He wrenched off the flimsy scrubs they'd given him to wear, kicked himself into his jeans, shrugged on the T-shirt and the jacket. He was getting out of here.

"We've got a long drive ahead of us," Irons said.

They followed Jones through the empty sheriff's station. "It wasn't just the arrest warrant," Irons continued. "The document of probable cause, the report on the discovery of the sock—shot all to shit, the entire thing. That Mayfield, he's been in this business how long, twenty years?"

"Twenty-three," Jones said, unable to keep a little lilt of satisfaction from his voice.

"You'd think he could type a statement by now."

"Nobody bothered to read it?" Jamal said, still not entirely convinced this wasn't another vivid dream.

Irons said, "Somebody was in a hurry to get you locked up."

Past the empty front desk, into the little lobby with its flags and its low ceiling, through the glass doors.

And then he was outside, smelling the air of a clear night, looking up to see the sun all but gone and the thin streaks of cloud fading slowly from ember to ash. He wasn't sure he'd ever spent so long inside in his life.

"It's the Mercedes," Irons said without breaking stride. "Might be wise if you ride in the back until we're over the county line."

CLARK

She'd been trapped in traffic outside Houston for nearly an hour. She'd called Joel twenty times. She'd messaged his mother on Facebook, messaged Kimbra Lott and Bethany Tanner asking if they'd heard any word of his whereabouts. As Bison halftime approached on the radio, she picked up her phone and prayed she wasn't making a mistake.

Clark had wasted the day watching her father sleep. On the phone this morning outside KT Staler's house, a nursing home attendant had informed Clark that her father's condition had deteriorated all week, that he'd had difficulty sleeping, refused to eat, and finally this morning had attacked another patient.

"Difficulty sleeping?" Clark had said.

"Yes, ma'am," the nurse had told her. "You don't read your emails?"

When she'd finally arrived in Houston, the home told her they'd had to sedate him. "There were mitigating circumstances," a sweaty doctor informed her. "But if he lashes out again we'll have no choice but to release him."

Release him. Like a tiger. There was nowhere else she could put him. If not for the discount the home offered to retired veterans—and could you really be surprised, in a house stuffed full of old soldiers, if one of them threw a punch over a plate of cold toast?—Clark could never have afforded to keep him there.

She'd stayed at the nursing home all day, watching her father sleep off his Ativan. On smoke breaks throughout the afternoon she had checked her phone but only received one message from Joel.

Just left Ranger M's house. Jason O is dead. Garrett/Dylan connection dubious. I think I know a little more about the Bright Lands. Call me.

She'd called. Joel's phone had gone straight to voice mail. Just like it did an hour later. And an hour after that.

Around seven thirty, Clark had found a radio in her father's room and tuned it to the game. When the marching band finally commenced with "My Herd, My Glory," she'd heard his breathing quicken, saw his eyelids flutter open.

He'd not looked happy to see her. "Did you shut them off?"

Oh boy. "Shut off what, Dad?"

"The lights!" he said to her sharply. "Those damn queer lights! Fuck it, girl, you *know*."

"Dad, Dad, please, listen to me." She grabbed his thin hand, squeezed until he shut up and stared at her. "I need to ask you something important."

He blinked: foggy eyes, the other hand scratching at the bedsheet.

"Dad, do you remember all that stuff Mom used to talk about back in the day? About the monster in the trench, and the dreams and—"

"Crazy as a fucking loon, that was her. Do you know how

hard it was living with a woman who said the ghost of her first love would keep her company at night? A woman who always knew exactly where you'd been because her favorite man was always whispering things in her fucking ear? Fuck him, fuck her, fuck me."

Clark frowned. "Her first love?"

"The boy on the team, the one ran off! She swore and swore, oh no, he ain't run off, 'he's dead in a concrete box,' whatever the fuck that is. 'It's why the catfish came to town,' she said. 'It came to drink his blood.'"

"Is that what it wants then?" Clark swallowed. "The… catfish—it wants blood?"

"Troy asked me the same goddamn questions right before you threw him out." Her father grinned. "You really ran him through the wringer that night, you know. Poor boy hadn't been able to sleep for a week when you went screaming at him like a banshee."

She flinched away.

"You think I went deaf that evening you called him over?"

"Then what did you tell him?"

"I told him his mother was the biggest mistake I ever made in my life."

Clark stood, put a hand on her father's arm. She said calmly, "You hit another soul in this home, you'll be walking the street."

What did Joel mean about the Garrett/Dylan connection being "dubious"? Everything about Garrett Mason—that giant boy who seemed to lurk at every edge of this investigation—was dubious.

A second message from Joel hadn't arrived until ten minutes ago, when Clark was stuck in traffic, though she saw that the message was timestamped 3:25 p.m.—over five hours before. Clark suspected Joel had sent the message at a moment when both he and she had no service. She knew from long experience that messages could become trapped in limbo around Bentley.

It was a link to a news article. Clark felt her scalp prickle when she saw the headline.

STAR PLAYER'S WHEREABOUTS REMAIN UNKNOWN.

There was her mother, looking happier than Clark had ever seen.

And there was her mother's first love. Corwin Broadlock.

"Her favorite man was always whispering things in her fucking ear."

She called Mayfield. It went to voice mail. She hung up, deliberated—she, like Joel, wondered if whatever force had been tormenting them all week might not have invented this little diversion to drag her miles from town—and rang a new number.

"Pettis County Sheriff's Department."

"Browder?" Clark said, crawling around a nasty wreck on the highway outside Houston.

"Clark? Oh Christ, Clark. Fuck me for drawing the squawk box tonight. I've got catastrophes every which way."

The tingling heat spread down her neck. "Catastrophes?"

"I got Mayfield heading to a gas leak all the way over in Rattichville. I thought Jones was supposed to be guarding that bank but he won't get on the horn so now *I'm* heading to a wreck in Lockpoint, the damn constables say they've never seen the likes of it. Clark, I swear those constables couldn't save grass from shit."

Clark held her phone against her shoulder, tapped her thumbnail to her teeth. She was suddenly very afraid for Mayfield. *"We inherited this town,"* he'd told her, as if it excused sabotaging an investigation. But then he'd worked her shift, he'd left hard proof on her desk that the department was covering up for the Bison's golden boys. And now he wasn't answering his phone.

And neither, apparently, was Deputy Jones. The man who'd last been seen with Jason Ovelle while he was still alive.

"Any of these catastrophes have to do with Joel Whitley?"

"Not that I know of. I saw his car outside the hardware store a bit ago. Want me to run back and check if he's there when I'm done with this pileup?"

Clark saw the highway clearing.

"I thought these were the best years of our lives," Coach Parter had said in that article Joel had sent.

Coach Parter, who had been so quick to defend Garrett Mason this morning.

She stepped on the gas.

"Don't worry about it," she told Browder. "I'll be there soon."

KIMBRA

Her head ached where she'd been struck; her back had gone numb from lying on the stockroom's concrete floor. She heard a knock on the back door of the hardware store. She flexed her shoulders, stretched her arms and legs, but it was no good: she was tied up tighter than a roast.

The door opened. Garrett Mason spoke from outside. "They said you needed me. I got here as quick as I could."

The other man said, "About time. Go get your truck."

There was a low moan from somewhere to her left.

"Fuck," Garrett said. "He don't look right."

"You've seen worse."

A minute later Kimbra heard the sound of the truck rumbling down the alleyway.

"...folks, we're only ten minutes into the second half and it's already hard to tell if this little Garcia boy is either brave or crazy," Buddy Laurie said from a crackling radio. "But he's throwing himself at these Perlin tackles like a dog at a bone."

"Christ, that's a tight fit," said Garrett, stepping back inside. "Grab his legs."

There was a rattling as someone was lifted off the ground. "He's heavier than his brother," Garrett said as he and the other man shuffled awkwardly to the door. A few minutes later they came back for her.

It was terrifying, of course, but being carried by her wrists and ankles didn't hurt as bad as she'd thought it would. Kimbra told herself that this was practically like tumbling practice. When they heaved her into the cold bed of the truck the zipper of her singlet dug into her spine.

"Grab that tarp."

"Is that a box of five-five-six?" Garrett said.

A pause. "Grab a couple of them too."

Kimbra heard a soft rattling noise that could only come from one thing: ammunition.

LUKE

The game was a nail-biter. After three quarters of deadlock, Perlin scored early in the fourth only to watch Stevey Turner stick a beautiful forty-yard running goal not three minutes later. Perlin paid him back hard, knocking both Turner boys to the ground. The twins brushed themselves off, and when Perlin took control of the ball again, stuttering Benny Garcia somehow took down a boy twice his size four times in a row and didn't give the Stallions an inch of room.

Luke had to hand it to Benny. When Garrett Mason had been called home to an emergency during halftime Luke had been certain the defensive line was fucked.

Now, with a minute-twenty left on the clock, Luke and the rest of the offense were on their second down, thirty yards from a goal and jogging slow, breathing hard. The Stallion defense seemed as fresh as could be. Luke shouted a play, bent down, clapped for the snap. The Stallions jumped the call and slammed into Whiskey Brazos before the ball was out of his hands.

The Bentley stands let out an awful noise, something between a boo and a hiss. All night long the town had screeched and screamed and bellowed like all three thousand people were in danger of losing their minds. Luke didn't want to imagine what this lunatic town would do to him if he spoiled their game.

The ref called the foul in Bentley's favor: five-yard penalty, still second down. The Bison shuffled up the field, Whiskey spat what looked like a mouthful of undigested chicken into the grass. The score stood 26–21 Perlin.

Luke's chest ached. His hands burned in their gloves. One minute two seconds left on the clock and he wondered how Dylan had done this, played entire games without a moment's peace. He wondered why neither of them had tried harder to stay friends.

One of the burly Stallion defensive tackles gave Luke a toothy smile from across the line that made Luke's nuts tighten in their cup.

"Blue Cherry Forty-Two," Luke called, the Bison's code for a sweeping play, and he caught the snap, faked a pass to Roy Birch—a receiver who'd been subbed in for KT—and instead slipped the ball into Mitchell Malacek's hands as the fullback sped past him. No good. A linebacker decked Mitchell before he could make it two yards.

Fifty-nine seconds. Third down. Luke called for a long pass, did his best to hurl the ball but felt his arm give out as he threw it. The ball flew low and for one ugly second it looked as if it might even stop in the hands of one of the Perlin guards. The ball grazed the guard's fingers, hit the ground. Incomplete. Thank you, Jesus.

Luke heard a heavy thud from very nearby and turned to see that the Perlin tackle with the hungry smile had come within a foot of sacking him, having been stopped only by stubby Danny Elgin's solar plexus. The Stallion tackle mouthed something to Luke as he climbed to his feet: *"You're mine."*

Forty-five seconds, the Bison's last down and the goal was miles away. Luke breathed, thumped his chest to keep his heart beating, looked at the faces of the boys assembled around him. What would Dylan do at this moment? He would make a call that Luke would challenge him on, would get in his face about. And what would Dylan do then? He would stick to the call. He would stick to the call and probably be right.

One fucking goal, Luke prayed. *Just give me one fucking goal.*

The clock ticked down. Luke called "Blue Cherry Forty-Three," and prayed the boys remembered the twist on the play the number represented. Judging by the incredulous looks on his teammates' faces he was being optimistic.

The Stallions certainly remembered the call from last time. They looked thrilled at the chance to stonewall the Bison again on the last play of the game.

The crowd went quiet as Luke bent low. "Forty-three!" he shouted again, clapped his hands, caught the snap.

Roy Birch angled for a fake position but the Stallions were smart, remembered that Birch had been bait last time and ignored him. Mitchell Malacek was knocked to his feet before he could even arrive for the play's fake handoff. Whiskey was in the grass, the other offensive tackles were falling and Luke felt the Stallion with the shark's smile bearing down on him—sprinting hard, his cleats slicking over the grass—*now.*

There, past the scrum, by a pure miracle, Ricky Turner had made it nearly to the goal line, just as Luke had prayed he would. Ricky, running like a man possessed, a backfield safety flying his way, raised a single hand. It would have to do.

Luke lobbed the ball, high and hard, and then he was on the ground, gasping for air. The Stallion had landed on top of him, the grills of their helmets clacked together, the other boy's cup pressed hard against Luke's thigh. Their eyes locked as the Stallion started to rise, but instead—instead—he let a hand linger on Luke's shoulder.

The moment passed. The crowd was screaming like a bomb had gone off. Luke knew from the mania in their voices which team they were cheering for. The Stallion tackle grimaced and spat and hauled himself up. He left Luke lying dazed in the grass as the entire town of Bentley rushed the field.

BETHANY

Bethany wove her way through the wilding crowd. She didn't hesitate, didn't look over her shoulder, didn't stop when she reached the little gap between the stands and the south end zone fence that was just—just—wide enough to squeeze through.

Bethany had seen something remarkable in the minutes before halftime. As the Bison had done their best to press through the last few yards to the Stallions' goal, Bethany and the other girls had kicked and cheered "WE GOT GAME, YES WE DO" and Bethany had waved her pom-poms and smiled till she thought it would break her goddamn face and felt a knot of rage and grief tighten inside her.

Nothing had gone right all week. Jamal was in jail. The school knew everything. The town knew everything—you could see it in their eyes, the way they covered their mouths to whisper to their neighbors and waved when they caught her looking. Oh yes. They knew everything and her father knew more.

Thank God Bethany was so naturally tan. Her bronzer had blended over her arms so seamlessly you'd never guess they were covered with bruises.

The moment she had dreaded all night had finally arrived: tonight's halftime routine had ended with the triple pyramid, the tumble they'd practiced all season, and Bethany had learned minutes before kickoff that she would, in fact, be middle bitch. Someone had gotten into Coach Rushing's ear.

"A chance for you to share some glory," the Boss Bull had said. "Middle support is almost harder, don't you think?"

Fuck her. Fuck that. And Fuck Jasmine Lopez too. Because Jasmine Lopez hadn't batted an eye when Coach Rushing told her *she* was riding on top, hadn't even tried to stick up for her best friend, Bethany, oh no. Jasmine had been more than fucking happy to take that shared glory, had smiled when Rushing told her like she'd known this moment was coming all her goddamn life. The whore. The scrawny fake fucking cunt.

God. Jesus. Bethany was tired. She'd suffered nightmares all week. The pit followed her everywhere now, a palpable darkness flickering always on the edge of her vision. Her eyes burned with exhaustion. Her joints ached. Her mind got caught in loops or else went entirely blank while her body apparently moved on its own.

So when she had arrived in the middle of the triple pyramid tonight, smiling out at the stands, Bethany almost missed the exchange that was occurring outside the field house. But she saw it, oh yes sir, she did: Coach Rushing and the gossiping whores on the squad might have tried to pull Bethany off the top of the pile but she still stood tall enough to see, oh yes.

Standing on the other side of the end zone fence, across from a line of bushes that concealed them from the stands, Bethany caught a glimpse of Coach Parter having an argument with Mr. Boone, the county attorney from the ads that always appeared opposite Bethany's and Dylan's pictures in the *Bentley Beacon*'s sports pages. Parter was poking a finger into Mr. Boone's chest and Boone was shaking his head no, no, *no*.

Strange. Bethany had never seen Coach Parter angry. Come to think of it, she had never even seen these two men together.

Boone strode away in a huff, Parter pushed open the door of the field house. The argument had only lasted a second— already Bethany could hear Coach Rushing behind them calling, "Dismount in five, four—" but it was enough.

"Tell Luke not to go tonight," Kimbra Lott had said, right after she'd given Bethany a nasty bruise on the back of her head to go with all the damage Bethany's father had done to her yesterday. *"It's dangerous."*

On her cue, Bethany and April Sparks tossed Jasmine and heard the soft thump as she landed in the spotters' arms. Awaiting her own cue, Bethany waved to the crowd and to her father smiling at her with a koozied beer to his lips like he wasn't planning some dreadful punishment for her this weekend— and she felt an idea forming.

Because she realized now there was a reason she hadn't passed on Kimbra's message to Luke Evers. Kimbra was a bitch—she'd abandoned her goddamn *responsibilities* tonight— but she was also very clever. If Kimbra was worried that something strange was happening after the game then it most definitely was. And whatever was going on, Bethany knew it was sinister enough that Jamal had to be framed for a fucking *murder* to keep it a secret.

And Luke Evers was the key. She had noticed the way Luke was suddenly hanging tight with *Dylan's* old friends, boys who never used to give him the time of day. Those boys wouldn't just suddenly start hanging out with someone like *Luke*. They didn't do anything out of the goodness of their hearts.

As Bethany fell back toward the spotters—a little early, but who cares—she recalled something Alisha Stinson had once asked her and Jasmine as they'd picked at salads at Bethany's house one weekend. *"Don't you ever wonder where those boys go after the games?"* Alisha had said, and Jasmine—the whore—had laughed and said, *"Not as long as they know who they're coming home to."*

Dylan and KT weren't the only boys who were hard to find on Friday nights, oh no.

Bethany had never cared back then, of course, had always been confident that Dylan would have told her if there were something serious going on, but clearly she had been mistaken. No more. Bethany wasn't going to let this continue. These people could smile and they could talk behind their hands and pretend that nothing was ever wrong but Bethany was about to smash their faces into everything they didn't want to see. She was going to stop this. She was going to fix everything.

Bethany landed hard in the spotters' arms. She opened her eyes, realizing she hadn't been entirely awake on the way down. For a moment, just a moment, she'd been certain she was falling, falling into the open mouth of the pit that had waited for her all week, the one that smelled of clay and rot, the one—

She trembled as she stood up, walking on boat legs.

She knew what she needed to do.

As the town rushed the field, as the marching band started braying, Bethany made her way to the parking lot. She turned back to see that no one had noticed her leave. She kept moving.

She would fix this. She would fix everything. Bethany was a very smart, capable, perceptive girl and she was going to fix *everything.*

She stuck to the dark tunnel that ran between the parking lot's lights, nervous of the way the spangles of her uniform glinted, but she needn't have been concerned. Every soul in town was on the field right now.

Bethany made it to the far side of the parking lot without incident, hurried down the line of players' trucks. Mitchell's Jeep, Tomas's red Ram, Whiskey's rusted Chevy. And there was Luke's silver Ford, parked in the darkest space between two lights like it had been planning for this moment all along. Waiting for her.

The truck still had the camper shell over the hood that Bethany had seen at school earlier this week.

The tailgate was unlocked.

LUKE

He smiled for pictures, shook hands, was buffeted with gratitude and relief. When Paulette Whitley gripped him by the arm and whispered in his ear, "You did him proud," Luke struggled not to cry.

He was saying something to a TV reporter with spooky smooth skin (how, Luke wondered, could he get himself cheeks as soft as that?) about how they'd all been training for this moment all their lives when Mitchell Malacek came up alongside him and shouted to the reporter's camera, "You can't stop the herd!" The reporter narrowed her eyes at Mitchell and thanked Luke and stepped away. Mitchell slapped Luke hard on the ass and murmured in his ear, "Get cleaned up. We leave in fifteen."

Luke rinsed off and dressed as quick as he could, all while accepting thumps on the back and cheers and bobbing his head to the music someone had turned on the soundbar, just like he was supposed to do. Scrawny little Benny Garcia was having his own moment near the water fountains, pointing out bruises on his pale body to a crowd of onlookers with a glee that smoothed away his stutter.

The only boys who failed to look impressed were Whiskey Brazos and T-Bay Baskin. They spoke in low voices in a far corner.

Tomas Hernandez laid a hand on Luke's shoulder. "Give it five minutes and meet us up the highway," the boy said, and slipped outside with Mitchell.

Luke laced up his shoes. He could all but taste his heart beating in his mouth.

Coach Parter had positioned himself near the door. His huge soft hands encompassed Luke's own. "I'll see you soon," Parter said, cool and serious, holding Luke's eye just a little too long.

Things were wild outside, the parking lot overflowing with people shattering bottles and setting off firecrackers, all of them exultant—batshit—at the end of a week that had worn the good folks of Bentley down to tendons and nerves.

Luke wove through well-wishers, past boisterous men who wished they'd had arms like that at his age, past Mrs. Malacek and Mrs. Mason asking him how a boy so strapping could be so single.

The crowd thinned out as he neared the edge of the lot, and soon he was alone but for someone standing by the tailgate of his truck. He approached the person cautiously, wondering with a jolt of excitement if this was part of whatever new code he was learning.

But it was only his father. Even when the man was smiling at Luke as he was now, regarding him with an expression that was novel to the both of them—it was a look of respect, Luke realized, the first he'd received from him in eighteen years—Luke couldn't help but scowl.

"You did well tonight," his father said, haltingly, when it was clear that Luke wasn't going to start a conversation.

"I know."

"You were tough out there, I mean. Strong."

"I always have been."

A beat. Clearly, the man was realizing the same thing that Luke was—this was the most he had spoken to his son since all that business in Rockdale over the summer. Mr. Evers smiled wider, and Luke saw on his fifty-year-old father's face a teenager's nervous desire to please someone they cared for, the fear that it would be rejected.

"You should go out tonight with the other boys, I think. Enjoy yourself. I'll take the heat with your mother. You've earned it."

Luke only shrugged to his dad, reached out to open his truck's tailgate, tossed his bag inside. He didn't care—he had a life of his own now, better obligations than his parents.

"Let her get mad—I already made plans."

"That's good, that's good, that's...you know, Luke, I always wanted to say—"

His father was interrupted by the sudden appearance of red-faced Mr. Tanner, the big man waving his arms, spraying spittle and demanding to know where Bethany was.

Luke left the two men where they stood. He'd wasted enough time—what if the others left without him?

He hurried up the side of his truck, never glancing into the camper shell, and swung up into the cab. He eased over the grass edge of the lot. He gunned the motor and took off up the darkened highway.

CLARK

Fifteen minutes later, Clark's truck roared to a stop outside the darkened windows of Lott's Hardware. She jogged to Joel's ruined convertible, parked just where Browder had told her it would be, and found it empty. She had a pretty clear idea of what had brought Joel here in the first place—she too had seen tiny little Mr. Lott in the photograph with Corwin Broadlock and her mother—but in searching the seats of the convertible Clark found no sign of where Joel might have gone.

Gone. Or been taken.

Reaching for the trunk-pull, she spotted something in the window pocket of the driver's door: Dylan Whitley's knife, still in its sheath. She took the knife with her as she dug her fingers in the corners of the empty trunk, ran her hand over the rug for anything someone might have dropped or left behind. Nothing.

Slamming the trunk lid, she stared at the warning carved in the paint. GET OUT NOW FAG.

There were no lights on in the hardware store. The back door down the alleyway was locked. She had never seen the town this empty. Wind moaned through the fiberglass chicken above the door to the Egg House. The gutted bank sat unguarded. No cops would miss the game, of course. She doubted any robbers would, either.

She heard the faint pop of firecrackers to the north. She headed to the Bison field.

The crowd in the parking lot buzzed with the lethal, giddy energy of a riot. Sparklers and cherry bombs burst against the pavement. She saw a shirtless man covered in green paint bash in the window of his own truck with a camping chair and let out a roar for a cheering crowd. There were no deputies in sight. These people would go on like this all night, Clark thought. The town's memories of a weary, terrified week were being demolished before her eyes, one bottle at a time.

Clark pushed her way through the gates and hunted for any sign of Joel.

She spotted Darren, Paulette Whitley's boyfriend, standing in the line for the toilets. She'd had her doubts about the man's alibi for last Friday night but now she grabbed him by the arm.

"Joel? Here?" Darren shouted over the noise. "Since when did he care about football?"

"Clark?" Paulette Whitley said, coming up beside Darren. "Is something wrong with Joel's phone? It don't even ring before it goes to voice mail."

Clark forced on a professional smile. "I'm sure he just let the battery die."

A few cheerleaders stood sipping water and taking selfies near the edge of the field. As Clark approached them the girls all suddenly remembered something they had to do else-where. She watched them leave, hoping to spot Kimbra Lott or Bethany Tanner, someone who might have spoken to Joel. But neither girl was here. Odd.

She glanced over her shoulder to the field house, searching for some sign of him among the players filing toward the parking lot, or of big Coach Parter with his idle smile and the best years of his life behind him, but she saw neither. She turned back to regard the cheerleaders one last time. She spotted Dashandre, the lone boy of the squad, eyeing her cautiously.

"You're friends with Kimbra, aren't you?" she asked him, stepping over to where he sat massaging his feet.

"I thought I was." He took a sip of water. "She left school early, didn't bother telling any of us."

Heat prickled between Clark's shoulder blades. "And where's Bethany Tanner?"

"Being Bethany."

Clark studied him. "Thank you," she finally said, and turned to go.

"Did y'all ever talk to that crazy guy on Grindr?" Dashandre said from behind her.

Clark froze. The noise around her faded.

"What crazy guy?"

"I tried to tell Mr. Whitley about him last Sunday night but he blocked me 'fore I could say nothing." Dashandre shrugged, tried to look bored, but Clark could tell he was spooked. "It's just this weird dude pops off on there sometimes. It probably don't mean nothing."

She held out her hand. "Show me. Now."

"It ain't that big a deal." He unlocked his phone, tapped it a few times, handed it over.

On the screen Clark saw a blue message that had arrived for Dashandre at 9:10 p.m. seven days ago, a little more than an hour before Dylan was last seen alive.

Right after halftime, Clark realized, when the Bright Lands

boys had been passing around links to Dylan's doctored escorting ad.

IF ANY OF U FUCKING FAGGOTS COME NEAR MY BOY I WILL FUCKING CUT U N MAKE IT LOOK LIKE A ACCIDENT.

Clark read the message twice. "Faggots?" she said softly to Dashandre. "Isn't this an app for gay people?"

"I told you, he's crazy. Look." Dashandre tapped a button and the screen reverted to a blank gray square. "This where you normally would have your profile and shit. This guy don't post nothing. For a while he used to come online when he was lit and try and get busy and then pretend he don't know you next time you say hey." Dashandre shrugged again. "He's trash."

Clark hit the Chat button, began to scroll up for older messages.

Dashandre tried to cover the screen with a hand, suddenly sounding nervous. "I don't want you to see nothing you don't want to see, Officer ma'am."

She hardly heard him. She pulled the phone away and read what the mysterious user had sent Dashandre on 5/19:

what's up yo 24 6'0 195 well built nice package vers masculine very dl looking for fun u down??

The message was followed by five pictures. The pictures had been taken in a dingy yellow bathroom, posed in front of a mirror flecked with toothpaste (or something equally creamy). The man was holding his phone in one hand and a middling dick in the other, posing a muscled backside, flexing a ridged stomach.

His face was cropped from the frame in every photo but Clark had no trouble identifying him. Those tattoos could only belong to one person.

She scrolled back to the picture of the man's ass, zoomed in, stared. A pair of Bison charged at one another from either cheek. Above the Bison floated two scrolls. On one scroll was written *2008*. On the other was *2012*.

IF ANY OF U FUCKING FAGGOTS COME NEAR MY BOY.

"D just got to run off with his boy every weekend."

"Some of the Bison I played with had more tricks than a deck of cards."

Browder. *Son of a bitch.*

"Excuse me, Officer, can we speak to you a moment?"

Clark looked up to see Whiskey Brazos and T-Bay Baskin standing behind her, their faces serious. While her head was turned she felt Dashandre slip his phone from her hand.

"Is it urgent?" she asked the boys.

"It's about Dylan, ma'am," T-Bay said.

Whiskey added, "And Luke. And Kimbra. And Joel."

"Shit's been wrong all week, ma'am. Us and the other boys, we've been feeling it in our gut."

Whiskey swallowed, studied Clark's boots. "Something bad is going down tonight."

Clark, her head still buzzing from the photos, felt something click in her head. "You think it's connected to that place?"

T-Bay chewed his cheek. "We've been having dreams."

Clark fixed the boys with a hard glare so they'd know she wasn't playing. "Dreams about where to find it?"

The footballers looked at one another, hesitated.

"Not exactly," T-Bay said.

Whiskey glanced over his shoulder before murmuring, "But we know someone who knows."

BETHANY

Bethany told herself that this was totally absolutely don't panic normal. Luke's truck bounded over the open country while she clutched on to a hook with two fingers and prayed a golf bag skittering around in the bed with her didn't come flying into her face.

The truth. They were heading toward the truth, Bethany knew, she *knew* it—heading toward the truth *she* would reveal, she would call the lady deputy with the ugly shoes and say, "Officer, Officer, I'm sending you my location now—" (because Bethany knew all the tricks to all the modern devices) "—come quick, tell everybody, I found the *TRUTH*."

Bethany had spotted the pile of stale clothes in the far corner of Luke's truck bed the moment she'd lowered the unlocked tailgate in the parking lot. She'd even been pleasantly surprised to discover that she could curl herself beneath the few old shirts and towels and hardly raise the pile at all. As long as nobody shone a flashlight in here, as long as she wasn't still here come daybreak, she could stay perfectly hidden.

Her resolution had lasted about thirty seconds before common sense had intervened and asked her what the fuck she thought she was doing.

Being brave. Bethany was a very brave person.

Once she heard Luke approaching the truck bed her bravery didn't much matter. Because shortly after Luke's footsteps stopped at the tailgate—*what was he* waiting *for, hurry, let's go*—Bethany had heard her father's voice shouting, "How the hell could she have left early when her car is in my damn garage!" and for a while Bethany hadn't thought about much of anything.

Once the truck started rolling she felt her fear abate for a moment. She had escaped that man again. She almost smiled at the thought of her father scouring the parking lot for her in a panic, experienced the same small pleasure she'd felt when she'd gotten Jamal inside her house a week ago. Whatever the consequences, Bethany would always love getting the better of that furious piece of shit, the man who, years before, had given her perfect mother and her perfect face a permanent lazy eye after a blow from Bethany's (surprisingly heavy) Disney Cinderella pumpkin chariot (with real light-up windows).

Bethany used to try telling people what her father had done but had quickly learned that nobody wanted to know. Bentley refused to doubt its men. But one of those men had hurt *her* man—they must have, why else would someone be trying so hard to pin the murder on Jamal?—and she would be fucked three ways if she let them get away with it.

They would listen to her now, oh yes. Everyone was about to start listening to her now.

Luke's truck had rolled north on the highway for what felt like a few miles, idled by the side of the road and then set off again. It had been joined by another truck. No—get it straight,

Bethany, you might need to state this in court—from what she could hear, it sounded as if Luke had started *following* another truck. Had followed the other truck east, scooted carefully down the highway's shoulder and set off bounding over open country.

The Flats. They had headed into the Flats.

Bethany might have been a very brave person but now, a few miles away from the highway, anyone—anyone!—would feel their courage falter. Pretty soon, at the rate Luke was going, she was going to be very, very far from any shelter. She'd once heard that the Flats were over a hundred square miles wide. Or had it been acres? Kilometers? Big enough, anyway, that anything could happen out here.

Anything.

Bethany decided to get in touch with Officer Clark now, get her and the whole sheriff's department mobilized and ready to roll the fuck out. But when she slipped her phone loose from her bra and looked at the screen the last of her courage left her.

She had no service.

The truck shifted course and rolled over a heavy stone. Bethany's head struck the lower wall of the truck's cab. She bit her hand to keep from screaming. Bit until she was afraid she was going to draw blood and didn't let go.

The thought finally occurred to her that whatever had killed Dylan, whatever Luke and the other boys were driving to, the *truth* that was so determined to stay hidden it had concealed itself all the way out here in the barren Flats: what would the *truth* make of Bethany finding it? Bethany, wielding nothing to defend herself but a useless phone and an expensive smile?

The thought finally occurred to her that she could—how was it possible?—die.

Peeking from beneath her towel, Bethany saw a pale hook of moon through the camper shell's window: brilliant and clear as an open wound in the sky. Fear struck the last of her composure from her head. Her mind went blank, her body cold.

That moon, that exact hook of moon, had watched her in her sleep every night this week.

They had crossed the threshold. They were going where the dreams were made. They were driving toward that thing, that pit that had been calling to her since the night Dylan died. It had been calling her here, all along.

JAMAL

The highway to Dallas was nearly empty. Night had fallen. Irons had flipped on his headlights and told Jamal that he could call his mother. Half this plan had been her idea in the first place.

"Won't it look bad that I've run?" Jamal had asked his lawyer, and Irons had insisted that whatever they did would look bad. Hopefully, Irons had said, once Jamal's cousin in Dallas had gotten him to Atlanta, the lawyer could subpoena footage from the security company that monitored the Tanner ranch and prove Jamal's alibi.

Jamal hadn't known what to say to that. However prudent or miraculous this escape may be, the fact remained that he was running away from a crisis he knew he had helped to create in the first place.

All this past summer, Dylan's mood had pitched wildly at any moment from giddy to morose, from generous to petty to irritable to enraged. As his friends' trips to the coast became more frequent, Jamal had never found the sack to say a word about what was clearly a dire (and worsening) secret.

With a queasy flood of shame, Jamal remembered the lazy afternoon three weeks ago when—a few minutes after he'd sent those fateful text messages to Bethany: Let's do it—Dylan had sighed through a cloud of weed smoke in his stuffy attic and said, with a faint trace of something Jamal recognized now, too late, as fear, "It's like a fever. It makes you crazy."

"The weed?"

"Like, love." Dylan laughed. He always laughed when he talked about his own feelings, as if it were some embarrassing insult of nature that he had any at all. But then he said it again, a tremor in his hands. "Love."

Jamal suspected that Dylan wasn't talking about Bethany. He should have pressed his friend, should have asked why he was seeing somebody if it made him so miserable, and yet all Jamal had done was mind his own business, take a drag on their blunt, say, "It'll chill eventually, right? You have to do what makes you happy."

That was Jamal, ever the backbencher. Cheerleading in the places the girls couldn't reach.

Just what, he wondered, had he cheered Dylan into doing?

Jamal hadn't called his mother yet. As he and Irons crossed the line into Burleson County, Jamal saw that Kimbra Lott hadn't answered the messages he'd sent her since his escape. The face that the girl had worn when she'd left the interview room this morning—stubborn, brash, curious—had haunted him all day.

"Don't let those guys fuck you up," he'd told her, because when Kimbra asked him about the Bright Lands, Jamal had remembered plenty of rumors about that place: weird gossip the backbenchers were smart enough to only whisper about when certain players came close. Stories about a party in the

Flats where boys swore a blood oath of secrecy, made pacts that followed them all their lives. It had always sounded so ridiculous, like the cheap seriousness of a fraternity in a movie. But now he wondered.

Kimbra's silence over the last hour had spooked him. She was never away from her phone.

Jamal called her. It went to voice mail.

KT sounded stoned when he picked up Jamal's call a minute later.

"Yo," Jamal said, dialing down the end of the game on the car radio. "Where's Kimbra?"

A long pause. "She's supposed to be meeting me here."

"After the game?"

"This afternoon."

"Then where is she?" Jamal stared at the empty road. Mr. Irons gave him a curious look. "Bro, she was asking questions today about that place you and Dylan used to go." Jamal paused. Why did the words frighten him so badly when they were poised on his lips? "The Bright Lands."

After a long silence, KT said, "That was dumb of her."

"She's in trouble, ain't she?" Jamal said.

Silence.

"Where are you now?"

"At home."

"Stay there."

Jamal lowered the phone. He choked on the smell of cinnamon cologne. Irons's knuckles were almost white on the wheel. "Change of plans."

"No," the lawyer said.

"Please. My friend's in trouble."

"And you're not?"

"Nobody will even know I'm in town. With the game—"

"You're not that stupid, son. Don't play me like I am, either."

"Turn around." Jamal swallowed, almost couldn't believe what he was about to say. He felt, suddenly, that he had no choice. "Turn around or I'll confess."

"It wouldn't stand up after we get the security footage."

"You're right, I'm not dumb. But if you think Mr. Tanner hasn't found a way to get that footage deleted—"

Irons spun the wheel of the car. The Mercedes fishtailed as it turned its way back to Bentley.

A silent hour later, Irons slid to a halt outside the dark Staler house, idled with one foot on the brake and said, "Don't do this, Reynolds. Please. If you get out of this car you're on your own."

Jamal tried to smile. "Thank you for the ride."

Irons said nothing. The moment Jamal stepped out onto the cracked sidewalk, Mr. Irons's Benz pulled away with a roar.

Jamal Reynolds, he thought to himself. *You are a fucking idiot.*

He started up the overgrown lawn toward the dark house, shivering in his leather jacket despite the warmth of the night. Before Jamal could make it to the front door, KT called from the backyard. "Around here."

There was something broken in his voice.

Jamal found him seated alone in a lawn chair in the middle of the yard, staring at the eerie hook of moon that hung above them. It illuminated the awful bruise on KT's cheek, the backpack at his feet, the phone in his lap.

"They let you out," KT said.

"I'm on the run."

"You ran the wrong way."

Jamal couldn't remember the last time they'd talked like this, just the two of them, Dylan nowhere to be seen. It might have been never.

"Kimbra's in trouble, man."

"We're all in trouble."

"I know you two didn't just go to the coast on those weekends you wasn't here. I know you went to that party first. You tried to act like it wasn't real that one time you saw me listening to you and D but you can't fool me."

KT snorted. "Oh no, sir, nobody could ever fool *you*."

Jamal refused to be distracted. "I know that's where y'all was going the night Dylan died, after the game. And I think Kimbra knows that too. I tried to stop her asking questions but—"

"It's not my fault it's awake now."

Jamal blinked. "Awake? What's awake?"

"I know what you want me to do." KT's eyes grew wide, the bruise bulging as a nerve worked in his jaw. "They'd kill me if I went out there again. They'd kill all of us."

"I think Kimbra might have learned something about that party. I think somebody's going to hurt her to keep her quiet."

"And you think you can stop it?" KT said. He started to laugh.

Jamal struck him, hard, on his bruised cheek. He grabbed the legs of KT's chair and wrenched it out from under him, spilling him into the grass. He kicked KT in the ass.

"All that time I knew you were getting yourself in trouble with those other guys and I didn't say shit!" Jamal shouted. "I didn't want to get in your business. But now my best friend is dead, your girlfriend's in trouble and someone in this fucking town is trying to put me on death row. So you and me are going to fix this. Now."

KT lay curled in the grass, a hand over his face. He didn't move.

"Was it your idea to frame me?" Jamal said.

KT trembled, bracing for another blow, but Jamal only adjusted his jacket. What did it matter?

"Get up."

After a long pause, KT dragged himself to his feet.

Jamal said, "They took her out there, didn't they? It's the best place to hurt someone if you want to hide it. I bet it was dumb luck Dylan's body was ever found. What do you want to bet they'd get luckier next time?"

KT scowled at him, rubbed his cheek. If he was going to tell Jamal anything else, he wasn't going to do it now. All he said was, "Where's your car?"

Jamal stopped. "What happened to yours?"

"It's impounded. Up in Dallas."

"What about your sister's?"

"Mom totaled it."

"You're telling me you ain't got a car here?"

KT picked up his chair. He shrugged. "Life's a bitch. You wanna sleep here tonight?"

Jamal couldn't think of anything to say. He watched KT lower himself into the chair, felt his heart slowing. This couldn't be happening. This couldn't be real.

And then a brilliant pair of headlights washed over the street out front. A truck rumbled to a stop at the curb. Jamal jogged around the side of the house to see Whiskey Brazos and T-Bay Baskin starting up the walk to the house. They gawped at him.

"You're out," T-Bay said.

"It's a long story."

Whiskey cleared his throat. "Are you here about Joel Whitley?"

"Joel?" Jamal looked between the two of them. "We're looking for Kimbra."

A second truck pulled to a stop behind the first and Jamal fought a violent urge to flee at the sight of the woman behind the wheel. It passed when he saw the way Officer Clark regarded him with nothing more than a cool interest.

"She's with us," T-Bay said. "We're going to that place."

Officer Clark rolled down her window and said, "Where's KT?"

Jamal heard something. He slipped back into the yard just

in time to pull KT down from atop the fence over which he was trying to escape. Jamal marched the shaking boy to the front of the house, a hand clamped over the back of KT's neck.

"Right here. And he's going to take us."

LUKE

Luke heard the sound of a few trucks pulling up in the dirt, heard boys leaping out of them with a whoop only to go quiet—reverent—as they drew near. He swallowed. The new boys took their place in the circle that Luke felt around him. He'd lost count of how many people had arrived since Mitchell had slipped a blindfold on him a few minutes before.

What Luke did not hear in any of the cleared throats or muted chatter was the sound of a single girl.

At some signal, the low murmur of voices died. Silence tightened the air, finally broken by the squeak of a foot across a wooden board. From ahead and above him, Luke heard a man's voice, gleeful and unabashedly smug, shout down to say, "This is a beautiful night, ain't it, boys?"

A mumble of agreement.

"Then let's not waste it," the man said, and Luke recognized that it was Mr. Boone speaking, some big deal with the city government his parents sometimes had over for dinner.

Mr. Boone clapped his hands and a moment later Luke heard two people step into the circle. They grabbed the hem of his shirt, tugged it off over his head. Luke's upturned face caught a glimpse of stars, the hooked moon, before the blindfold was fastened back in place.

He began to panic—the fuck *was* this?—when one of the boys locked an arm around Luke's bare chest and clasped a hand over his mouth while the other boy wrenched loose Luke's belt and tugged his jeans down over his thrashing legs. Tugged down Luke's briefs.

Luke shouted into the boy's hand as he was lifted up and his pants were pulled over his shoes. They struck the dirt nearby. His belt buckle clattered.

"Evers!" Mr. Boone shouted. "You've got some words to answer."

The hands released Luke. He shivered with his hand over his naked crotch.

Not real, this wasn't real.

"You are standing on hallowed ground, son. The edge of goddamn greatness, you hear me? I said do you hear me?"

Luke nodded.

"Say it!"

"I hear you."

A hand struck the back of Luke's head.

Boone shouted, "Boy, you will address me as *sir*."

"I hear you, sir!" Luke's teeth were chattering. When had the night gotten so cold?

"Do you swear to keep secret all that you see here, boy?"

"Yes, sir!"

"And do you swear to protect it, even with your own life?"

Luke hesitated. Could this man possibly be serious?

"That's not a good answer, boy."

"Yes, sir!"

"Very good."

Boone and someone else began to clap. A moment later and the circle around Luke joined in, a steady one-two, one-two, one-two. Through the noise, Luke heard a new pair of feet approach him. The hands that had stripped him naked now grabbed his wrists and ankles, wrenched his arms back. The clapping grew louder. A new hand rested on Luke's shoulder—a man's hand, calloused and dry.

"To seal the oath you have just made, son, this old place will mark you. It hurts us a little so we know it can hurt us a lot. Do you hear, son?"

Luke's throat had gone dry. It was all he could do to nod his head.

"Very good!" Boone shouted. The clapping grew wild. A cowbell began to ring, a noisemaker rattled, whoops and shouts echoed over open country.

The grip on his wrists tightened. From down near Luke's feet, Mitchell Malacek murmured: "Whatever you do, don't scream."

A sudden, icy pain spread across the back of Luke's thigh, just below his ass, and a moment later he felt warm blood spilling down his leg. He gasped. Something firm and cool and sticky came to rest on his shoulder, a few inches from his neck. A knife.

"And just like that, you're in the end zone," Mr. Boone shouted above the din. "You, my boy, are in the Bright Lands."

Luke's hands and ankles were released. The blindfold was pulled free. He was dazed by a brilliant flash of light. A sudden boom of a marching band coursed through the speakers, and when Luke's senses returned to him he saw a tiny figure holding a Polaroid camera start up a tall set of wooden steps.

At the top of the steps—and it was a good ten-foot climb—there was a triple-wide trailer, skirted by a wooden porch.

Mr. Boone, clad in nothing but a black leather harness across his chest and black leather chaps, smiled from the porch like a priest. Coach Parter, wearing a green Bison jacket and a pair of Lycra football tights, looked impatient to get on with something.

Luke turned and saw that he stood in the center of a wide circle of trailers: campers, double-wides, a little silver Airstream. Between Luke and the trailers there stood maybe fifteen boys. Boys in jockstraps and high socks, boys naked but for pads and sneakers.

Pale Tomas Hernandez. The Turner twins and their mirrored smile. Luke recognized some of the other boys from games—a few had played for Rattichville last week, others he knew from past seasons—but many were strangers.

Strings of Christmas lights ran between the trailers, little footlamps burned in the dirt and, high above them, a pair of tall halogen field lights rendered every hair on every boy's head, every groove of every boy's hard body, brilliant and crisp and unbearable.

Mitchell Malacek, wearing nothing but green face paint, rose from where he'd pinned Luke's feet. Luke could only stare at him, feeling the blood trickle down his leg, and marvel at a reality that put eighteen years' worth of wild rumors to shame.

"You did good, bro," Mitchell said with a smile, and smacked Luke hard on his bare, bloody ass.

JOEL

Pain. The blaring horns awoke him to a pain in the back of his head so terrible he wondered if his brain was trying to wrench itself out through his skull. Joel strained to touch the wound, certain he would feel the soft gray matter exposed, but he couldn't move his hands. His arms were spread wide, shackled to some sort of bar suspended from the ceiling above him that rattled when he moved. His feet had been secured to the floor. He heard a rustling noise somewhere ahead of him. Through the darkness he could just discern a shape on the floor maybe ten feet away.

"My Herd, My Glory." That's what those fucking horns were playing. Somewhere outside—outside meaning he was inside, his battered mind told him, okay, he was getting somewhere—there was the chatter of a small crowd of people. Joel tried to scream for help but found that his lips were sealed together. He tasted adhesive. Oh boy.

God, the pain. It brought back a jumble of memories: Deputy Browder shouting that Kimbra had been hurt. Seeing thousands of dollars spread around the floor as he ran inside the hardware store. The young cop going very quiet behind him. A blinding rush of—

Joel's eyes burned as a door opened and light spilled in from outside. The shapes of two men appeared, one tall and heavy, the other shorter, more tightly packed. The two were followed, a moment later, by a lithe, muscled form that could only be Browder.

"Don't let that door bolt," said Mr. Boone, the county attorney. "My key—fuck, what did you *do*?"

Deputy Browder closed the door softly. There was a click and a bare red light came on overhead, illuminating what looked like the inside of a small camper trailer. Joel was standing, he saw, in what had once been a living room but had long ago been emptied of all furniture but a black leather sofa. Hanging from nails across black walls were a range of instruments that Joel recognized from sex shops and some of the stranger corners his nocturnal adventures in Manhattan had taken him: riding crops, paddles, ball gags, chains.

The three men paid him no attention. They were standing in the camper's bare kitchen, staring at the shape Joel had earlier seen on the floor. It was Kimbra Lott, he realized: her feet bound with black tape, her hands cuffed to something on the wall.

"Christ Jesus," said Coach Parter.

"Why the hell did you bring her here?" Boone said.

"She'd been asking questions around the school," Deputy Browder said. "I was watching the bank while Jones was on his break—I saw her go into the store. I just wanted to talk to her, figure out what she'd heard. I didn't know she was going to scream."

"Christ Jesus," Parter said again.

"Has her father heard yet? That she's here?" said Boone.

"Are you smoking that ice now too?" said Parter. "Can you imagine what the little blossom would do if he knew about this?"

A long moment of deliberation. Boone played his nails along a black metal refrigerator that rested near the kitchen's doorway. "There might be some leverage in it."

Parter pulled a face. Joel caught, in the coach's scowl, decades' worth of dissatisfaction with the county attorney. A fraying patience.

Boone rounded on Joel. "Mr. Whitley, how are you?"

Joel stared at him.

The man motioned to Browder. The tattooed young deputy slid a long knife from a sheath at his waist—*The wound to the neck was caused by a serrated blade about six inches long,"* Clark had told him Wednesday night (really, you don't say?)—and tossed it casually in the air. Caught it. Tossed it. Caught it. Browder wore only a pair of baggy jeans and a leather jacket over his bare chest.

A jacket, but no shirt. A costume like the ones these men were wearing. Like Dylan had been wearing.

"You ain't gonna holler on us, are you?" said the deputy, drawing close, holding the point of the knife a few inches from Joel's eye.

Joel pulled back, shook his head no.

Browder ripped the tape from Joel's mouth. Joel didn't make a sound.

Boone gave Browder a dismissive little flick of his hand.

"Mr. Whitley, it's good to finally meet you. I apologize for the circumstances."

Joel said nothing.

"You must be awful curious about all this." Boone gave the implements along the wall the broad gesture of a TV hostess revealing a prize. He said with more than a touch of pride,

"It's like the sort of thing you might find in the city, no? Look, here, this way."

Boone stepped to the wall to swing open a black shutter and reveal a barred window. Joel saw other trailers outside, strings of lights, young men. Naked young men.

Joel caught one of those young men—was that Luke Evers?—glance at him, an eyebrow raised, a moment before Boone pushed the shutter closed.

"I want you to imagine something, Mr. Whitley," Boone said, and immediately Joel realized why Clark had spoken of this man so dismissively: he was a born jackass. "I want you to imagine three young men in Nowhere, Texas, who were given the chance to carve out a little piece of country where they could be themselves. Maybe invite a few folks they knew was like them, some other boys who was just a little bit peculiar. Different. Harmless."

Browder and Parter grimaced, shifted on their feet in the kitchen and looked impatient. Kimbra lay motionless between them. Mr. Boone adjusted the leather harness strapped over his chest and gave Joel a politician's nod, all gravitas.

"Things ain't changed much around here since Korea, Mr. Whitley. The crazy seventies, that was all going on someplace else. We was still living in a town where the old ways was the *best ways*. And we didn't feel no need to change that. We *valued* it. Everyone knows your name in Bentley, holds the door at the grocery, brings over food in the hard times. It was our home." Boone wiped his eyes. The man, to Joel's astonishment, was suddenly buckling under real emotion.

"Bentley was beautiful. There just wasn't room there in it for all of us."

Joel's eye fell on a row of wooden instruments on the wall.

"Mr. Whitley, when that opportunity to make something beautiful fell into our laps, you can bet we took it, yes, sir. The chance to make a place where we could go release a few urges and then head back to our brothers on the team, head back to our girls, our wives and children. Could go back to the right sort of life. We made a safe space for us and the boys who came after. Can you imagine the pain we've relieved here over the years? Can you imagine the good we've done?"

Joel was too injured to be clever. He said only, "If it's so safe then why is my brother dead?"

The three men all looked away. A faint tremor in the earth set a pair of long metal rods—God, not even Joel could imagine what those were used for—clacking together on the wall.

"Dylan's death was unfortunate," Boone said, acting as if he hadn't noticed the trailer shake. The man nodded to Parter. "By the time us Old Boys heard what the young ones had done to your brother—well—things was too far along to smooth over. We would have saved you a lot of heartbreak if we could have, Mr. Whitley. We're truly sorry."

Joel's arms were starting to burn. He'd gotten sick of this man. Hoping to jostle him, perhaps play on some of the frustration he had caught earlier between Boone and the coach, Joel said, "Is that the same comfort you offered Clark's family?"

"Troy was—"

"What about Corwin Broadlock's parents?"

The name had a much stronger effect than Joel had intended. Coach Parter seemed to fly across the trailer—for such a big man he could certainly move—one thick arm pulled back to throw a punch. Joel felt a distant pain in his temple as his mind went dark again.

LUKE

Luke couldn't pull the smile from his face: even in his most lubricated fantasies he could never have imagined a place as perfect as this. Mitchell wandered around the Bright Lands like it bored him, nodding at one boy, cupping another's nuts with a brazen little smile that suggested more to come later. Luke, clutching his clothes in one hand, trailed naked behind him, doing his best to hold on to all that Mitchell was saying while his mind threatened to flit away into the sky, giddy as helium.

"If you need to tidy up we got the Water House there." Mitchell pointed at a long blue trailer that sat at one end of the circle, opposite the massive elevated triple-wide that Luke had seen when the blindfold was removed.

He noticed a steady line of boys filing into a brilliant red trailer that rested up the circle from the Water House, all of the boys grinning and chugging from red Solo cups.

"We'll get you into Glory Days over there later. You've stopped bleeding, yeah?"

Luke touched the wound on the back of his thigh. It would leave a scar. His smile wavered. "For now."

"Let's get you changed then."

As they started across the circle, Luke heard two boys cackling at something. He glanced over his shoulder just in time to spot a man who looked an awful lot like Joel Whitley appear in the window of a black camper trailer that stood next to the tall triple-wide.

Luke felt his first pulse of misgiving. What was Whitley doing here? And why did he look so terrified? Luke recalled Garrett Mason, in the truck last night, saying of Joel, *"He's on the list for tomorrow."*

"Word of advice." Mitchell put a hand on Luke's shoulder. Joel's face disappeared behind a black shutter. "That black one's Mr. Boone's special trailer. It's the only one that locks. You steer clear of Boone, you hear? He's short a favorite right now."

Mitchell guided Luke toward a double-wide trailer painted Bison green and chuckled as he pointed out the tall words painted above the trailer's door: HELLO DARLIN'.

"Don't mind the names," Mitchell said with a bemused little shake of his head. "The old guys have a boner for the faggy details."

A handful of boys stood inside the trailer, sipping from more red plastic cups. They went silent the moment Luke stepped through the front door.

Mitchell led Luke into a large room where hideous wallpaper peeled around a bank of rusted green lockers. An old bed was buried beneath a mountain of jockstraps and socks and jerseys. Costumes.

"Don't let them see you with a phone," Mitchell said, heading into an attached bathroom.

Luke tossed his jeans and his dusty shirt into a locker,

plucked a pair of shorts off the bed, told himself he felt no misgivings about leaving his keys and his phone out of reach. Mitchell emerged from the bathroom with a grimy first aid kit and handed Luke a roll of gauze and an alcohol wipe.

"You guys think of everything," Luke said.

Mitchell shrugged. "If you see something you want around town you can just take it. Nobody's gonna hassle you anymore."

In a cramped kitchen, Mitchell showed Luke a counter full of orange Gatorade coolers labeled TRASHCAN PUNCH, VODKA MONSTER, RUM. A pair of glass cutting boards rested near a rusted sink. The boards were covered with lines of powder. Arrayed behind the cutting boards were foil pouches that Luke saw contained lube, candy dishes full of tablets, empty pill bottles like he'd find at a pharmacy. FEEL FREE 2 TAKE HOME—COMPLIMENTS OF THE BAG BOYS.

"Do those guys in the living room play for Spricksville High?" Luke murmured to Mitchell.

"Better don't ask questions," Mitchell said. He sidled up to the counter, ran a thin line of crystal up his nose and plucked a small glass vial from a candy dish; the shape of it alone looked illicit. "Do you like poppers?"

"Are they sour?"

Mitchell grimaced, rubbing his nose. "You don't drink it. Take one of the big ones—Garrett refills all this shit later. You want some Oxy? You want—oh what's up, bro, where you been?"

The most beautiful redhead Luke had ever seen appeared with a boy of his own in tow and twisted Mitchell's nipple with a sneer. Mitchell popped his nuts. Luke studied the floor until the redhead and his boy stepped past him.

"You're sort of shy, aren't you?" Mitchell said, leading Luke back toward the living room.

Luke smiled, shrugged. "Dylan must have been popular here."

The living room suddenly went silent. Mitchell grabbed Luke by the wrist and yanked him outside.

"Let's pretend you never said that name," he said with his father's political smile. "Now, some guys spend their whole night in Glory Days—that's where the cards and the titty porn is." Mitchell pointed at the red trailer, then turned to nod at the tall triple-wide Luke had seen earlier, the one with the big porch. Tomas Hernandez was stepping out of its door and tucking something into his sock as he walked, a cigarette on his lips. His fingers were shaking. "If you're ever short on cash you can go in that one there but, well—you'll see."

Luke saw the dark spots in the dirt where his blood had fallen earlier. He remembered the cop with all the tattoos who had cut his thigh. He glanced again at that little black camper with its dark windows. "Do you get to keep coming here after you graduate?"

"You're all about the questions. But yes, you *can* come back to be a Hand, but you don't want to. And you *definitely* don't want to start dating one of the Hands off the clock." Mitchell let out a funny, humorless laugh. A few more boys arrived, Luke saw, and now they milled around the doors of the trailers in twos and threes, drinking, smoking, talking without meeting each other's eyes. It was strange, Luke thought: the way two dozen guys could feel like a wild party. If this was what a party felt like.

Mitchell stopped near a silver Airstream. The trailer was surrounded by a white picket fence and a bed of fake flowers. White foil packets of lube glinted among their stems like eggshells.

"Listen, man, it's simple. Don't think about this stuff. Let what you do at home stay at home. Let what you do here stay here. 'Cause what we've got here is just a few guys doing what we feel. It don't mean we're about that faggot shit, yeah?"

Over Mitchell's shoulder, inside the dim silver trailer, Luke saw Garrett Mason throw his head back in a moan. Stevey Turner was braced on a couch.

Luke knew one thing and one thing only: he was definitely, definitely about that faggot shit.

He forced a smile. "Of course, bro."

"Perfect. Now repeat after me."

Mitchell fished an amber vial from his sock, shook it briskly, unscrewed the cap and pressed it to his nostril. He took a snort, switched sides. Let out a long quavering breath.

Luke did just as he was told. The liquid inside smelled of paint thinner. By the end of his first drag he felt a tingling in his face. By the end of his second he was flush all over with a warmth anchored somewhere inside his balls. He saw spots. He said, "Oh shit," and it felt like the most profound thing to ever come out of his mouth.

Luke felt a finger run up his ass. He turned to see the stunning redhead from earlier regarding him. The boy jabbed the finger deeper. Luke winced—even with the poppers it hurt like a bitch—but smiled back and told himself this was exactly what he'd always wanted.

BETHANY

Dear Jesus. Bethany wasn't sure what exactly she was seeing from the windows of Luke's truck parked on the dark side of the ring of trailers, but she knew in a heartbeat that more than one boy here would kill her to keep it a secret. She saw Tomas Hernandez step out onto the porch of the tall triple-wide and light a cigarette. His eyes seemed to settle on hers.

Bethany ducked down, her heart thudding.

Steps in the dirt outside. A truck's door opening, slamming. A laugh.

She pressed her hand to her lips and counted to thirty. Thirty-five.

The laugh faded. Quiet around her.

Deep breath. Deep breath. Bethany reminded herself that she was a very strong person, a very capable person, a very—

No. Stop. Bethany realized, in that cold quiet moment, that if she wanted to survive this mess she was going to have to stop telling herself what kind of girl she was and start living like that bitch while she still had the chance.

Get your shit together, Tanner.

She noticed something. During the entire ride here, she had been certain that the golf bag sliding around the truck bed was going to strike her in the face. Now, however, she saw that it wasn't a golf bag at all.

It was a black vinyl rifle case.

What had Dylan called her that one time, that rainy morning this past spring when Bethany (and her .22 bolt-action) had rounded on him in the shelter of her father's deer stand and asked (possibly demanded) to know why her man hadn't fucked her in weeks?

The Sharpest Shot in the West.

Bethany pulled the rifle bag toward her and spun the business end outward. She fumbled with the zipper.

JOEL

He was vomiting, though he felt only vaguely connected to the throat clenching and burning as bile fell to his feet. Such bright new floorboards down there, he noticed, so out of place in this moldy old trailer.

"Don't you ever say Broadlock's name again, you fucking faggot."

Parter stood so close his spit struck Joel's eye.

"You're only alive out of the goodness of Mr. Boone's heart, Whitley." Parter jabbed a finger into Joel's chest. "Me? I'd have killed you the minute I heard you'd found out about Mason's arrest, but our beloved County Attorney said we should at least offer you a deal. All we're doing here is keeping hold of the past for a little while longer, Whitley—we're just a few folks trying to get some satisfaction out of life, alright? So here's our offer. We take you from here, safe and sound, and we put you on the first plane back to New York. *You* drop this. You never come back. In return, your family is safe—your mother, that little oil slick of a boyfriend she has now, they go on living like nothing's happened. But if you ever say a word to them, if you so much as step foot in Pettis County again, well—you've seen what we can do."

Parter took a step back. Joel thought of Deputy Grissom, burned alive in his bed. He started to vomit again.

"For Christ's sake," Boone said. His arrogance had fallen away. He sounded near to tears. "Why'd you hit him like that?"

Hearing the quaver in Boone's voice, the bottom fell out of Joel's stomach. He looked from one man to the next, went very cold. This deal of Parter's was an empty promise. He'd already seen too much, heard too much: this place—these men—they would never be safe while Joel was still alive. Joel thought of the scowl Parter had fixed on Boone a few minutes before, the disgust and the frustration. He saw the way Boone was cracking up before his eyes. The county attorney, Joel realized, was the sort of man who had to be backed into a corner before he could commit to something unsavory.

All of this had been a pretense, hadn't it, the latest round of some old argument between the two men? Boone's proud sales pitch, Parter's angry offer, they could have done it all back at the hardware store if they'd really wanted to. No: these Old Boys had brought him (and Kimbra, sweet Jesus) out here to kill them. There was no better place to commit a murder in Pettis County. If they'd been smart and buried Dylan then the boy would have never been found. Joel knew they wouldn't make the same mistake again.

He did the only thing he could think of. He let his head fall, burped up a little bile, tried to look more dazed than he felt, if that was even possible.

It worked. He felt the cuff on one wrist come free, then the other. Parter murmured something and a moment later

Joel's arms prickled with heat as Browder lowered them from the spread-eagle bar. Joel's hands were cuffed back together above his crotch. He wished they would give him a chair to sit in, but he supposed this was better than standing like he'd been crucified. His hands tingled as blood slipped back into his fingers.

Joel opened his eyes. He saw where Kimbra lay, motionless, on the kitchen floor. What had she learned? What had he done?

"But what about her?" Joel said, his voice slurring. Delaying these guys seemed as smart as any other strategy.

Boone cocked his head like a stuffed bison. "What about her?"

"I'm not leaving this place without her."

Browder made a disgusted noise. "He's wasting time. Clark might be on her way already."

"Then we take care of her," Parter said.

The ground shook again, so violently Joel nearly lost his balance. Mr. Boone studied the shaking tools on the wall, shook his head. "And what would that accomplish? For God's sake, ain't we dug this hole deep enough? Why let it grow?"

Parter rounded on him. "The fuck did you just say?"

"You can feel that damn thing moving down there." Boone pointed to the floor. "If we stop feeding it now it's bound to calm down again like it did the first time. If we don't—"

Parter strode back into the kitchen and struck Boone with the back of his hand. "Don't you dare tell me what I can do on *my* property. In *my* town."

Boone held a hand to his cheek. He looked pathetic, deflated, though whether out of sadness or fear Joel couldn't say. The man shook his head at Parter, at Browder. "You're dealing with a beast from the absolute depths of hell and you want to ride it like a bull."

Parter shrugged, straightened his jacket. "How else do you expect to keep tradition alive?"

The big coach nodded to Browder. The deputy turned his attention from Boone back to Joel, swiveling the knife in his hand like he was using it to twist open a lock in the air. In the stark light of the trailer's single red bulb, Joel caught a glimpse of something much more dangerous than excitement in Browder's eye. A brief, black shimmer. A momentary appraisal from something not entirely human.

"We tried it your way," Parter said to Boone. "Now let's do what needs to be done."

Blood leaked from Boone's lip. He looked away. Browder crossed the threshold of the kitchen.

A moan of pain rose behind him.

Every man in the trailer froze. Kimbra Lott struggled to rise from the kitchen floor only to collapse again.

Oh Christ, Joel thought. What was she doing?

When Kimbra moaned again, Browder and his knife turned back in her direction.

JAMAL

Like a dream forming and dissolving, familiar objects loomed up out of the darkness of the Flats. KT asked Whiskey to slow the truck so he could look out for way-markers.

Take a right at the rusted stop sign that sat bereft of any road.

Left at the stand of dead brown cactus.

Straight past the burned-out Chevy sedan, a Texas flag bolted over its back window frame. "They've moved it since last time," KT said blandly as the Chevy slipped past them. The other boys, Jamal included, were too anxious to say a word.

Earlier, Jamal had become convinced that KT was leading them nowhere, that he planned to drive them until Whiskey's truck ran out of gas and then abandon them in the wilderness. Jamal had pulled his phone from his pocket to text Officer Clark, who was following them in her own truck—Jamal had been certain to get her number before heading out—but had discovered he had no service. He'd opened the compass on his phone and felt his throat tighten. He'd watched the compass's red needle spin wildly, hunting in vain for north.

"He should never have brought me there," KT said in the front passenger seat. "He should have known I couldn't handle that place."

Whiskey tightened his pale knuckles on the wheel and said, "Couldn't handle what, bro?"

"I heard they had party favors. I heard everyone who went out there got special treatment in town. He kept saying, D kept saying, it ain't meant for boys like you but I said, shit, I'm open-minded, ain't I? I like to let loose, don't I?" KT shuddered. "I didn't know what that place would do to me. I didn't know what *letting go* would do to me."

T-Bay, seated beside Jamal in the back, twisted and twisted his fingers in his lap.

"I wasn't made for it, he was right. But shit, maybe only them Old Boys is made for it. Pretty soon I was Mr. Boone's favorite. In his special trailer. I was the one always had to teach him his lessons. Some nights he wanted the paddle, some nights he wanted the whip, some nights—" KT stared at his right hand for a long time. He said, "Coach is easier, he just sucks you off, but Mr. Boone, he needs his lessons, oh yes, sir. Did you know someone can make you hate yourself even when *you're* the one putting *their* dick in a cage? It's fucking funny. I'd have never believed it. Go right. I said right."

"Dear Jesus," T-Bay said. They had reached an old wooden roadhouse, the road it had once serviced long since dissolved by time. A sign painted in wobbly white letters reading BURGERS GRITS NO COLOREDS hung on what remained of its door. The building's windows had long since been busted out and boarded over. A lone gas pump sat in the dirt, its nozzle bobbing at its side like a busted arm.

"Oh, but Dylan, was *he* ever popular. All the boys wanted

a piece of *Dylan*. And when the Old Boys' Hand showed up in town again, fuck me running, you should have seen those two lovebirds strutting around the Bright Lands like they was celebrities, Dylan always touching his hair and Mr. Deputy following him like a fucking dog. They was fucking shameless! *'Let's go camping out west, sweetheart, let's go fishing.'* Never a thought paid to your buddy KT, huh, Dylan? Your Bison buddy who didn't have no college recruiters to come get him out of here? Who had a girl who wanted you to make her money, money, always more money so you can run away together? *I* was the one locked in Mr. Boone's special trailer every fucking Friday night because if KT don't show up you can bet Boone and his fucking deputies would take your mom away come Monday morning. You didn't have Garrett and Jason hounding you to sell your product together, didn't have a friend up in Dallas with an idea how you could make some coin off other sirs doing the special things that Mr. Boone taught you, did you, D? I just got so tired, Reynolds. I got so *tired*."

KT turned back to stare at Jamal. Jamal had forgotten how to breathe.

"I remembered what they done to Joel Whitley with those dirty pictures and I thought, hell, maybe Dylan could get him some rough treatment for once in his life. I just wanted D to know what it was like for *one* goddamn night. To know what it felt like to have your brothers look at you like you was the scum of the earth, to be so ashamed you would cut yourself open to stop it. Is that so wrong?" KT's mouth had twisted into a pout. "How was I supposed to know the deputy would see my ad once I put Dylan's face on it? How was I supposed to know he'd drag Dylan into the special trailer? *It was Dylan's fault.* Last year, back when I threatened to tell people about the pictures I found on his phone if he wouldn't take me, he should have known I was bluffing. He should have warned me it wasn't just a party."

Something new had appeared on the horizon.

No, not quite new. Jamal had seen it all week.

A pale dome of light, quivering wrong against the night.

T-Bay said, "What the fuck is that?"

"The best years of my life." KT sobbed like he'd choked on a nail.

CLARK

Clark saw the light too, recognized it though she'd never seen it before. *"Those queer lights."* Maybe her father had been trying to tell her something after all.

She took a deep breath. If she wasn't much mistaken her nose caught a smell of rot on the breeze. She pulled up beside Whiskey's idling truck, shouted through the open window, "You boys stay here for now."

It sounded to her ear like the right thing to say, the dutiful thing to say—and she had put enough weight on her conscience by bringing these terrified kids out here in the first place—but dear God did Clark not want to do this alone. With every strange new sight on this desolate plain, with every mile spent drifting farther from civilization, she had felt a cold dread growing in her mind. Whatever monster had been haunting this town's dreams, whatever force had stalked Bentley's beds all week, she knew it awaited her now. Right over there, on the other side of the fence her mother had always warned her about.

She checked the chamber of her father's old revolver, though she wondered if it would do her much good against the thing awaiting her under those lights. She holstered the revolver on her left hip, pulled her 9 millimeter service pistol from the holster on her right, socked a round into the chamber.

She rolled up the hem of her jeans to leave Joel's hunting knife exposed on her ankle where she could grab it easy. She popped free the safety strap of the knife's sheath.

She took a long breath. Every inch of her skin was alight with prickling heat.

"If you hear trouble, you turn back and run," Clark said to the boys, and she rolled up her window and drove.

LUKE

Luke stepped from the dim silver Airstream and blinked at the brilliant lights. Two boys were pissing into an empty Igloo cooler outside the red trailer across the circle. They nodded to him and looked away. Luke wiped some lube from his crotch, glanced back inside the silver Airstream and, when no one tried to stop him, he walked away.

Before a cop had caught him fucking a random trick from Rockdale ("Tyson," the boy had called himself, though the student ID in his cupholder had carried a different name) in a Chili's parking lot back in July, Luke had been convinced that he and Tyson were destined to be boyfriends. His heartbreak when the boy had evaporated afterward had hurt Luke far more than any of the predictable grief he'd caught from his father. Later, when Luke had realized there was a reason Wesley Mores seemed to understand him so well, Luke had felt a brief spark of hope, a silly spell of adoration, but when he'd finally succeeded in getting alone with Wesley last Friday night he had been disillusioned again.

Wesley had pushed Luke's lips away from his mouth and down to his lap, had accepted head with the same grimace Luke saw on the faces of the boys here tonight in the Bright Lands. They all scowled and forced their eyes closed and pretended that they didn't need this.

It was pathetic, really. Luke had no heart for it.

Instead, he wandered. He hurried past that squat black camper trailer in which he'd seen Joel Whitley earlier—that trailer spooked him bad—and ambled up the creaky steps of the tall triple-wide. He stopped at the porch. Nailed to the triple-wide's door frame was a sign: PLEASURE THIS PRETTY BEAUTY: $50 LICK PUSSY $100—

Luke stopped reading. It was rather a long list, and the sight of some of the things on it made his dinner roil in his stomach. There was a smell coming from inside the triple-wide— an awful mix of decay and cheap citrus candles—that really wasn't helping.

And when Luke saw something worse than either the sign or the smell he hurried back toward the steps.

The entire front wall of the triple-wide was shingled in Polaroids. The subject of each photo was identical. A boy, surrounded by a naked gang of others his own age, bled from a cut to the arm or the leg or the chest and stared at the camera with a numb shock Luke recognized very well. The only thing in the pictures that changed were the hairstyles, from shaggy pelts to baggy mullets to bleached-tip spikes and buzz cuts. The Polaroids rattled on their nails when the breeze stirred.

Luke recalled the flash of light he'd seen when his blindfold had been pulled free earlier. The message on this wall was simple enough, he supposed: *Talk at your own risk.*

A note of alarm had been sounding, all night, in a distant corner of Luke's head. It grew too loud now to ignore. What would the men here do if they discovered that the only reason Luke was still in the closet was simply because no one had ever asked? If they were to discover that he had no fear of anyone knowing the truth about him?

A warped little voice called from the triple-wide's door, "Is someone there?"

Luke kept moving. He skirted a massive chugging generator that reeked of gasoline. He heard a loud moan of ecstasy come from the red trailer but he didn't care. After years of solitary nights and empty weekends, Luke was so saddened by the brotherhood he'd found here that all he wanted to do was leave.

He noticed something odd: the dark spots of his blood in the dirt at the center of the circle were gone. There was no breeze that could have blown the bloody dirt away (and besides, wouldn't the blood make the dirt too heavy for the breeze to lift?) and surely it hadn't been so long the blood could have dried away so thoroughly it left no trace. It was almost as if the ground had swallowed it.

He didn't like that idea. He didn't like that idea at all.

He hustled past the generator toward an orange RV that looked (mercifully) empty. He was only spooking himself—surely that's all it was—but the longer he stayed out on this thirsty ground, here under these lights, the more certain he became that something—not some*one*, his mind told him, some*thing*—was watching him. That coming out here might have been an enormous mistake.

HOME ON THE RANGE read the sign above the orange RV's door, and sure enough, the dim trailer was stuffed inside with cowboy kitsch: Indian rugs, cow skulls, a lovingly lit photograph of some twink named Roy Rogers. An old television in a walnut case was playing grainy porn. Luke supposed it would pass the time.

Lowering himself onto a couch in the dark, he almost sat

on a boy's face by mistake. He jumped, turned back, apologized to the kid sprawled over the seat beneath him. The boy had a buzzed head and a dirty blond crotch and he gave Luke a carnivorous little smile that was the first welcome sight Luke had seen all night. It was the defensive tackle from the Stable Shootout.

"You sacked me at the game," Luke said.

"It was an honor and a privilege." The tackle sat up, handed Luke his beer. "Cheers."

Luke hesitated, smiled back. "Cheers."

They passed the bottle in silence for a time, watching the desultory porn, their knees just barely touching. Luke leaned against the arm of the sofa and unwittingly released a sigh.

"It's a lot to handle, isn't it?" the Stallion said finally.

"The nineties?" Luke said, nodding at the TV.

"All of this."

Luke nodded, drank, said, "I don't understand—are the guys here actually straight?"

"Not the angry ones." The Stallion laughed. "The angry ones are gay as hell—the old dudes are good at spotting fags. But some of the dudes here are straightish, sure. They like to try some no-strings shit like they could in the city, see what the fuss is about. Mostly I think they like having a secret, you know? Getting out of trouble around home. Getting pampered."

"And there's drugs."

The boy nodded. "And there's drugs."

"It's kind of like a dream. At first, I mean."

The Stallion hesitated before he drank. "It ain't free, you know. Those Old Boys, they always want some gratitude from you eventually."

Luke studied him. He saw a pain on the other boy's face, the mark of something Luke knew would never be named. "Were you hiding in here?"

"Maybe I was just waiting for you." The Stallion smiled, extended a slippery hand. "Bryan, by the way."

"Luke."

"How come you're all the way over there, Luke?"

Mitchell Malacek found them joined together at the mouth a few minutes later. He waited until Luke looked up with a line of spit dangling from his chin. Mitchell said with a snicker, "Can I borrow your gloves? I swear I'll get them—"

Luke waved vaguely toward the door. "They're in the back of my truck. The gate's unlocked."

Luke forgot about Mitchell almost the moment he was gone, forgot all his earlier misgivings, forgot most everything. With every second his lips lingered on this boy with his toothy smile, Luke hoped that dawn would never come.

BETHANY

When Mitchell Malacek dropped the tail of the truck, Bethany had the rifle aimed directly at his forehead. His mouth dropped into a cartoon's "Oh" of surprise.

In a tight, dangerous voice Bethany said, "Don't move."

The fucker bolted.

She followed him with the rifle's barrel. Her finger hesitated on the trigger for one second.

Another.

She couldn't do it.

Malacek was gone.

Shit.

Run, she told herself. *Run* now.

Bethany rose into a crouch, clutched the rifle carefully by the stock and frogwalked down the bed of the truck. She leaped into the grass and collapsed when she tried to stand. Blood burned as it flooded back into her veins.

She threw an arm over the truck's open gate. She dragged herself up.

Run.

JOEL

Parter crouched over Kimbra, pressed his fingers to her neck.

"Dad," she moaned. "It hurts."

"Christ," Boone said to Joel, shaking all over, tears in his eyes. "You see what you've done? What'll her father say?"

Parter and Browder exchanged frowns. Browder tightened his grip on the knife.

"Wait!" Joel shouted, straining at the clasps on his ankles and nearly falling on his face.

Browder grabbed a handful of Kimbra's hair. He placed his knee in the small of her back. He brought the knife to her neck.

"Coach!"

A boy was shouting outside, pounding the trailer's door. "Coach, there's someone here."

Browder pulled the knife away, sprang to his feet.

Boone opened the refrigerator and retrieved a handgun

from inside (*because of course*, Joel thought: *what Texas fantasy would be complete without a gun in every crevice?*) and gave Parter a resigned nod. Boone stepped past Joel and found Mitchell Malacek waiting outside, pointing furiously to something Joel couldn't see.

"Bethany Tanner!" Mitchell said. "Luke's truck. She's got a gun."

"Where is she now?" Parter pushed Boone aside.

Mitchell's face went white. "I—I—"

Parter let out a roar and shoved the boy off the porch. Mitchell landed on his ass in the dirt.

"Go find her!"

A cry of alarm went up outside. Boone followed Parter out the door a moment later, the gun in his hand trembling.

Browder did not. No sooner had the deputy reached the open doorway than he stopped as abruptly as if he'd struck a wall. He stood very still as boys started running and shouting.

When he looked back, Browder's eyes were not his own. They were flat and glassy black and they were regarding Joel with the smug reptile's intelligence that had fixed on him the moment he'd arrived back in Pettis County, that had watched him in the park ten years ago, that had watched countless boys in this place endure all manner of tender treatment.

Browder's mouth opened in a smile and Joel saw that past his teeth lay a deep, infinite black.

A whisper slithered out from that darkness.

imissedyou

BETHANY

Blood flooding back into her veins like liquid fire, Bethany limped away from Luke's truck, his rifle clutched to her side. Parked outside the circle of trailers was a loose cluster of other trucks, some of them unlocked, none with keys anywhere obvious. Bethany heard boys shouting. The entire camp was on alert: there were more angry men here than Bethany could hope to hold off on her own.

There was nothing behind her but empty country. They would hunt her down in seconds if she ran that way.

Only one option.

She bolted to the nearest trailer, a rusted silver Airstream, and threw herself into the dirt. Took a quick breath, scrambled beneath it.

Clay smeared her cheeks. Someone rushed past the trailer behind her a moment after she pulled her feet out of sight. Boys shouted from the trucks, from inside the circle.

The boys behind her moved on. Bethany adjusted her grip on the slick rifle.

A hand wrapped around her ankle.

Bethany kicked at the hand and felt another grip her free foot. She screamed. She struggled, she flailed but there was no resisting it: soft-eyed Tomas Hernandez dragged her wailing from beneath the trailer.

Bethany's head struck the base of the Airstream on the way out, her outstretched wrist was sliced by a rock. The loaded hunting rifle dropped, soundlessly, from her hand and settled into the dark.

JOEL

"You were the boy on the side, weren't you?" Joel said as the commotion raged around them.

Browder stepped back into the trailer and let the door close slowly behind him. He blinked and for a moment the deputy was himself again: furtive, bloodshot eyes, the teeth in his mouth a dull red in the light.

"Dylan was the real deal." Browder swiveled the knife in the air. He took a step forward and a moment later Joel felt blood running down his cheek, a flare of pain. "Football hadn't touched him."

Joel started babbling. It was a primal reflex: delay, delay, don't die.

"But it touched you? How did it touch you, Browder?"

"Jason had his foot. Ranger had his arm. Troy had his neck. I had my head. Bosheth likes us broken boys the best. He likes the way we *taste* inside." Tears streamed down the deputy's cheeks. He touched his forehead tenderly and said, "But not Dylan. The game never touched Dylan, no. It's why he was leaving. College was going to take him away from me."

Joel thought of the force that had tried to possess him last night at the park, the darkness that had overwhelmed his mind and nearly driven him to murder. He said, "You have to fight it, Browder. That thing inside you. You can't let that thing take you—"

"This was all your fucking fault!"

Joel felt a pain in his shoulder so excruciating he thought a sparking wire must have fallen loose from the rickety ceiling and come to rest there. He looked down and discovered that it was, in fact, Browder's knife, buried halfway to the hilt in the joint.

Joel fell backward. The knife slid back out again, grazing cold across the bone, and Joel landed hard on his ass. He stared at his ruined shoulder, gleaming black and bright in the red light, and fought the urge to vomit again.

"Do you hear me, Mr. Whitley? I said it was your fucking fault."

Joel felt the knife press against his neck, just like Dylan must have felt. Joel closed his eyes. Was he even surprised to learn he was going to die this way? After all, he'd spent all week learning that he and his brother were far more alike than he'd ever thought.

A strange croaking noise came from the kitchen. Kimbra tried to rise to her feet, struck something, slid down again. She moaned.

"For fuck's sake," Browder shouted. His voice was no longer quite his own. He spun toward the kitchen and hustled in her direction. The wet knife left a string of black beads across the pale floor. A furious hiss seeped from the darkness in his mouth.

Joel heard, from a great distance, someone who sounded an awful lot like Clark shouting somewhere outside.

Kimbra moaned again.

Faintly, very faintly, Joel heard another truck approaching.

LUKE

Luke joined Bryan, the Perlin tackle, as the boy rushed outside the orange trailer at the first sound of distress. Bethany Tanner—*how in all holy fuck had she made it here?*—was being dragged across the dirt by her feet, the spangles peeling from her green Bisonette's uniform like a fish's scales under a knife.

Tomas Hernandez dropped her precisely where Luke had stood just a short time before, dead center in the circle of trailers. Mr. Boone awaited her. In his leather jacket and motorcycle chaps, surrounded by a small army of naked boys, he resembled some sad parody of a warlord in a decimated future.

Mitchell Malacek descended the creaking stairs of the triple-wide bearing a handgun of his own. Parter followed him, a pump-action shotgun in one hand. To Luke's horror he saw the big man slipping something that looked an awful lot like a red .38 buck shell into the pocket of his old Bison jacket.

The hulking frame of Garrett Mason, sheathed in his pads and helmet, emerged behind them, a long, black AR-15 semi-automatic rifle braced across his chest.

"The fuck are they doing?" Luke said to Bryan, appalled.

Bryan was shaking. "Shut up, fuck, shut up."

Mr. Boone and Coach Parter and Garrett and Mitchell all came to stand above Bethany, regarding her. The generator rumbled. Bethany struggled to rise. Mitchell lowered his gun to within a few inches of her face. She went still.

Mr. Boone started to talk, turning to take in the two dozen boys standing on porches or framed in windows, their hands over their crotches and their mouths.

Boone couldn't quite keep a nervous stammer from his voice. "I know none you boys want trouble here. None of you—"

"What's that?" Garrett said.

The other boys stirred. Luke heard it too: the crunch of tires on dirt.

A sturdy-looking old Chevy rumbled to a stop between the green trailer (the trailer, Luke realized with a start, that held his phone and his keys) and the blue Water House. Four guns all swiveled around to face the truck's driver.

The Chevy shifted into Park. Slowly, slowly, its door swung open.

CLARK

She saw the old sign as she pulled in. A dingy relic from another age, it was secured to two metal poles, looking sad and limp and desperately cheery.

WELCOME TO THE BRIGHT LANDS, it read. Pink flamingos and green bison smiled and charged around a landscape of mobile homes that reigned over tended lawns, around pies cooling on windowsills and men draping their arms over the shoulders of their teenage sons. A NEW KIND OF COMMUNITY.

Oh sweet Jesus. Oh sweet Jesus.

She rumbled to a stop between two trailers—a blue one to her right, a green one to her left, a tall triple-wide dead ahead across the circle—and took in the scene.

Why hadn't she brought more guns?

Four armed men (boys, she thought, two of them were boys) stood before her, weapons drawn in her direction. A ghostly face framed by two plaits of brown hair slid up behind a window of the tall triple-wide and studied her with a loathing that didn't seem human. Clark blinked, and the face was gone.

Hadn't it looked a lot like Mr. Lott?

When no one lowered his gun, Clark saw no choice but to open her door. She took a careful step out of the truck, hands held high, and stood where her metal door still covered half her body. Where it concealed the pistol and revolver on her hips.

"Aren't we flattered, boys?" Mr. Boone said. "More company."

On the ground in the middle of the circle, Bethany Tanner looked about ready to rip these men's balls off with her teeth.

Clark saw no sign of Joel or Kimbra.

"I apologize for the interruption," Clark said. "I'm just here to collect a couple friends."

There was a brief hesitation, a consideration.

"It was Luke!" shouted Mitchell Malacek suddenly, a black Glock trembling in his hand. "I found Bethany Tanner with a gun in his truck. This bitch must have followed him here too."

All eyes turned to Luke Evers. He stood on the concrete porch of an orange RV, a low string of white Christmas lights turning his hair incandescent. The handsome kid next to Luke now stepped away with a look on his face like he'd stumbled into roadkill.

Luke turned in Clark's direction, mouth open, panic rising on his face. His eyes darted to a black camper trailer situated close to the tall triple-wide and returned to her. Did it again.

"I came alone," Clark shouted. "And if you'll just let me see Joel Whitley I'll be on my way." After a moment's hesitation she added, "I can take any girls you might have lying around off your hands too."

Parter said something to Mitchell and Garrett Mason that

Clark couldn't catch. The boys adjusted the grip on their guns. Clark inched one hand down toward her hip.

Boone struggled to get hold of the proceedings. "Well, maybe y'all leaving would be best for all involved."

The breeze stirred.

"Son of a *bitch*," Garrett said from behind the grill of his helmet.

Clark heard it too. *Oh sweet Jesus, no*: another truck was heading fast for the ring of trailers. Its chugging muffler was unmistakable. She turned and saw Whiskey Brazos racing toward a gap between the black camper and silver Airstream to her left. KT Staler was sitting wide-eyed in shotgun, T-Bay Baskin gawping behind him.

It happened so quick Clark couldn't stop it, so slow she couldn't miss a moment. Whiskey's face stretched with shock as the guns turned his way. Jamal, seated behind Whiskey, bent his body toward his door. T-Bay screamed. KT Staler was holding out his arm, mouthing, *"No!"*

Garrett Mason brought his AR-15 semiautomatic assault rifle to his shoulder and aimed down the sights with a hatred Clark could see through his helmet's grill.

Garrett fired.

KIMBRA

Well then. All summer long Kimbra and April had giggled whenever fresh young Deputy Browder in his tight khakis and polished boots had stepped into the Egg House, when he'd grinned at the waitress with that little twist in his lip that seemed sly and abashed all at once. Deputy Babe, all the girls had called him. He'd never seemed to pay Kimbra a minute's attention until this afternoon, when he'd waved to her from in front of the busted bank building.

And now here he was, hustling in her direction with every intention of killing her because she'd been dumb enough to help Joel Whitley, and she was handcuffed to a goddamn pipe. It was really something, *oh shit, no sir, you don't get this every day. Better think of something, darling, he's almost here.*

Now.

Thank God she'd been conscious enough on the truck ride here to realize that the duct tape around her ankles had been loose. While the men's attention had been elsewhere earlier she'd worked a leg free of the tape's binding. When Browder got close enough to smell—and Jesus, he suddenly had a stench on him that would skin a cat—Kimbra braced her elbows on the trailer floor, tightened her stomach, arched her back and blindly swung a stiff, meaty leg in the best goddamn kick of her high school career.

Her foot connected with Browder's ankle and the deputy stumbled. Kimbra spun out with her other leg and through pure luck caught the man behind the knee. The knife in his hand clattered to the floor.

Browder let out a little grunt as he fell. Kimbra felt his hand grasp at her ankle but she was too quick for him. She slid the foot away, pulled it up and drove it back. The kick knocked the deputy's head into something hard. She heard a wet thud.

She felt Browder's nose fold under the sole of her shoe with a snap.

Kimbra kicked him again, catching him on the forehead and knocking him back.

She kicked a third time and caught nothing but air. Her mind went white with panic.

But she was fine. She heard Browder slump to the floor beside her, smelling of clay and blood and spoiled meat.

"Holy shit," Joel said.

"Is he dead?" Kimbra said.

Gunshots came in reply, one-two-three-four quick pops. Glass shattering. Screams.

Five-six.

A bullet punched through the wall of the black camper and clanged against the pipe above her head.

LUKE

Luke saw KT's hand go up, saw the other boys in Whiskey's truck all struggling with their seat belts, saw Garrett's shoulder buck ever so slightly as the AR-15 fired.

The truck's windshield puckered. KT's head snapped back like a doll's. His eyes bulged. A piece of his forehead disappeared. His open mouth was empty one second. The next it was full of blood.

Boys started screaming, sprinting for cover, the doors of trailers, anywhere they could hide. Luke watched as Bethany sprang to her feet and bolted toward the Water House. Coach Parter raised his shotgun. Mitchell Malacek, his eyes glassy with meth and adrenaline, turned toward Luke with a raised Glock—

A memory chimed in Luke's mind. He remembered the sight of kerosene cans in Dylan's truck the morning after the church burned down, remembered the way Dylan had laughed when Luke had confronted him about it. Luke finally realized something: these boys hadn't brought him here to be their friend.

Luke turned back toward shelter.

The door to the orange RV was closed. Luke slammed against it in surprise, his head striking the frame. The door budged but held firm. Bryan the Stallion was inside, pressed against the door to keep it closed, and Luke was trapped out here on the porch.

"Bryan!" Luke shouted. "Bryan, open the—"

Thump-thump. Two rounds passed over Luke's shoulder and pierced the door of HOME ON THE RANGE. A shotgun boomed. A windshield shattered.

Thump-thump.

Luke tried to slam his shoulder against the door but he felt a cool pain in his side, felt his knees folding under him. Felt the cold porch strike his cheek.

CLARK

She shouted "Freeze!" in the seconds before Garrett started firing, fumbled for the pistol on her hip, but it was too late. Garrett fired four quick shots into the cab of the truck, two more at the blurry boys fleeing toward the black camper.

"Stop!" Boone was screaming, waving his handgun in the air. "What are you doing? What are you—"

Garrett glanced at Parter. Parter gave a little nod of assent.

Garrett made a quick swivel and planted two rounds in Mr. Boone.

The county attorney gawped at Mason. Coach Parter turned the shotgun her way and Clark ducked beneath the open door of her truck a moment before the windshield exploded.

Clark finally got hold of her pistol. She didn't bother asking herself if this was real, to ask how any of this was possible, no. She heard a few stray beads of the shotgun's spray *ting* against the old truck's door. She didn't plan to find out what a concentrated round of buckshot would do to this old Chevy metal. She took a breath.

One-two-three go.

Clark spun out from around the door, arms locked out, knees bent, praying that she remembered enough tactical training to survive this second, and this second, and this. She brought her pistol up, trained her eyes on the sight, aimed at the big man pumping a round into his shotgun.

She fired twice.

Her first shot grazed Parter and whizzed on to strike something behind him with a loud metallic *whang*. The second bullet struck the coach somewhere in the arm. He threw a hand over the wound and bolted for cover.

Clark readied herself to fire again and saw Mitchell Malacek turn his attention from the orange trailer—Luke Evers, blood smeared over his stomach, was collapsing outside its door—and turn a black Glock in her direction.

Clark fired first. She didn't hesitate. A warning shot, but good enough to spook Mitchell. The boy took three steps backward and squeezed off a round but Clark had already cleared the short distance to the jaunty green trailer on her left and heard the bullet strike the dirt where she'd just been standing.

She touched her father's old revolver, felt it tucked tight against her waist, ready and eager.

Anything would help.

Silence fell over the Bright Lands, broken only by a chugging generator.

Clark poked her head around the green trailer to survey the scene. The circle was deserted. No men, no boys, no Bethany. With a stab in her heart, Clark saw Luke Evers lying on the concrete porch of the orange RV ten yards away, on the far side of the circle from her. *So much for brotherhood*, Clark thought: Mitchell Malacek had shot him in the back.

She heard a faint, high shriek beneath her feet, a sound like a nail dragged across a brick. When the ground shook a moment later the force of the quake was so strong the field lights above the circle trembled on their stalks, threw wild shadows around the trailers. That thing down there was almost here, and Clark had an ugly suspicion it would find a way to get aboveground soon enough. If she didn't get Joel and the others out of here they might just have to introduce themselves to Bosheth himself.

Luke wasn't moving. Nothing she could do for him now. Instead, Clark thought of what he'd done earlier, before the shooting had started. Luke's eyes had gone twice from her face to the black camper trailer and back again. It might have been nothing, or he might have been trying to tell her what she needed to know. It was all she had.

Go.

Hustling through the darkness behind the green trailer, Clark strained to track this place's geography. From this trailer, moving up her side of the circle should bring her first to the silver Airstream, then to Whiskey Brazos's truck, then to a long exposed space and then the black camper.

If Joel was still alive, and if he was there in that black camper—so many if's—then maybe Kimbra was alive and with him as well. Maybe Clark could salvage some of this situation. Maybe she wouldn't spend a lifetime choked by the shame she already felt for involving KT, Jamal, T-Bay and Whiskey in a firefight.

Go.

As Clark reached the end of the green trailer some strange monster composed of nothing but pale flesh and black leather threw itself across the ground in front of her. She raised her gun to fire, thinking it was the twitchy thing from her nightmares, but no: it was only Mr. Boone, heaving himself along on his elbows with what little life was left in him. Boone turned to look up at her, blood pumping from his nose, a black Glock held loosely in his hand.

He said something choked and wet. His eyes strained to find her in the dim light. "Bloated. The others are bloated."

Clark didn't move until blood came puddling up from Boone's mouth and the light left his eyes and then she grabbed the Glock in his hand and kept moving.

She was hoarding guns like the government was coming for them. The Glock was customized, very lightweight. An elegant tiger stripe ran along the grip, the letters HB monogrammed on the base like the vanity plates Mr. Harlan Boone always fastened to his new trucks. Clark thought of a similar gun she'd seen in Mitchell's hand earlier and wondered if the two Glocks didn't form a pair.

She dropped the new pistol into the empty holster on her hip and bolted the short distance to the silver Airstream. Nothing. No shouts, no gunshots. Clark pressed her back to the trailer's cold aluminum wall and breathed.

When she looked to her right, her eyes settled on Whiskey's truck parked a few feet away. She fought a wave of nausea at the sight inside. KT Staler's face—or what was left of it—lay pressed against the glass of the truck's passenger window like a specimen on a slide. Awful as that was, Clark didn't feel herself slipping loose of her bearings until she saw T-Bay Baskin, sitting dead in the seat behind KT and wearing a great bib of blood on his shirt.

The crackle of splintering wood from up ahead cleared her mind. She kept moving.

JAMAL

For a very long time all Jamal could see were T-Bay's bright eyes: they had locked on to his the moment the bullet had slid into his neck. Jamal had fumbled blindly with the handle of the truck's door, unable to look away from his dying teammate, and then a bullet had shattered the cab's back window and Jamal had thrown himself in the dirt and run.

"Let me talk to them," KT had said.

"She said for us to wait," T-Bay had said.

"They'll never listen to her," KT had said.

After a long silence, Whiskey had said, *"Are you sure?"*

Oh, these guys had listened alright. KT was dead, T-Bay was dead and now Jamal was crouched behind a black camper, Whiskey Brazos shaking and puking on his shoes beside him. Jamal stared at the black horizon and saw T-Bay's wide white eyes staring back at him.

When Jamal returned to himself—how long had his mind

left him? A second? A year?—he heard metal screeching inside the black camper against which he and Whiskey were sheltered. He realized that he and Whiskey were holding hands. The portly boy was mumbling something: "It feeds help it feeds help."

Jamal smacked Whiskey and pressed his hand to the boy's mouth. "There's someone in there," Jamal whispered, nodding his head at the black camper.

But Whiskey wasn't listening to him. The pale boy had gone paler. A moment later and Jamal heard it too. To their left, footsteps were coming rapidly around the back of the bloody truck. Coming their way.

KIMBRA

When the gunshots quieted, Kimbra raised her head. She heard footsteps somewhere nearby, heard silence. *Move.*

Kimbra blinked at the red light of the black camper, the things on the wall, the bare kitchen. Browder was slumped on the ground near a black metal refrigerator with a sharp corner on its door. He didn't appear to be breathing.

From a few feet away Joel whispered, "Do you see a key to these cuffs on him?"

She turned back and saw Joel seated, his ankles cuffed to hooks in the floor, his hands pressed to his shoulder as something black and bright seeped through. "What did he *do* to you?" she said.

"No keys?"

She ran her eye over Browder's body and didn't see anything useful on him. "I think he's dead."

Joel said weakly, "That pipe looks loose."

Kimbra turned away from Browder's corpse and followed Joel's eyes up the kitchen's wall. Her hands had been cuffed— so tightly her fingers were numb—around a rusted pipe that ran between two exposed joists. Kimbra lifted her arms to situate herself well back on her ass. She pulled her legs up, easing them past Browder's slack body, and braced a foot against the wall's joists.

She jerked the chain of her cuffs against the pipe and felt it shift, loose in its casing. *Dry rot*, she thought. Her father would have just the fix.

"Try it again," Joel said in a low voice. "I think you can pull that pipe loose."

She pulled again. The pipe did, indeed, move a little.

From behind the trailer's back wall she heard a man's voice. *Hurry*.

Joel was right: with enough leverage, she might just be able to wrench the pipe from the wall and free herself, though her numb fingers refused to help her. She listened to the way the chain of the cuffs click-clacked against the rusty metal and grimaced. This wasn't going to be pleasant.

She braced her other foot against a joist, took a long breath, bit her lip. She pushed with her legs and pulled against the pipe with the cuffs' chain and choked on a squeal. A sharp bite of metal on her wrist, a sudden cold ache in the bone. *This*, she thought, *must be what it's like to use a rowing machine in hell*.

When she stopped to catch her breath, Joel said behind her, "You've got this. Please."

"Easy for you to say," she said through a gasp. Kimbra saw blood beading around the tight cuffs. She braced her legs again. Pulled.

She'd never felt pain like this before. She pulled until she thought her arms would tear free of her shoulders, pulled until she thought every bone in her wrists had been ground to powder. She bit the top hem of her Bisonette's singlet and screamed into her teeth.

The pipe shifted an inch. Another. She heard a crack, a low moan of old wood and then, in a shower of splinters and dust, the pipe snapped free of its casing and came plummeting toward her face.

She fell back, hit the kitchen's linoleum, twisted her head away. The pipe landed an inch from her ear with a dull thud.

Kimbra rose, panting, to one elbow. Browder still lay motionless. Joel, in the living room, gave her an exhausted thumbs-up. Even in the red light Kimbra could see that his face had gone very white. You didn't have to be a doctor: the guy had lost an enormous amount of blood.

Kimbra stumbled along the length of the pipe, pulled her wrists free over its little cap of splintered wood and fumbled off the loop of tape that clung to her ankle. She checked Browder's pockets—empty—and grabbed the long hunting knife from where it rested a few inches from his fingers. She carried it with her into the living room.

Someone rapped on the trailer's shuttered back window. No sooner had she heard the sound than the trailer's lights dimmed, died and shook back to life again.

"Joel?" said a muffled voice.

"Clark." With his good hand, Joel tugged at the cuffs around his ankles that bound him to the floor.

Kimbra fumbled with the latch of the window shutter.

Officer Clark was outside, looking up at her through the bars over the window—because *of course* there would be bars over the window—while Jamal Reynolds and Whiskey Brazos—of all fucking people—stood trembling behind her. Kimbra raised her bleeding, cuffed wrists and said, "Joel's hurt bad. We need keys."

Clark fumbled at her belt, said, "Can you raise that window?"

It didn't budge. Kimbra returned a moment later with a

metal paddle the size of a fly swatter. She shattered the window with the butt of the paddle, swept the glass away with its business end. Clark raised an eyebrow, passed Kimbra a small ring of keys. "Hopefully those cuffs came from the department," Clark said.

"Is KT with you?" Kimbra asked.

The stillness that settled over the three of them told her everything she needed to know.

Oh.

"Here." Joel held out his hands. Kimbra uncuffed him first, let him take the keys and free her a moment later. Her wrists burned. KT was dead. "Are you alright?" Joel asked her, and she tried to smile. She honestly didn't know the answer to that question.

"Dadders would say I'm better off," she finally said, and touched her dry face as if she expected to find a tear there.

"What's going on out front?" Clark asked, and as Joel worked at the cuffs on his ankles Kimbra crept to the trailer's other window. She swung it open and took a quick breath. She was here, in dreamland.

Two guys she didn't recognize stared at her—their mouths agape, their faces jaundiced with fear—from the windows of a red trailer on the other side of the circle. Directly across from her, past the tall triple-wide that had lorded over her all week in her sleep, Kimbra saw a boy slumped on a concrete porch outside an orange RV. The boy rose from a puddle of blood, reaching for the RV's doorknob, and fell back down. It was Luke Evers, she realized, struggling but alive.

Kimbra saw a tall man step from the far side of the triple-wide, a shotgun in his hands, and Luke's survival suddenly became much more tenuous. Kimbra had given up being surprised tonight. The fact that Coach Parter would be here, shotgun in hand, slipping a shell of buckshot from the pocket of his Bison jacket, seemed just as logical as all the other nightmares she'd experienced since Dylan Whitley had gotten him-self murdered.

A moment later, Mitchell Malacek emerged from the red trailer. He locked eyes with Parter. Kimbra watched Mitchell and Parter engage in a terse, wordless deliberation.

Parter pointed Mitchell toward the blue trailer at the far end of the circle. Mitchell nodded at Luke. Parter made a big gesture and pointed to his chest: *"Mine."*

CLARK

"Officer, Luke's alive," Kimbra said, hurrying back across the black camper but speaking calmly, logically. Clark was coming to like this competent girl. "I think he's in trouble though—Coach Parter's out there. He's got a gun."

"What about the others?" Clark said.

Kimbra didn't hesitate. "Mitchell Malacek has a pistol. Parter told him to go do something in that blue trailer down the other end."

"I saw Bethany Tanner run in there," Whiskey said.

"What about Garrett Mason?" Clark said. "He's the last person armed."

"I didn't see him. There's some other guys hiding but they look too scared to do anything. I—" Kimbra paused. "Joel says the keys aren't working for the cuffs on his feet."

"I'll get Parter." Jamal touched Clark's arm. "Do you have another gun?"

Did she ever. "Do you know how to shoot?"

"He can't be hard to miss."

With a heavy lurch of apprehension, Clark pulled her father's revolver from the back of her jeans and passed it to Jamal. "There's no safety on this." She tapped the hammer. "You pull this back till it clicks—"

"I can figure it out."

Jamal disappeared around the other end of the black camper before she could say another word.

Whiskey said, "Let me help Bethany."

Color was finally coming back into the boy's cheeks. Clark said, "Can you fire a pistol?"

"My brother's in the Guard."

It would have to do. Clark pulled Boone's fancy Glock from her hip. "Go around the back way," she said, nodding in the direction she'd just come.

The boy accepted the gun, sighed at the grisly sight of his truck and nodded to Clark over his shoulder. He took off, bent low at the waist like he was prepping for a snap.

"Officer," Kimbra said. "If they stop Parter and Mitchell I think I can help Luke."

Clark heard the sound of fabric tearing. She rose onto her tiptoes to peer into the black camper—with a woozy rush of déjà vu she finally recognized that Joel was seated precisely where Clark's bed had been situated all week in her dreams—and saw Kimbra tying a strip of Joel's shirt around his bloody shoulder and knotting it tight. The girl was coming in handy.

"Alright," Clark said. "Wait for my signal."

A gunshot echoed from the direction of the triple-wide. They froze.

Jamal shouted, "Clear!"

A moment later, Whiskey shouted, "Clear!"

She heard the screech of stone shearing from stone beneath

her. Louder now. Closer. The lights above the circle flickered again.

Clark met Joel's eye through the window. A quick, silent conference—*This is fucked/I agree*—before Clark nodded to Kimbra. "Remember—wait for my signal," she said, and headed around the side of the black camper.

BETHANY

Mitchell Malacek collapsed into the blue trailer, falling face-first into the basin of a long metal urinal that ran the length of the trailer's wall. Whiskey Brazos panted in the open door, the butt of his handgun still raised where he had coldcocked Mitchell a moment before. Bethany was pressed into the trailer's back corner, grasping a toilet seat over her head like a club, ready to swing. If Whiskey hadn't knocked Malacek unconscious the moment Mitchell had stepped through the door Bethany supposed she probably would have killed the guy. She was unsurprised to realize this didn't bother her.

Whiskey bent down to grab the handgun that Mitchell had dropped and stuck the pistol down the back of his pants.

Bethany lowered the toilet seat to the floor. She looked first at Whiskey and then at Ricky Turner, bent over one of the trailer's many toilets, tears in his eyes, a rubber douche trembling in his hands.

Whiskey shouted "Clear!" through the open door.

Mitchell groaned in the urinal trough. Bethany crossed the narrow trailer briskly and slammed the toe of her shoe into his groin. Mitchell let out a yelp of pain and stared at her, aghast. She smoothed the hem of her Bisonette singlet.

"Now," Bethany said. "Does anyone want to explain what the fuck is going on here?"

JAMAL

Jamal wasn't entirely certain what a generator was supposed to sound like, but he didn't care one bit for the wet sputtery noises the Bright Lands' generator was coughing up. The trailer park appeared to be run entirely off a single massive black box that stood taller than Jamal by a good six inches. The name on its face—MITSUBISHI—was dancing violently a few inches to his right. He wondered if the thing had been hit in all the gunfire. Frankly, he didn't want to find out.

"I hope you understand the arrest weren't nothing personal, Reynolds," Coach Parter said, hands over his head. "When Boone told Mason to hold on to Whitley's socks I never thought we'd find a use for them. But once Staler started setting you up with the cops, saying you was mad at Dylan for some reason, well…"

Jamal said nothing. The big man stood a few feet away, just past the front of the triple-wide, the shotgun somewhere in the dirt. Parter had dropped the .38 easy enough when Jamal had come around the back of the trailer a moment before. The warning shot Jamal had fired had certainly helped the coach over any hesitation.

Ahead and to the left of Parter, on the steps of the orange RV, Luke Evers lay in blood.

Parter glanced back at Jamal over his shoulder. "It was all just bad luck."

Jamal cocked the hammer of the revolver and felt the gun tremble in his hand with a supple, satisfying *clunk*—why didn't every black man in this state own a gun? Jamal wondered— and Parter froze at the sound.

"You ever notice the only brown kid here is light enough to be white?"

Parter swallowed.

Jamal shouted to the others. "We doing this or what?"

CLARK

She pressed herself to a corner of the black camper and trained her gun on the windows of the silver Airstream into which she was certain—ninety percent certain—she had seen Garrett Mason and his military-issued assault rifle flee earlier. Ninety-five percent certain. Ninety. It had been so hectic when the bullets had started flying a few minutes ago, young men had been running in every direction, but surely she wouldn't have mistaken Mason making a break for the Airstream. In his pads and his helmet he couldn't have been that hard to miss, could he?

"We doing this or what?" Jamal shouted.

Or had he been bolting for the green trailer?

Silver or green. Silver or green.

Nothing moved in either window.

Silver. She trained her gun on the Airstream and shouted, "Clear."

KIMBRA

Kimbra took up a place by the camper's door. She eased it open, taking in the trailer park, judged the distance to Luke's orange RV and wondered for the first time if she weren't making a colossal mistake. Hadn't Luke come out here of his own accord? Hadn't he had sense enough to know that nothing good came of boys like Mitchell Malacek or Garrett Mason (or, for that matter, their good friend, poor broken KT Staler)?

Too late. When Kimbra saw Luke struggle to rise again in his pool of blood she knew she couldn't do anything but try to help him. Luke could be aloof, could be embarrassingly alone, but he didn't deserve to die here.

And besides: Kimbra suspected that if it weren't for all her plans and tricks over the summer Luke probably wouldn't have been brought here in the first place.

"Good luck," Joel said.

Without looking back, Kimbra said, "I think you need it more than me, man."

A brief silence. The night held its breath. She tightened her grip on Browder's knife, just in case any of the frightened boys she saw watching her from their windows suddenly decided they wanted to get in her way. Better safe than sorry.

Clark shouted, "Clear!"

Kimbra leaped to the ground outside. The moment she landed she heard a strange chugging noise, saw the lights of the trailer park go dark around her. Before the lights went down she saw it: the truck parked near the side of the black trailer, the truck full of blood, the truck full of bits of the beautiful boy she'd spent far too many years of her life hoping to fix.

Kimbra saw KT's corpse before the lights went out and hesitated for just a moment before she started running.

There were two pops of gunfire. The sound of glass shattering. She ran faster.

And then a third shot—furious and deafening as a thunderclap—burst over the Bright Lands. A strange, sharp heat seeped across Kimbra's chest.

The ground swallowed her feet.

The lights kicked on again. Above her, staring out from inside the tall triple-wide, Kimbra saw the long barrel of a high-caliber hunting rifle extended in her direction. She even imagined she saw a trail of smoke rising from the tip.

And above the gun? It was the face that had haunted her all week in her sleep.

Kimbra saw herself—her twin, her mirror image—staring at her through the triple-wide's window, eyes wide with surprise under a head of perfect brown hair, clad in a tight Bisonette singlet.

But no, not quite an identical twin: Kimbra had never managed hair that pretty.

And when, she wondered, had she grown such a funny mustache?

CLARK

The moment Clark shouted "Clear!" she saw movement in the green trailer. Garrett Mason appeared in the window Clark wasn't covering and aimed his AR-15 in Kimbra's direction.

She pivoted, squeezed off two shots at him.

The lights died. The trailer's windows shattered. Garrett tumbled out of view. And behind Clark there came the sound of a rifle crack—a gunman, there was another gunman here—and Kimbra—

Clark spun around the front of the black camper as the lights came up again. She saw the way Kimbra hit the dirt: you didn't get up again after falling like that.

Clark saw a flash of metal above her in the window of the triple-wide and let her momentum carry her up the step of the black camper. She leaped across the threshold and threw the door shut behind her. Something in the door's frame let out a loud, heavy *clunk*.

"No!" From the direction of the tall triple-wide, Clark heard Mr. Lott let out a scream. *"No!* How is she *here*? Why did no one tell me she was *here*?"

Joel stared at Clark. *No,* his eyes said.

She could only nod her head. *Yes.*

JAMAL

The rifle shot sent Parter running up the steps of the triple-wide before Jamal could think to fire his revolver.

"Shit," Jamal shouted. He bolted after the big man.

He didn't make it far. Just past the generator he felt his feet slip out from under him. He barely got his elbow down in time to break the fall.

Pain spiked up Jamal's arm. Someone was screaming. Jamal was choking. He had landed with a splash in something cool and oily that flew up his nose and down his throat.

Gasoline. The chugging old generator was bleeding gasoline.

BETHANY

"What the fuck just happened?" Whiskey said, the rifle crack still ringing in their ears.

"Don't take your gun off him."

Mitchell groaned behind her. Bethany stood in the door of the Water House and watched as Coach Parter seemed to fly up the steps of the tall triple-wide. Mr. Lott—he looked hideous in a wig, God bless him—screamed from inside one of the triple-wide's windows, wailing like a piece of his soul was being pulled out through his mouth. Bethany's mind was moving fast. She refused to look at Kimbra's spangled corpse, clad in a singlet identical to the one Bethany was wearing.

Bethany knew—*knew*—that that rifle's bullet had been meant for her own heart.

Coach Parter made it through the triple-wide's door. Mr. Lott shouted something at him that Bethany couldn't hear.

She didn't need to. A moment later Lott had the barrel of the rifle in his mouth.

Bethany saw Jamal leaning against the corner of the tall trailer's porch, breathing hard, his clothes soaked. He met her eye. Bethany prayed that the little nod she gave him said everything she wanted to say: *I'm sorry* and *Good luck*.

She looked back up at the triple-wide's window in time to watch Mr. Lott's wig come off with the top of his skull.

And there was Jamal, revolver in his hand, climbing the steps of the tall trailer's porch two at a time.

JOEL

"Fucking knockoffs," Clark said under her breath, crouched in Joel's drying vomit, struggling with the handcuffs on his ankles.

A second rifle crack. Clark didn't pause.

"Hey," Joel said, his voice sounding very soft to his own ears. "I'm sorry."

"You can explain later," Clark said, and the cuff around his left ankle finally popped free.

"No. I mean about Troy."

Clark started work on the other ankle.

"You deserved to know everything," Joel said.

Clark opened her mouth to speak, but instead she let out a grunt of pain when Browder's boot struck the side of her head.

She fell. Browder took two staggering steps forward and kicked Clark hard in the stomach. She went limp. Browder bent over her body.

Joel's brain struggled to think. His hand was heavy. He laid it over the cuff that remained latched around his right ankle and fumbled with the key Clark had left in the lock.

Browder rose to his feet, swung Clark's pistol to within a foot of Joel's face.

"Do you know how hard it is to get a text message out here, Mr. Whitley?"

Browder's eyes were black. His teeth were black. It wasn't a trick of the strange light. From somewhere deep inside Browder came the voice Joel had heard whispering to him the day he arrived. It was slick and it was deep and it was *old*.

It wasn't whispering now.

"And yet would you believe that's just what happened when Dylan Whitley was sitting exactly where you're sitting now, swearing to our poor young Browder that he had no plans to leave the man."

I'm getting you out

"Deputy Browder, he was so convinced that Dylan was trying to get away from him. Your brother kept swearing and swearing that the whoring ad was fake, that he hadn't asked you to come back to Bentley to help him, that he didn't want money from you or anybody. He swore he was going to college in Waco so he could come home on the weekends. They'd be lovers for life, Dylan said. Forever and ever." Browder's face opened in a smile. "And then Dylan's phone buzzed."

Joel remembered every word of the message he had sent to Dylan on Friday night after the game, back when he'd been driving the rainy roads of town and was certain he could save his brother with a few swipes of his credit card.

"And it was beautiful old you."

Don't worry. I'm getting you out of this shit hole.

"Can you blame the poor deputy for coming off his head at that moment, Mr. Whitley? Can you blame me for whispering a little encouragement in his ear?" Browder brought his gun to Joel's temple.

For a moment, Joel forgot his pain or his fear. He lost all of the resolve he'd gathered over the week. He was, instead, so crushed with shame at his own arrogance that he found it impossible to breathe. Pressing a hand to his ruined shoulder, marveling at the cost of his negligence—a dead brother, a dead cheerleader, the only person who would ever have come to his rescue about to be murdered—Joel felt all his hope seeping out between his bloody fingers. If only, if only. If only he'd gone home to the city last night. If only he had foregone one long white night to call his brother in the last ten years. If only he'd ever fucking cared.

"I'd waited so long, Mr. Whitley. I just needed a boy's worth of blood."

Browder opened his mouth. A hideous sucking noise came from inside his head—a sound like a straw slurping at the bottom of a cup—and Joel could feel the creature inside the deputy sucking something from the air of the trailer. Feeding.

"What are you?" Joel said.

Browder smiled wider. "Hungry."

With a roar, Clark threw herself against the deputy, grabbed for the pistol. A gunshot rang in Joel's ear, singed his hair.

Browder and Clark landed against the wall together. The gun tumbled to the floor.

JAMAL

The inside of the tall triple-wide smelled of lemons and cordite and rot. It was some strange approximation of a man cave: big-screen TV occupied by a pair of chicks with dicks, a half-deflated sex doll with a mouth open in permanent surprise, a long berber couch. Shelves full of football trophies lined the walls, scented candles burning amid the cheap metal like shrines assembled at a strip mall.

The walls, just like the wall Jamal had passed outside on the porch, were papered with Polaroids of boys: boys laughing under the white Christmas lights outside, naked boys drinking, boys wrestling in the dirt.

Mr. Lott's body lay near the open window through which he'd fired at Kimbra, just past the couch, the barrel of the rifle now jutting through what remained of his head. Jamal stared. It took real commitment to shoot yourself with a rifle that big.

Coach Parter, standing across the couch from Jamal, raised

one hand again when Jamal brought up the revolver. He pressed the other hand against a wound in his arm.

"The fuck is wrong with you people?" Jamal said.

"That's a very good question, son," Parter replied. He took a little step to one side and revealed a long hallway that stretched into the back of the trailer behind him. "You've made mistakes yourself, though, haven't you?"

Jamal hardly heard him—something had grabbed hold of his mind. His feet seemed to move on their own. He stumbled forward until he stood at the threshold of the hall, staring at an open bedroom a few yards away, a room whose walls were paneled with mirrors. In the center of the room there was a hole in the floor.

A pit.

"I thought so," Parter said, very close by.

A strange hissing noise rose from the pit like steam escaping an overwrought radiator.

"That creature—it found us a long time ago, back when we was boys and we made our first mistake. It's slept down there ever since. I think it's even helped keep us concealed out here, I really do." Parter chuckled. "Who knew all this time it was just waiting for someone to spill a little more blood?"

shamefulboy, whispered the voice in Jamal's mind. He lowered the revolver and let it dangle loosely at his side. His arms prickled like they'd died in his sleep. *yourfault*

The thing was right. It *was* his fault. All of this—Dylan dying, KT dying, Kimbra dying—he could have stopped all of it months ago, could have made Dylan talk, could have stopped everything if he'd only asked—

He blinked and the pit had grown wider, was spreading, the walls of the trailer dangling where their floors had fallen away, the Polaroids fluttering. Without realizing it, Jamal had taken a step closer.

A new voice came from the pit. A younger, brighter voice,

but Jamal recognized it all the same. It was Coach Parter, years ago, speaking to him now. *"But don't you like it, Cor? We made all this for us."*

"Christ, Parter, for us?" Another young man spoke, one Jamal didn't know. He sounded appalled. *"What do you think I am?"*

"You're a man like us," said another boy, pompous and scared.

"There's nothing wrong with this," said quieter, younger Mr. Lott.

But the boy Parter called Cor was having none of it. *"Y'all queers got the wrong end of things. Don't you got any fucking dignity? Don't you—"*

A gunshot rose from the pit. A heavy thud of a body falling. A gasp of pain.

The pit had come right to Jamal's toes. He couldn't move as the wooden floors began to buckle under his sneakers. He didn't *want* to move. Maybe it was best if he let things end here. He wasn't sure he could bear to live in a world that could ache with a shame like this.

"Alshoth Bosheth Toloth." Parter spoke with a deep voice that wasn't quite his own.

It was over, Jamal thought. And just as well: he'd fucked everything royally.

But as Jamal watched the boards under his toes disappear, he saw a sudden small flare of light glint at him from deep in the dark.

It was an eye.

Horror brought his mind roaring back. He pushed himself out of the hallway a moment before the floor on which he had just been standing collapsed.

He turned in time to see Coach Parter reaching for the rifle in Mr. Lott's hands.

"Hey, Coach," Jamal shouted.

Parter glanced over his shoulder, hesitated.

Jamal didn't. He lobbed the cocked revolver across the

couch. The gun spun gently through the air, end over end, and landed at Parter's feet.

It worked better than Jamal could have hoped. When the revolver struck the floor its hammer sprang into the chambered round and the spark of the bullet's detonation ignited the gasoline that had soaked the gun's other chambers. Five bullets fired at once, and because only one bullet had anywhere to travel the other four could only explode with a furious burst of shrapnel. The gun had become a hand grenade.

Jamal had only been hoping to distract Parter. Instead the small explosion tore most of the skin from the coach's legs. Parter collapsed against the wall, knocking a scented candle from a shelf of trophies and into the lap of Toby Lott's Bisonette singlet. The singlet ignited in a *whoosh* of crackling polyester, the fire leaped from the uniform to the Polaroids that papered the wall and in a second four decades' worth of boys were alight.

Parter tried to escape. Jamal was too fast for him. He pushed the couch against Parter and pinned him to the burning wall. He felt Parter struggle, heard the big man scream for him to stop, stop please *stop*, but Jamal closed his eyes. He had no doubt that the man would kill him if their places were reversed.

The room filled with smoke and whispers and the shit stench of decay. Jamal held his breath.

A cluster of dull pops that sounded like firecrackers came from Parter's jacket a few feet away and Jamal felt the couch first convulse and then go as still as a line when a fish slips free. Jamal rose, panting, and saw that the fire had reached Parter's open, unblinking eyes.

"You still say I got no strength in my legs?" Jamal said, mostly to himself.

He looked toward the hallway and saw, somehow without surprise, that the hole was gone, the floor restored. *Jesus.*

He didn't linger. The fire was real enough, and he smelled gasoline in his hair.

Outside, hurrying down the triple-wide's steps, Jamal heard a strange chugging noise. He saw that the wall of the trailer was alight, burning just a few feet away from the generator.

That generator. Hadn't it been leaking—

"Get down!" Bethany screamed from the door of the Water House, but it was too late. The shock wave of the explosion caught Jamal as he reached the ground and sent him flying through the night.

JOEL

The lights died, and the explosion knocked the triple-wide into the black camper. Like a capsizing ship, the camper tipped into the dirt, the shutters swinging closed and sending Clark—who had just lodged an arm over the Browder thing's windpipe—rolling off of him and tumbling into the sudden inky dark.

Joel heard Clark strike something hard in the kitchen. She righted herself as Browder ran toward her. Joel grabbed for the deputy but caught nothing but air.

Between the damage to his skull, the blood lost from his ruined shoulder and now this canted floor, Joel felt hopelessly disorientated, jet-lagged, as if his mind had left his body in a safer, colder time zone. He wasn't sure how he was still conscious. When Browder and Clark collided with the far wall, some cracked piece of Joel's brain wondered what the queens with whom he'd gone to Tulum would say when they heard that Joel Whitley—the brooding boy with the chest and the black card and a drug dealer in every city—had run out his brief clock in a mildewed mobile home in the middle of nowhere.

"I'd say you deserve better."

A sudden warm draft lifted the hairs on the back of Joel's neck.

"I'd say you deserve more of that fifty-k."

A dull amber light came from somewhere just over his shoulder. Years later, Joel would imagine a thousand explanations for the voice he heard in his head at that moment.

But Joel knew something he would never tell a soul: his brother's voice came not from inside his head but from *behind* him. He heard it a few inches from his ear. And his brother's hand had pivoted his head, ever so slightly, to show him exactly what he needed to see.

Browder was pinned between Clark and the kitchen wall, his hands around her throat, hoisting her into the air. She grabbed for his black eyes—her feet convulsing, her strength failing.

But what was that on her ankle?

"He needs vessels," said Dylan's small voice. *"But you can break them."*

Joel felt the little key in his hand turn smoothly and the cuff around his ankle pop free.

"Go."

He stumbled down the canted trailer floor in a crouch—careful to avoid the pipe Kimbra had pulled loose earlier—and when he reached Clark, he somehow moved his bad arm enough to touch her leg. To still her.

With his good hand he slipped his brother's hunting knife free from the sheath on her ankle. He stood up straight. He met Browder's black, empty eyes over her shoulder.

The knife was so sharp it slid into Browder's side as easy as sex after a long night. When the hilt of the blade reached the skin Joel turned it once, turned it farther, then turned it back around, just as he had seen Browder spinning his own knife earlier. Joel studied the pain in the deputy's blackened face and wondered when he would find the exact combination of turns to take the life from his twisted body.

Browder shuddered. His mouth opened wider and wider, the jawbones cracking free of their sockets, and a horrible smell of blood and clay and rot seeped out.

A blink, and Browder's eyes were his own again. The young deputy focused on Joel with an expression of absolute, desperate tenderness.

From his ruined mouth, Browder said, "You look just like him in this light."

Joel pulled the knife free. Blood splashed onto the old linoleum. Browder's fingers fell from Clark's neck. His eyes died.

Clark was saying something that Joel couldn't hear. She was pulling him away from the wall. He stumbled back up the canted floor and felt the bloody knife fall from his fingers.

Joel raised his head to see the place where his brother's voice had spoken to him. He saw nothing there. No shadows, no light, no bends in the air. No ghostly presence to give him one final nod of encouragement.

Instead he could just make out the trailer door rattling. "Fire!" screamed a voice outside. "You're on fire!"

BETHANY

It was a piece of paneling off the side of the tall triple-wide that did it. She saw a wooden board come loose from the triple-wide's wall, hit the grass and a second later there was a flash bright enough to blind her.

The generator's explosion blew out the windows of the Water House. Mitchell Malacek stirred. Whiskey brought his Glock to within an inch of the boy's head. "Don't even," he said.

Someone was screaming outside. Jamal. Bethany saw that he was rolling in the grass, his fake leather jacket burning on his back. His hands were slapping at the flames, his arms were tangled in their sleeves. He was panicking, she saw. Panicking and trapped.

Bethany and Whiskey traded nods.

She rushed across the circle. She saw boys watching her from the shattered windows of the trailers, some she knew and some she didn't, all looking terrified and appalled and nobody making a move to help Jamal. They hadn't done a thing to help anyone, friend or foe, from the moment the shit had hit the fan. She wasn't surprised at this—men were noted pussies, after all—and she supposed she really should be grateful that they weren't all wielding guns or bricks or toilet seats, but she couldn't help but think less of them for it. You'd think that after years of lies and secrets they'd have some fight in them.

What had happened to these boys?

Did she care? Not really. When Bethany reached Jamal she pulled her Bisonette singlet off over her head and thumped at the flames with it, just like she'd seen in safety videos at school. Those videos didn't warn you putting out a fire burned like a bitch.

She was able to damp the flames enough for Jamal to get hold of a sleeve and pull his arms free. A moment later her singlet ignited. Bethany dragged Jamal away and the two of them stared, dazed and fascinated, as their clothes burned together a few inches from Kimbra Lott's outstretched hand. Bethany pressed her singed palms together between her thighs.

The fire from the burning triple-wide leaped to the black camper. It spread up the camper's walls.

"Fuck," Jamal said. "Joel and the cop are in there."

But Bethany was already running.

The black camper's door was locked so firmly it hardly moved when she pounded on it. "Fire!" she shouted. "You're on fire!"

Clark's face appeared behind the bars of the trailer's broken window. "Find something to force the door—" She turned her head to listen to something behind her. "—Joel says Boone mentioned something about a key. I left him back by the Airstream."

Jamal said, "Whiskey has a toolbox in his truck."

"A crowbar, a hammer, anything," Clark shouted. She started to cough. Smoke poured from the barred window.

Bethany said, "I'll check the body."

JAMAL

Jamal hustled to the truck. He glanced back, saw that the generator's explosion had set fire to the roof of the orange RV across the circle. Luke Evers wasn't moving. With a lump in his throat, Jamal realized that Kimbra had died for nothing.

When he reached Whiskey's bloody truck he kept his eyes on the ground. He arrived at the tailgate, doubled back, held his breath. He reached a hand into the cab—brains on seats, shards of glass in open mouths—and pulled Whiskey's keys from the ignition.

He tripped around a pair of gym bags in the truck bed, over some empty beer cans and found the rusted metal toolbox he'd seen earlier when he'd clambered into the cab at KT's house.

He got it open with the third key on the key ring.

Jackpot: hammers, a long crowbar. He loaded his arms with as much as he could carry and started back.

BETHANY

She didn't give herself time to be disgusted. Mr. Boone's body
came up from the ground with a wet squelching noise and she
dug her hands in the pockets of his leather chaps. Nothing.

A key could be anywhere around here.

"Son of a bitch!" Whiskey shouted from across the circle.

He was leaning against the door of the Water House. He
looked dazed, blood dripping from a cracked lip, pointing his
Glock past the far rim of trailers.

Bethany heard a truck's engine turn over.

"Malacek's getting away," Whiskey shouted.

Sure enough, through a gap in the distant trailers, Bethany
saw a pair of red taillights go bouncing away over the dark
country.

She shook her head, wiped her sticky hands in the dirt.
Mitchell and the others here had killed her man and ruined

her life and nobody—*nobody*—was escaping from this place on her watch.

Bethany Tanner was the Sharpest Shot in the West. And she knew just where to get a rifle.

CLARK

Inside the black trailer, the flames were consuming the kitchen and Browder's body—or whatever Browder had been there at the end—along with it. The camper had a tin roof, thank God, but the fire was chewing up the walls. It would reach her and Joel in a few minutes. Even with both windows shattered open the smoke had already gotten deep inside her. Every breath was a little fire of its own.

Clark felt the camper's door shake as Jamal struggled to fit a crowbar in the frame. "Ready!" he shouted.

"On three!"

She counted. She pulled on the knob. He pushed the bar. Nothing. The camper was locked like a bank vault.

A quick pair of rifle shots cracked somewhere in the distance. "Don't worry," Jamal said. "That's just Bethany."

Clark could worry about this later, just as she could spend the rest of her life wondering about these sad men and this dark little trailer and the hungry force that had possessed Browder. She could spend her life wishing she'd paid more attention to her mother's warnings about the things that hid across the fence.

Now, right now, Clark felt in her bruised bones that she was missing something obvious and vital and that if she didn't find it *now* none of that shit would matter much longer.

"Fuck!" Jamal shouted.

Clark leaped away from the door the moment the fire raced up the wall.

Joel gave a nasty cough from where she'd left him on the floor. "Stay low," she told him, though she'd started to wonder if it wouldn't be wiser to just start sucking down smoke—it must be better to black out for good than feel your skin charring off your body—because the flames had caught on every wall. She saw a long chain whip hanging from a nail that was burning blue in the heat.

Joel propped himself on one elbow to give her a thumbs-up. He stopped.

Clark saw it too.

The floorboards. Did her eyes deceive her or did those bright new boards wobble when Joel leaned his elbow on them?

"Crowbar!" she shouted through the window, her voice cracking, her bruised throat tightening and tightening. A moment later Jamal slid the tool through the bars of the window and pulled back from the flames with a curse. Clark fished it away from the burning wall with her foot, ignored the heat of the metal in her palm and dug the crowbar's wedged end through a gap between two boards.

They were loose.

The first board was the hardest. It bumped and squealed against the crowbar but refused to budge. Finally Clark stood tall, closed her eyes against the smoke—*don't breathe it in yet, Star*—and pushed down against the bar with all her strength.

The board snapped loose. Clark kicked it free and hooked the curved end of the bar on to the next. Joel dragged himself through a thin skein of dried vomit to get out of the way. He tugged at the loosened board with what little strength remained in his good hand.

When they got the third board up he said faintly, "There must have been so much blood."

Clark bent down to examine the space they'd created. No wonder the floor had come up so easily: the crossbeams that undergirded the trailer were blackened with rot. Whoever had laid these cheap new synthetic boards—and the fact they were cheap and fire-retardant, Clark thought, was no doubt the only reason she and Joel weren't dead already—had nailed them into gummy wood that should have been ripped out years ago.

Clark drove the sharp end of the crowbar down into the beam that crossed the hole they'd made. Again.

The beam broke at the same moment the roof finally collapsed into the kitchen. Clark shielded her eyes from the scalding dust that billowed up with it. She kicked out the crossbeam. She shouted for Jamal to be ready. She prayed he heard her.

"It's just a few feet to the wall," Clark said, gripping Joel by the armpits and lowering him into the hole. "Just drag with your legs—"

She couldn't say more. Her throat had finally closed. She watched Joel disappear down into the hole and she turned her head to give the roof above her a dubious look. It would fall at any moment.

Clark looked back down. Joel was already gone.

No time like the present.

She braced her arms on either side of the hole and lowered herself into the dirt. She slipped at the last moment and landed hard on her ass. She stretched herself backward and crabwalked toward the front wall on her elbows and heard the roof collapse onto the hole she'd made. A dizzying wave of heat struck her face.

A pair of strong hands grabbed her ankles. A moment later Clark was sliding forward, forward until she saw the stars.

Jamal helped her to stand. The ring of trailers was ablaze. The crackle of it was almost comforting, like the logs she had always hoped would burn at her house at Christmas. Blank-eyed boys had poured into the night, hunching their naked shoulders. They looked sullen and humiliated—caught out—and terrified to within an inch of their sanity. They all looked so young. Something was raining down from the sky that Clark at first mistook for leaves until one landed at her feet and she saw that it was a singed Polaroid, the naked boy in its frame staring back at her with much the same expression as these shivering young men.

With Joel's good arm over her shoulder, Clark and Jamal made their way into the circle away from the flames. The little sea of boys parted and she saw Mitchell Malacek, his hands on his head, stepping toward her in the orange firelight. When he reached the dead center of the circle he stopped, a few yards from Clark, and sank to his knees and studied her feet.

Bethany Tanner, naked but for a bra and panties, strode behind Mitchell with a rifle braced against her hip. Clark recalled the two rifle cracks she had heard earlier—*"Don't worry, that's just Bethany"*—and fought the urge to smile at this girl's dedication.

Whiskey Brazos joined Bethany from the blue trailer and rubbed at a swollen lip. Clark saw with some relief he still held Mr. Boone's custom Glock.

Clark forced her bruised throat to swallow. She allowed herself to breathe.

Four fast pops tore through the crackling fire. Semiautomatic fast.

"Everyone on the fucking ground!"

Clark turned in time to see Garrett Mason, his pads and his Bison helmet covered in soot, step from the burning green trailer, the AR-15 braced against his shoulder.

"That means you, Officer."

Clark tried to ease Joel gently to the ground—*oh Christ, think, Star,* think—but gave up when Garrett sent a bullet whistling over her head. She dropped Joel in a heap and threw herself down beside him. Jamal, stretched out on her other side, whispered, "Piece of shit," into the dirt.

The Bright Lands boys fell on their faces without a second's hesitation.

Bethany Tanner hadn't moved fast enough: her rifle was still frozen, aimed at the back of Mitchell's head. Clark prayed the girl wouldn't try to be a hero.

Bethany clearly considered it, but when Garrett turned the AR-15 in her direction she settled for giving the boy a long, baleful scowl. She tossed the rifle into the dirt. When the gun landed, Clark felt the strangest ripple pass through the earth and reverberate in her fingers, like the rifle had landed on the tight skin of a hollow drum.

"You too, Brazos," Garrett said, and Whiskey threw the custom Glock down by Bethany's rifle. Garrett growled. His voice was growing deeper. *Older.* "I see what you got tucked in your belt."

Whiskey sighed. He withdrew a matching Glock from the back of his jeans and tossed it into the dirt with its mate.

The earth began to shake and this time it didn't stop. It sounded so close now: the screeching stone, the thuds of a massive body moving—climbing—just a few yards beneath her.

When Clark turned again to Garrett she saw that there

was no face behind the grill of his helmet. There was only darkness.

"Malacek," Garrett said. "Grab a gun."

But Mitchell, still on his knees, shook his head. "No."

"The fuck did you say?"

"I said no." Mitchell looked at that blackness, then turned away. "We never should have helped Browder with the body. We never should have taken the sock to the auto shop. We should have ended all this last week. Garrett, I'm—"

Mitchell was interrupted by the loss of his brainpan.

Garrett lowered the rifle from his shoulder. Screams rose from the Bright Lands boys as Mitchell's body collapsed in the dirt. Clark saw Bethany twitch when his blood spattered her cheek. The girl never blinked.

"You mean to tell me there ain't a single goddamn man here to finish this job with me?" Garrett shouted from the void behind his grill. The rumble in the ground shook Clark's teeth.

"Maybe they were right about you queers after all," Garrett continued. He took a few steps through the sea of boys, panning the gun over their heads. "Maybe I'll have to do all this work myself."

"I'm good."

There was a gasp. From the bloody porch of the burning orange trailer Luke Evers rose to his feet and made his way across the circle. He was agleam in blood from the waist down, so much blood Clark wondered how he could possibly be alive.

But alive he was.

"Luke, don't do this. Don't *help* him!" Clark called to him.

"Shut your fucking mouth," Garrett shouted.

She felt the AR turn her way but she didn't stop. "They shot you, Luke. I saw it—they tried to kill you."

Clark should have saved her breath. Luke bent down slowly and rose up with one of the monogrammed Glocks. He tested its weight in his hand.

The ground quaked.

Garrett let up a twisted whoop. *"Altoleth golesh shah."*

"It's been feeding on you." Joel's voice cracked. "It's been feeding on all of us. It sucks on our shame and our fear and our pain. It wants us to hurt. It wants us to bleed."

In response, the ground opened with a crack beneath Mitchell's body. One moment the boy lay there, the back of his head scattered over his feet, and the next he had slipped silently, smoothly, into a hole in the earth. From very far below, Clark heard water sloshing, the sound echoing and warping up the walls of the stone hole—the trench, of course, even the trench her mother had spoken of had been real—but she never heard a splash when Mitchell's body landed.

She and several boys tried to push themselves away from the hole. They froze at the sound of gunfire.

"Nobody moves!" Garrett said. "He's coming."

Luke gave the hole little more than a glance and stepped around it.

"Garrett—Luke—the fuck are you doing this for?" Whiskey shouted. "We're your fucking brothers!"

Garrett answered with a bullet in the back of Whiskey's knee. The boy keened into the dust.

A singed Polaroid drifted gently into the hole. Dirt whispered as it slipped over the spreading edge, just like Clark had heard in her dreams and a moment later, with a humid rush of air, the smell of rot billowed up from the open earth and overwhelmed her. The whispering voice rode on the stench, forced itself up Clark's nose and down her ears and into her mouth and noosed itself around her mind and choked off every thought.

hatedhim, Bosheth whispered. *youhatedhim*

Clark couldn't breathe. She couldn't move. She couldn't see her hands in front of her face. She was blinded by a vision of her brother, standing at the kitchen sink, telling her how afraid he was of this town, this county, this filthy trailer park where God knew what had been done to him. And how had she answered Troy?

By cursing him, running him out of her house, spitting on his truck. Troy had been trying to ask her for help—it was so obvious now—and Clark had been too petty and jealous to imagine that the man against whom she was always compared might need her help just as bad as she needed his. Cruel. Had anyone ever been so cruel as Starsha Marilynn Clark?

couldhavesavedhim

The voice was right. She could have saved him—could have loved him—but she had despised him instead. And now she couldn't save anyone—not her brother, not her town, not a single soul here at this awful place. She had failed them all. She had always, would always

failthem

All around her, Clark heard a hungry sucking nose as the creature drew air into the pit, feeding on every doomed soul in the circle, because

—because now now now was the time, now was the time he had been waiting all these many years for, the reason he had hidden here, sleeping and licking old wounds and leaking with dreams. Now—at last—now he had burned enough blood to break open the trench and take shape in the dirt world, had found a vessel that could keep him tethered there, this boy who would help him stare at the stars again, yes.

Now was the time again for the stonethings and the bloodthings, the sandthings and the bonethings, all the things the carpenter had banished to the far place, all the things that now would beg to follow Bosheth across the trench, the things that would cry and the things that would weep and the things that would shout please, Bosheth, please forgive us, please: please give us a taste of your men.

And he would smile and he would tell them, When I'm through.

"Some of you we'll keep in chains," Garrett shouted. "And some of you will bring more people here. And some of you—"

Jamal was sobbing. Joel was struggling to rise. Clark couldn't even imagine moving. The moment that voice had finally entered her head she'd felt her lungs fill with lead.

Only Luke seemed unbothered. As the rumble in the hole rose to a roar of delight, as the ground crumbled beneath Clark's fingers, Evers calmly made his way over a few whimpering boys and stopped a foot from Garrett.

"Celebrate, boys!" Garrett shouted. "These are the best years of your life!"

Luke raised the Glock and fired two shots into Garrett's chest.

NO! The whispering voice in Clark's head started screaming. The screeching of nails on the stone below grew louder, Bosheth climbed faster. *NO!*

Garrett fell back with a cough of surprise. The rifle fell from his grasp. Clark raised her head in time to watch him try to crawl away from Luke but there was something wrong with his legs. After struggling to escape, Garrett gave up, clutched his hands to his Bison helmet and pressed it hard to his head as if it might shield him from the fruits of a life of shame and hate and all the hush-now pillow games his brother had taught him. He let out a child's whimper. Luke took a step toward him.

A blink, and Clark saw behind Luke—though she wished for the rest of her life she hadn't—a great white hook of a claw, pale as the moon and long as a school bus, throw itself over the edge of the hole. Saw a clutch of whiskers, tall as cornstalks, bleached white after centuries in the water, rise, dripping, from down below.

Saw a single eye, black and infinite and cold, emerge to stare at her.

"Luke!" she shouted.

But Evers seemed to notice none of this. He only regarded Garrett, regarded Garrett's helmet.

"It's just fiberglass, you idiot," Luke said, and emptied the Glock into Garrett's head.

Clark buried her face in the dirt as a wail of rage rose from the mouth of the hole, the sound so high and sharp she was certain it would burst her ears. She felt blood run from her nose. She screamed.

She grabbed hold of Joel and Jamal.

From somewhere in Garrett's direction she heard the pin of the Glock clicking when it struck an empty chamber. Heard a shaking in the dust as Garrett's body gave up the last of its life.

There was a great splash from deep below a moment later and the wailing stopped.

It took all sound with it. The whispers. The roars. The crackle of the flames. For one long moment, all Clark could hear was her heart, galloping in her chest.

Before her strength returned to her, Clark looked up and saw not Bosheth or the empty hole of the Bright Lands but Troy, standing at her kitchen window, opening his mouth to speak.

AFTER

DYLAN

Now *there* was a party that had gotten out of hand. Pills and speed, the age-old story: to think these substances had become so pernicious in this country they could ensnare not just the Bison and the new Sheriff's Deputy but such pillars of the community as Mr. Lott, Mr. Boone and stalwart Coach Parter. The men at the bar agreed that it was a bad business, but it could have been worse. After all, just think what would have happened if Officer Clark hadn't arrived armed?

From their smoky den at Mr. Jack's Steaks, the members of the Chamber of Commerce saw to it that the only thing to make the papers were the obituaries. The only soul not memorialized was Garrett Mason, mass murderer and meth addict. The ladies at church folded their hands and shook their heads. Between this and his brother's suicide, how would Garrett's family ever bear to be seen in public again?

Offensive coach Bill Wesford was named the new athletic

director, despite murmurings of inappropriate conduct from members of the girls' softball team. The consensus at the Egg House was that you couldn't let gossip like that slow you down. The boys still had a shot at the state championships, after all. The town still had a dream.

A naked redheaded boy named Baker Channing, delirious and seared with sunburn, stumbled onto the highway the week after all that business, raving about play-offs and blow jobs; he had apparently escaped the violence on foot and become lost in the Flats for days. Baker was loudly and insistently informed of how blessed he was to be alive, reminded of this until he stopped feeling the need to discuss what he may or may not have seen that night.

In his cursory search of the premises, Investigator Mayfield discovered the charred body of Bryan Weissman, a defensive tackle for the Perlin Stallions, propped against the orange door of HOME ON THE RANGE. The boy had taken two 9-millimeter rounds to the back. The bullets matched the shell casings of the customized Glock which had killed Garrett Mason, a murder that Officer Clark ensured was written off as self-defense on Luke Evers's part.

In the back bedroom of the triple-wide, beneath a heavy pink bed surrounded by shattered mirrors, a trapdoor was discovered in the floor. It was determined that the door must have provided access to the cavernous crawl space that spread among the stanchions of the elevated trailer. It was never determined precisely how a skeleton had come to rest within that crawl space, though Officer Clark had a few theories she kept to herself.

The skeleton was discovered still clad in football pads. It wore a jersey with the name BROADLOCK printed across its back.

The skeleton had been preserved from the explosion overhead by the strange concrete coffin in which it had been enclosed. Beneath the skeleton's crossed arms there was a photograph that had likely been taken on the same day as the team portrait which Joel Whitley had seen online, after leaving Ranger Mason's house. Standing in the center of the photo was handsome Corwin Broadlock. To his left was nervous little Toby Lott. To his right was cocky Harlan Boone. And standing there with his arm over Broadlock's shoulder was hulking, bashful Tom Parter, smiling like he couldn't believe his luck.

The sole concession the school made to grief was to postpone the Bison Homecoming game. Instead, on the Friday night following all the trouble, a formal memorial was held in the school's gymnasium. A line of wreaths stood beneath the basketball goals as Bethany Tanner and Luke Evers were awarded Most Valuable Player—the only honor for which the cash-strapped school had medals at hand—and smiled grimly for photographs.

Tomas Hernandez and the Turner twins watched them from the stands with frowns. It had been made clear to Luke and Bethany and the others that there were still plenty of folks in this town with a vested interest in keeping the exact nature of the Bright Lands obscured.

Jamal awaited Luke and Bethany outside the memorial. They rode in Luke's truck to Joel's house, where they found him less stoned than might be expected. His arm, fresh out of yet another shoulder surgery, was suspended in a cast, his head shaved from the operation to relieve the pressure in his cracked skull. Very few flowers stood on his nightstand.

"The charges got dropped," Jamal told him.

"You told your mother to send me the legal fees?" Joel said.

"Can we come visit you in New York?" Luke asked.

Joel smiled. "I wouldn't be able to keep you out of trouble."

Mrs. Whitley shushed the kids out the door a few minutes

later, more insistently maternal with her surviving son than they had ever seen her with Dylan.

Paulette sat on the edge of Joel's bed. She stared at his bruised face. Joel had learned that although Dylan had hidden his queerness from his mother he needn't have bothered. Paulette had known about both her boys from the day they were born.

She never mentioned to Joel that the fiery demise of Bentley First Baptist may not have been entirely Dylan's idea.

"Did I do good?" Joel asked her.

She rested a hand on his hand. She never did start to cry. "You always have."

At the dam, Bethany and Jamal and Luke sat on the tall walkway and ignored the stars.

Bethany lit a blunt. "So why did it stop when Garrett died? Didn't it want people to get killed?"

"I was texting with Mr. Whitley about that," Luke said, taking an inexpert drag, coughing. "I think it needed someone it could get inside, someone who'd given themselves over to it. Someone to help keep it over here, somehow. Like a circuit helping it connect our world to…wherever it came from."

"A vessel," Bethany said. They'd all heard that thing speaking—thinking? screaming?—at the end there, just before it made it aboveground.

The three of them watched the water a long time, the flat line of nothing out there. They had put a stop to something that had ruined a hundred lives. Why didn't it feel like a victory?

Luke opened his mouth to say more but Jamal cut him off. "That thing's someone else's problem now."

CLARK

She was jogging when she saw the little convertible crest the rise in her road and draw slowly toward her like a shadow fleeing the Sunday dawn. She stopped when he came close, but Joel said only, "Take your time. I'll meet you at the house."

She found him inside a few minutes later, brewing coffee in her machine. She sat at her family's old table, not even bothering to change out of her sweaty clothes, and accepted the cup he carried to her, carefully, with his one good hand.

"Are you sure you have to leave so soon?" she said.

Joel brought a cup to the table for himself. "There's business in the city. No such thing as bad press, I guess."

"And that's what you'll do? Go back and analyze property values?"

He shrugged with his good shoulder. "Maybe if I get absurdly rich I'll fight crime. The one-armed Batman."

She sipped her coffee. She tried to smile at the sling suspending his shoulder. "How does it feel?"

"Like I've pressed my last bench press. But I can hardly complain."

Unspoken memories of Dylan's belated funeral yesterday morning—the end of a long week of such proceedings—hung briefly between the two of them.

Joel said, "Dylan must have known that KT was up to no good on those weekends they were supposed to be at the coast together. Why do you think he didn't try to stop the tricking and the drugs?"

Clark played with a napkin. "Because KT was too convenient for the narrative. I went and checked—Browder moved back to town on May second. The first trip the boys took to the coast came three weeks later. My guess is that Browder went back to the Bright Lands sometime soon after he arrived and met Dylan there. Apparently there's phone records showing that your brother and Browder was texting each around the clock by the end of the month. With KT's help, Dylan and Browder could disappear together. Guess which of our deputies was off-duty for seven of those ten weekends Dylan and KT told people they were in Galveston?"

"Mayfield must be sick that he never put that together."

"He's sick about a lot. But to his credit I think he'd had his misgivings ever since the sock was found. If I had to guess, framing Jamal was too much, even for him. He botched the booking paperwork eight different ways. And once Grissom was killed, well—" Clark twirled her mug. "He'll be sheriff soon enough, I'm sure."

Clark and Joel regarded the window, the broad copper Flats outside.

Joel said, "They never found Mitchell's body?"

"No. I don't know how the department is going to spin the story but I'm sure they'll find a way." Clark shook out her damp hair from its bun. "Of course, that pit explains why Troy never turned up."

"You think he got swallowed by that thing?" Joel said.

"I'd rather not think about it, frankly."

"But Ranger Mason said Troy left town the night I was arrested."

"Ranger lied about plenty. It would be the perfect way for him to have Troy killed—just get him dumped in that hole and no one would ever find him. Ranger said it himself, he hated y'all that summer." She drank. "You've seen what happens to jealousy."

Joel shook his head. He touched her hand. "That doesn't make sense. Think about it. That thing down there, whatever it was, it started moving when people died. Mayfield said everyone got bad dreams after Broadlock disappeared forty years ago. The dead lady at the bank'll tell you the same thing happened after Dylan was murdered. But, Clark, back when Troy ran off—" Joel smiled. "There weren't any dreams. There wasn't anything."

"Troy told my father he wasn't sleeping before he disappeared."

"Neither was Dylan."

Clark thought about her mother, thought about Troy, but finally she only cleared their cups from the table. "We owe Luke plenty."

"Clark, you're not listening to me."

"I hear you fine. And I appreciate what you're trying to do, really." She struggled to smile. "But, Joel, listen—it's easier to know that Troy's dead than to eat dinner with his file at the table. When's your flight?"

"Soon. Sadly. Will you be alright?"

A stone caught in Clark's throat. Would she?

"You'll always have a friend here, Joel. Truly."

He smiled. "Maybe not *here*, here. I saw the sign in your yard. Where will you go when the house sells?"

"Somewhere I'm not Troy Clark's sister."

When they reached the door, Joel touched her arm. He lowered his voice for one final question. "The night Dylan started all of this he said he'd texted me by mistake. Do you think that's true?"

"How would I know?" The words had come out sounding colder than Clark had intended. Like always. She readied herself to apologize but Joel only wrapped her in a one-armed embrace.

Neither of them spoke for a long time.

Her phone rang as she let him out the door. Detroit, MI, the screen read. Clark didn't know anyone in Detroit, MI. Another reporter, she supposed. She had nothing to say to them—she'd turned in her resignation days ago.

But when Detroit, MI rang again (and again and again), when she finally relented and answered, was it any wonder that her first response, upon hearing the voice at the other end of the line, was to feel just as much resentment as relief?

"Star," a man said—ten years older, ten years the same. The only man who had ever been allowed to call her that.

She sank to the floor. She pressed a hand to her mouth.

"Star, it's me."

JOEL

His brother sent him one final message. It came when Joel was in flight, somewhere over the Mason-Dixon line. It came when he was somewhere between the past and the rest of his life, again. It came in a dream.

Yet when Joel awoke a few minutes later he could already feel its memory—like all the other memories of all the other dreams—slipping away from him. By the time his plane broke through the clouds and empty Manhattan thrust itself up before his window like some glimpse of a dubious future, Joel found that the dream had all but faded.

By the time he touched down all he could remember was this:

The sound of insects whirring in late afternoon. The expectant hush of an empty highway. The aubergine sky and the swell of hot light, an afternoon in autumn finally slipping into dusk.

They were at the football field, Dylan and Joel, alone. Dylan tottered along beside his brother, the top of his wobbly helmet barely coming to Joel's waist, the fingers of one small gloved hand clutched tight in Joel's palm. Dylan was speaking. Joel, for the first time in his life, was listening.

When they reached the fifty-yard line, Dylan stopped. He turned up his head to ask, "Are you going to stay for the game?"

Joel took in the empty stands, the empty road, the empty Flats in the distance that bore him, now, no ill will. "If they'll let me."

"I'll see what I can do."

Dylan slipped his hand free. He pointed to the stands. Joel started across the field.

"I texted you Sunday night because I thought I could learn to be like you," Dylan yelled.

Joel couldn't bring himself to turn back. Be like him? A solitary man so broken he'd thought he deserved every minute of pain he'd ever received?

"I wouldn't wish myself on anyone," Joel said.

"You've always played yourself short, you know."

Joel sat in the front row of the rusted stands. He looked across the pitch, hoping to catch some glimpse of Kimbra Lott or KT Staler or T-Bay Baskin or any other member of the idle dead. But there was no one. Only an empty cascade of bleachers charged with all the promise of youth and time and the thin, irresistible potential for glory.

"Did you really hate football?" Joel shouted to his brother.

"Nobody ever taught me how to ask for help."

Before Joel could think how to answer this, Dylan bent low on the line, his back rigid, his helmet up. Joel broke off. There was only so much you could say, he realized, even to the dead.

The sun finally faded. The spindly field lights came on, one by one, each a little storm of hope and halogen thundering to life over his brother's head.

"Out here I can still be everything I always wanted me to be," Dylan shouted, his voice echoing against the empty metal and the flat horizon. He clapped his hands for the snap. "And I love it."

Joel heard the *smack* of a rubber ball striking a leather glove and awoke in his seat with a start. He reached out to touch his useless arm and froze: a warm breath was stirring the hairs on the back of his neck.

It was enough.

Joel was adequate. He was loved.

For a moment—for a breath of a moment—he wasn't alone.

★ ★ ★ ★ ★

ACKNOWLEDGMENTS

While all published authors are inordinately fortunate, even fewer are fortunate enough to be represented by Ross Harris. Authors are infamous for describing the strains they put on their agents—frantic late-night emails about errant characters, sprawling lousy drafts, strained social calls that thinly mask a plea for news (any news!) about the fate of their novel—and all I can add to this litany is: *mea culpa*. This novel would, very literally, not exist without Ross and as such he gets my first and loudest acknowledgment. Thanks also, to Stuart and to everyone else at SKLA. I can't believe it's finally worked out.

Deep thanks are also due, in no order of preference, to Carter, James, Tom, Megan and Ed, for reading this book in manuscript form, providing dozens of notes and hours of encouragement.

My parents, Rose and David, deserve an award for their unflagging support. I can't think of another American family who would actively urge their son *not* to go back to school and complete his degree, but I'm glad they did. Sorry for all the bad words.

I will always owe Peter Joseph more than I can give: he saw this story and decided it deserved to be told. Peter and John Glynn guided me through three rigorous rounds of edits that made the book immeasurably stronger. Also, my thanks Grace Towery for her endless attention, to Emer Flounders and Roxanne Jones for championing this book harder than I ever thought possible, to Eden Church for her limitless savvy, to Linette Kim for getting the novel into the hands of so many librarians, to Margaret Marbury for her boundless encouragement, and to Natalie Hallak and all of the intrepid copy editors and designers at HarperCollins. Any mistakes that remain in this novel after such assiduous guidance are mine and mine alone.

On the West Coast, I have to thank Brooke Ehrlich for her enthusiasm and her savvy. Thanks to her I've met Drew, Andy and Kyle, all of whom have changed my life for the better.

Helen and Winnie deserve special love for putting up with my neuroses when I was at the end of drafts or shirking my responsibilities to tease out a nice sentence on a square of scratch paper. I'll always remember our time fondly.

Carson and Brian were kind enough to offer me a stunning view of Lake Saratoga and the chance to escape the city while under the pressure of editorial deadlines. I still owe them a bottle of rosé.

I must thank the many footballers in Central Texas who were kind enough to answer my questions about the sport and their private lives. I withhold their names here because I remember very well the way guilt works by association in my old neck of the woods, and I would hate for any of these young men to be tainted for helping me a write a novel that is, to put it mildly, concerned about the world in which they live.

To the survivors whose stories informed characters like Deputy Grissom and the Old Boys, I'm sorry, and thank you. I hope things have gotten better. You know who you are.

And finally, to all the young people living anywhere there isn't room for you, whose stories have yet to be heard, whose lives will never be normal: I see you. You're loved.

THE BRIGHT LANDS

JOHN FRAM

Reader's Guide

HANOVER
SQUARE
PRESS

1. *The Bright Lands* has been described as both a thriller and a horror novel and it draws freely from both genres. Did you enjoy the way the author melded these forms, or did you find yourself growing lightheaded when the food started to touch on your plate?

2. When asked in interviews why *The Bright Lands* features a supernatural monster, the author has responded, "I wish I knew." Does this answer satisfy you, or do you see other motives at work in the inclusion of Bosheth that perhaps the author doesn't wish to disclose?

3. While the novel stars a queer man as a protagonist, many readers have also found themselves drawn strongly to the book's female characters. Would you classify *The Bright Lands* as a "queer novel?" Why or why not?

4. Building on the last question, was this your first time reading a novel centered on a queer man? If so, did you discover anything surprising about the queer experience in doing so?

5. While football runs throughout the novel, we see very little of the game actually played, and the author has stated that this was a deliberate choice. Why do you think he might have done that?

6. By centering the novel on the effects of football on the town of Bentley, rather than on the game itself, do we gain some insight that we might otherwise have missed?

7. The revelation of what The Bright Lands actually are, and the chaos that surrounds that discovery, has been both lauded and criticized for its intensity. How did you respond to the final hundred pages of the novel?

8. In an interview, Fram states that he wanted to "take no prisoners" with this novel. How do you interpret that statement, and do you feel he succeeded?

9. Finally, the novel is threaded with a great deal of dark humor, and the author has stated that some of the book's most honest lines are in its jokes. Was this true for you? And did the novel's wit balance out the horrors of the story?

10. At the end of the novel, one of the surviving characters says that Bosheth is "someone else's problem now." What does this line mean to you? What, if anything, have our heroes achieved?